Quest of Eight Part Seven: Ad Paria

Richard Reda

I0647594

Quest of Eight Part Seven: Ad Paria

Richard Reda

The Quest of Eight
Part Seven: Ad Paria

Quest of Eight Part Seven: Ad Paria

Richard Reda

The Quest of Eight

Part Seven: Ad Paria

By

Richard Reda

Quest of Eight Part Seven: Ad Paria

Richard Reda

Published 2013

ISBN-13:
978-0-9890729-0-8
ISBN-10:
0989072908

This book is dedicated to our first eight Grandchildren

Summer

Lochen

Solveig

Sean

Natalie

Stella

Quinn

Liam

With a special thanks to my wife, Karren, for her support and her editing and to Melanie Simon for her editing. And a special thanks to Quinn for the names of many of the characters.

Quest of Eight Part Seven: Ad Paria

Richard Reda

Quest of Eight Part Seven: Ad Paria

Richard Reda

Quest of Eight Part Seven: Ad Paria

Richard Reda

The Quest of Eight

Part Seven: Ad Paria

Chapter one

Two thousand years ago, a band of renegade sorcerers were defeated in their attempt to control the different peoples of the world. They were picked off one by one by a very cunning Alchemist and a very powerful Enchantress. These Kelpies, as they were called, were cast under spells into separate, and well-hidden keeps – frozen in time. Near the end of the battle to contain the sorcerers, a pendant – the source of power of the Enchantress – was destroyed: broken into four parts.

Quest of Eight Part Seven: Ad Paria

Richard Reda

One of those parts was discovered by a wandering Rebbercand, as was the axe of the person who sent an arrow into the back of the Enchantress. That axe, now permanently attached to the Rebbercand's hand, and empowered by the pieces of the pendant in his possession, have allowed him to locate the Kelpies and break the seals of the crypts holding them.

He and the Kelpies that have been released so far, have stayed one step ahead of those who have been hunting them – those who represent the various peoples the Kelpies once sought to control. Five of the eight Kelpies have been freed. The race to the remaining three is coming to a close.

Akmen Milzu, the Mountain Kelpie, reflected on the events that brought her and her party to this time and place, as she led them at a reckless pace through the Swamp. As she had predicted, the beasts and the vegetation posed no threat to them. She had enveloped her group in a spell that repelled all the toxins and poisons in their path. B'nair watched in the fading light as the vines and shrubs curled back away from them as they passed. The moss and branches that hung above them did the same.

As more of the Kelpies were released, it seemed that their powers not only returned, but that they increased. It probably had something to do with their combined strength. Throughout the night as they continued to drive deeper and deeper into the Swamp, the cold of the Ice Kingdom fell further and further behind them.

Quest of Eight Part Seven: Ad Paria

Richard Reda

The air became thicker and heavier. The humidity was trapped under the canopy of the trees and moss, seeping up from the moisture in the ground beneath them. B'nair could feel the marshy ground and several times the path they took was no real path at all. Instead, they tromped through bogs where the water rose to his mid-thigh. He could only imagine what sort of vile creatures lived in these bodies of water.

He decided he preferred not to imagine them. He would never have led his own soldiers through this place, and certainly not at night. In spite of the overcast skies in the daytime and the lack of any sunlight at all in the night, the heat and humidity were becoming oppressive. He felt like he was breathing under water.

Sweat saturated his clothing. It ran down his face from his head and seeped beneath the patch he wore over his one dead eye. The salt from his perspiration burned his good eye, even though he continually tried to wipe it away.

He stole furtive glances at the others. He could barely see their features. Their figures were blurs of motion to his right and left. None of them seemed to be affected as he was by the rising temperature. Neraka Ferr probably welcomed the heat, he thought. He wondered if it was as hot beneath the ground where Saldeti had disappeared. He realized he didn't really care.

It felt to him as if it took forever for the daybreak to appear. He was glad that the sky was still overcast. He didn't want to think about how much more uncomfortable the Swamp could get with

13

the twin suns beating down on it. He hoped, but didn't expect, that they would stop. He was not surprised when they didn't.

As the day brightened, he could see his traveling companions more clearly. He had been right about the Fire Kelpie. He seemed to be reveling in this heat. The sorcerer was still half person, half mist. More of the top portion of his body was taking shape, but his legs still disappeared into the cloud his entire being had been when they first discovered him. He wasn't floating as much as he was bouncing. Soon, thought B'nair, he'll be walking like the rest of us.

He could see the imp still riding on the sorcerer's shoulder. Her wings were beginning to regenerate. Long wisps of filament extended from the center of her back, not yet connected by the fiber from which her wings were made. Neither of them seemed to be adversely affected by the thickness of the air. Why only him, he wondered.

Shortly after dawn Akmen Milzu slowed down nearly to a stop. She was staring at a clump of brush off to the right. B'nair followed her gaze. He saw nothing particularly unusual and wondered what had caught her eye. He was turning his head back towards her when she raised her arm and thrust it at the pile of leaves and branches. The resulting explosion startled him.

"What did you do that for?" he asked, angry at having been so surprised.

"It was a supply cache for one of those who have been following us," she answered once again picking up her pace.

"One of who?" he asked.

"The one they call the Pathfinder," she answered. "The one who calls this miserable place his home. He has these storage stations all over the Swamp. That's how he's able to traverse it and not return to his home base. I just wanted to make things a little harder for him if he ever makes it back here."

B'nair thought that this was somewhat shortsighted on her part, although he said nothing. There could have been things in that cache they could have used. Had she given any thought to that before she simply blew it up? Apparently not.

After several more hours of hiking, he could take no more. He was hot, uncomfortable, tired and hungry.

"I'm sorry," he said slowing down. "I'm not immortal. I need to rest. Some food would be nice, too, but for now I will be satisfied with a brief stop. If you must continue, you can do so without me. I'll catch up or take my chances on my own."

Without waiting for a response, he slowed down to a stop, looked around and found a suitable log and sat down. He rested the axe head on the ground and wiped the sweat from his brow with his free hand. He didn't bother to look up to see what the others were doing, but he heard them stop walking.

Quest of Eight Part Seven: Ad Paria

Richard Reda

Akmen Milzu clenched her fists and clamped her jaw. She stopped and turned on her heel, glaring at the Rebbercand. She fought to control her anger at being delayed by his weakness. She watched him for a few seconds as the others looked at her and then to him and back, waiting to see what her response would be.

She turned away from B'nair and looked at the surroundings. Off to their left was a shallow stream covered with a thick layer of green scum. The water looked stagnant and had an odor of decay about it. She walked over to the stream and stepped into it, bending over and peering through the murky surface into the water.

After a few seconds, with a flash, she thrust her hand into the stream and yanked out an eel. It was mottled green and black and had a wide, gaping mouth filled with long, sharp teeth. She was holding the creature tightly behind the jaw as it wound itself around her arm.

She gave a quick squeeze, crushing the eel's throat. It slowly unwound from around her arm and hung limply, extending its full five feet in length. She waded out of the stream and over to B'nair. She stopped immediately in front of him and held out the eel to him, having dragged it across the dirt.

"Here," she said. "I should have realized you needed sustenance. Please excuse my oversight. This is a sludge eel. They're actually quite a delicacy once you get used to the texture. I think you'll find that this will provide you with both food and liquid nourishment. Enjoy."

She didn't wait for him to take the eel from her. Instead, she dropped it to the ground at his feet. B'nair looked from her to the eel. He had eaten many strange items in his life, but nothing that looked so far from appetizing as this. After making such a display, he could hardly refuse to eat the thing.

He reached down and picked it up. The skin felt like slime. He looked up to see the others all watching him. His brow lowered and he raised the eel to his mouth. He hesitated only a second and then bit into it, forcing himself not to grimace as he chewed through the foul tasting, rubbery skin.

"Mmmmm," he said. "You're right. Very tasty."

He finished chewing and prepared to take another bite. The others were still watching him with fixed eyes. He raised his head back from the eel, cocked it slightly to the side and raised the eel towards them.

"I'm sorry," he said. "Did you want some?"

They all turned away wordlessly. He took his time, biting and chewing, gagging the slime-covered morsels down his throat until the entire eel had been eaten. The Kelpie had been right about one thing – it provided the nourishment he needed. Unless he threw it all up.

Akmen Milzu had waited patiently for the Rebbercand to finish the eel, and was somewhat surprised he had eaten the entire thing. She had to give him credit for his strength of character, or whatever it was that allowed him to meet her challenge as he did. She didn't wait for him to say anything, and as soon as he was done, she began leading them all forward again.

The entire group trudged ahead in silence for the most part. Late in the afternoon, the Mountain Kelpie once again slowed down, having spotted another of Liam's supply stores. She swept her hand sideways and a blast of energy destroyed it and everything in it.

"I don't mean to second guess your motives," B'nair said to her as he came up from behind.

"But you already have," she said over her shoulder. "What is it?"

"Before you destroy the next one of these storage bases," the Rebbercand continued, "you may want to see what's inside first."

She turned to look directly at him and a slight sneer appeared on her face. She raised one eyebrow.

"Why? Are you hungry again?" she asked in a taunting voice.

His stomach rolled slightly at the thought of the eel, but he kept his face stern.

"No," he answered when he was sure his meal wouldn't make an unwelcome return. "But there could be something useful inside."

"What could any one of those miserable little creatures have that would be of any possible use to us? Food? It seems you're the only one craving food. Weapons? You already have a weapon and none of the rest of us has such a need. Protective clothing? Blankets? Cookware? Tell me. What?"

With each item she listed she had taken a step towards him, causing him to finally begin to back away from her. He knew she was trying to assert her authority over him. He decided it was time to push back. He stopped retreating and not only held his ground, but took a step closer almost coming in contact with her.

"I was thinking more of transportation," he said defiantly.

His comment took her by such surprise that she was unable to hide her reaction. Her face wore a look that spoke of a lack of comprehension. B'nair allowed a slight smile to show. He moved slightly closer to her, taking advantage of her lapse of control. She involuntarily reacted by stepping back from him.

"Yes," he said, not having waited for any kind of response from her. "Transportation. You don't seem to have considered that."

"What method of transportation could they have? Sleds? Carts?"

She had not regained her composure. Instead, she spit the words out at him, angry that he had embarrassed her; angry that he had dared to challenge her; angry that she had underestimated him. He refused to back away.

"I don't know," he said. "If you hadn't destroyed those places, we might know. When I was releasing the imp," he pressed on, making a point of the fact that he was the one with the power to release the Kelpies — including her, "they showed up in the desert on some kind of vehicle that sailed across the sands. It's logical to assume that this Pathfinder, as you called him, moves about this Swamp with a certain degree of ease. I'm sure he doesn't walk."

Akmen Milzu hadn't been aware of the details of the encounter in the desert. She shot a glance at Angin Topan. The small Kelpie tried to speak, but her voice froze when she saw the fury in the eyes of her friend. She could only nod that the Rebbercand was correct. When it was clear that Akmen Milzu expected more than the simple bobbing of her head, she found the words.

"He's correct," she croaked. "I was still weak at the time, but I saw them arrive in a large craft of some sort. There were wheels and a sail. They had lost control of it and it crashed into the sand, but it had arrived with considerable speed."

Questions began to flare up one after the other in the Mountain Kelpie's mind. How was it made? How was it propelled? Were there others? Could they use them to get to Scirios faster? Her mind raced, but her pride prevented her from engaging in any discussion, and certainly not with B'nair. She turned back to him.

"You could have mentioned this earlier," she said wryly.

"You didn't ask," he answered, holding her stare.

This only infuriated her more. She eventually broke eye contact first. She stepped back and turned away from him. She looked back at the destroyed storage base, and then back at the others. She considered that they were not even half way through the Swamp. They could be much further along if they had not been forced to walk.

She was angry with B'nair for not having suggested the possibility of some kind of vehicles before now. Then she realized she was angrier at herself for once again underestimating him. However, she would not apologize. He had challenged her authority; her leadership. His behavior and the way he confronted her had been a clear attempt to shift power. She would not yield. Not to him.

"You have my permission to search the next one," she said as she resumed walking.

That will show him his place, she thought.

"If there is a next one," he murmured.

He didn't shout, but he had said it loud enough for everyone to hear. It was another dig to let her know that he was not to be so easily dismissed. It also left an uneasy feeling with Ena Ray. He was unfamiliar with all of these individuals. He had initially thought to ally himself with Angin Topan, but he was viewing the Rebbercand in a different light now.

He understood that the imp, like Akmen Milzu, was a master Kelpie, but he thought that this might be a factor that would divide the two of them. He took for granted that the Neraka Ferr would follow the Mountain Kelpie wherever she led. He was correct in that assumption, though he couldn't know that for sure. He wished he knew about their history with each other.

There had to be a way to find out without revealing his interests. He allowed for a little bit of distance to grow between him and the others – not enough to draw attention, but enough to speak with the imp without being overheard.
"Do you think the Rebbercand was right about there being some kind of supplies we could have used?" he asked.

"It's possible," Angin Topan answered. "He was right about the strange vehicle that appeared in the desert. The one they call the Pathfinder was in it when it crashed. I suppose he could have had others like it."

"Still," Ena Ray went on, "it wasn't right to make such a point of it with Akmen Milzu – especially not in front of us. It undermines her...authority over us."

He was careful in choosing his words. He didn't want to seem to be provoking anything, but he wanted to see the reaction from the imp about his "impression" that Akmen Milzu was what amounted to their commander.

"She has no authority over us," Angin Topan answered. "She doesn't command us. I am a master – the same as she is."

It was the reaction Ena Ray expected. Now he had to be careful not to alienate the imp.

"A poor choice of words," he said. "I'm sorry. I meant her leadership."

He could see Angin Topan's brow furrow. He decided to push a little more and see where things would go.

"I know she's not in <u>charge</u> of us – especially not you – but she <u>is</u> leading us to our next destination. She's the one making the decisions about where we go and when or if we stop. That's all I meant."

"Yes, I could see how that would be perceived," the imp answered. "But you're right. She's not in charge. We have allowed her to set the pace and take the forefront. That's all."

Ena Ray noted that she had not addressed the challenge B'nair had made to the Mountain Kelpie's authority. She had focused on the perception he left with her that Akmen Milzu was their leader. When he had been released from his prison, he had been given the impression that these Kelpies were a united force. He wasn't so sure about that now.

At least some of them seemed to have their own self-interests; and those interests differed from the Rebbercand's, as he could already see. He decided right then and there that he would keep a low profile and see which way things evolved before committing himself to one or another of this group. He had grown up fending for himself and saw that the lessons he learned then would probably serve him well now.

As they continued to hike through the Swamp the tension between Akmen Milzu and B'nair increased. They came across no more caches, so B'nair's assertion that there may have been something of use in them could not be contested or confirmed. Her inability to squelch that assertion only aggravated the Mountain Kelpie further. When they approached their second night and they were still in the Swamp, and there was still no end in sight, the Kelpie slowed down and turned to the Rebbercand.

"I assume you'd like to stop and rest for the night," she commented.

"You don't need to stop on my account," he answered.

As exhausted and hungry as he was, he refused to show her any weakness. She had set a demanding pace and was feeling the effects herself. She needed to rest. She knew the Rebbercand was tired, and regretted giving him the upper hand with her comment.

"You're right," she told him. "I don't, but stop we will. I need to reconnoiter and I expect you to study your map so that once we are out of this Swamp, you can provide the most direct route to the mines of Djall."

B'nair wanted very much to point out to her that she hadn't asked him the most direct route the entire time they had been traversing this miserable Swamp, but he thought it might be better not to alienate her any further than he already had.

"Of course," he said, instead.

Without asking anyone else, Neraka Ferr wandered off into the marshes in search of something. A few minutes later he returned with a large and very unusual looking reptile. He found a long, thin branch and impaled the creature on it. Then he gathered some nearby stones and small rocks, making a bed with them. He routed around for some dead branches and leaves and made a fire on the bed of stones. Over the fire he extended the branch with the reptile skewered onto it.

As it cooked and the skin crackled, it emitted an odor that was far from appetizing, and the smoke that rose from it turned yellowish-green in color. B'nair wondered if it would be safe to eat, assuming the Kelpie decided to share. He realized that he hadn't cared if the eel he had eaten raw was safe. He had been so hungry then it didn't matter. In spite of the foul odor and the toxic looking smoke, he was once more so hungry that he didn't care now, either.

At some point the Fire Kelpie either determined that the meal was fully cooked, or that further heating would make no difference. He ripped a piece off and tossed it to Akmen Milzu. She hadn't been expecting this and fumbled to catch the hot chunk of meat without dropping it. Another piece was torn off and tossed to Ena Ray, whose hands and arms had regenerated enough to grasp the meal. He tore smaller pieces off from the piece he had been given and passed those to the imp.

Without any pause, Neraka Ferr tore one last chunk and tossed it to B'nair before he began to eat what remained. The Rebbercand was grateful for the offer and wasted no time debating over the wisdom of eating a creature that smelled so bad. He bit into it hoping it tasted even only slightly better than the eel, but expecting it to be worse.

It was neither. He concluded from what he tasted now that, even if the eel had been cooked, it would not have been any more palatable. He tried to take his mind off the meal and wondered what the Pathfinder could possibly find in this place that tasted good. Did he eat anything at all?

When everyone had finished eating, Neraka Ferr stomped out the fire. The air was still hot and humid. There was no need to have a fire make things hotter. Akmen Milzu waved her hand in a sweeping motion around the surrounding area.

"Get some sleep," she directed. "We'll start again early in the morning."

The others found flat spaces near the extinguished fire and stretched out. B'nair looked around as the darkness engulfed the marsh, the plants, the trees and whatever creatures were hidden from view. He took a step away from the others and stretched out his hand.

He couldn't see anything but after taking a few more steps his hand came into contact with something. He pushed against it and it didn't yield. He slid his hand as high as he could reach and then down to the ground. Then he moved it to the left and then to the right.

There was some kind of wall there – invisible, but hard and solid as stone. He looked up, wondering how high the barrier went, assuming it was dome-shaped. He hoped it blocked whatever might crawl underground.

Giving that concern no more thought, he kicked at the dirt, smoothing it out with his foot and looking for a dry spot. When he was satisfied he had found the driest area, he lowered himself to the ground, rolled onto his back and closed his eyes. Within seconds, he was asleep, but his sleep was not sound, nor was it untroubled.

Almost immediately after sleep had overtaken him, the dream began. He felt like he was falling. He thought this was odd. Even in his dream state, he recalled that he had nightmares before. In those nightmares, whenever he had a falling sensation, it was at the end of the dream and was the reason he woke up.

This time, though, his dream began with him falling. He felt a rising sense of panic and told himself to simply wake up. He was unable to do so. Is this real, he wondered. And then as suddenly as it started, the falling stopped. He didn't crash. Instead, as in a play, the scene merely changed. He was on a bridge somewhere deep inside a cave.

He looked around. The cave looked familiar, but he was certain he had never been there before. How can it look familiar then, he asked himself. Because this is only a dream, he answered himself. He looked behind him, expecting to see the Kelpies, but none of them were there.

Quest of Eight Part Seven: Ad Paria

Richard Reda

He faced forward and on the other side of the bridge he could see in the very dim light something that looked like a door. Where was the light coming from, he wondered. Who cares, he told himself. This is only a dream.

He had the strange sensation that something was behind him and he jerked his head around. Nothing was there, but the feeling lingered. He turned back to the front and then looked to his left and right. He was alone in this strange place. Where is everyone else, he wondered. What does it matter, he asked himself. This is only a dream.

He looked back towards the door. It was clearer now. There was more light. Where was it coming from? He felt a tingling against his chest. He looked down and saw a flash of light. It was coming from the stone – the piece of the witch's pendant that he wore around his neck. He pulled the charm out from under his tunic.

The cave, or wherever he was, filled with the light from the small stone. But it wasn't the only source of the light. There was something in the center of the door on the far side of the bridge. He tried to cross the bridge but his feet wouldn't move. It felt like they were part of the bridge on which he was standing. A wave of panic swept over him. Relax, he told himself. This is only a dream.

He looked back towards the door. He could see a circle of some kind. It was beginning to glow. He realized this circle –

whatever it was – was the second source of light. He tried to move closer, but was still rooted to the bridge. He bent forward as much as he could. The circle was some kind of band.

As if a curtain had been pulled aside revealing something that had long been hidden, B'nair knew instantly that he was seeing the band the Kelpies had mentioned, but failed to explain. In the same instant, the band flashed brilliantly. He could see strange markings all around the outside. This was not just a dream, he told himself. This is a message.

At the same time he was thinking this, he felt a burning sensation in the center of his chest. A sharp pain came on suddenly and was driving deep into him. He looked to his right hand that hung at his side. His axe was still in his hand, but one of the blades was driven into the ground. The pain increased. It was becoming unbearable.

He moved his free hand to the spot where the pain was most intense. He could feel, but not see, something protruding from the center of his body. He couldn't recall anything burning so intensely. He felt the object from where it seemed planted in his chest and reached outward. He opened his eyes.
When he did, he saw he was face to face with Neraka Ferr. The Fire Kelpie had his finger pressed against the Rebbercand's chest, exactly where he had felt the sharp pain. B'nair looked startled and pushed the Kelpie's hand aside.

"What are you doing?" he demanded. "What do you want?"

"Get up," answered the Kelpie. "It's time to leave."

Neraka Ferr removed his finger from B'nair's chest and the pain immediately disappeared. It happened so fast that B'nair wondered if he only imagined it. He felt his chest. There was no indication of any heat. There was no sensation of pain or any residual soreness.

The Kelpie stood up straight and turned away, moving towards his partner, Akmen Milzu, who was waking Ena Ray and Angin Topan. B'nair sat up, still not feeling any pain or discomfort in his chest. He tried to recall the dream. Fragments of it were already fading, but the one thing he remembered was the band.

He felt for the pendant and noted that it was still hanging around his neck and inside his tunic. He patted it gently, realizing more than ever that he needed to retain possession of it. This, the remaining piece that he didn't yet have, and the band were all key – to something. He just didn't know what. But that would change. He was sure of it. He had to pay attention, he told himself. He would discover what they were key to, if he paid attention.
He picked himself up and looked around. During the night something had attempted to penetrate the spell the Kelpie had cast. There were carcasses of various sizes and shapes, not to mention vines and creepers that had shriveled up and died along the edge of the invisible shield.

Quest of Eight Part Seven: Ad Paria

Richard Reda

Akmen Milzu snapped her fingers and began walking. Whatever had protected them in the night was gone; replaced by whatever spell she cast to protect them during the day. They marched most of the day. The Mountain Kelpie never once asked if anyone was tired or hungry – she certainly didn't ask B'nair – but she stopped once or twice.

During these stops she drove her finger into the dirt and created a small spring of drinkable water, and she found edible plants, nuts or berries, and a few unfortunate animals. She also stopped shortly after dusk for the night. It was the last one they would spend in the Swamp. After that it would be another two days hike to reach the mines at Djall.

When they reached the southern edge of the Swamp, it seemed to simply end. There was no specific natural formation such as a ravine or river that separated it from the open plains. It merely stopped.

They reached the end late in the afternoon. No one asked about stopping and making camp. Everyone knew it wasn't going to happen. Akmen Milzu called to B'nair and consulted with him about the most direct course, as if all that had gone on before never happened.

"How far do you estimate it is?" she asked.

"It seems to be about two days journey," he answered. "Assuming there are no obstacles. I've not been to this part of the world before, at least not very long. I don't know what the terrain is like. I don't know if there are impassable sections."

"There are not," she assured him. "I've been here before – a very long time ago. I don't imagine it's changed much."

He wondered why she had to ask how long it would take to complete their journey if she had been here before. As if reading his mind she told him.

"Scirios commands the Lightning Riders," she said. "They conveyed us when I was last here. They will make our trek to find Rovek much quicker."

B'nair only nodded. He had no idea who or what the Lightning Riders were. He assumed they were some kind of creature like the Yokais. He hadn't particularly liked them and hoped these Lightning Riders were more agreeable.

He looked out at the plains. All he saw was a seemingly endless field stretched out to the horizon. It was a pleasant change from the Swamp, although he knew it, too, would be filled with potential dangers. They would cross this for a little more than a day, and then reach a more desert-like terrain.

Akmen Milzu kept the procession moving until after dark, but not throughout the night. When darkness settled in, it felt like they were inside a deep cave. The sky had remained overcast and the low clouds lingered, blocking out the moon and the stars. It was so black, that B'nair could not see the horizon.

He thought it was foolish to continue walking in this blanket of night. They could easily come upon animal holes in the ground or ravines. If they did, they could get injured or killed. In spite of his concerns, he refused to object. He did, however, let the Kelpies take the lead. He stayed close enough to be able to see them, but not so close as to fall victim to whatever danger they might encounter.

He was inwardly relieved when the Mountain Kelpie stopped to make camp, and Neraka Ferr found enough fuel to make a fire – not so much for warmth, as the air was still hot, but for light. No one objected.

Before the middle of the next day, the plains disappeared and the way ahead was nothing but flat sand and rock. Late in the day they came to a long, low rise. It continued for several miles, steadily climbing upward. When they crested the hill, they came upon the mine field of Djall: tens of thousands of holes in the ground, extending for untold miles.

They had arrived. The trick now would be to discover which of these holes held the Kelpie.

Chapter two

Lochen had been studying the front edge of the forest for some time. It was apparent, even though no one asked him – and no one would understand his answer if he had been asked – that he was trying to decide on the best approach. Quinn was standing next to him, astounded by the density of the trees. He had never seen anything like them.

"Wow," he said. "How are we going to get through this?"

Lochen didn't understand the words Quinn spoke, but knowing him as he did, he could well imagine the nature of his question.

"Stajahat ilhodak," he said. "Jistu dajaw streffi ghallat xizm enissa, u M'noxot certl-ah jarrott li jienhush." I've been studying this forest for some time now, and I'm not sure of the best route.

Quinn nodded as if he understood, although he didn't. Lochen turned in the other direction and faced Liam.

"Meilla modin tijirrak komwaddin?" he asked.

Liam turned to face him and gave him a blank stare.

"I haven't been able to understand a word you've said since you woke up," he eventually said. "What makes you think that's changed?"

Lochen gave him a puzzled look. They stood facing each other for a few seconds, each waiting for the other to attempt to clarify communication.

"Satamakau," Lochen finally said. He gestured towards the forest and repeated, "Satamakau?"

Liam nodded his understanding, then frowned and turned towards the woods. He looked left and then right, looked up to the sky and then back behind them. He scratched his head. After careful consideration, he turned back to Lochen.

"That way," he said, pointing slightly towards the right of where they were standing.

"Dan zkiensh hsiev tieghetta, wiszx," Lochen replied. That was my thought, too.

As this discussion was taking place, Sean had been pacing back and forth, muttering about the strange and unknown creature that did unspeakable things to all who entered these woods.

Quest of Eight Part Seven: Ad Paria

Richard Reda

Liam had dismissed his fears, but he had always trusted the ancient taboos of the Forest Creatures.

Sean was becoming so agitated that he looked like he was doing some kind of jungle dance. He hopped from one foot to the next, his head swiveling back and forth, looking at the forest and then jerking his head away from it, as if looking at it would, all on its own, evoke the evil spirit he envisioned lived within.

Summer poked her head out of Lochen's hood to see what was going on with Sean. His antics were becoming distracting. She watched him for several seconds before she turned to Stella.

"Isn't there some kind of potion you can conjure, or root you can feed him to calm him down?" she asked.

Stella looked as Sean and then back at Summer and merely shook her head.

"He knows nothing," Solveig shouted from deep inside the hood.

"Yes," replied Summer, looking back into the hood where Solveig was curled up. "We've already established that, but there must be something we can do or give him. After all we've faced I can't believe he's afraid of a bunch of trees. What's up with that? He lives in a forest! How is this different?"

"Because," Sean snapped at her. "The forest I live in isn't home to some ruthless demon. The forest I live in doesn't have people disappear and never return. Unspeakable things don't happen to people in the forest I live in. The forest I live in is my home – where my family and friends live."

Quinn turned around at the sound of Sean's outburst. He walked over to him and put his hand on Sean's shoulder. He lowered his head and waited until Sean was looking at him eye-to-eye.

"We're your family, now. And your friends," he said. "We'll face whatever is in there right alongside you. You won't be alone. We all come out or none of us comes out."

Sean breathed deeply, somehow calmed by Quinn's comment.

"I was all right until that last part," he said. "Why did you have to add that last part – about none of us coming out?"

"What else was I going to say?" Quinn asked. "That if anything happened to you we'd leave you behind?"

Their discussion was cut short. Liam turned around and announced that they were about ready to begin. Despite the language barrier, he and Lochen had agreed on where to start. They all crowded around so Liam could set out his thoughts about who would go first and who would follow after that.

"Look," said Liam. "I think Lochen and I have to take the lead. Stella, you should be up front with whoever is going first. "

He stole a glance at Sean and added, "Just in case." He hurried on before Sean could ask, "Just in case of what?"

"Quinn, since you're carrying Natalie, you need to be in the middle, between Stella and Sean. With the two of us who can cast spells up front, I think you'll be safer there. Sean, you need to help cover our backs.

"Do you think Lochen can lead us?" asked Summer. "No one can understand a word he says."

Turning towards the back of Lochen's head, she added, "No offense."

"Why are you apologizing?" asked Solveig, struggling to her feet and climbing up to the edge of Lochen's hood. "He can't understand anything you said. He doesn't know if you meant to be offensive or not."

"That's why I'll be up front with him," said Liam. "I'll be helping him lead."

Before any further discussion or debate could ensue, Lochen took a bold step forward and entered the forest. Solveig and Summer flopped back into the folds of the hood.

"Hey," shouted Solveig. "Aren't we going to talk about this first?"

"Apparently not," mumbled Summer.

Solveig and Summer got back to their feet and climbed up his hood to his shoulders – one on either side – and looked to the left and right, stealing glances behind them to make sure the others were close behind. The cold air from the Ice Kingdom quickly disappeared; replaced by a thick fog. There was a heavy, dark moss growing up the trees. It was as black as the bark, but gave the trunks a furry coat.

Quest of Eight Part Seven: Ad Paria

Richard Reda

The trees were so thick, within seconds he was nearly gone from sight. The others lurched forward before he got too far away, and then followed him tentatively. He snapped his fingers and generated a small orb of light that floated a few feet above and ahead of him to light the way. What little light came from the gray sky above was lost under the giant limbs and black leaves that towered above.

The ground was covered with layers of leaves and dead branches, but the air was so moist that everything they walked across felt like a damp sponge. What little sound their footsteps made was swallowed in the surrounding humidity and the ominous growth that was wrapped around the trees.

Sean had readied his slingshot and was alternating between walking forward while looking backwards and walking backwards while looking forward. He backed up to trees and then spun around, jumping into a defensive crouch. His odd behavior caught Quinn's eye.

"What are you doing?" he asked impatiently.

"Keeping an eye out for trouble," he mumbled. "You know – for that...that...thing – those things – oh, man, I hope there isn't more than one. Actually, I hope there isn't even one of them...it"

"But why are you," Quinn tried to find the right word to describe the way Sean was walking, "dancing?"

"I'm not dancing!" he insisted. "I'm being unpredictable."

He spun in a complete circle and nearly tripped over his own feet. Recovering, he jumped into the air and landed once more in a crouching position, pulling back on his slingshot and quickly shifting his aim from right to left and back, as if someone or something had begun an attack. Quinn merely rolled his eyes.

"You're being a dope," Quinn muttered. "Which is hardly unpredictable."

Sean continued his antics, unfazed by the criticism. Lochen continued forward, climbing over and around large roots, trying to avoid contact with the moss, fungus, or whatever it was that clung to the trees. Every once in a while a space would open up, revealing a small clearing. Sometimes there even appeared to be a hint of a path. After little more than two hours of exhausting travel, Lochen stopped at the next such clearing.

"Nathsab li ghaddack mistriecht," he said. "L-arxa hijatta tannis ohxjonn, huwatti finddikki lin fins." I think we should rest. The air is so thick, it's difficult to breathe.

Liam looked at him, still not comprehending a single word, and said. "Thanks. I think we need a rest. The air is so thick, it's hard to breathe."

Lochen only nodded. He didn't understand Liam's words, either, but he could see by the fatigue on Liam's face the meaning behind his words. There were some fallen trunks on the edge of the clearing. Lochen examined them and found nothing threatening. He motioned to the others and signaled they could sit. They didn't think twice about any danger and quickly sat.

While the rest of them dropped to the large logs and relaxed, Lochen wandered a few feet away, poking through the leafy coverage with his foot. Eventually, he found what he was looking for. He picked up a branch that was about three feet long and had broken to a point at one end. He tested it and found that it had not yet become as sodden as so many of the other fallen limbs and twigs.

He moved to the center of the clearing, looked up at the treetops and took a step or two to one side as if aligning himself with some unseen marker. When he was satisfied that he was in the right position – whatever that was – he raised the stick above his head with both hands and drove it into the ground. It sunk about halfway.

He wiggled it back and forth as he mumbled some indistinguishable and unintelligible incantation and then jerked the stick from the ground. At first nothing happened. Then there was a gurgling sound, followed by a gush of water that sprung up like a small fountain. Lochen reached into the flow of water with a cupped hand and drank it.

"Are you crazy?" shouted Quinn. "You don't know where that water's been."

"Huwatta ghansho toffuma pjuttotta qawwixita," he said smacking his lips and taking another drink. "Izdatta nemm enli huwattom tajjebli tirox." It has a rather pungent taste, but I believe it's safe to drink.

He looked up to see them all staring at him blankly. He nodded to the spring and scooped out another handful of water, taking another drink. He smiled and nodded again. Liam didn't need a second invitation. He reached his hand in and cupped the water into his mouth. He winced as he swallowed and struggled not to spit it out.

"Oh, brother," he coughed. "That's going to leave a pretty bad aftertaste. It reminds me of...never mind. You don't want to know."

The others watched him and were put off by his words. The grimace he made when he swallowed was far from encouraging. He took another handful and then another, filling up on the water.

"It's not so bad once you get used to it," he said. "Go ahead. It may be a while before we find any more."

Stella took a small cloth from one of her pockets and soaked it. She squeezed the water from it over Natalie's mouth, coaxing it into her. When she had done this several more times, she scooped up her own drink. The others had been drinking their fill as she tended to Natalie.

After a while Quinn asked, "I thought you said it's not so bad once you get used to it. When do you get used to it?"

"You don't," Liam answered. "I lied. The taste just gets worse, but we need to stay hydrated. I only hope it's safe to drink."

"Now you tell us you hope it's safe?" spouted Sean, spitting a mouthful out. "Now? Really? After we've all probably poisoned ourselves?"

"Look at the bright side," said Solveig as she shifted in Lochen's hood. "Maybe it'll make you taste so bad that this so-called monster you've been whining about – and that no one's seen, by the way – will find you too disagreeable to eat."

"I never said it ate you," Sean shot back. "I said it did unspeakable things to you. There's a difference. And I never said there was more than one."

Their debate was cut short by a sudden rustling across the dead damp leaves. They all turned in the direction of the sound, but saw nothing. They waited expectantly; all eyes wide open, staring into the forest. Then they heard it again.

"What was that?" squeaked Summer.

"Maybe it was the wind," suggested Quinn.

"What wind?" challenged Solveig. "We're in the middle of some kind of demonic forest where the air doesn't have room to move and you think that was the wind?"

"It's them," whispered Sean, his throat suddenly dry. "Him. Her. It. Whatever. Please let there be only one. It's going to do unspeakable things to us."

"If these things are unspeakable," said Summer, "I wish you'd stop speaking about them. And why do you hope there's only one? Why can't there be none? None is a whole lot better than one, don't you think?"

They each looked in every direction and strained to listen. They could see nothing but the trees. They heard nothing at all. The

44

absence of sound was even more terrifying than the rustling of the leaves had been.

"Ghaddah nzommat jekkaqlaqat," said Lochen. We should keep moving.

No one tried to get him to explain what he said, and he didn't wait to see if they understood. He turned away from the spring, which died out as suddenly as it had appeared. He looked around and then started off. He led them, twisting and turning in between the trees for several more miles until he came to another clearing.

Here, what spaces Lochen had followed as a path now opened in two separate directions. This was something new. He stopped for a second, as if trying to decide which one to take. He turned to Liam.

"Satamakau?" he asked, and gestured to the two openings.

Liam looked at both, then up to the sky. He closed his eyes for a second and when he opened them he pointed to the right.

"That way," he said. "That's the way to Satamakau."

Lochen nodded his understanding and turned in that direction. As soon as he did, they all heard the same rustling in the leaves they had heard at the spring. Everyone stopped and looked around. This time, the noise continued. All eyes darted in several directions at once. Eventually, they each found the source.

In the middle of the path that Lochen was about to take, the leaves on the ground were fluttering – being pushed aside by something unseen beneath them. Everyone backed away a step or two. The leaves were pushed up and away as something emerged from the ground.

Ants. It seemed as if they had come upon a colony of fire ants. Several of them had broken from the ground and were pushing the leaves out of the way. More were following right behind.

"Ants," said Quinn with a sigh of relief. "It's only ants. That noise that scared all of us. It was only ants."

"I wasn't scared," objected Sean.

"Are you kidding?" countered Summer. "You were the scaredest of all of us."

"I was not," Sean shot back.

"You should have been," Liam cut him off. "Those are fire ants. They can be very dangerous."

"Maybe we can step around them," suggested Solveig.

"Daska jidruhu lihu manem el tanzanar," said Lochen. "Forsikki nist ghupanz madawarhonna." Those appear to be fire ants. Maybe we can step around them.

Without waiting for any acknowledgement of understanding, Lochen took a step forward down the path to the left of the ants. They suddenly changed direction and moved in his way, cutting him off. More of them were emerging, climbing on top of one another, bubbling up out of the ground.

He stepped back and moved to the other side. Hundreds more burst out from beneath the dead leaves and spread out, cutting him off from that direction as well. He stepped back and considered what alternatives he had. He thought about casting a spell on them, but was reluctant. He didn't know what other enchantments lingered in the forest or protected the ants. Anything he cast could react differently than intended.

As he watched them, Stella stepped forward and raised her hand. Lochen caught the motion out of the corner of his eye. He reached out and grabbed her hand, stopping her.

"Muhx! Mana fuxxim pattack jespli citaw jistanta 'jkollchka. Nahzek lidan stiref hikja xededka ew natcheden." No! We don't know what impact a spell might have. I think this forest is hexed or enchanted.

"I hope you know what you're doing," Stella responded.

Although she didn't understand the words, she comprehended their meaning. She lowered her arm and looked back at the ants. They had continued to pour out of whatever hole in the ground from which they had come. Instead of spreading across the ground as expected, though, they stacked themselves on top of each other, rising higher and higher.

After a few seconds, they began to rise up and spread outward to the front, back and sides. Within minutes a low, wide tree with long extended branches and no leaves stood before them. Only this one was made up of thousands and thousands of fire ants. The movement of the ants made it appear as if the "bark" on the tree was moving.

"Hanfunta santinnestixi," said Lochen as he cocked his head slightly to the side.

"I know that look," said Solveig.

"What look?" asked Summer

"The look on his face," Solveig replied.

"You can't see his face," objected Summer. "You're leaning against the back of his shoulder."

"I don't need to see his face," she argued. "I can tell by the sound of his voice and the tilt of his head. He thinks this is interesting. He'd probably like to stay here and study them."

Even as she was speaking, Lochen stepped slowly and carefully toward the ant-tree, leaning his head forward to see it more clearly. He was gradually extending his hand as if to reach out and touch the ants, when Solveig whistled as loudly as she could into his ear.

"Are you completely mental?" she shouted.

She reached forward and smacked his shoulder, trying to get his attention. He stopped in mid-reach and turned his head slightly in her direction. Just as she could tell what he was thinking, he could tell by the sound of her voice what she had said.

"Muhx, neji manen lentak. Neji sibbisti juzruk," he replied. No, I'm not mental. I'm only curious.

He took a step back and refocused on the problem at hand. He saw that the way Liam had designated as the direction to Satamakau was completely blocked by the ants. He looked at the other path, and then back to the ants. There was no telling how long they would remain in the way, and he knew they could not wait.

"Jihdre ghandanna l-ediba ghaxxala liheffi lijm orrufidin id-zzojodni," he said.

He looked to Liam and frowned. He was trying to think of a way to communicate what he had just said. Liam looked at him, and raised his arm towards the open path.

"I get it," he said. "We have to go this way. Let's get going then."

Lochen led them away from the ant-tree and away from Satamakau. After a few miles they stopped again to rest.

"I'm thirsty," said Sean. "But I don't know if I'm thirsty enough to drink that sewage Lochen dug up."

At the sound of his name, Lochen looked to Sean. He stood up and motioned as if he was driving a stick into the ground. He raised his eyebrows in question.

"No," said Sean, signaling to Lochen. "Thanks, but I'm fine. Really. My stomach hasn't settled from the last time."

As they were talking Liam was looking at the forest and the sky. He looked back the way they had come and then forward through the trees. He turned from one direction to another, checking and double checking what he thought he was seeing.

"I don't know how we did this," he said, "but we're back in the right direction. I think we went a little bit out of our way, and maybe lost a little time, but we're back on course."

Lochen looked at him blankly. He pointed up the path and said, "Satamakau."

Lochen looked at the path and then back to Liam and smiled, nodding his understanding. Whatever elation this discovery had brought them vanished when they heard the rustling in the leaves again. Everyone was on alert, looking in every direction, but there was nothing to see.

"Don't say it was the wind," cautioned Summer.

"I wasn't going to say that," said Quinn. "I mean it could be the wind, but I wasn't going to say that."

No one waited for the decision to be made. They all got up and continued on their way. As they moved deeper and deeper into the forest, the tiny orb of light that Lochen had generated was providing less and less light. They couldn't see more than a few feet in any direction. Sean was getting even jumpier in his rear guard position.

"If I don't believe in you, you can't exist," he muttered. "I don't believe in you. I don't believe in you. I don't believe in you."

Quinn looked over at him and frowned.

"You're not real. You don't exist. I don't believe in you," Sean kept mumbling.

"What are you doing now?" demanded Quinn.

"I'm telling the creature that I don't believe in it...in him...in...whatever," Sean answered. "And if I don't believe in it then it can't exist."

"But if you're talking to it, doesn't that mean you really believe it exists?" asked Quinn.

"What's with you," snapped Sean. He stopped, put his hands on his hips and said, "Do you think you're Lochen now? Mr. Sensible?"

"No," muttered Quinn. He stopped and turned back to Sean. "I don't think I'm Lochen, but I don't have to be. You don't make any sense. Come on, think about it. If you're talking to this thing, then you already think it's real, and just saying you don't believe in it isn't going to make it not be real. Besides, we haven't seen any signs of any living thing here, except for those ants."

"Maybe it isn't a living thing," said Sean. "Did you ever think about that?"

"What do you mean it isn't a living thing?" asked Quinn. "You mean a dead thing?"

"No," said Sean. "I mean like some kind of para norma lacktivity thing."

Quinn stopped walking again, turned and stared at Sean. Sean stopped and looked back at him, seeing the frown on Quinn's face.

"What?" Sean asked.

"I'm beginning to think that Lochen, who is speaking in some unknown language, makes more sense than you – even if I don't understand anything he says."

"What are you talking about?" asked Sean, indignantly.

"What are YOU talking about?" Quinn shot back, pointing his finger at Sean.

"I was talking about the creature in this forest," said Sean defensively.

"You said something about a pair of norma lacktivity. I thought there was only one of these things in the forest. Are you telling me now that there are two? And who is Norma?"

"Two what?" asked Sean. "Norma who? What are you talking about?"

"I don't know," said Quinn. He took a step close and bent his head down closer to Sean, whispering, "You're the only one who seems to know anything about the monsters. You tell me."

"Tell you what?" asked Sean, who began to whisper only because Quinn had.

"Is there only one or are there two?"

"Who said anything about two?" asked Sean.

"You did," Quinn whispered forcefully.

"I did not," Sean hissed back.

"You said there was a pair of them."

"I said that this monster didn't necessarily have to be a living thing. It could be…you know…like a ghost, or something – a para norma lacktivity kind of thing."

"That's just stupid," said Quinn, standing upright. "That's really…"

Quinn suddenly realized that it seemed darker. It was also quiet. He looked at Sean, who he could barely see once he straightened up. Then he looked to the right and saw nothing. He turned to the left and saw the same nothing.

"What are you looking for?" asked Sean.

"Where did everybody go?" asked Quinn

Sean's head jerked around. He couldn't see more than ten feet in any direction. He looked up at the sky, but it was completely blocked by the leaves. He squinted, searching for the small ball of light that Lochen had created, but it was nowhere to be seen.

"Where did everybody go?" Sean squeaked.

"That's what I just said," Quinn said in a shaking voice. "They wouldn't have just left us, would they?"

"Maybe it got them?" gasped Sean.

"Don't say that," demanded Quinn. "They're all all right. We only got separated. Which way should we go?"

"How should I know?" Sean hissed. "Weren't you paying attention?"

"Me?" countered Quinn. "What about you? Weren't _you_ paying attention?"

"I was guarding the back," snapped Sean. "That's what I was supposed to do. I wasn't supposed to be paying attention to where we were going – only where we had been. What were _you_ doing?"

"I was listening to you," Quinn snapped back. "Which, I can see, was a big mistake."

"Nobody forced you to do that," Sean sniped. "Don't blame me for your mistake."

"Don't worry," shot Quinn, "It won't happen again. I won't listen to a thing you ever say."

"Fine!" said Sean.

"Fine!" Quinn answered.

They both stood there glaring at one another. Sean folded his arms and poked his head forward, intensifying his stare. Quinn folded his arms, but realized he was still carrying Natalie in the straps around his neck. He tried to shift her one way and then the other so he could fold his arms and glare back at Sean.

When he realized this couldn't be done, he put his hands on his hips instead and leaned his head forward and hovered over Sean's head. They stood like that for a minute or two, Quinn staring down and Sean staring up. After a while, they both looked to their right and then to their left and then behind them.

"Which way should we go?" asked Quinn.

"I don't know. Maybe we should stay where we are," answered Sean. "Sooner or later, they'll see we're not with them and they'll come back for us. Besides, what if we go in the wrong direction? They might never find us then."

"What if something has happened to them?"

"I don't think something would have happened to all of them," said Sean. "At least I hope not."

Then they heard the rustling in the leaves.

"What was that?" gasped Sean.

"OK," said Quinn. He started chewing on the end of his thumb and rested his other arm on top of Natalie's still sleeping body. "If I was facing you and they were on my right, then we should go to the right. That seems to make sense."

"What was that?" Sean repeated. He stood frozen in place like a statue.

"I don't remember turning around," said Quinn. "Do you remember turning around? No, wait. You were turning around all the time. That's no good. I'm pretty sure I didn't turn around. If I didn't turn around, then that's the way we came and that's the way we were going. I think we should go this way."

He pointed to his right.

"What was that?" Sean asked again.

"Will you stop asking that?" Quinn snapped. "I don't know what it was and neither do you. Do you expect there's someone else here that can answer you? I hope not."

The leaves rustled again and they both froze in place.

About the time their initial debate had begun, Lochen had reached another clearing with another split in the passage – not that there was much of a passage to begin with. Still, there was enough of an opening to force him to have to make a choice. As Liam stepped up to him, Lochen turned back to face him.

That was when he noticed something odd. It had been nearly impossible to gauge what time of day it was, since the little bit of daylight was almost completely unable to penetrate the canopy of leaves. However, it was clear that by now night had fallen. Lochen couldn't see more than a few yards behind him, even with the illumination from the orb.

He knew that Solveig and Summer were safe in the folds of his hood. Liam was right next to him and Stella was close behind. Where were Sean and Quinn? And Natalie, who was still in a sling attached to Quinn? He pushed past Liam and took a few steps back along the way they had come. There was no sign of them.

"Sean," said Lochen. "Quinn." He turned to face Liam. "Fejhan humazak?" Where are they?

"Where are they?" Liam asked, not knowing that was Lochen's same question.

"They were right behind me," said Stella.

"We have to go back," said Liam.

He started back down the way they had come, but Lochen stopped him.

"Jiensh serra imorrtu. Intotti gghodd wahawn," Lochen said. I'll go. You stay here.

He motioned for Liam to stay with Stella. He didn't wait for an answer. He snapped his fingers and created a second tiny light. When he did so the light from the initial orb dimmed slightly and discolored from its original level as some of its power was diverted to the second one. Lochen flicked his finger and the second light shifted over towards Liam and Stella and hovered there.

Then he reached back, removed Solveig and Summer from the hood of his robe, turned and disappeared into the woods.

Chapter three

Akmen Milzu stood next to B'nair as they and the others gazed upon the vast expanse of holes in the valley before them. They were of varying sizes, and, B'nair guessed, depths. He couldn't imagine the Trepans digging anything like this, but they were the only miners he was aware of. He was at a loss as to who or what could have created so many mines.

He had heard of this place, but his travels never brought him here. The mines of Djall had been a myth among his people. Everyone knew about them, although, to his recollection, none of his people had ever seen them. How did they know about them, then, he wondered. He thought that if he ever made it back to his own people, he'd explore that. For now, though, that time seemed like it would be a long way off – if it ever came at all.

"Which one?" Neraka Ferr asked. "Which hole is he in?"

"I can't tell from here," answered B'nair. "I need to get closer."

They moved across the crest of the hill and descended into the valley. It was more than an hour later that they reached the first of the holes. These were rather small – most less than a foot in diameter. B'nair knew the Kelpie wasn't in any of these, but he stopped anyway. He lowered himself to one knee and felt the edge of the nearest hole.

The ground was hard; almost like stone, although there was a layer of soft dirt on the surface. He ran his hand along the inside wall of the opening. It was hard, smooth and charred, as if something had burned it. He turned to look back at the Mountain Kelpie.

"What caused this?" he asked. "Where did all these holes come from?"

"They were created by a meteor shower," Akmen Milzu responded.

B'nair looked at the hole immediately before him and then at the field of the thousands of others stretched out over the valley. He couldn't imagine a meteor shower that was this compact or localized. He thought there was more to this than the Mountain Kelpie was ready to explain. He debated about pushing her for more information, but discovered that he wasn't the only one who was so inquisitive.

"A meteor shower?" asked Ena Ray. "How is that possible? Why would a meteor shower be limited to this valley and nowhere else?"

"Do you doubt my word?" snapped Akmen Milzu.

"No," Ena Ray quickly replied. "Not at all. I'm merely curious about this location; about what happened here. I don't need to remind you that, like most of you, I have been imprisoned for centuries. There is much for me to learn."

B'nair thought Ena Ray had recovered nicely and had posed his question in such a way that the Kelpie would be forced to explain. He was right; and she did.

Two thousand years ago the Valley of Djall had been a lush and fertile field. It was a vast valley, nestled in between low lying hills that separated it from the Swamp on the north and the range of mountains to the south that divided the land almost in half. The mountains had been the home of Akmen Milzu and Scirios had been her sorcerer.

Scirios had also been one of the mountain people, but had spent his youth under the mentorship of the prime sorcerer – Vezeto Landoo. All Sorcerers serve the leader and the people from which they came, much the way that all Enchantresses serve their people and leader. However, both Sorcerers and Enchantresses must spend several years under their respective mentors, honing the skills with which they are born.

The Enchantresses were mentored by Ceannaire, one of the most powerful of her kind. Most Enchantresses are women, but on rare occasion, an Enchanter has been part of their elite group. At the telling of this part of the history, Akmen Milzu reflexively glanced at Neraka Ferr. This movement was not lost on B'nair or Ena Ray. They both wondered if the Fire Kelpie was one of these rare Enchanters, but both held that thought to themselves.

Not long after Scirios had completed his mentorship, the Kelpie uprising began. Battle lines were drawn and sides were taken. Scirios followed the lead of Akmen Milzu. At one time during the conflict, the Kelpies had convened in this valley. Vezeto Landoo had tried to destroy them.

Using his powers, and with the aid of the Alchemist, he rained down a devastating meteor shower on the valley. The resulting fire and ash turned the valley into a desert, scarred with thousands of holes. Over the centuries, the residual debris from the meteors was dug away by Trepans. Now there was a honeycomb of mines that interconnected the shafts, deep below the surface of the earth.

Some of the shafts, however, were dead ends, coming to a stop several miles underground. Others opened to aquifers – large expanses of streams and lakes at different levels. And still others opened to rivers of lava and fire. Only a few led to tunnels that were safe. One had to be very careful in descending any of the pits.

When the Kelpies were separated and trapped, and the Alchemist imprisoned them, he chose locations near to their origins. Although the Valley of Djall had not been Scirios' place of birth, apparently the Alchemist had seen some degree of irony in burying him here.

"So this Scirios person is in one of these mines?" asked Ena Ray.

"So it seems," answered Akmen Milzu. "Since our friend, B'nair, has led us here."

"And how, exactly, are we supposed to figure out which one?" Ena Ray asked. "Do we go down each one, or just guess?"

"Leave that part to me," the Rebbercand answered. "Getting down into the mine itself will be much more difficult."

"I will address that when the time comes," said Akmen Milzu.

"We don't all have to go, do we?" Ena Ray wondered. "As you can imagine, after being in a black hole in the ground for two thousand years, I'm not anxious to return."

"That won't be necessary," said Akmen Milzu. "Only one of us will need to accompany B'nair – someone to ensure that Scirios doesn't mistake our friend here for an enemy."

"Scirios will need time to recuperate," said Angin Topan. "The sooner we find him the sooner that will happen. He'll also need time to summon the Lightning Riders."

"Yes," agreed the Mountain Kelpie. "We've spent enough time on the history lesson. B'nair, if you would, please lead the way."

B'nair turned from the Kelpie towards the valley. He reached up and held the pendant in his hand and closed his eyes. The vision of the map returned. He could no longer see the locations of the Kelpies that had been released. Not only were the markers of their prisons gone, but those areas of the map itself were now nothing more than blurs.

The features such as mountains, rivers, and forests were completely obliterated. However, the mines of Djall were even more vivid than before. He scanned the terrain in the vision, looking for a sign as to which of the holes held the Kelpie.

He felt a wave of panic when nothing jumped out at him. His mental eye swept the field, moving from front to back. There was nothing but black hole after black hole – and then a slight flash. It was so slight and so quick, he almost missed it. At the same instant that the flash appeared, he felt a tingling in the pendant.

He fixed his vision on where the flash had appeared and opened his eyes. The image in his vision was repeated identically before him. His gaze was fixed on an opening off to the right and well into the distance.

"This way," he motioned.

He began to weave his way in and around the mines. The spaces between them varied as much as the size of the holes. In some places there was barely enough to walk across. In others, there was room enough for all of them to walk abreast.

Akmen Milzu stayed close to B'nair's side, with Neraka Ferr close behind. Ena Ray's legs were becoming more and more solid, but he still glided across the ground with the imp on his shoulder. Angin Topan's wings were beginning to fill back in. It wouldn't be much longer and she would once again be able to fly. By then, with any luck, another Kelpie would be counted among them – and these Lightning Riders; whatever they were.

B'nair would stop periodically, close his eyes and hold his pendant. He was fairly certain he knew which mine was the correct one, but he used these opportunities as reminders to the Kelpies how much they needed him. He refused to identify the mine at the onset, saying only that the vision told him they were in the right place, but it only grew stronger the closer they got. None of this was true.

He could easily have taken them directly to the mine after first locating it. He didn't need to go through the charade of closing his eyes and grasping the pendant. He chose to do this solely for dramatic effect and to enhance his own self-importance.

Like Ena Ray, he had no fondness of mines. He had somehow escaped the disaster in the Trepan mine when the Scyllas had attacked. And he had miraculously escaped when the bridge he had been standing on collapsed, nearly dropping him into the river of magma, only to be saved by the hobgoblins.

He didn't like pressing his luck, and he viewed going down one of these shafts just that – pressing his luck. He knew there was no way around it. He alone could release the Kelpies from their prisons. He would have preferred more than Akmen Milzu's assurances that his descent into the pit would be "addressed." How and by whom, he wondered.

After several hours of winding back and forth, they came upon an opening that looked much like all the others. There was nothing particularly different about the one at which B'nair stopped. It was smaller than most – barely two feet in diameter.

The top edge was hard and crusted, like all the others. The entryway of the shaft was black and crystallized from the burning meteor particle that formed it.

"This is it," B'nair announced.

He hadn't leaned over to peer down the hole. He didn't need to. He knew he wouldn't be able to see anything and he needed no visual confirmation to be certain this was the location. The tingling in the pendant stopped as soon as he arrived at the edge of the mine.

He wondered what would happen next. Although he knew the Kelpie was in this specific shaft, he had no idea how far down, whether the shaft narrowed further down, or what was at the bottom, if anything. He had no interest in finding out. In spite of his apathy about discovering the answers to these questions, though, he was about to learn them.

"Angin Topan," said the Mountain Kelpie. "If you could fly, things would be so much easier. However, this will have to be sufficient."

She didn't wait for an answer. She waved her hand and a dragonfly appeared out of thin air. It hovered for a second and then darted over to Ena Ray's shoulder. The imp looked over at Akmen Milzu. Being forced to ride such a creature was highly insulting. Angin Topan clenched her jaw in anger.

"My deepest apologies," said the Mountain Kelpie. "If there was any other way, I would gladly use it; but there's not. We must know where our friend is and what lies beneath. Only you can tell us."

Angin Topan swallowed her pride and mounted the dragonfly. With a sudden jerk, the insect flew over the shaft and immediately disappeared from sight, pulling its reluctant rider along. Once it was gone, Neraka Ferr stepped to the edge of the hole and flicked a finger. A ball of fire burst into the air and slowly sunk into the shaft following behind the imp and the dragonfly, providing light for them to see.

The dragonfly spun in circles, dropping lower and lower. The light from the fire glistened off the sides of the shaft; the reflective surfaces of stone that was heated and melted by the meteor acting as mirrors. The tiny pair descended more than a thousand feet to the bottom of the mine.

Once there, it opened to a giant crater, like the base of a flower bulb – round at the sides and bottom and tapered at the top where it connected to the mineshaft. Hovering in the center of the open space was a mass of black crystal.

The ball of fire created by Neraka Ferr slowly descended through the shaft and into the cavern. It struck the top of the crystal and shattered into hundreds of small embers, falling to the ground. The smaller blazes shed light that bounced off the walls of the cavern, multiplying the light sources a hundred-fold and illuminating the entire area.

Angin Topan steered the dragonfly closer to the black crystal. It was streaked with fine jagged lines of white, as if lightning itself had been frozen in the stone. Deep inside, the imp could make out a form. She moved closer, almost touching the crystal, squinting to identify the image. What she saw staring back at her was a face: the face of Scirios contorted in a scream of fear and petrified for two thousand years.

The imp steered the dragonfly upward, back to the surface, and reported, "He's encased in a black crystal of some kind. It's floating in mid-air at the bottom of the shaft. The cavern at the base is not very big. If the Rebbercand can fit down the shaft, he can reach the crystal standing on the bottom of the cavern.

"If I can fit down the shaft?" sputtered B'nair. "You can't expect me to go down there. You can't conjure up some insect to carry me down and back, and if you don't have a guaranteed way of bringing me back…"

"What?" asked the Mountain Kelpie when B'nair didn't finish his sentence. "You'll refuse to go? I don't see that as an option. Not really? Do you?"

B'nair hated her sarcastic tone, but he knew she was right. He had no options. If there was any way to bring the crystal to the surface, it would have risen here long ago. He looked at the shaft. It was barely big enough for him to fit into. How would he ever be able to get back out?

"Angin Topan will accompany you," said Akmen Milzu. "You both will stay below while Scirios recovers. He will be able to bring you back to the surface once his strength returns."

"Just like that," muttered B'nair.

"Just like that," Akmen Milzu replied.

"And how am I supposed to get down there without falling a thousand feet?" B'nair challenged her. "If I don't survive the fall, then he doesn't get free and you're missing another Kelpie."

Akmen Milzu smiled at him. She walked up to him and put her arm around his shoulder, guiding him to the edge of the mine. He was fairly certain she wasn't going to simply push him in — fairly certain, but not completely certain. He tried to prepare himself for the unexpected without betraying anything.

"You will float on the air," she said.

With that she waived her free hand, took a deep breath and then blew into the mine. The air expelling from her body at first whistled and then turned into a roar. When she stopped, the breath that had filled the mine and the cavern below began to push outward. At that moment, she did exactly what B'nair couldn't believe she would do. She pushed him in.

At first he dropped quickly. Reacting instinctively, he tried to dig the axe into the stone to get a hold or to at least slow down. It only clanged against the stone. As quickly as he dropped, he began to be buoyed by the wind fighting to reach the surface. It blew past him around the sides of his body, counteracting his weight.

His descent slowed gradually. As it did, he overcame his panic and looked up. He could see the imp on the dragonfly silhouetted against another ball of fire sent down after them by the Fire Kelpie. B'nair wondered what would happen when he hit the end of the shaft.

The thought was barely out of his head when it happened. With a whoosh and a pop, he exited the shaft, bounced as he hit the black crystal and landed unceremoniously on his back-side on the bottom of the small cavern. Angin Topan followed right behind, but with a little more dignity.

When the ball of fire came through right behind the imp and the dragonfly, striking the black crystal as the first one had, B'nair raised his arm to protect himself from the shower of burning embers. Several of them landed on him and began to burn.

"Why didn't you tell me this was going to happen?" he demanded of the imp.

"It wasn't a problem for me," she responded.

He beat his hand against the cinders that had attached themselves to his clothing and were beginning to smolder. When he was sure he had removed all of them, he glared at Angin Topan, who took no notice. Then he turned his attention to the chunk of crystal hovering in the center of the cavern.

He walked around it, looking at every angle. That was when he discovered the face, deep within. He gasped at the sight: a pained expression, the mouth open in a scream of terror, and dead, black eyes staring back at him. He reached up and pushed against the rock. It didn't move. He pushed harder, but nothing happened. Then he put all his weight into it, leaning against it. It remained solidly in place.

"I don't think you're going to be able to move it," said Angin Topan.

"I don't either," replied B'nair. "But I wanted to make sure before I swung this axe at it."

He moved around to the back of the crystal and spotted a point where parts of it created a small notch. Striking this location would keep the axe blade from ricocheting to one side or the other. The Rebbercand looked behind him to make sure he had enough room and adjusted his swing accordingly.

He brought the axe back, clearing the ceiling and, focusing intently, struck in the center of the notch. The clang of the blade resounded in the enclosed area. Even before the echoing stopped, it was joined by a plaintive wailing noise. Slowly the crystal cracked open and the Kelpie inside broke through like a chick hatching from its egg.

The person that emerged was tall and thin. His skin was so pale it was almost white as snow, but his hair was as black as the stone he had been curled up and compressed inside for the last two millennia. He straightened out slowly and turned to face B'nair.

His face, like his body, was long and thin. He had a large, beak-like nose that separated two dead, black eyes – shark's eyes, thought B'nair. His arms dangled at his sides, large hands with long thin fingers hanging limply. He seemed confused.

"Who are you?" he asked, staring at B'nair, his eyes shifting from the Rebbercand's face to the axe and back.

"He is a friend," interjected Angin Topan.

The Kelpie turned and looked at the imp, still not showing any signs of comprehension. He tried to take a step, but staggered.

"It is your old friend, Angin Topan," the imp said. "You have been released from your prison. Sit down while you regain your strength."

Scirios looked to the tiny Kelpie and then back to B'nair. He slowly looked around him at the small cavern, at the embers burning in scattered piles, and at the broken remains of the crystal in which he had been held captive. He staggered again and then lowered himself to the ground.

"Where am I?" he asked.

"In the mines of Djall," replied Angin Topan.

"Mines?" he questioned.

"The Valley of Djall," the imp corrected herself. "You knew it as the Valley of Djall. Before the uprising."

"The uprising," Scirios repeated. "Yes. The uprising. I remember. What happened?"

"We were defeated," Angin Topan told him. "The Alchemist and his witch outsmarted us. They divided us and captured us one by one, casting spells that imprisoned us. But we are free now."

"Yes," Scirios said. "Yes. I remember. I was battling Vezeto Landoo. He was at my mercy. Then...something happened...I can't recall what. It was as if the sky exploded. I was swept away. Everything went black. I felt like I couldn't breathe."

His voice was becoming thinner and faded to a whisper. His face was beginning to contort, reflecting a growing sense of fear.

"That is all over now," said Angin Topan, trying to calm her friend. "You are with friends. We are here for you. Akmen

Milzu and Neraka Ferr are above, waiting for you. Saldeti will be with us soon."

The Kelpie turned to the imp, recognition of the names slowly sinking in.

"You will feel better when your strength has returned," Angin Topan assured him.

"Does he need food?" B'nair asked.

"No," replied the imp.

She stretched out one arm and gestured towards a piece of the black crystal that had broken away from the larger piece in which Scirios had been embedded. It slid across the ground and flew up to her hand. It was nearly as big as she was, but she suspended it effortlessly a few inches in front of her.

She muttered an incantation that B'nair could barely hear, not that he would have understood the language she was speaking. The shard then floated upward and over to Scirios, hovering over his head.

"Nourish yourself," she said to him.

The Kelpie leaned his head back and opened his mouth. Angin Topan moved the stone over his head and held it there. In seconds droplets appeared from within the crystal and fell into Scirios' mouth. He reminded B'nair of a baby bird taking food from its mother – it was another similarity to birds that he noted: first, hatching from the crystal as if from an egg; second, the beak-like nose on the Kelpie; and now the way he was taking the droplets from the crystal.

B'nair wondered if there was some other reason for these connections. Could this Kelpie fly, too? Would he sprout feathers? He continued to watch in silence. The drops from the rock fell like thick sap from a tree, but as black as the stone itself.

When Scirios had taken all the crystal could offer, he looked around and found another piece. This one he moved on his own, grasping it in his long, thin hand and squeezing it. More droplets fell and he lapped them up. This went on for some time.

B'nair watched as for the next several hours, the Kelpie gathered pieces of the broken shell of crystal and extracted the thick liquid from the stone. He noted that neither of the Kelpies still on the surface called down or made any effort to find out what was going on down here. Did they already know what was happening? That was certainly possible. Each of them required some kind of replenishing and time to recover from their captivity.

When it appeared that Scirios was done, his eyelids grew heavy and he slumped against the side of the cavern, his long, thin legs stretched out before him.

"He will sleep now," said the imp.

"And what do we do in the meantime?" B'nair asked.

"We wait until he awakens," said Angin Topan. "Do you have a pressing engagement elsewhere?"

The little Kelpie smiled at the question. B'nair found nothing amusing. He noticed, though, that the imp's wings had filled in considerably in the time they had been down here. He wondered if she would fly out and leave him behind. Not with two more Kelpies to be released, he thought. After that, who knew?

He closed his eyes for a few seconds, but then thought better of trying to sleep. If he was to be left behind, it wouldn't be without a fight or while he was asleep and unaware. He opened his eyes. Scirios was sound asleep, but the imp was wide awake and watching him.

"You were close to him?" B'nair asked.

"We were all close...are all close," she answered.

B'nair couldn't understand such a bond between two people, not to mention more than that. He had no friends, close or otherwise – not even his own brother. Not having this experience himself, he didn't believe it could exist between others. His people had never been known to put others first, or to put their trust in others. They collaborated with no one. It was always everyone for himself. He didn't believe the Kelpie.

The heat from the embers that were still scattered around the floor of the cavern was making the air heavy. Try as he might, B'nair could not stay awake. As soon as sleep overtook him, the dream started.

It started the same way as before. He felt like he was falling. His rising panic didn't force him awake. Instead, the falling suddenly stopped. He was on a bridge somewhere deep inside a cave. The cave looked familiar, but he knew he had never been there before.

He faced forward and on the other side of the bridge he saw the same door in the same dim light. He had the same sensation that something was behind him, but nothing was there. He was alone in this strange place.

He looked back towards the door. He knew he was dreaming the exact same dream as before, but he could do nothing to change things. He felt a tingling against his chest. He looked down and saw a flash of light. It was coming from the stone. He pulled the charm out from under his tunic.

There was something in the center of the door on the far side of the bridge. He tried to cross the bridge but his feet wouldn't move. It felt like they were part of the bridge on which he was standing. He looked back towards the door. He could see a circle of some kind. It was beginning to glow. The circle was some kind of band.

He remembered. This was the band the Kelpies had mentioned. In the same instant he recalled what this was, the band flashed brilliantly. He could see strange markings all around the outside. And then, he felt the same burning sensation in the center of his chest. The sharp pain was driving deep into him. He looked to his right hand that hung at his side. His axe was still in his hand, but one of the blades was driven into the ground. The pain increased. It was becoming unbearable.

Quest of Eight Part Seven: Ad Paria

Richard Reda

He moved his free hand to the spot where the pain was most intense. He could feel, but not see, something protruding from the center of his body. He couldn't recall anything burning so intensely. He felt the object from where it seemed planted in his chest and reached outward. He opened his eyes.

When he did, he saw he was face to face with Angin Topan. The Kelpie had her finger pressed against the Rebbercand's chest, exactly where he had felt the sharp pain. B'nair looked startled and pushed the Kelpie's hand aside.

"He's awake," Angin Topan said. "It's time to go."

B'nair shook the sleep from his mind and stood up. Scirios was standing, squeezing more fluid from another shard of the broken crystal. He didn't look much different. He was still thin and very pale, but his eyes looked much more alert. When he saw B'nair staring at him as he swallowed the last drop from the crystal, he smiled. There was no warmth in his face.

"One for the road," he said in the same reedy thin voice.

"Good for you," B'nair muttered. "Now how do we get out of here?"

Scirios gave the crystal in his hand one last squeeze and then flung it to the ground. It shattered into tiny pieces, and, as it did so, released a tiny electrical charge. The charge rose up from the ground and flickered in the air, dancing like a miniature bolt of lightning.

B'nair looked from the lightning to Angin Topan. The imp was smiling. B'nair turned back to the charge, waiting for something more to happen. Scirios pointed at the floating electricity and then motioned toward Angin Topan. The charge hovered for a second and then floated over the imp, inches above her head. She looked upward as the lightning spread out and enveloped her. Then the Kelpie, cocooned in the electricity, rose into the air and up through the shaft.

"What did you do?" demanded B'nair.

"She's safe on the surface," Scirios answered. "Are you ready?"

Without waiting for an answer, the Kelpie pointed to another shard of crystal, lifted it into the air and smashed it on the ground. Another small charge escaped and was moved over B'nair's head. It slowly began to expand.

"Wait," objected B'nair. "What are you doing to me?"

Scirios didn't bother to answer. He watched as the electrical threads vibrated erratically, spreading a spider's web of thin, hair-like flashes of lightning over and around the Rebbercand and then lift him into the air and through the shaft. Once B'nair was gone, the Kelpie looked around at the place that had been his prison for two thousand years.

"I hope I get the opportunity to return the favor, Alchemist," he said.

His strength had fully returned. He no longer needed the shards of the black crystal that had been formed from the exploded meteor in which he had been encased. He waved his hand over his head, and one last bolt of lightning appeared. He let the electricity wash over him and take him to the surface.

He watched patiently as the sides of the mine rushed past him. Rock and bits of meteor that had been burned and fused two millennia ago sparkled, reflecting the brilliant light from the electrical charges that surrounded him. A few seconds later, he was on the surface. The lightning that carried him fizzled and evaporated into nothing, leaving the odd odor of electrical discharge in its place.

"Welcome back, my friend," Akmen Milzu greeted him.

"It's good to see you," Scirios answered. "And you Neraka Ferr. Where are the others?"

"Saldeti is making arrangements elsewhere," answered the Mountain Kelpie. "We will join him in a few days."

"We will set Rovek free next," continued Neraka Ferr. "And then Ollos Foscos."

Scirios took all this in. He looked around, noting the stranger.

"And what of Pantano Izaki?" he asked.

"He had been lost to us," Akmen Milzu answered.

"Lost? How?" Scirios asked.

"When I was being released," explained Angin Topan. "We were attacked. It happened then. He was out of my sight, so I can't be certain exactly how it happened."

"Who did this?" the Kelpie demanded. "Vezeto Landoo? Ceannaire? Traina? Who?"

"None of them," Akmen Milzu answered. "They are all gone. But it seems that their descendants have gathered."

"Although we may have disposed of some of them," Neraka Ferr added.

Descendants, wondered B'nair. What or who were they talking about. Who had gathered? Were they talking about the ones who had been following them? That couldn't be right. His thoughts were interrupted by Scirios' next comments.

"And who is this...Rebbercand? And that other?" he demanded.

"The Rebbercand," Akmen Milzu quickly cut him off, "is a friend. He is called B'nair. He has a piece of the witch's pendant, and has the vision of a map that will lead us to our friends. He has been a valued member of our group."

Even B'nair could tell that the Mountain Kelpie was trying to stop Scirios from giving any more offense. The Lightning Kelpie stared at B'nair as the message Akmen Milzu had been trying to communicate sunk in. His aggressive posture slowly softened. He then turned to Ena Ray.

"I meant no offense," he said by way of apology. "I'm sure you understand that after two thousand years, a lot has changed. It is difficult to grasp it all."

B'nair noted that the apology didn't seem to be directed to him – the one in this group who actually released the Kelpie from his prison.

"This is Ena Ray," said Akmen Milzu. "He was a protégé of the witch before she turned on him. He will serve as Pantano Izaki's replacement."

Scirios looked him up and down as if evaluating a purchase he was about to make. B'nair had thought the other Kelpies were arrogant. This one, he realized, could give them lessons.

"He will complete us," added Angin Topan. "But first we must release our remaining two friends. We will need your help."

Scirios continued to study Ena Ray for a few more seconds before acknowledging the imp's comments. He turned to her, and then to the others. Without being told, he knew what was needed. He nodded his understanding and then stepped back from them a few feet. He raised both arms to the sky and then swung them down quickly and dramatically.

The air around them was filled with a clap of thunder and the spark of electricity. Over their heads a small burst of lightning appeared. Ena Ray was about to comment that this, surely, couldn't be what they all expected would transport them. He turned to B'nair for confirmation, but could tell by the look on his face that more was about to come.

And more did follow. The small arc of current flickered over their heads and then doubled in size. It flickered again and doubled once more. The crackling sound grew louder as the charge grew in size. Then it began to multiply at a quicker rate, spreading out in a large umbrella over the entire group.

From there it descended to the ground, encompassing them completely. Slowly, the spaces inside the shell of electrical current began to fill, surrounding each of them in a web of lightning. Ena Ray fought to remain calm. Even B'nair, who had been through this only minutes before, had to force himself to not panic.

When the blanket of lightning surrounded each of them and consolidated them as a single unit, Scirios said, "Which way do we go?"

B'nair tried to raise his arm to point the direction, but only seemed to set off a fury of sparks.

"Don't move," ordered the Kelpie. "Just think it."

B'nair closed his eyes and brought forth the image of the forest – the same forest in which Solveig had been lost; the same forest in which she encountered the tree people; the forest that held Rovek.

Chapter four

The forest had gone so black that Sean could barely see Quinn, who was standing only a few feet away from him. They no longer heard the rustling of the leaves, but neither of them was sure if that was a good thing or a bad thing. It was so silent they could hear each other breathing. By now, they had no idea of which way to go, even if they thought searching for the others was a good idea.

"You've really gotten us into a mess this time," said Quinn, his voice little more than a whisper.

"Me?" sputtered Sean. "What do you mean I got us into a mess? I didn't do anything!"

"You didn't do anything?" Quinn repeated. "Are you kidding? You were the one that was dancing around and going on about this so-called monster not being real and if it wasn't real, it couldn't get you."

"And your point is?" asked Sean.

"You were supposed to be paying attention to potential dangers behind us, not dancing a jig."

"I wasn't dancing," argued Sean. "I already told you. I was being stealthy. Besides, no one said you had to pay any attention. I was doing just fine until you stuck your nose in."

"Doing fine?" Quinn asked incredulously. "Fine? You looked like you were about to wet your pants."

"Wet my pants? Really?" asked Sean. "And what were you going to do? Loan me one of your diapers?"

Quinn was so insulted he didn't know what to say next. He folded his arms across his chest, squashing Natalie. He quickly lifted them up and tried to find a place for them. Finding no alternative, he dropped them to his sides, and then resumed his fuming and glaring at Sean. Sean folded his arms across his chest, and glared right back. The fact that Sean could fold his arms across his chest and Quinn couldn't, irritated him even more.

"I was just trying to help!" finally snorted Quinn.

"Pa-leeze!" Sean spat out, rolling his eyes. "I didn't need your help then and I don't need it now."

"Oh, really?" asked Quinn.

"Really," answered Sean.

Quinn had no idea what to say or do next, he was so angry. He continued to glare at Sean while he tried to think of some way to show Sean how wrong he was. Sean staring back at him in the same obstinate pose only aggravated Quinn further.

"Okay, then," he said and he took two steps backwards.

It was far enough for him to be swallowed by the blanket of the night. Sean was out of sight and he assumed he was, too.

"Oh," said Sean. "That's really clever. Like I don't know where you are."

Quinn took two steps to the left and one more to the back. He wished he had something to throw to make Sean think he was someplace else. He held his breath to be as quiet as he could.

"Well I can do that, too," Sean finally said.

He then took two steps to the right and one step back. Quinn could hear Sean's steps. He sensed that they were still standing in front of one another. He took another step back and two to his right.

Sean heard Quinn move and took a step back and one more to his right. Quinn, hearing Sean move, decided to move again. He stepped backwards, and tripped over something. He tried to keep his balance by waving his arms. His right arm brushed up against the thick moss coating on one of the larger trees, startling him.

"Ewwww!" he shouted. "What was…"

He lost his balance and fell onto his back into a thicket of shrubs, scrub grass and roots. Natalie fell with him, knocking the breath out of him. Low hanging leaves brushed across his face, but in the dark he couldn't tell what they were.

"Agkkk!" he choked. "Something's got me. Help."

Sean immediately forgot about their argument and turned towards Quinn's voice. He started to run, but quickly stopped. It would do neither of them any good, if whatever had grabbed Quinn grabbed him, too. Oh, please don't let it be a monster, he thought.

"Where are you?" Sean shouted.

"Right here," Quinn answered.

"That's not helping," said Sean. "I don't know where 'right here' is."

Quinn struggled to free himself, but in the darkness all he was doing was wrapping himself tighter in a thicket of vines and tangling the straps around the sling in which Natalie was held. In seconds he was trussed up tightly.

"Can you follow my voice?" he squeaked. "I'm really, really stuck."

Unfortunately, his voice was muffled by the foliage he was burying himself in, and was bouncing off one tree after another. Sean had no idea where Quinn was calling from. He got down on his hands and knees, feeling his way around.

"Are you being eaten?" Sean asked.

"N...n...no," Quinn answered. "I d...d...d...don't think s...s...s...so."

The thought had now been planted in his mind. Nothing was eating him. There was nothing in this area of the forest but the two of them. However, frightened by his own thrashing, Quinn was certain something was there and that it was coming for him.

"H...h...hurry," he pleaded.

"Keep talking," said Sean. "I'm trying to find you."

"But if there's something that's going to eat me," he wailed, "won't my talking lead it right to me?"

"No," said Sean. "Yes. Maybe. I don't know. But if you don't keep talking, I won't be able to find you. Take your pick, either you keep talking or I leave you all alone. And don't tell me that this is a mess that *I* got you into."

"Okay, okay," stammered Quinn. "I'll keep talking." And then, under his breath, "But this is all your fault."

"I heard that," Sean shot back.

Quinn tried to cover Natalie the best he could while he continued to yammer about whatever popped into his head.

Sean inched his way right, left and forward, trying to focus on Quinn's location. He flinched whenever a leaf or a branch or a root brushed up against him. He could see the ground between his hands immediately beneath him, but not much further than a foot or two past that.

"What's taking you so long?" whined Quinn. "I think I feel things crawling on me."

"I'm going as fast as...what?" Sean stopped. "Something's crawling on you? Is that what you said?"

"Yes," answered Quinn.

"Yes, what?" replied Sean. "Yes, that's what you said or yes, something's crawling on you?"

"Yes," Quinn said again. "That's what I said and that's what I think is happening. I can feel something moving on top of me."

Something was definitely moving across Quinn's chest. Whatever it was pulled the straps tighter and was pressing against him. He tried to brush it off of him, but both his arms were tangled in vines. He could move his hands, but his arms were stuck at his elbows. Then he heard a sound.

It was a soft whimper, almost a squeak. It was right under his chin. His first thought was that this creature of Sean's was on top of him and was eating Natalie. He struggled more, but only tightened whatever was holding him. Then he heard a voice.

"Why is it so dark?" the voice asked.

"Wahhhhhh!" he and Sean screamed at the exact same time.

"What was that?" they both shouted at the exact same time.

"Why am I tied up?" the voice asked.

"Wahhhhh!" Quinn and Sean screamed again at the exact same time.

"There it is again," they both shouted.

"Wahhhhh!" the voice screamed. "Who's there?"

Sean had curled up into a ball, covering his head and trying to make himself as small as he could. Quinn stopped struggling long enough to recognize the voice. It was Natalie.

"Natalie?" he asked. "Is that you?"

"Quinn?" she asked. "Where are you? Where am I? What's going on? Why is it so dark?"

"Sean," Quinn shouted. "It was only Natalie. She's awake."

"Are you sure?" shouted Sean.

"Sean?" asked Natalie. "Where are you? Will somebody please tell me what's going on? Why am I all tied up?"

"It's a long story," said Quinn. "Well it's not all that long, but it can wait. Right now all you need to know is that we're in an evil forest, it's nighttime, and we got separated from all the others. But everything's going to be all right."

"Evil forest?" she repeated. "Separated from the others? Then why were you screaming?"

"Um...well," he stammered. "I was just taken by surprise. That's all."

As he was trying to avoid explaining everything to Natalie, Sean had resumed his efforts at locating them. He followed their conversation, focusing intently on where the sounds of their voices were coming from. He was sure he was near. He reached forward with one hand and felt something different. At that same moment, Quinn felt something grab his foot.

"Wahhhh!" he screamed and he began to kick.

"Wahhhh!" Natalie screamed, startled by his sudden reaction.

"Wahhhh!" Sean screamed when whatever it was he touched jerked away from him.

Quinn kicked harder and his foot came down on what had grabbed him.

"Yeow!" Sean shouted. "That hurt. Is that your foot?"

"Was that your hand?" Quinn asked as he stopped kicking.

"Yes," the both answered at the exact same time.

"I found you," Sean shouted.

"You found us," Quinn shouted.

"Now," interjected Natalie. "Will somebody please tell me what's going on?"

"Let's get you both untangled, first," said Sean.

He pulled away the vines that Quinn had been wrapped in so that he could sit upright. Then they fumbled with the sling in which Natalie was held. Without being able to see very much, this was all somewhat disconcerting for Natalie. The wound in her shoulder was still quite painful and the gyrations the other two were making trying to undo the straps in the dark only aggravated things.

When she was finally freed, Sean suggested they all reach out to touch one another and maintain that contact while he backed up. He thought that if he tried to go back the way he had come in reaching them, he could get them out of the thicket and to a more open area.

Quinn put one hand on Sean's back while Sean led the way, and he held Natalie's hand in his other. Sean inched his way backwards a few feet until he could feel that he was crawling on fallen leaves and not on whatever it was that Quinn had landed in.

When he stopped, he rolled over and sat on the ground. Quinn could feel Sean stop and groped his way to a sitting position next to him. He then helped Natalie position herself next to him opposite from Sean.

"The last thing I remember was being in a bubble and getting tossed around by that Strelka," Natalie said. "You were carrying Lochen around on your back. And then everything went black. I remember waking up briefly in some kind of cave. I don't remember where it was or who was there."

"You really missed a lot," said Sean. He laughed nervously and added, "You were really in the dark. Get it? Like right now? You're still in the dark. Don't you get it?"

"I get it," she answered. "I just didn't think it was funny."

Quinn was about to begin explaining when something caught his eye, breaking through the darkness. There was a dim flickering of some kind.

"What's that?" he asked, pointing towards the dim, yellow light, although no one could see his finger.

"It looks like an eye," said Sean. "But there's only one."

"How many eyes does that monster of yours have?" asked Quinn. He had dropped his voice to a whisper.

"It's not 'my' monster," Sean whispered back. "And I don't know how many eyes it has."

"Why are you two whispering?" asked Natalie.

"Shhh," hissed Quinn. "There may be a monster of some kind in these woods. If that's it, we don't want it to know where we are."

"Monster?" Natalie whispered. "What kind of monster?"

"One that does unspeakable things to all who enter this forest," said Sean. "I tried to warn everybody about it, but no one would listen. It does unspeakable things to everyone it finds. No one has ever returned."

"If no one has ever returned," asked Natalie, "then how do you know it exists or what it does?"

"Liam asked him the same thing," said Quinn.

"And what was the answer?" Natalie asked when no one said anything.

"He didn't have one," said Quinn.

"This is stupid," she said.

"OVER HERE!" she shouted, waving her hand to no avail.

"Shhhh!" Sean and Quinn hissed. "You don't know what that is."

The yellow "eye" appeared to be bounding through the forest. It was weaving from left to right and back. At the sound of Natalie's voice, the movement stopped and then the light headed straight towards the trio.

"Now you've done it," said Sean. "It knows where we are. We're doomed."

"Can you shoot it?" asked Quinn. "You know. With your slingshot."

"I know what to shoot it with," snapped Sean. "I need some stones. I don't have any stones."

He and Quinn ran their hands across the ground, feeling for stones. Sean located one and groped for his slingshot. He took careful aim and fired. He could hear it whiz through the air, but the "eye" didn't change course. He felt Quinn's hand on his arm, nudging him.

"Here," he said to Sean. "I found a few more."

He handed Sean three small stones, an acorn and a bit of bark. Sean loaded one of the stones and fired again. And again, the "eye" didn't change course. It was still galloping through the woods, coming right at them.

"How could you miss?" shouted Quinn, seeing there was no longer any reason to be silent. "You never miss."

"I didn't miss," Sean shouted back. "It's one of those para norma lacktivity things. I told you. It's a ghost or something."

"Shoot it again," shouted Quinn.

By now he had gotten to his feet. He felt around for Natalie and helped her to her feet. Sean was already on his. The eye was getting closer. Sean sent off two more missiles, one right after the other. He was positive they had struck the yellow light, but nothing seemed to phase it. It was still moving quickly towards them.

"We need to run," said Sean.

"Are you crazy?" asked Natalie. "In the dark? We could get killed."

"We could get killed if we stay put," he snapped.

"Let me cast a bubble," suggested Natalie.

"Are you sure?" asked Quinn. "That didn't work out very well the last time."

Sean loaded the piece of bark, not having anything better. He knew it would do no damage, but he was out of options. Whatever was coming at them was only a few yards away. He heard it drop harmlessly into the foliage.

"I'm out of stones," Sean announced.

"Great!" said Quinn. "What do we do now?"

"We need to get out of here," demanded Sean.

"And go where?" asked Natalie. "Be reasonable. We can't see two feet in front of us. Where are we going to go?"

"We should split up," said Sean. "That way at least two of us will be spared."

Natalie tried to lift her arm to cast a bubble around them, but the pain in her shoulder stopped her short. She started to lift her other arm but it was so dark, she couldn't see exactly were Sean was. Quinn, she thought, by the sound of his voice, was still within reach, but she couldn't tell where Sean was and didn't want to exclude him. The bounding eye was only a few yards away. Soon it would be too late.

"Run," shouted Sean.

Instead of going in opposite directions, he and Quinn ran into each other. Quinn grabbed Sean's shoulders in an effort to keep his balance. Sean tried to pull away, but only managed to shift his weight enough to make Quinn's efforts futile. As he tipped sideways, one of Quinn's feet tangled between Sean's ankles, tripping him up even more.

The other one of Quinn's feet slid backwards as he still tried to keep his balance. He slid across the dead, damp leaves, almost doing the splits, skidding back into the growth of shrubs and vines. In a panic, he tightened his grip on Sean and pulled him down, too. Sean was lifted into the air.

Quinn swung one leg over his body, trying to land on his feet instead of his back, but he hadn't let go of Sean. He lost the battle to keep his balance and didn't quite complete his turn. He landed on his side in the same thicket he had been before, his arms wrapped around Sean who was nearly smothered under Quinn's side.

Natalie could see none of this, but she heard the thrashing. She was torn between trying to see what was happening with Quinn and Sean, which was futile, and the approaching light. She readied her uninjured arm, preparing to envelop whatever it was that was about to pounce on her in its own bubble. A split second before she waved her arm, the source of the eye appeared.

"X'qeddach jigiri wahawn?" asked Lochen. What's going on here?

"What?" asked Natalie.

"Lochen?" Sean and Quinn said together.

Lochen moved the light in the direction of their voices and saw that they were stretched out on the ground, holding each other in their arms in a bed of Night Creeper. His first thought was how much they were going to be itching before the day was out, and then, how ridiculous they both looked.

"Intidi riditt?" he asked, not really expecting an answer. Are you all right?

"Why is he talking like that?" asked Natalie.

"Natalie," Lochen said. "Kifint intidi thokosht?" How are you feeling?

"What?" she asked again. "What's going on? Why can't I understand anything he says?"

"Don't worry about it," said Quinn. "No one can understand anything he says."

"How did this happen?" she asked. "<u>When</u> did this happen?"

"Uhm," pondered Sean. "We don't know and we don't know."

Lochen raised the light a little higher into the air and looked around. Then he turned to the two on the ground and said,

"Bhazonn. Ghanata zonn il-teraggah 'luragh allt-ohrjahan." Get up. We need to get back to the others.

Sean and Quinn didn't need to understand his words. The meaning was clear. It was not safe here and they all needed to get back together. They struggled to their feet, moved closer to Natalie and then looked to Lochen. He could see that all three of them were unharmed and he quickly turned back the way he came and started off. The others followed quickly behind.

"Where are we?" Natalie asked as they traveled through the forest. "And why are we here?"

"Lochen and Liam decided that our best chance at stopping the Kelpies was to quit chasing after the ones that are free and try to get ahead of them," Quinn explained.

"Liam can understand Lochen?" Natalie asked.

"Well, no," said Sean. "Not exactly, but they both figured out a way around that."

"Anyway, we had to cut through this forest to get to a place called Satamakau," Quinn continued.

"I voted for going around," Sean interjected. "This place gives me   the   creeps."

"It's a forest," Natalie said. "Aren't you a Forest Creature? How can you be afraid of a forest?"

"Don't get him started," said Quinn.

Their discussion continued as Lochen led them through innumerable twists and turns, around trees and over roots. Along the way, Sean and Quinn managed to fill Natalie in on all that she had missed, including the fact that Solveig was shrinking. By the time they were done, the glimmer of the second orb of light that Lochen had left with Liam was visible.

By the time Lochen returned with Sean, Quinn and Natalie, morning light was beginning to inch its way through the blackness of the forest. The orbs of light faded into nothing and the group continued on its journey. The ones who had stayed behind while Lochen made his search managed to get a little bit of sleep, taking turns standing guard.

During the night they had heard nothing – no crickets, no owls, and no more rustling of leaves. In spite of the short respite, no one was rested. Everyone was still on edge and stressed by the oppressive air and the ominous silence.

Almost without stopping, Lochen scooped Summer and Solveig up and put them back in his hood. He motioned to Liam, indicating they needed to continue. Stella had barely enough time to give her Princess a hug and they were all on the march.

Shortly after they continued their trek, they came upon another break in the trees and another choice of paths to take. Once more, Liam pointed the way to Satamakau, and once more the ground erupted. This time, though, instead of fire ants, a gush of tiny spiders broke through. As before, thousands of them created a barrier, blocking the way that Liam had identified.

Lochen crept closer to the barrier, studying the spiders. They appeared to be tiny viper spiders – very poisonous and very aggressive; however, none of them left the formation of the barrier. He reached out to touch one of them, but Liam grabbed his hand before that could happen.

"I don't think that's a good idea," he said.

"Manash izbix lida wanzhuma dakka lijid herlij kunz," Lochen replied. I don't think these are what they appear to be.

"I have no idea what you said," Liam told him. "But I still don't think touching them is a good idea. They look even more threatening than the last time."

He made what he hoped Lochen understood to be a signal to leave them alone.

"This happened before?" asked Natalie.

"Yes," replied Stella. "Only the last time it was made of fire ants."

Lochen continued to study the formation, respecting what he thought might be Liam's wish that he not touch anything. There was something unusual about these creatures – more unusual than normal, if that was possible.

"Someone or something is trying to keep us from getting out of here," said Summer.

"Or maybe just from going in that particular direction," suggested Liam.

"It's the monster," moaned Sean. "Its toying with us, making us go deeper and deeper into the forest where it can dispose of all of us. No one's ever going to find us."

"Aren't you a ray of sunshine?" said Solveig, as she pulled herself up from inside Lochen's hood.

Natalie recalled being told that Solveig was shrinking, but when she rejoined the other half of the group, she was so happy to see Stella, that she forgot about everything else. There was no time to speak with the others; they immediately moved on. Lochen had bent over to pick something up, motioned to Liam, and the two of them headed off into the woods.

Quinn followed them, mumbling something about not getting distracted again by Sean. Stella grabbed her hand and pulled her into line behind Quinn, and Sean followed right behind her. It was still so dark that she lost sight of Liam and Lochen. In fact, until the dawn, she could hardly see Quinn who was a few feet in front of her.

When they reached the place where the so-called paths diverged, everyone stopped and gathered. When Solveig poked her head out of Lochen's hood, which was the first time Natalie had seen her since Angin Topan had cast her spell. She hadn't realized the extent to which her friend had shrunk. She was smaller than Summer by more than a head.

"Oh, my!" she gasped. "Solveig! What's happened to you?"

"Didn't anyone tell you?" Solveig asked. "I'm shrinking."

"Yes," said Natalie, trying unsuccessfully to regain her composure. "But I had no idea how bad it was. There must be something we can do. Stella! Can't you create a potion or cast a spell? What about Lochen? Surely he can do something."

"We've tried," said Stella.

"Well, try harder," demanded Natalie.

"There's nothing from which to make a potion," Stella explained. "And even if there was, we don't know how the spell was cast, and a potion may do nothing, or worse, may only accelerate the shrinking."

"Lochen's already tried a few spells," said Solveig.

"When did that happen?" asked Stella. "I thought he didn't want to try anything; that he was afraid it may make things worse."

"I made him try," said Solveig. "When we were alone."

"I thought no one could understand anything he said," Natalie commented.

"We didn't need to understand each other's words," Solveig explained. "He knew what I was asking. And I knew why he didn't want to try. It doesn't matter, though. Nothing worked."

"But how much longer can this go on?" Natalie persisted, her anxiety rising. "You could get too small for any of us to see. That can't happen!"

They had forgotten about the barrier of spiders that had blocked their way. Lochen wasn't able to understand the conversation, but he guessed correctly from the stress in Natalie's voice what the topic of their conversation was.

"La-jahar hagal nistangha namlugat huwali kitseb id-zzajoni tagnashk," he said, raising his voice over the discussion. "Forsicht hemmah naser izzbik xi-rook." The best thing we can do is get to our destination. Maybe there we will find a cure.

"What?" Natalie nearly shouted. "What did he say? What does that mean?"

"We don't know," said Liam, trying to calm her. "He's been like this ever since he pulled you and Quinn to where we were waiting for you in the Ice Kingdom."

"But he was unconscious," she said, and then recalled what Quinn had told her.

Stella moved closer to her and put a calming hand on Natalie's arm.

"A lot has happened," she said. "None of that is important. Right now, we have to focus on getting through this forest. If we don't stop the Kelpies, none of this will matter at all."

"Look," said Liam, trying to make the best of a bad situation. "The last time we were diverted, we ended up back on track. That'll probably happen again. Let's just go."

He didn't wait for any further discussion. He turned towards Lochen and motioned towards the passage that was open to them. Lochen nodded his understanding and continued on. The others fell in line, each of them feeling the frustration and hopelessness that Natalie had expressed.

As the day wore on, they entered a different section of the forest. In addition to the trees that grew so thick and close, they encountered vines that covered the ground, wound around the trees and hung from the branches. To make things worse, the effects of the Night Creeper were beginning to become apparent on Sean and Quinn.

Natalie was trying to focus on where she was walking, while at the same time, keeping an eye out for hidden dangers. She heard Sean behind her mumbling something about not believing in something. She leaned forward to whisper to Stella.

"What is Sean muttering?"

"You don't want to know," replied Stella. "And, please, don't ask him."

How long was I unconscious, Natalie wondered. So much had happened and so much had changed. She looked up ahead to where all the others were wending their way through the foliage, and then cast a glance over her shoulder to see if Sean was staying close. What she saw was such a surprise that she was certain she had been mistaken. She stopped walking and turned around to face him head on.

"Oh, wow," she gasped. "You're...you're. Sean, you're green."

"What?" he asked.

He stopped and looked at his arms. On the outside, near the elbows, there was a greenish hue. He tried to twist his arm around to get a better look, but only ended up turning in circles.

"What is this stuff?" he asked.

"It's on your legs," said Natalie. "And your face, and neck. It's everywhere."

"Get it off me!" he shouted.

His yelling attracted the attention of the others. They all stopped to look back, searching the area in all directions looking for the threat. Nothing was there. All eyes turned back to Sean. It was still too dark for most of them to see him clearly. As they moved in closer, Summer climbed up on Lochen's shoulder and leaned forward.

Her focus was on Sean, until Quinn stepped in the way. That was when she got a clear vision of the back of his neck. Was his hair turning green, she wondered. She looked more closely. That wasn't his hair, she realized. Something was crawling on his neck. She was about to say something when she noticed the same stuff was on the backs of his arms and legs.

"Lochen!" she shouted, pulling on the edge of his hood, and pointing to Quinn.

Her shout caught Liam's attention, too, and he looked where she was pointing. As he did, Quinn was reaching back to scratch his neck.

"Quinn!" Liam shouted. "Stop. Don't scratch."

"But I itch," he objected.

"Let it itch," Liam quickly said. "Or it'll spread."

That brought Quinn to an immediate stop. He froze like a statue, his eyes shifting left and right.

"What will spread?" he whimpered. "What's on me?"

"Lyjal Proznac," said Lochen. Night Creeper.

"Night Creeper," said Liam at the same time. "Sean!" he shouted. "Don't scratch yourself."

The direction to not scratch only made him want to do it. He reached up as if he was forced, ready to dig his fingernails into the green fuzz on the back of his neck.

"No, Sean," Natalie shouted. "Don't do it."

"Why?" he wailed. "It itches like crazy. What is it?"

"It's Night Creeper," shouted Quinn. "He just said what it was. Didn't you hear him? What else did you get us into?"

"I heard him," Sean shot back. "That doesn't mean I know what he meant. What is Night Creeper anyway? And I wasn't the one who was crawling in the weeds. That was you. And come to think of it, it was you who pulled me into them. Aw, man, this itches!"

He could resist no longer. He feverishly scratched his neck and arms and legs. When he was done, he sighed in relief. At first nothing happened. Then the fuzz suddenly got thicker and longer. It resembled the moss on the trunks of the trees. It looked like Sean was wearing a green fur. In spite of the warnings and what he saw was happening to Sean, Quinn couldn't stop, either. He dug in and suffered the same results.

"What kind of place is this?" moaned Stella.

Chapter five

Stella was especially upset, since she could find nothing she could use to create potions that would counteract what they were running into. She could see that Natalie was still in a great deal of pain, and she was powerless to help. If they had been any place else, in any other forest, she would have found roots and leaves she could use. She could ease Natalie's pain and the suffering Sean and Quinn were experiencing. This place was awful.

She wasn't the only one who was feeling the stress. Everyone's nerves were on edge. The added groaning from Sean and Quinn as they fought with all their strength not to scratch at the maddening itch, and then succumbing and bemoaning the spreading and thickening of the green fuzz, only aggravated everyone's already raw nerves.

In addition to being tired, hot and sleep deprived, they were hungry. There had been no sign of edible nuts or fruit. Lochen had summoned forth another spring, but the water tasted so foul that none of them drank as much as they should have. They had to rest more frequently than Lochen and Liam were comfortable with. They were taking far too long to get through these woods.

Summer and Solveig were sweltering inside Lochen's hood. When they flopped onto his shoulders, he could feel their body heat penetrating through his clothing. He was overly aware and sensitive to their presence, but he knew that there was no other way they could keep up. He found he was constantly thinking about them, and that this was distracting. Normally able to focus his attention with pinpoint precision, his failure to do that now was maddening.

When they came to another break in the path, they heard the same rustling of leaves and brush as in the past. Still, nothing was visible, which further irritated all of them. Liam indicated which way they should go, but Lochen was blocked once more. This time, scorpions dug their way out of the ground. As before, there were thousands of them, rushing to form another barrier.

"Why is this happening," Liam spat in frustration. "We keep getting moved out of our way. It's as if something knows where we're headed and is trying to keep us from getting there."

Lochen couldn't understand his words, but he could feel the exasperation in the tone of his voice. Little did they both realize, he was thinking the exact same thing. He forced himself to try to reason this puzzle out. The shape of the obstacles had been identical each time, but the makeup was different.

Each time, the blockade was made up of something that would normally be threatening, but at no time did any of the creatures break their formation and attack, which is something each species would have done, especially in an environment like this. Why hadn't they attacked, he wondered.

He was beginning to figure out what this all might mean, but his silence and their inactivity served only to wear on them all, rather than as a time for them to rest. It was too much.

"This has got to end," muttered Stella.

She pushed Quinn and Liam aside and stepped closer to the wall of vicious black scorpions. She raised her hand, and before Lochen could stop her, she thrust her arm forward, casting a spell on the barricade.

"Muhx!" shouted Lochen.

He immediately stepped between her and the formation of scorpions, just as the spell she cast struck and bounced back. The full force of her hex crashed into Lochen, throwing him into the air, over her head and onto the ground and a thicket of vines several feet behind everyone.

"Nemmahn lidan huwskar fomarta fishkar," he shouted as he sailed through the air. I believe this is a shape shifter.

And as he hit the ground, he finished, saying, "Another sentinel sent by the Alchemist."

Everyone was staring at him in disbelief. Everyone except Summer and Solveig. They had tumbled together and got tangled in each other's arms and legs inside the folds of his hood as he was flung up and over everyone else. They landed as unceremoniously as he did when he struck the ground.

"What just happened?" cried Summer, as she struggled to climb out of his hood, and then, seeing the vines that had given Sean and Quinn their green rash, she scrambled back.

"What did you just say?" Liam directed at Lochen.

"I said that I believe this is a shape shifter – this blockade in the path. I believe it is another sentinel sent by the Alchemist."

"But we can understand you," said Quinn. "We couldn't understand you before."

"I couldn't understand him half the time when I could understand him," said Sean.

"Did my spell do this?" Stella asked.

"If it did," said Solveig as she poked her head out of Lochen's hood, "maybe she should try to cast a spell on me to stop me from shrinking."

"Maybe she could cast a spell on the forest to get rid of the monster," piped in Sean.

"There is NO monster," Liam, Stella, Summer, Solveig and Quinn all shouted back at him.

"Oh, yeah?" responded Sean. "Then why did the Alchemist need to put a sentinel in here?"

The others looked at each other, all of them unable to come up with an answer. After a short silence they all began talking again; each suggesting the casting of a multitude of different spells for different reasons. Lochen got up from the ground and stepped into the center of the discussion.

"I don't think any spells will do any good," he said. "Allow me to elucidate and to begin from the beginning. At the time we – Quinn, Natalie, Summer and I – encountered the Kelpies at the site of the volcano, I had been reading the book I obtained from the sentinel, Nevarnik, in the forest of the Navedi. He handed it to me on his deathbed, if you recall. He had taken it from the Alchemist. I was translating it with the alphabet key provided by the gnome sentinel – Oryxx was her name. For those of you who missed the opportunity to meet her, I must say, she was quite unusual."

He turned to Quinn and Natalie and continued, "You recall her, don't you? Oryxx spelled with two zekkas. At any rate, the scroll she gave me allowed me to transcribe an ancient language with which I was totally unfamiliar. I thought at first that a language based on six hundred and ninety-two letters and three hundred and twenty-seven symbols would be rather daunting. On the contrary, I found that it lent the language a flexibility I now see has been lacking in several other ancient languages."

"I think I liked it better when we couldn't understand him," said Sean, as he fought against scratching his skin, and again lost the battle.

"Me, too," added Quinn, as he joined Sean in scratching the growing green coating. "He said shorter sentences when we couldn't understand him."

"Lochen," interjected Solveig. "The abridged version, please."

"What?" he asked, turning his head to face her perched on his shoulder. "Oh, yes. Of course. I surmise that when the Mountain Kelpie cast the spell causing the landslide, the language I was translating became imbedded in my subconscious. I had been focusing so hard on understanding it that I began speaking in that exact language. As to the spells, I believe the Alchemist has covered this forest and the sentinel with layers of protective spells, which ours are unable to penetrate."

"Then why did my spell change you?" Stella asked.

"I don't believe it changed me," said Lochen. "Not exactly, anyway."

"Apparently not," mumbled Sean. "You still talk too much."

"I believe the shock wave of your spell," he went on, ignoring Sean, "was repelled by the sentinel and merely jostled my brain the same way the earlier spell from the Kelpie did. It cleared the ancient language and returned me to my normal speech. But it didn't erase it completely. I seem to be able to still understand it. Remarkable."

"You're right," Quinn whispered to Sean. "Too many words."

"You mean you were reading that book when the Kelpies came out of that cave and attacked?" asked Natalie.

"Re-reading it, actually," Lochen answered. "I had already read it once before."

"I thought we were all supposed to be ready to launch our own attack," said Quinn, astonished that Lochen was busy doing something else.

"Precisely," answered Lochen. "And I <u>was</u> prepared."

"No you weren't," countered Natalie. "You were fixated on that silly book."

"It's not a silly book," he responded. "Furthermore, reviewing that compendium did not distract me from completing my role in our siege. Unfortunately, our plan was foiled and we had no contingency plan. I'll have to improve upon that for the next time."

"Were you able to translate anything?" asked Natalie.

"No," he said. "I was still working my way through the letters and symbols from the scroll."

"So it was all a waste of time," mumbled Summer.

"Great," added Quinn. "And now the book is gone. We'll never know what was in it."

"The book is lost," said Lochen, "but given a little time, I should unlock the key."

"Was the book locked with a key?" asked Sean. "I thought it was just a book."

"I meant that I expect I'll be able to complete translating it," clarified Lochen.

"How are you going to do that?" asked Sean. "I thought it was lost."

"It is," Lochen answered. "But I recall what was in it."

"I thought you said you only read it once," said Summer.

"I did; that's correct," he answered. "I read it once. I only needed to read it once. I committed it to memory. And once I can compare it to the information in the scroll, I'll have a suitable translation."

"You read it once and you memorized it?" asked Quinn.

"Yes," answered Lochen. "I believe that's what I just said."

"You know something, Lochen?" asked Sean.

"I'm sure I know a lot of things," he answered, "but I don't know what you're referencing specifically."

"You're even freakier than I thought you were," Sean told him.

The others laughed, glad for a little comic relief in the midst of the tension. Lochen wasn't sure how to respond.

"We need to keep moving," said Liam, bringing them back to the issue at hand.

"Yes," said Lochen. "I agree. And if I'm correct, that this barrier is a shape shifter, and a sentinel, then we should take the way that isn't blocked."

"Why do you think it's a shape shifter, and a sentinel?" asked Solveig.

"Because each of the barriers we've encountered has been essentially the same," he explained. "They've been dangerous creatures, meant, I believe, to deter us from going the direction they have been blocking. But they've all been similar."

"Why not the same?" asked Summer. "If it's a shape shifter, can't it take the same shape each time?"

"That's an excellent question," answered Lochen.

"And the answer is...?" asked Solveig, when he didn't continue.

"I have no idea," he said. "I can only venture a guess."

All eyes were on him, waiting expectantly. Solveig knew he wasn't going to answer a question that hadn't been asked, especially if the answer to that question was as plain as day to him – even if it was plain only to him and no one else.

"Are we going to have to force this out of you?" she asked again, when he was once more less than forthcoming.

"Oh, no; of course not," he said. "I think it might have to do with the nature of the spell cast upon him and the fact that when he creates these barriers, he shifts into multiple entities – in fact thousands of ants, or spiders or scorpions."

"Wouldn't it be easier for him – or her – to just appear to us normally?" asked Natalie.

"Probably," Lochen answered. "I imagine that his – or her – natural form may be either frightening to us, or he is unable to appear naturally for some reason. Unless he takes a form that can communicate with us, we may never know. For now, though, all that's important is that we can't take the more direct route."

"Yes," agreed Liam. "We shouldn't waste any more time. I don't know how much further we have to go, and I'd like to avoid spending any more nights in this place than we have to."

He turned and headed down the opposite passage with Lochen right next to him. Summer and Solveig dug their feet into Lochen's hood and leaned over each of his shoulders – Solveig on his left and Summer on his right. Natalie and Stella followed them, and Quinn and Sean covered the rear.

They were still tired and hungry, but at least one of their problems – understanding Lochen (as much as they could under normal circumstances) – had been solved. It was enough to lift their spirits, if only temporarily.

Once they were out of sight, the scorpion tree began to whirl in a cyclonic circle, slowly breaking apart. The scorpions faded away, turning into the wind as the shape shifter dissolved into nothing but the air.

Lochen had been right. The barriers that had blocked their way had been a single person. Valta Radenie had always been a shape shifter. However, until he ran afoul of the Alchemist, he could change shape to whatever or whomever he wanted, returning to that same form as often as he chose. Most of his life he had used his skills irresponsibly, serving only his own self - interests.

When the Kelpies had begun banding together and the wars between them and the leaders of the various peoples escalated, Radenie had chosen poorly. He allowed himself to be too easily seduced by promises of power and riches. Those promises had all been lies, but he had made his choice, and by the time he realized how wrong that choice had been, it was too late.

He had been discovered by the Alchemist shortly after Scirios had been captured and imprisoned. He thought he could hide in the depths of the forest in which he now resided. He was wrong. When the Alchemist found him, he immediately cast a spell on him. The spell prevented him from returning to any previous shape other than the air itself. Then he was offered a chance at redemption. He had agreed, without condition, thankful to be out from under the Kelpies and willing to do anything to save himself.

"There may come a time when you will meet some travelers," the Alchemist had told him. "You must ensure their protection."

"How will I know them?" he asked.

"It will be apparent to you from your first encounter with them," the Alchemist replied as he began to cast the first of several spells. "You will sense their need and provide assistance."

"What am I expected to do," he asked.

"Guard them from the threats of those who would do them harm," the Alchemist told him.

"Wouldn't they be safer if you protected them?"

"I will be otherwise occupied," said the Alchemist. "Do you want to help, or shall I return you to the Kelpies?"

"No," Radenie answered immediately. "I'll help."

"I thought you might."

"When will this happen?" Radenie asked.

"Not for a very long time," came the answer.

"What if I'm gone – you know – what if I die first?"

"You won't die first. You will live well beyond your lifetime. I have slowed your aging process down."

"My aging is being slowed," Radenie asked almost excitedly.

"Yes," the Alchemist answered. "But you can never leave this forest, and the spells I am casting will limit your abilities."

"Limit them? How?"

"Your basic form will be unlike your former self," the Alchemist answered, completing his spells. "You will exist only as the wind. When the time comes, the shape you take can be taken only once and never again. The forms you take will be creatures without voices; creatures feared and despised by others."

"Sounds wonderful. How long must I do this?" were the final words Radenie was able to utter.

"Until your task has been completed," said the Alchemist. "And then you will be released from your pledge and this life."

He had roamed the forest from one end to the other for two thousand years. No people and no animals came through these woods. A few entered, but soon left when the oppressiveness of the air, the heat and the darkness proved too much. Until two days ago when the shape shifter spotted the figures of Ena Ray and Angin Topan.

He knew immediately what would be expected of him. He watched as the two moved through the forest, traveling quickly from the edge near the Ice Kingdom towards the far side of the woods near the coast of the Viridian Ocean.

He saw that they were casting spells – setting traps – for anyone who came through the forest in this direction. Over time, the protective spells the Alchemist had constructed on the forest became vulnerable. Radenie wasn't sure how effective the traps the Kelpie was setting would be, but they would be enough to present a danger to whomever fell into them. He knew it was only a matter of time before those he was meant to protect would appear. Then his debt would be paid; his purpose would cease.

It had been centuries since anyone had traveled this forest. It was a cursed place, made even worse by the sudden presence of a Kelpie. Radenie, already invisible in the form of a puff of air, rose high into the treetops to watch what these visitors were doing. Less than a day passed before more strangers appeared.

At first Radenie saw only six. They were led by one who spoke in the ancient language of the Alchemist. Later he saw there were two more. They had been hidden in the folds of the hood of the strange one. His mind flashed back to the wars that led to his presence here. There had been eight leaders that fought the Kelpies. He wondered if there was any connection between them and these strangers. He realized he would never know; and that it was not important whether he did or not.

Not long after they entered the forest, they approached the location of the first trap that had been set. Radenie assumed the trap had been set for them. He was certain his task was to shield them from this ambush. He had followed them to this point and now had to decide a way of warning them. The Alchemist had told him he could only assume the form of creatures that were feared and despised.

He began shifting his form into the shape of fire ants. His twisting motion made it appear as if the ants were emerging from under the ground. He rose higher and wider, spreading like a tree, duplicating his form a thousand times over until the passage was completely blocked.

When the two had become separated from the others, he darted back and forth, keeping watch over both groups. He hadn't been prepared for this situation. He wondered if the Alchemist had considered this could happen. They were arguing like children, he noted. There was no way they could be connected to the ancient leaders. How could the Kelpies be concerned or threatened by these people?

He was also unprepared when the small Enchantress had cast a spell in his direction when he had taken the shape of the scorpions. The Alchemist had been true to his word: no spells would affect him. Instead, it bounced off and struck the strange one. Somehow the deflected spell had altered his speech. Now he spoke like the others.

Radenie watched as they all continued their trek through the forest. Once they were gone and he had left the shape of the scorpions and was once more nothing but the wind, he darted across the leaves, making them flutter in his wake, as he spun around those he was tasked to guard. It didn't take long before they reached another place where the small Kelpie had set a trap.

Now that these strangers had concluded he was a shape shifter and was assigned to protect them, he thought it might not be necessary for him to completely block their way. Shifting into swarms of ants, spiders or scorpions had been exhausting for him. He decided he could resort to something less dramatic.

When Liam and Lochen reached another split in the barely distinguishable passage, they both stopped.

"What are you thinking?" Liam asked.

"I'm thinking we should wait a second or two to see if my theory about a shape shifter is correct," Lochen answered. "If nothing appears soon, then I think we're free to take the more direct route."

"Why do you think we're being blocked?" Summer asked.

"I have to assume the Kelpies came this way and set traps for us," answered Lochen.

"Wouldn't some of them have stayed behind to try to finish us off?" asked Sean.

"That's what I would have done," said Quinn, "if I was in their place."

"I think they may be more concerned about how close we've come each time," suggested Lochen. "They will have taken the most efficient route to free their colleagues, while we have opted to bypass the others and head for what is likely the last one they will attempt to release."

"Why wouldn't they do the same thing we are?" asked Solveig.

"I think it's imperative that all eight of them are free," said Lochen.

"Why?" asked Stella.

"I don't know," he replied. "I haven't gotten that far in the Alchemist's book."

As they were talking, the shape shifter had drifted to the ground and began to transform. He had thought about several options, but when he tried to take those forms, he was prevented. The Alchemist's spells on him had held fast over the centuries. His choices were limited – something feared and despised.

He began to twist and turn. The bottom of the whirl of wind he was becoming touched the ground and rustled the leaves. In seconds he had converted himself. Six small items popped up from the ground. They slowly stretched from front to back. Snouts appeared; then mouths with sharp tiny teeth. Their bodies were low to the ground and larger towards the back where long tails extended.

"Look out," shouted Sean. "Rats. A whole bunch of them."

He whipped out his slingshot and crouched down to the ground searching for stones, while keeping his eye on the vermin. They scurried in haphazard circles, covering the path, but not advancing or retreating.

"I think we've been given our sign," said Lochen. "This way."

He pointed down the path that led in the opposite direction. When they were out of sight, the rats disappeared in a rush of wind. Sean looked back when he heard the rustling of the leaves, but saw nothing.

"I've got to find some stones," he said to himself.

This diversion was taking them in a direction that was completely the wrong way. Previous changes to their route had presented similar problems, but nothing as clearly wrong as this one. Liam had expected the passage would wind around and get them back on track, but it wasn't happening.

"Maybe we should go back," he suggested.

"No," said Lochen. "I think we have to trust that the Alchemist was looking out for us. Besides, the lack of choices in our direction is giving me time to complete more of my translation."

"What's this book about?" asked Summer.

"It's still too early for me to say," Lochen answered. "Part of it seems to be a history, but it also seems to include information about spells. There are sections that address tactical strategies and others that are more instructional in nature."

"How can you know about different sections?" asked Solveig. "Are you translating it out of order?"

"There is no specific order," said Lochen.

"You mean there's no beginning, middle and end?" asked Stella.

"No, there's not," he told her. "It's not linear like other books we are familiar with. It's multi-dimensional. As a part of it is translated or revealed, that text seems to overlay a section that is completely different and independent of the surface text. I'm not sure this makes sense."

"What else is new?" groused Sean.

"Is there at least a title for this thing?" asked Quinn, and then laughed. "You know, like, 'The Guide to Conquering Kelpies.'"

"Yeah," said Sean. "Or Everything You Ever Didn't Want to Know About Creepy Forests."

Quinn laughed and added, "Or what about Weird Things You Only See in Nightmares?"

"Oh, that's a good one," answered Sean. "Come on, you guys. What are some others?"

"How about 'Surviving in the Company of Nitwits?" added Summer.

"I like that one," said Solveig. "Or maybe 'One Hundred Ways to Make the Brainless Useful.'"

"Actually," interjected Lochen. "It does, in fact, have a title."

"Probably not one of those suggested," said Liam.

"No," said Lochen. "Not one of those. It's simply called, 'Quest of Eight.'"

"Oh, poop," muttered Quinn. "You're joking. Right?"

"On the contrary," answered Lochen. "I'm quite serious."

They were all silent for several seconds as they absorbed the implications of what they learned. By the time any of them had recovered enough to say anything, they had reached another fork in the woods. Earlier there had been nothing that even closely resembled pathways. More recently, though, they seemed to be following more clearly defined passages.

It was as if whoever made these had come from the direction they were now heading, and stopped long before reaching the other side – the side from which they originally started. The choice they faced gave them the option of turning slightly to the right, or nearly doubling back the way they had come. The second option looked as if it went deeper into the woods and towards much higher ground.

The familiar rustling of the leaves drew their attention to the first path. They watched as an unseen wind spun small bits of debris, drawing them into the air to be replaced by several cobras intertwined among each other. The center one raised its head and spread its hood, quickly followed by three more.

"It looks like we have been given our sign," Lochen said.

Everyone had, for the moment, forgotten about the book and its prophetic title. They carefully stepped around the snakes and onto the switchback path. They wound in and around the trees, climbing steadily uphill. The light was diminishing sooner than they expected.

Liam tried to see the sky through the trees. From what little he could see, the clouds overhead were getting darker. Then he heard the distant booming of thunder. Everyone stopped at the sound, taking the opportunity to catch their breath. The hill had gotten steeper. Then it started raining.

"At least this should cool things off a bit," said Natalie.

The humidity in the forest was so thick it was hard to breath. The rain didn't change that, nor did it cool things off. The loud splattering sound of the drops hitting the leaves on the trees after about two days of no sound whatsoever was deafening.

As the water fell from leaf to leaf and then to the ground, it soaked into the dirt, converting whatever wasn't covered with dead foliage into a slick mud. Where the ground was covered with fallen leaves, those leaves became so slippery that the travelers looked for areas of mud for steadier footing.

Liam had taken the lead and was pulling himself up the hill by grabbing low lying bushes and vines. He extended one hand back towards Lochen to pull him up, waited until he was stable, and then thrust his other hand forward to the next cluster of rooted vegetation to pull again.

Natalie was holding on to the back of Lochen's robe with one hand and to Stella with the other. Quinn was far too heavy for Stella to pull him up. He had motioned to her that he and Sean would pull themselves up. She kept an eye on them, though, to make sure they didn't get separated again.

Liam reached another string of Night Creeper, knowing he would suffer the same fate as Quinn and Sean. There was no choice. There was no place for them to stop. At one point the shrub he grabbed pulled free of the ground and his feet went out from under him. He fell into the mud face first, pulling Lochen with him.

They started sliding back down the hill, taking Natalie's legs out from under her. She rolled to one side to keep from being swept away and knocked Stella over – also falling face first into the mud. Quinn managed to plant one leg, and Sean pressed his back against Quinn's leg, digging his heels into the slime.

It was enough to brace against the others who were skidding down the hill. They all plowed into Quinn, who was able to keep his balance and stop their descent. Sean kicked harder, digging his heels deeper as Quinn reached down and lifted the others up one by one.

Liam, Lochen, and Natalie were smeared with mud, but Stella had nearly been buried in it. She was covered head to toe. It was all over her face and in her hair. It had oozed into her clothing, which was already soaked through. And worse, it smelled like decay.

"Oh, brother," shouted Quinn over the rumble of the raindrops. "You all smell like..."

"Don't," snapped Stella. "Just don't."

She spit out a mouthful of the muck as she glared at him.

"What?" he asked defensively. "I just stopped you from rolling down the hill. This is the thanks I get?"

"I didn't want to hear you tell us what we smell like," she said somewhat apologetically. "I got a mouthful, and didn't need an image in my mind worse than the one I already have."

Sean leaned around the side of Quinn's leg and wiped the rain out of his face.

"You mean you already had an image of walrus poop in your mind?" he asked.

"Not until now," she snarled at him.

"Oh," muttered Sean. "Sorry."

Liam managed to get back to his feet. He stomped his feet into the mud to secure himself and then retraced his steps more slowly and more deliberately. He tried to walk through the brush. It took a little longer, but the footing was better. They had to stop several times to rest. Their legs were burning with the strain.

After was seemed like an eternity, they crested the hill and could see the end of the forest. Lochen had expected to see the coast, but instead what stretched out before them was a vast field. It was still a ways off, but the density of the trees was lessening and they all could see more clearly than before.

The thought of finally being out of the woods was enough to give them a shot of energy. Until they saw the wolf. Standing about twenty feet in front of them was a dark gray beast with red eyes. It was crouched low to the ground, its lips pulled back revealing a mouth full of needle sharp fangs.

"Where did that come from?" asked Solveig, who had to shout to be heard by Lochen.

"I think it's the sentinel," he shouted back. "At least I hope it is."

They inched forward until they had closed half the distance. It was then that they saw the run off path to the right. It appeared to lead back into the forest. A wave of defeat rushed over all of them. The wolf growled at them, but made no sign of advancing. One by one they squeezed by and down the trail back into the woods.

Sean was the last to slip past the wolf. It watched him the entire way. Keeping his eye on the animal, waiting for it to attack, he didn't see where his feet landed, but he could feel the small stones. He looked ahead and saw the others in front of him.

"Quinn," he hissed, trying to be quiet, but still be heard over the rain.

"What?" Quinn asked as he turned back to Sean.

"Hold on a second," Sean said to him. "I need to go back for something."

"Are you crazy?" Quinn said in astonishment.

"I won't go far," said Sean, "and it'll only take a second. Keep watch for me."

Without waiting for an answer, Sean turned back towards the location of the wolf. He crouched down and felt for the stones he had stepped on earlier, while watching for the beast. He found the stones and started picking them up. He quickly glanced up at the wolf.

It had been dark, almost black, only a few seconds ago. Now it looked a lighter gray. Sean wondered if the light or lack of light was playing tricks on him. He gathered a few more stones and looked back at the wolf.

It hadn't changed position, but it looked less threatening – as if it was relaxing. Then it sat on its hind legs and slumped its head. Sean picked up another stone or two, but his eyes were glued to the wolf.

Its massive mouth seemed to shrink. Its front legs receded and seemed to change shape. They became arms. The head became human. The wolf had changed into a man – a man who was rapidly aging before Sean's eyes. The man's head lifted and turned towards Sean. He nodded acknowledgement and then lowered himself to the ground.

Sean stood to see him better. Within seconds the body made its final shift – from man to dust. Valta Radenie had paid his debt. His task was done.

Chapter six

When Sean caught up to Quinn he asked if Sean had gotten what he needed. He could see that Sean was troubled by something, but didn't press the issue. The others hadn't gotten too far ahead and in short order they rejoined them. It was two more hours of slogging up the hill through the mud and rain before they reached the edge of the forest and could see the open field stretching to the horizon.

"I suggest we stop here," said Lochen. "We have at least some protection from the rain with these trees."

"Are you kidding?" asked Solveig. "Summer and I have been inside your hood, and we're soaked through. Fat lot of good these trees did."

Her voice was little more than a squeak. She was now slightly more than half Summer's height. When she dropped to the bottom of Lochen's hood, it took considerable time and effort for her to climb back to the top.

"I suppose you're right," Lochen acknowledged. "Still, I think we're better served staying here for the night and heading out across that field in the morning."

"How much further is it?" asked Natalie.

"I estimate about another day," said Liam. "Barring any new obstacles."

To the south of the field they could see the edge of another forest. It wasn't as foreboding as the one they had just come through, but it still didn't look inviting.

"Is that the same forest?" asked Quinn, pointing to the line of trees.

"No," said Liam. "There's a valley that separates them. I think that's the one we were in before."

He pointed towards the northwest and added, "I think those towers we went through are in that direction."

"We're not going back there, are we?" asked Sean.

"No," said Lochen. "Our objective is out to sea."

"Oh, poop," muttered Sean. "I'd almost rather go back to the towers. Why does there have to be so much freaking water?"

"Are we close to one of the other Kelpies?" asked Summer. "Shouldn't we try to take that one out if we can?"

Stella closed her eyes to bring forth the map. When she did, she saw that the markers that had indicated the locations of the Kelpies that by now had been released were all gone. There was nothing in her image that told where they had been. She noticed something else, too. The marker indicating the location of the Kelpie in the mines of Djall was fading.

"Oh, no," she gasped.

"What's wrong?" exclaimed Natalie.

"Another one has been freed," she answered. "They've already reached the one in the mines. They'll be headed to the forest next."

"Maybe we shouldn't wait," said Summer. "We should get to the ocean as fast as we can."

"We need to rest," said Liam.

"Besides," added Stella. "the Kelpie that was released will need time to regenerate. Still, we don't have much of an advantage. We can't afford to lose any time."

"At least we can clean ourselves off," said Quinn.

He stepped out from under the trees a few steps into the field. He raised his head towards the sky and stretched out his arms, allowing the water to pour over him, washing away the mud. He rubbed his face, his hair and then his body, until it was as clean as he could get it.

"That feels better," he announced as he stepped back under the minimal cover of the trees.

"That looks like an excellent idea," chimed in Natalie, and she did the same.

One by one the others joined her and helped one another scrub off the muck and slime. When they were done, Natalie constructed a bubble to protect them from getting even more wet than they already were and to fend off any nocturnal visitors they may have. Stella ventured into the field a short way, picking up items here and there. When she was done, she returned to the bubble.

"Lochen," she asked. "Can you conjure up a pot or two?"

"Certainly," he replied.

He waved a hand and created two of them. She indicated that this was enough. She then snapped her fingers and generated a small fire. She waved her other hand in a small circle and created a shaft of air that carried the smoke up and out of the bubble.

She had found a number of leaves, roots, and plants. She dropped some in one of the pots that she had filled half way with rain water. She dropped the rest in the other pot, with a smaller amount of water, after she crumpled them up into tiny pieces.

"How about some small bowls or cups?" she asked Lochen, who quickly obliged.

She poured the liquid from the first pot into the cups and passed them around.

"I know this isn't much," she said, "but it's an old potion that will reduce the hunger and replenish our strength. There's nothing I can do about drying our clothes."

"I may be able to help with that," answered Lochen.

He waved his hand in an arc, high in the air along the shape of the bubble. A wave of heat slowly began to float down on them, warming them up and drying their clothes. They all drank the broth Stella had provided. There wasn't much taste to it, but after gagging down the water that Lochen had brought forth from the ground, it tasted like ambrosia.

After a few more minutes, Stella took the second pot off the fire and let it cool. When it was safe to touch, she pulled Sean closer to her, scooped out a handful of the mixture and smeared it on the green rash.

"Yeow!" he howled. "That burns."

"Quit being such a baby," she ordered.

"It stinks, too" he continued to whine.

"Do you want to let it keep itching?" she asked. "And spread?"

"No," he mumbled.

"Quinn," she said when she was done. "You're next. And Liam, I should probably put this on your hands, too."

Within seconds of her smearing the goo on the rash, the itching stopped. A few minutes later, the fuzzy coating began to fade away. About an hour later, there was no sign of the inflammation.

With their stomachs fuller than they had been in days, the rain being held at bay by the bubble, and the warm air drying and soothing them, it didn't take long for them to fall asleep. All of them, except Lochen.

Since he could go several days without sleep, he used this time to continue his translation of the Alchemist's book. The sentinel who had given it to him faded away before he could explain how it came into his possession. He had forced it into Lochen's hand as he gasped his last breath. Lochen had glanced at the text and could immediately see that it was written in a language with which he was totally unfamiliar.

He had no idea what the source of the book was or what its relevance or importance was. Not until he encountered the gnome. She had recoiled at the sight of it. That was when he learned that the book had originally belonged to the Alchemist. The gnome had seen the book before. Lochen could only assume that she knew the sentinel who last had possession of it – perhaps not.

He closed his eyes and recalled the image of the manuscript. He had never seen anything like it before. He reached in his pocket and pulled out the scroll the gnome had given him. It was the key to translating the text.

At first he thought it would be relatively simple – substituting letters and symbols and converting them to a language he understood. He was wrong. The conversion was simple, but the outcome was not.

He found the information was revealed in layers. There was no specific beginning, middle or end. If he used the letters from the scroll, the text exposed one facet of information. However, if he used the symbols, the same text revealed a different facet of information. Only recently he discovered that if he applied both the letters and the symbols the gnome had provided, the same text told yet another story. It reminded Lochen of playing three-dimensional chess, except that the additional dimension of time was superimposed over all of it.

"Simply amazing," muttered Lochen.

He opened his eyes again and looked at the scroll neatly rolled in his hand. It was too dark for him to see it clearly. Night had fallen – not that it had been especially bright before. The rain was steady and heavy. The sound was muffled to a dull thudding as it struck the bubble and rolled down in rivulets from the top.

Traveling in this weather was going to be very difficult, he thought. But that was still several hours off. In the meantime, he needed to take advantage of the quiet and solitude. He put the scroll in his lap and rubbed his hands together softly. A small arc of light appeared and extended from one hand to the other as he separated them.

"Not so bright," he whispered to the tiny electrical charge.

It dimmed slightly.

"A little more," he whispered.

The light dimmed further. Satisfied that it was sufficient for him to be able to read the scroll but not so bright as to awaken his friends, he turned towards the side of the bubble and moved the light between it and him, shielding the sleepers. Then he opened the scroll and read.

After studying it for about an hour, he had the letters and symbols committed to memory. He put the scroll back in his pocket, cupped the small arc of light in his hand, dousing it, and once again closed his eyes to bring forth the opening pages of the book.

He sat in the dark, still facing the wall of the bubble, concentrating on his recollection of the text. He had translated the initial pages before, but only with the use of the letters. In that translation, he had seen a chronicle of the figure he and the others had faced in the Crystal Citadel. How long ago had that been? He dismissed his wandering thoughts and returned his attention to the book.

Ena Ray – that was the name of the young man who had been rescued and taken in by Meri Hocto. Lochen let his mind's eyes float over the account of how the Enchantress had mentored the young sorcerer; how another had been trained by her as well –

the one now locked in a tomb in a cave deep in a volcano far out in the Viridian Ocean: another figure he and the others had encountered.

He read how they had both been pupils of the Enchantress, and both had betrayed her, as the Alchemist had predicted. He read how the Rebbercands, among whom Meri Hocto resided, had been manipulated by these two individuals. And he read how she had, with her last breath, cursed the two of them and those who followed them – those who would become the gargoyles and hobgoblins.

This section of the book ended with the arrow piercing the Enchantress' back, her spell that shattered her pendant, and the splinter that creased the axe held by the Rebbercand before it struck his head. Lochen had seen that axe in the hand of another Rebbercand. He wondered, for a brief moment, if he would discover how B'nair had come by the axe.

When he was done, he took a deep breath and rubbed his eyes. He looked over his shoulder at the others. They were all still deep in sleep. Sean was face down, with his knees pulled up under him and his butt in the air. Natalie and Stella were curled together. Quinn was spread-eagled in the center and snoring.

Liam was on his side, pressed up against the side of the bubble. The rain that was still drumming down on it must be comforting to him, Lochen thought. Summer was wrapped in a leaf Stella had found. Her wings seemed to have completely restored. She would be able to fly now, he considered.

He then turned to look at Solveig. He shook his head in dismay. She was less than two inches tall now. He had conferred with

Stella and neither of them could think of a way to stop the shrinking. He wasn't worried that she would shrink to nothing. He knew that wouldn't happen, but he also knew that she could become so small as to no longer be visible to them.

He wished he had been able to communicate with the shape-shifting sentinel. The sentinel may have had an antidote. They needed to get to Satamakau soon. They might have better luck finding a cure there. At least he hoped so.

He turned back to the side of the bubble and closed his eyes again. His mind shifted from the letters on the scroll the gnome had given him to the symbols. Once these were fixed, he returned to the same passage he had just completed.

The translation through the symbols told a different story. It focused on the figureheads of the six different realms that comprised the world: the small people, which included the faeries, the pixies and the imps; the forest creatures, the mountain people, the sea sprites, the people of the jungle – that jungle which would become the Venomous Swamp – and the Ice Kingdom.

These individuals were not exactly the commanders of their respective peoples, but they were revered and consulted. None of the peoples had anything like chiefs or commanders, but these figureheads were the closest thing to that. The Rebbercands had originally come from each of these groups of people.

Initially, the Rebbercands were not a separate people but members of each of the six nations. However, they gradually began to isolate themselves. They refused to change or to grow.

They became entrenched in the "old ways." Their thinking and creativity stagnated and they refused to view anyone who was different than they were as equals. Without opening themselves to new and different people and ideas, they inbred so much that they grew apart from all the other civilizations. They had no real leadership and wandered aimlessly.

In addition to the principals of the six nations, there were two other factions that played key roles: the sorcerers and the enchantresses. Both of these groups were as prominent as the separate nations and had their own leadership. The fact that this resulted in eight leaders was not lost on Lochen. He wondered if that was what the title of the book referred to.

As a sorcerer himself, he was aware that they, like the enchantresses, could come from any one of these six groups. However, they were different in that they were born with special powers. These powers set them apart from their own people. In his case, his powers set him apart from Solveig – his own sister.

He was of the Mountain People, as she was. But she was their Princess, while he would never hold such a position. Sorcerers were raised and trained apart from their people, but then were bound to them. More specifically, they were bound to the leader of their people. He was Solveig's to command, and would give his life to protect her.

It was similar with Enchantresses. Enchantresses were raised and trained by different mentors, since their powers and skills were different than those of sorcerers. But when their training was complete, they, too, were bound to their people. Stella was bound to Natalie in the same way Lochen was to Solveig.

As Lochen read, he learned that Ena Ray and Tebaga were both anomalies. They were not traditional sorcerers. And they were from people quite different than the six nations – outcasts for the most part. But their special powers needed to be developed and disciplined. Meri Hocto took on that role. The Alchemist had warned that they would betray her, and she was certain he was probably right. But she felt that there was still a chance that they could be saved. She had proven to be wrong about that.

At the time she was developing them, though, there was a split among the sorcerers. A number of them, once their powers had been fully cultivated, rebelled against the expectation that they would be bound to their people and the leaders of those people. They revolted. They called themselves the Kelpies.

To show their powers, they began to attack and destroy the homes of the people they had been destined to serve. They were out of control. The Alchemist and the Enchantress tried to negotiate a peace, but the Kelpies were beyond reason. Things got even worse when they discovered the source of power of all Enchantresses, which had been in the keeping of Meri – the pendant she often wore.

At the Alchemist's suggestion, she kept it hidden in the Sanctorum deep within her Citadel – the same Citadel in which she was schooling Ena Ray and Tebaga. They then devised a strategy to divide and conquer the Kelpies. Their code of ethics prohibited them from destroying the Kelpies, even though the Kelpies would not hesitate to destroy either one of them. Consequently, the best they could do was to lock them away.

They knew this was not a permanent solution, but it was the best they could do. Even when Ena Ray and Tebaga betrayed

Meri Hocto, she could not allow herself to destroy them. Instead, she cast them into deep, dark and secret prisons. The Kelpie revolt occurred at a time when the planets were all aligned.

The Alchemist knew that the spells he and Meri cast would be at their weakest and the powers of the Kelpies would be at their greatest the next time the planets aligned. In spite of this, they also knew that as long as the pendant was safe, the prisons would hold. But then Ena Ray located the gem, and everything was in jeopardy.

It became even more perilous when Meri shattered the stone and was then shot in the back. The Alchemist had to come up with another plan, as he started his search for the broken pieces of the gem. That was when he created the Boravak.

Lochen stopped translating. Boravak? What was that, he wondered. He hadn't seen that word before. He snapped his fingers to re-ignite a spark as he pulled the scroll from his pocket and re-examined the letters and symbols. He tried different combinations, but nothing cracked the puzzle. All the words translated to the same one: Boravak.

"That can't be right," he muttered out loud. "I must have misread something."

"What can't be right," mumbled Quinn, still deep asleep.

"Nothing," snapped Lochen. "Go back to sleep."

He waved a hand over Quinn's face as it contorted with a wide yawn. Before Lochen's spell had been fully cast, Quinn's body and face went slack and he slumped, mid-stretch, back to the ground, and resumed snoring softly.

Lochen doused the light and once again closed his eyes. Try again, he told himself. It simply doesn't make sense to throw in a word without any context by which to determine its meaning. He was convinced that he had memorized something incorrectly. After almost an hour of re-examining, re-translating, and re-evaluating, he conceded that he would have to give up and move on. Perhaps the meaning would become clearer later on in the manuscript.

He read in great detail the methods by which the Alchemist and the Enchantress, until her unfortunate discovery and confrontation with Ena Ray and Tebaga, had trapped the Kelpies and hidden them. The descriptions also confirmed what he had suspected about the locations of the crypts.

Each of the Kelpies was secured in the same location as the people they had come from and were now ravaging. Lochen marveled at the sense of irony. They were almost hidden in plain sight, so to speak. The two exceptions seemed to be the Kelpie who was interred in the mines of Djall, and the one they had seen in the depths of the volcano. He realized that these two had been separated from their people – Scirios from the Mountain People and Neraka Ferr from the sea sprites.

Scirios was a sorcerer from among sorcerers – an extremely unique situation. Neraka Ferr had been an Enchantress, Lochen realized. An Enchanter, he corrected himself – one of those rare instances of a male enchantress. He wondered what the implications of this discovery were, if any.

The description of the capture of Scirios included the telling of the destruction of a giant meteor. Such power was inconceivable to Lochen. How strong was Scirios to have required such a drastic attack to capture him? And then there was Neraka Ferr. Was the Fire Kelpie more powerful? Was he more vulnerable? More mysteries he hoped would be resolved later in the text.

He began to see how the ancient lore of the different peoples had been formed. The names of the Kelpies were the ones they were generally known by among themselves and other sorcerers. They were not the names they were known by among their own people.

He remembered Summer's reaction at seeing the imp. What had she called the Kelpie, he tried to remember. The Malkia. That was it. She was screaming about the Malkia. Lochen scanned the book, moving past several pages until he found the part that discussed the lore of the little people.

Their leader had been someone named the Wakuu. Yes, he recalled that name, too. The Wakuu had been confronted by an imp that the small people called the Malkia. Lochen read the description of the Malkia and researched the name of the sorcerer from the small people who had joined the Kelpies.

It was Angin Topan, the imp. They were one and the same. Summer had been right. The personification of evil that was the basis of the folklore of the faeries was Angin Topan, who was now alive and well.

Lochen mentally flipped pages, searching for another example. The problem was that only Summer had seen the Kelpie that had risen from her own ancestors. None of the others had. None of them had faced these ancient evils as she had. The sorcerers, he thought.

He looked for the lore of the sorcerers. He recalled the stories he had been told as he had grown up. The ancient leader at the time of the revolt was Vezeto Landoo. Landoo had been destroyed – lost forever – at the hands of a person Lochen had been taught was named Kurat. He matched the descriptions from the accounts of the Alchemist with the lore of the sorcerers. Kurat was Scirios.

These ancient myths had all been real, he now understood. He searched for another. He knew that Solveig had shared with him the teachings of the Mountain People – the history he had missed while he was raised as a sorcerer. Their leader was a princess named Traina. She was the one who had tried to keep the peace between the faeries and the forest creatures.

She had been close with both of these civilizations. When it was evident that peace was no longer possible, rather than be forced to choose a side, or, worse, to stand by and watch as they tried to annihilate one another, she moved her people further and further into the mountains, and ordered the creation of the palace, carved from the pink and purple granite of the mountain itself.

She had been crushed in a battle with the vilest of villains – one named Jainkaso. Lochen went back to the part that described the Kelpies. Jainkaso was Akmen Milzu: the Mountain Kelpie. The same one Lochen had seen firsthand. The same one who had brought down a mountain on him, Quinn, Natalie and Summer.

This was worse than he thought. He had understood that the Kelpies were powerful, but he hadn't connected them all with the horror stories that had been handed down generation to generation among the different civilizations. In fact, he had limited knowledge of the myths – although now he no longer thought they were myths – of more than one or two of these other peoples.

He looked down at Summer and realized how much the sight of Angin Topan must have affected her. The devil himself had come alive before her very eyes. No wonder she was so frightened. He might have reacted similarly if he had seen Scirios without the benefit of the knowledge he now possessed.

Lightning Riders, he immediately thought. Scirios will summon the Lightning Riders. We have less time than we assumed, he said to himself. And the Kelpies will be able to cross the sea. He would have to see if Stella could be more precise about when Scirios had been released. He needed to calculate exactly how much time they had to get to the one in the Ocean.

He thought about waking her, but then decided against it. They would all awaken soon enough. Right now, they needed to rest. He looked up at the rain again. There had to be a way of getting to Satamakau faster. Maybe one of the others would have an idea. He decided that could wait and he continued with the translations.

He returned his focus to the book and the history of the other Kelpies and the evolution of the folklore surrounding each of them. He knew a little bit about the legends of the Sea Sprites. He turned to that section. Their ancient leader had been a Princess called Liderra. He had discussed with Natalie the question of whether or not she might be a descendant of Liderra, but she didn't think that was possible.

In their discussion Natalie had told about how Liderra had moved the Sprites to the bottom of the ocean not long after the onset of the fighting between the faeries and the forest creatures. She had been responsible for creating their home on the ocean floor.

She hadn't been in this new location long before she was called upon by the Alchemist to help defeat another Sprite who had split away and joined the Kelpies. She was referred to as Banrian. There was nothing Lochen could find in the book that explained if this name, or any of the other names for the villains of the other myths, meant something specific. He supposed that was part of the individual cultures.

He noted the description of Banrian, and made a mental note of it. He expected they would encounter the Sea Sprite Kelpie soon enough and would know then if this was the same person or creature.

He read the other accounts and saw similarities in all of them. The leader of the Sprites was the Liderra. The leader of the Enchantresses was a woman named Ceannaire. Quinn's people told stories of a leader named Galvenais. He had already read about the sorcerers and the Mountain People and their leaders – Vezeto Landoo and Traina. He had heard Summer mention the Wakuu. The forest creatures were lead by the Kiongazi, and Liam's people had someone named Ketua.

In each instance, these people had been powerful and charismatic leaders at a time when their world was being torn

149

apart. The stories all varied as to what happened to these leaders, but the consistent thread was that they had either disappeared or been destroyed in a conflict.

Lochen then began to read about the source of this conflict. The alignment of the planets that he had read about before seemed to play a significant part in all of this. The timing of this alignment coincided with the efforts of the various leaders to keep the Rebbercands and the separatist Kelpies engaged and a part of their respective nations.

The power generated by the intense gravitational pull and other cosmic factors resulted in the generation of an immense electrical storm – the Fury: a storm of incredible and evil force. The weak-minded succumbed and the rift became irrevocable. Civil war broke out. The Kelpies were formed and went on a rampage of destruction.

Lochen recalled the storm that had appeared when the planets were recently aligned. It had devastated the land. It was what had brought all who were now inside a bubble, protected from the rain, together for the first time.

The Kelpies struck first, joining forces and singling out one nation after the other. No one had expected this. No one was prepared for it. The leaders were too slow to unite and fight back. It wasn't until the Alchemist and the Enchantress mounted defenses that the tide began to turn. But even they could not defeat the Kelpies in a head-on conflict.

They divided and conquered; singling out the Kelpies with the aid of the surviving leaders. Even those tactics were not without sacrifice. The lore of the different peoples all told of ancient leaders placing their own lives in harm's way to save their homes.

Lochen had heard Summer talk about the Malkia – the personification of evil that he now knew to be the Kelpie Angin Topan. He knew of his own tradition's villain – Kurat, who he was certain was the Kelpie Scirios. He knew of Banrian and Jainkaso – the banes of the Sprites and the Mountain people.

He had read and absorbed everything about the Enchantress's mythical Bathala, the Nelabas of the Ice Kingdom, Paligu of the forest creatures, and Mengassi from the area that was now the Venomous Swamp.

He couldn't imagine the chaos that had erupted at this time so long ago. Trying to maintain and then restore the peace seemed like an impossible task. It had clearly called for severe and decisive action. He understood now why these Kelpies had been imprisoned in such remote and ruthless conditions. And now they were being released.

He had translated through most of the night. It was still dark outside, and would be for several more hours. Even after the first sun rose, Lochen doubted the day would be much brighter. He was tempted to reread the same section again, this time applying both the letters and the symbols from the scroll. He wasn't sure what to expect, but hoped this version of the story would fill in the blanks between the past and the present.

It would have to wait. What he had read about the Kelpies was much too disturbing. More than ever he was convinced that they needed to stop them from resurrecting all eight of them.

Once that happened, their combined powers would be insurmountable. Lochen shook Liam awake.

"We need to move," he said.

"What?" mumbled Liam. "Did something happen? Are they near?"

"No," Lochen answered. "It's what I've read. We have no time to waste."

"What you read?" asked Liam, trying to clear the fog of sleep. "What did you read? What's changed?"

Lochen started waking the others.

"We need to go," he told them. "Nothing's changed," he answered Liam. "I've only discovered how dire the situation is."

"And you didn't think it was dire before?" asked Stella, who was awake instantly.

"Yes," he said as he scooped up Summer and Solveig and plopped them in his hood. "I thought it was dire before, but I hadn't fully appreciated the scope of the pending threat. We must reach the last Kelpie before they do – at all costs."

"How far are we from Satamakau?" asked Natalie.

"Another day," said Liam. "At least. If this rain doesn't let up, it may take longer. And that's assuming we don't run into any trouble."

"Is there anything either of you can do about the rain?" Quinn asked Lochen and Stella.

"What about another bubble of some kind?" Sean asked Natalie.

Everyone turned to Natalie.

"Is that possible?" asked Lochen. "You cast one around us in the volcano."

"And what about the one you created in the Ice Kingdom?" added Quinn.

"That one didn't work out too well, if you recall," she answered. "They're not really meant for traveling. They don't exactly steer well."

"I may be able to help with that," said Lochen. "Make it large enough to give us all room to spread out a bit."

Natalie moved to one side of the bubble that currently enclosed them. She raised her arm, wincing at the pain in her shoulder, and waved it in an arc along the top. The bubble expanded to more than twice its size.

"Is that big enough?" she asked.

"Yes," said Lochen. "That should do. Can you make it so that it's movable?"

She swept her arm downward and across, sealing the bubble across the ground beneath them to the sides. Now they were completely enclosed.

"Good," said Lochen. "Now if everyone will assume the same positions as we did coming through the forest and stay close to one another, we can see if my theory is sound."

Everyone lined up and moved close to one another. Liam and Lochen again took the lead. Lochen looked over and then nodded to Liam, indicating that they should start walking forward. Lochen extended his hands, making a motion like he was shooing ducks or some other small animal ahead of him. The bubble started rolling. Everyone shuffled their feet as they tried to get into rhythm behind Liam and Lochen.

"It might help if we all took the same stride with the same feet, as if we were marching," Lochen suggested.

"Then take shorter steps," Stella piped up. "Some of us are not quite so tall."

Lochen adjusted his stride and the others fell in step behind them, Stella following Lochen, and Sean following her. Natalie fell in line behind Liam and Quinn stumbled along behind her. Once they were all in step, Lochen announced that he was going to increase the pace. They all followed suit and soon the bubble was moving more quickly across the sodden grass.

"This is working out pretty good," declared Sean. "And the best part is that we're not getting wet."

"Wait until we start rolling down hill," cautioned Quinn. "It won't be so great then."

Chapter seven

'nair had closed his eyes and envisioned the location of the Forest Kelpie – the one called Rovek. As he did so, he noticed that the indicators for the locations of the Kelpies that had been released were no longer visible. The locations of the two who remained were sharper than they had been before. He wondered what would happen to the map when the last one was released.

When he opened his eyes, he found himself high in the sky. The sudden and unexpected change took his breath away. He hadn't felt any movement lifting him into the air. There was no change in the sound or the feeling of the air around him. Now, though, he was several hundred feet above the ground, wrapped in a spider's web of interlocking electrical charges.

"Relax and breathe," Scirios told him. "We need you. It wouldn't do us any good if you asphyxiate yourself."

The Kelpie had to repeat himself. B'nair hadn't heard him the first time. The sense of vertigo he experienced in his dreams, and the same sensation he felt when he fell from that bridge in the Trepan's caves, washed over him — immobilized him. He closed his eyes again and forced the breath out of his lungs.

Concentrating only on his breathing, he sucked in air and quickly blew it out. He couldn't slow himself down. He was beginning to hyperventilate; his head felt light and dizzy. The muscles in his back had gone so rigid that he could feel the pressure up through his neck to his head. His teeth were clenched so tightly that his jaw hurt. Get a hold of yourself, he demanded. He forced himself to control his breathing.

Once that had been done, the dizziness in his head subsided. Then he forced himself to open his eyes. He did so slowly, and concentrated on the back of Akmen Milzu, who was immediately in front of him. Gradually, he looked to his right and saw Ena Ray and Angin Topan. They seemed to be unaffected by the altitude.

He slowly moved his head to the left. His gaze swept past Neraka Ferr and turned towards Scirios, who was next to him. He couldn't resist the urge to look downward. As soon as he did, the feeling of falling that he sensed in his dreams and in the caves swept over him once more. Panic gripped him and he immediately shut his eyes again.

He admonished himself mentally. He hadn't felt this way when crossing high narrow bridges. Why was this bothering him now? He hated the fear that was boiling up inside him. He hated this sign of weakness. What was making this happen, he wondered. And why now? All he could think of were the dreams. Were they a premonition of things to come? Or were they warning signs of things to be avoided?

"A fear of heights?" asked Scirios. "It's nothing to be ashamed of."

"No," B'nair answered, a bit too forcefully.

He opened his eyes and turned to the Kelpie, his eyes fixed on the black holes that studied him. He clenched his fist and swallowed hard, forcing back the bile rising in his throat.

"I was only taken by surprise," he said, hoping the quivering in his voice went unnoticed.

"Of course," Scirios replied. "I meant no insult to your courage."

B'nair wasn't sure if the Kelpie was being genuine or ridiculing him. The face peering back at him was expressionless. It took all the strength the Rebbercand had to appear calm. Eventually, he relaxed slightly and looked beyond the Kelpies, but refrained from looking down.

They were passing through thin, gray clouds. A mist surrounded them, but the electrical charge caused it to evaporate rather than penetrate the dull blue air that enveloped them. Beyond the mist to the south he could see the long, low valley littered with holes drift by. He had no idea how fast they were going.

As much as he hated the way he was reacting to being so far aloft, he had to agree that this was better than walking. He wasn't sure, yet, if it was safer. The mines of Djall seemed to go on forever; but as suddenly as they had appeared, they were gone. B'nair judged it was midday by the time they had crossed over the valley.

He could feel the air getting colder and sensed they were rising. He was still not comfortable looking down. There was something unsettling about seeing so much open space between your feet and the ground. He glanced to his left again and saw the foothills of the range of mountains that ran east to west across the center of the continent.

He knew that south of this range of mountains was the beginning of a forest. This particular forest was one of the more peaceful places his people had encountered. He recalled an expedition in which he led a team that removed several trees on the western side. They had encountered a group of Dozors. It was his first meeting with the forest creatures. It hadn't turned out so well for them.

He was lost in his thoughts when he noticed the forest fade away and the foothills began to rise higher and higher. He could see the ground change, too. It went from forest land to rock. The rock rose up quickly and changed to granite. At first the granite was so dark it looked black. But then it started to lighten in color.

B'nair also noticed that they seemed to be changing direction. Akmen Milzu was in the lead. She must be the one altering their course, he thought. But why? He kept his focus on the mountain as it neared.

As they moved closer, he could see that what he had mistaken for the black color of the stone was in actuality a deep, dark purple. Once the mist cleared away, he saw the top. The mountain rose into the sky, turning a lighter purple, streaked with lines of pink. He had never seen anything like this before. Out of the granite had been carved a castle. It was immense. And, he had to admit, beautiful.

In addition to the spectacular colors, its design was breathtaking. There were spires and turrets and intricate walkways. There were sculptures at various locations that demonstrated an extremely high level of craftsmanship. These were impressive, but less so to the Rebbercand than the strategic design.

The walls grew up from the rock and slanted outward at a slight angle. It would be impossible to lay siege to such a structure. In a word, it was impregnable. Scirios could see how thoroughly B'nair was studying the palace.

"Incredible, isn't it?" he asked.

"I've never seen anything like it," B'nair answered.

"It was home to Akmen Milzu," he said. "A very long time ago," he added when B'nair jerked his head towards him.

"The Kelpie lived here?"

"Yes," answered Scirios. "She is a Mountain Kelpie. Her family was of the Mountain People. They helped build this fortress when her people moved here from the foothills – not long after the infighting began between the forest creatures and the faeries."

B'nair gave a puzzled look to the Kelpie.

"Why would they run from the faeries and forest creatures?" he asked. "Surely, they could have defeated both of those civilizations – probably in the same day."

"Their leader at the time," explained Scirios, "was a Princess named Traina. She chose to avoid the conflict. She didn't want to take a side for or against either of those peoples."

"How ridiculous," sneered B'nair.

"Akmen Milzu agreed," said the Kelpie. "With you, of course. It was ridiculous. The Mountain People were strong and powerful. It was their leader who was weak. She offered to meet with the faeries and the forest creatures to help them resolve their differences. All she wanted to do was talk.

"Akmen Milzu had been trained as a sorceress. She had been trained for action, for leadership. What good was having such power, she argued, if it was never to be used? This argument was rejected – vehemently. When all that talking failed and the spats between the faeries and forest creatures escalated, Traina opted to move away. Again Akmen Milzu urged a different path. The time was ripe to take over the lands these two warring peoples occupied. They could be easily eliminated.

"Traina chastised Akmen, and did so publically. This was no way to treat such a powerful sorceress But Akmen held her tongue. Once the castle was constructed, she again tried to persuade Traina to send a war party down to the forest and take advantage of the situation.

"Once again, she was refused and humiliated. She was challenged in an open forum and reminded of her duty as a sorceress. Traina threatened to have her exiled and stripped of her powers. She was being advised by another, instead of her own sorceress."

"Another?" asked B'nair. "Who?"

"The Alchemist," answered Scirios.

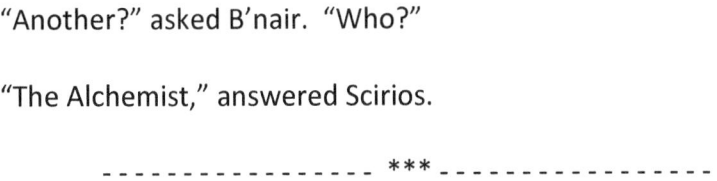

From the moment of Akmen Milzu's birth, it was known that she would be a sorceress. At the earliest time, she was enrolled in training with others like her. She excelled quickly and was a leader among the sorcerers. Another from her people, born not long after her, was also discovered to have this same calling. He was also enrolled in training. Since they came from the same civilization and Akmen Milzu was of noble birth, the other sorcerer was bound to her.

By the time her training was complete and she returned to the Mountain People, she was a master – one of a few select sorcerers who had an exceedingly high level of skill. In her training, she became close to another who would become a master. This one was from the small people; the faeries, pixies and imps. Her name was Angin Topan.

At this time the Mountain people lived in the foothills between the mountain range that extended from the Cerulean Sea to the Viridian Ocean and the forest in which the Forest Creatures resided. To the east of this great forest lived several colonies of faeries, pixies and imps. Their community extended from the

161

forest to the shore of the Cerulean Sea. Along the coast and into the sea lived the Sea Sprites.

For centuries these communities lived side by side in harmony. Akmen Milzu had done well in learning her craft, but she had failed to understand that the proper use of her skills was for the benefit of everyone; that as a sorcerer of the Mountain People, it was her duty to protect and enhance the lives of all of them. Instead, she viewed the common people as less than worthy. She believed that she was destined to lead the powerful to even greater heights, even if that meant at the expense of those who were less fortunate or less capable than she.

When she expressed these views with Traina, the leader of the Mountain People, she was gently, but firmly, told that this was not the moral code of their people, nor of the sorcerers. Akmen Milzu did not agree, and she resented what she perceived as being chastised. She persisted and was repeatedly rebuffed.

Could no one see that what she was telling them was the only way to ensure the survival and prosperity of the elite, she demanded. Her continued insistence and narrow-mindedness resulted one day in a public confrontation with Traina. Akmen Milzu was forcefully overruled and was threatened with dismissal as sorcerer to Traina.

Shortly after this incident, the second sorcerer from the Mountain People returned from training, and became bound to her. He was in complete agreement with her position on the matter of securing the rightful place of the leaders, and suggested that there were other sorcerers who felt the same way. Among them was her friend, Angin Topan.

A clandestine meeting was arranged with the imp, who brought with her a friend – another who believed their powers were wasted on anyone of lesser stature. He was the sorcerer of the Forest Creatures, a man named Rovek. This first meeting with Akmen Milzu, her sorcerer, the imp and Rovek, was to be the first of several.

Initially, all that was accomplished was an exchange of complaints and what they all believed to be summary dismissals of their opinions by the leaders of their respective peoples. Angin Topan told of her own incident of public humiliation and ridicule by the Wakuu of the faeries. She had exaggerated, of course, in an effort to make her stand against her leadership as defiant as Akmen Milzu's had been.

Rovek added his own stories of how Kiongazi, a Dozor in the Lodge of the Forest Creatures, had threatened to ban him from Lodge meetings if he persisted. He had suggested implementing measures that Lodge members be exempt from the duties of the rest of the Forest Creatures, and that they were in some way more important than the other Forest Creatures.

After a while, it became apparent to all of them that their complaining was not resolving anything.

"We need to do something," said Rovek.

"But what?" asked Angin Topan. "Our leaders have made it clear that they don't share our views. We can't force them. And we risk banishment if we persist."

"We need for them to come to this conclusion on their own," said Akmen Milzu.

"It would be easier to move the mountains," said Rovek.

"Something needs to happen to demonstrate that our powers are essential to their well-being; that their view of the masses is inaccurate," offered Angin Topan.

"Yes," agreed Rovek. "Something that makes us indispensible to them."

"Something that threatens their positions, their security," added Angin Topan.

"Something that will force them to ask us to intervene, to use our powers to save them," said Rovek.

"War," said Akmen Milzu.

"Yes," agreed her sorcerer, greedily. "A war. But with whom?"

"How can we get them to go to war with anyone?" asked Rovek.

"We don't," said Akmen Milzu. "It will have to erupt on its own."

"How is that going to happen?" Rovek questioned.

"Carefully," she replied. "And we can't do this alone, or at the risk of being discovered."

"What do you propose?" asked her advisor.

"There are some others who I think can help," Akmen Milzu said. "Others who I am confident share our views – that we who have been granted our special powers were meant to rule. We should lead our people, not those who currently do."

"You're talking insurrection," said Rovek.

"Does that frighten you?" she asked.

"No," he said. "But once we start down this road, there can be no turning back."

"I agree," she replied.

"As do I," said the imp.

"I am bound to you," said the advisor. "As you go, I shall follow."

"Good," said Akmen Milzu. "First, we should reach out to some of the other sorcerers. I have met the sorcerer of the Sea People, and her Enchantress. I believe they are of the same mind."

"I studied with a man named Pantano Izaki," said the imp. "He has already expressed the same views. I am sure he will join us."

"Excellent," she replied. "And we will need to meet in a more remote location."

"I studied with the sorcerer from the Ice Kingdom," said Rovek. "I am sure I can bring him into our fold and he will know of a place that is secure."

"The Ice Kingdom?" asked Angin Topan. "So far away? It will take too long to go back and forth."

"I can arrange transportation," added the advisor. "The distance will present no difficulty."

"Then it's settled," said Akmen Milzu.

"You realize that if this is not successful," said Rovek. "We will become outcasts. We'll be branded as Kelpies."

"We are already outcasts," replied Akmen Milzu. "And the label of Kelpie suits me just fine."

After that fateful meeting, Akmen Milzu met secretly with Ollos Foscos and her Enchantress, who was, in fact, the Enchanter, Neraka Ferr. The predominant population of the sea creatures was the Sea Sprites, but Ollos Foscos was not one of them. She was descended from the Krakens. Her Enchanter, however, was part Sprite.

Neraka Ferr, in addition to being a rare male member of the society of enchantresses, was born of a Sea Sprite father and a mermaid mother. He should have been a liaison between the two civilizations, but, instead, was aligned with neither. He had been bound to Ollos Foscos. The Krakens were a small clan that was quickly dying out. As such, Ollos Foscos already viewed herself as an outcast, and Neraka Ferr, who was bound to her, had the same status. They were eager to become a part of the Kelpies.

Angin Topan arranged a meeting with Pantano Izaki, who had for a long time had an overly exalted opinion of himself. He felt honored to be visited by a master sorceress; it fed his ego. To be asked to join an elite group who all held themselves above everyone else was impossible for him to resist.

After several months, the seven were transported far to the north and met in a deep cavern in the Ice Kingdom as hosts of Saldeti, the sorcerer to the Guardians. Initially, he was reluctant to agree to their plan, but he was basically weak, and eventually gave in, when he understood that little would be expected of him.

"Half of the civilizations we represent are in close proximity to one another," Akmen Milzu began. "It would be more manageable if our rebellion began there and then spread outward."

They all nodded their agreement.

"I suggest that we begin by secretly fomenting dissent between the faeries and the Forest Creatures," she went on.

"Why them?" asked Pantano Izaki.

"They live in and share the same forest," answered Rovek.

"Yes," agreed Akmen Milzu. "And that closeness will serve our needs."

"And what will cause a war between them?" asked Ollos Foscos.

"We will" answered the imp. "But not immediately. We need to create suspicion and mistrust between them."

"And then let them spark the war themselves," added Rovek.

"We can add to the confusion by creating some conflict among the faeries, the pixies and the imps, as well," said Akmen Milzu.

"And how do we do that?" asked Saldeti.

"The pixies, imps and faeries have the reputation of being able to cast small hexes," said Rovek.

"And they can't?" asked Pantano Izaki.

"No," said Angin Topan. "It's a myth we created to protect ourselves – themselves. Being as small as they are, they are vulnerable to attacks by almost anyone. Only those who were born with special powers have those capabilities."

Angin Topan had originally included herself in her descriptions of her people, but eventually disassociated herself from them. She had committed herself to the Kelpies.

"Has anyone ever attacked your people?" asked Saldeti.

"No," said the imp. "But they are a very suspicious and paranoid people; especially the pixies. And they are quick to fight. We will take advantage of that flaw in their character."

And so the strategy was implemented. It started off slowly. The Kelpies cast simple spells on a few of the faeries. A small group was flying near some pixies that were gathering honey. Angin Topan, who was able to shape shift even then, took the form of one of the pixies. As the faeries flew by, she cast a spell and the faeries' wings dissolved. They dropped to the ground. At the same instant she cast a spell on the pixies that caused them to laugh uncontrollably.

The faeries were certain the pixies had destroyed their wings. Angin Topan could see the fury on their faces. They screamed at the pixies, and threatened revenge. Two days later, Angin Topan called upon a local woman who could create powerful potions. Her name was Beebee. The Imp convinced her to contaminate the water supply of the pixies, which she did. When they drank from it, the water turned them red – a color they would remain for eternity. After that, no further intervention between these two communities was needed by the Kelpies. Things escalated on their own.

"We need to expand this conflict," said Rovek, after Angin Topan reported on the success of her efforts between the faeries and the pixies.

"I agree," said Akmen Milzu. "We need to draw in the Forest Creatures."

"We need to make them appear to be collateral damage," said Angin Topan. "At least initially."

They initiated a series of "mishaps," to occur to the Forest Creatures. The first ones were minor – reactions to plants that had been hexed, causing some of those who had been gathering berries to break out in horrible rashes. Watering holes became polluted; trees became infested with insects; small fires broke out.

Kiongazi, the lead Dozor, went to visit the faeries to get them to stop their attacks on the pixies. He met with the Wakuu.

"Your people must stop casting spells and hexes on the pixies," he urged. "They are doing damage to our environment."

"You know that's a myth," she answered. "We have no real power to hex or spell."

"But you have to agree that the relationship with the pixies has become strained," he said.

"Yes," she admitted. "I don't know what caused it, though. I've tried to meet with the pixies, but they see me as an enemy rather than their leader. They have refused to talk any further."

"We should seek help," he suggested.

"What do you recommend?" she asked.

"I was thinking of seeking out the Alchemist," he answered.

"Alone?" she asked.

"If necessary," he replied, "but I would rather that you join me. We should be united in this. It will also send a message to our peoples."

She agreed and a few days later the two of them set off towards the Alchemist's fortress at Virkio. The Kelpies took this opportunity to escalate the conflict. They discovered two faeries alone in the woods, returning from the Lodge of the Forest Creatures, and made them disappear. At the same time, they did the same thing to a small party of pixies who were foraging nearby.

The first reaction from both groups was to blame the other. It soon became evident that each had lost people. Their attention then turned to the Forest Creatures. Without their leaders to instill reason, chaos ensued. The war had begun.

Full-scale invasions took place. There was no further need of spells from the Kelpies. The warring parties developed their own attacks. The pandemonium that resulted grew to a frenzied level. Evil had quickly displaced intelligence. It no longer mattered how things began. Each group was committed to eradicating the other.

It spread like a cancer, as the Kelpies had planned. Soon it spilled over to the Mountain People and the Sea Sprites. However, instead of drawing them into the conflict, as the Kelpies had hoped, the opposite happened.

Liderra, who was the leader of the Sea Sprites, evacuated the shore. It was her intention to create a giant bubble on the ocean floor and shelter her people there. As she prepared them for the move, she met with resistance from her sorceress, Ollos Foscos. She turned to the Enchantress, Ceannaire, who agreed with her, that this was the wisest and safest course of action. Ollos Foscos turned to Neraka Ferr for assistance.

Liderra and Ceannaire were unaware of the plotting and conniving that Ollos Foscos and Neraka Ferr were engaged in. The two Kelpies did what they could to stall the departure of the Sea Sprites, urging, instead, that they stand their ground and take a position.

Liderra traveled to the foothills of the mountains to discover that Traina was already moving the Mountain People high into the nearby peaks. She had commissioned their master builder and stone carver to create a castle from the granite itself – one that would be impregnable. The master carver was Yannis Milzu – father to the Kelpie, Akmen.

By the time Kiongazi and the Wakuu returned with the Alchemist, the disease of war had spread even further. The Forest Creatures and the faeries were in an all out battle. The pixies had fled to the gardens of a nearby valley only to run into resistance that had been fomented by Pantano Izaki. He had planted seeds of dissention and doubt among the people who were the ancestors of the Pathfinder.

In an effort to thwart the Alchemist, Pantano Izaki foolishly attempted to engage him in a battle of spells. He attacked a peace envoy, seriously wounding the Alchemist, but that moment of surprise was the only encounter in which he had the advantage. He had struck the Alchemist full in the face with a near lethal spell. The Alchemist deflected it at the last moment, saving his own life, but the blast covered his eyes with a milky white film that robbed him of his vision. In spite of this, he was able to fend off every challenge after that, and the Kelpie, sensing defeat, took flight.

Thinking he could escape, he ran to the meeting place the Kelpies had used in the Ice Kingdom. He found no refuge there, and only managed to reveal this location to the Alchemist. The old sorcerer was relentless in his pursuit of the Kelpie, cutting off one avenue of escape after another. In a final act of desperation, Izaki returned to his garden home and destroyed it, hoping the Alchemist would attempt to reverse the curse he placed, thereby giving him more time to hide.

The spell he cast was irreversible, and the Alchemist knew it instantly. As much as he wanted to save the gardens and their people, he knew it was futile. He had to stop this mad man. Eventually, he trapped the Kelpie along the river that separated an enchanted forest from the gardens, which were even now quickly devolving into what would become the Venomous Swamp.

When he caught up to Pantano Izaki, he sealed him in a block and hid him in the vegetation that was choking off the garden along the river. He managed to divert the Kelpie's spell enough to use it against him. The poisons he created would serve as the guardians of his prison.

He could not destroy the Kelpie; he had been too weakened. He knew that this one fallen sorcerer was not alone. He knew that there were several others who were launching an attack across the land. He knew he would need help to defeat them.

The Alchemist returned to the Forest Creatures only long enough to assess the damage being done by the remaining Kelpies. Their power was growing at an alarming rate. He discovered that the Mountain People had already fled, moving as far away as possible, but that their efforts were being met with resistance from their own sorcerer.

He learned of the Sea Sprites' intent to move deep under the sea, and that those plans were also being met with resistance. It was clear to him that there was a well-coordinated effort being made to disrupt the normal lives of several of the civilizations. He left to secure the aid of a very powerful enchantress – Meri Hocto.

When she appeared, she was wearing the source of her power – a stone of unusual color and beauty. The center seemed to have captured a small storm. Deep inside the stone there were miniature flashes of lightning behind swirling clouds. The color shifted as its power built. Around the stone was a gold band with peculiar markings on the outer edge.

When she wore this pendant, her powers were incomprehensible, as if from another world. She knew that they had to take quick and decisive steps to stop the momentum of the rebellion and the damage the Kelpies could do and were doing. She also knew that she and the Alchemist were no match for the Kelpies collectively, and that they would have to separate them to defeat them.

She and the Alchemist came into contact with the imp first. Meri Hocto began an assault and chased the small Kelpie across the mountain range to the Cerulean Sea and then north along the shore. As her partner in crime had done, she cast a devastating spell over the forests the imps and pixies had called home, turning it into a desert.

It was her final act. As the spell was cast, the Alchemist trapped her and drove her deep into the sand of the desert she had created to be buried for the next two thousand years.

"We must be more efficient in separating them from one another and capturing them," he said to the Enchantress. "If they continue to cast these spells, there will be nothing left of this world."

"I agree," she replied. "We should probably go to the most remote locations and work our way inward."

"That may leave the most dangerous for the last," he said.

"I don't see any alternative. Once word gets out about the two we've dispatched, it will become even more difficult to overcome them. What's worse is that they have helpers – minions it seems."

"Yes," the Alchemist said shaking his head. "I've come across a few of them already. They have been either swayed by promises the Kelpies will never keep, or threatened and intimidated by the Kelpies' wrath if they don't comply."

"You know, too, that the prisons we're creating for these sorcerers won't last forever," she added. "The forces that caused them to rise in the first place will resurface."

"Not for another two thousand years," he said.

"Great," she said with a hint of sarcasm. "And what happens then? Are we merely delaying the inevitable?"

"No," he answered. "Other leaders will rise to defeat them. In the mean time, I will create a Boravak to hold them all, and a portal to a new place."

"What about the minions?"

"Leave them to me," he said. "I have a special task in mind for them – a penance for their crimes. They will serve to guide and serve those who come."

"We must keep a record," she said as an afterthought. "In case neither of us is successful. There must be an accounting so those who follow will know what happened here and why."

"I have already begun such a book," he told her. "It's in an ancient language that will not be easily discovered or translated should it fall into the wrong hands."

"All right, then," she said.

They were standing in the desert, south of what was now the Venomous Swamp. Two Kelpies had been captured and the remaining six were, as yet, unaware of the efforts being made to defeat them. Meri needed to return to her citadel, but shortly after she and the Alchemist would search the Ice Kingdom for the renegade hiding there.

"You should leave your pendant in a safe place," the Alchemist said. "Perhaps in your Sanctorum. If it should be taken by one of the Kelpies, all would be lost for certain."

"I would destroy it before I would let that happen," she answered.

With that, they departed. The Enchantress returned to her citadel to continue training her protégés and the Alchemist went in search of those who had allied themselves with the Kelpies. He also began to plan the strategies for isolating and conquering the six remaining sorcerers. He raised his hands to his eyes. Pantano Izaki had robbed him of his sight, but not his vision.

Chapter eight

’nair listened patiently. The story the Kelpie was telling him filled in several blank spaces in his knowledge of his traveling companions and the forces they were facing. It also explained the increasing sense of power he felt emanating from the stone he wore around his neck. It was part of the pendant of the Enchantress – the one the Kelpies referred to as the witch.

"How do you know so much about all this?" the Rebbercand finally asked.

"I was sorcerer to Akmen Milzu," he answered. "I was her advisor. I still am. I am bound to her."

B'nair didn't know what it meant, that Scirios was bound to Akmen Milzu, but he could guess. Scirios' commitment to Akmen Milzu was the same as Lochen's was to Solveig. It was a commitment to the death, if necessary. That certainly explained how he knew so much about the history of the Kelpies. He was in at the ground floor.

"So why are we coming so close to this castle?" asked B'nair. "Nostalgia?"

"I think the master has another purpose in mind," Scirios replied.

The Lightning Riders stopped moving and hovered a few hundred yards away from the castle. Akmen Milzu stared at the structure. Her father had been the key architect. He had created this fortress to keep at bay the wars that she had been instrumental in starting. His very actions were an effort to thwart hers.

When he discovered what she had done, she expected him to disown her. That's what she would have done in his place. Instead, he forgave her. He pleaded with Traina to make peace with her. She resented him for forgiving her. She resented him for pleading on her behalf. But what she resented most was that Traina had actually extended her hand in peace.

"This can all be undone," the leader of the Mountain People has said to her.

That was when the Kelpie brought the full force of her power down, crushing Traina and burying her under the black mountains to the east. Akmen Milzu made sure her former

178

leader would never live inside the palace her own father had constructed.

Her vengeance, however, was also her downfall. She had deceived Traina into meeting with her alone. The Kelpie's mistake was in arriving at the meeting alone herself. She had separated herself from her cohorts. After she destroyed Traina, she stayed behind, reveling in her triumph. The burst of power she had exerted to make the mountains open up and swallow her nemesis had also served as a beacon for the Alchemist, pinpointing her location.

She lingered too long. Before she could escape, the Alchemist and the Enchantress had her cornered. Their combined spells were too much. She was turned into stone and whisked away to another mountain range, deprived of the same thing she had withheld from Traina – buried in a mountain that was not her home.

Now she looked down upon the structure her father created. She stared at the memorial to her disgrace. Hovering at the front of the group of travelers still held in the electrical web of the Lightning Riders, she raised her hand, stretching it out towards the palace. She then clenched her fist and brought it down in a quick jerk. At first, it seemed as if nothing was happening.

Then there was a rumbling sound. Cracks began to appear like threads in the walls. They slowly widened as an invisible force applied incredible pressure. Akmen Milzu still had her hand clenched, squeezing as tightly as she could. The uppermost spires shook and then collapsed. They fell inward, one after the other, crumbling into small pieces.

Then the elaborate carvings that decorated the outer wall broke away. Some tumbled down the mountainside while others dropped backwards into the castle. The turrets collapsed as she squeezed her giant hand even harder, her power crushing them like paper. The granite screeched as pieces broke apart and scraped against one another.

It seemed to take forever, but was over in seconds. The once beautiful castle of the Mountain People was reduced to dust and rubble, heaped in an ugly pile, smashed and broken. As hard as B'nair's heart was, he felt this was a wasteful display of power, and found it repugnant. Scirios simply smiled.

Akmen Milzu's entire body was rigid. Eventually, she relaxed her fist and it dropped to her side. Her shoulders released the pent up tension. Then she turned to look at her party.

"This used to be my home,' she said to them. "Now it's home to no one."

The castle had been vacated some time ago when the Fury had rampaged over the countryside. Lochen had made sure his Princess and their newly discovered friends – a faerie and a forest creature – were on their way to a safe destination, and then he led the people to an alternate location. There hadn't been any residents here since that time, but until now, there was an expectation that the Mountain People would eventually return to this home.

Scirios motioned with one hand. The crackling of the Lightning Riders rose up again, signaling that they were moving once more. B'nair watched the castle until it was once again shrouded in mist and then disappeared from sight. His own people were somewhat reckless about the places they chose to live, but he couldn't recall an instance when they engaged in such wanton destruction.

He reflected on something the first Kelpie – Pantano Izaki – had said. He mentioned that it was he who poisoned the Swamp; it was he who made it uninhabitable for the residents. It was uninhabitable for all of them, except for the one who managed to track them all down and attack them in the desert – the desert where Pantano Izaki had been destroyed. His freedom from two thousand years of imprisonment had been very short-lived.

Scirios had also told him that Angin Topan had destroyed lush gardens in the seconds before her capture by the Alchemist. Then he remembered what Ena Ray had done to the Ice Kingdom. He had destroyed that community, turning the few people they could find into stone. And now this? Did these people destroy everything with which they came in contact? Was there any end to this, he wondered.

The day slipped into night and the Lightning Riders carried them on. At least in the dark B'nair wouldn't be able to see how far below the ground was, or if they were leaving any more destruction in their wake. He took little consolation in that. He saw the others were able to fall asleep. That was a luxury denied him, although given the nightmares he found himself recently plagued with, perhaps calling sleep a luxury was not entirely accurate.

At least the heat generated by the electrical current was keeping them all warm. That was a comfort, especially at this altitude. As the first light struggled through the gray sky, he could see that they were getting close to their destination. The edges of another forest were looming on the horizon. This one looked less threatening than some others he had seen. Regardless, though, he would be glad to feel his feet on solid ground again.

The web of electricity slowed down and gradually lowered to the ground. Once everyone was back on land again, the lightning began to dissipate, and eventually fizzled to nothing. All that remained was the odd odor of the aftermath. They were still miles from their destination, but B'nair assumed that landing here was safer than trying to maneuver through places where the trees were thicker.

By now, the imp's wings had fully restored and she was able to fly on her own. She rose from Ena Ray's shoulder and darted back and forth, anxious to find their companion. B'nair didn't wait to be asked. He closed his eyes and summoned the map. Once the destination was imbedded in his memory, he nodded to the Mountain Kelpie that he was ready and they all set out.

B'nair remembered being in this forest once before, but much further to the south. He remembered facing a hunting party of Forest Creatures. They had been very naïve, expecting him and his Rebbercands to stop their logging while the Dozors conferred with one another. That encounter hadn't worked out so well for the Forest Creatures.

As he also recalled, there were several kinds of animals that inhabited it, but nothing that would pose any threat to them. He almost laughed at that thought. The animals had posed no threat to the assembly of Rebbercands he had led here so long ago. Those animals would run in fear from this current group.

They wound their way through the woods at a steady pace. The Rebbercand didn't really have to pay attention to the direction in which he was headed. His internal compass and the image from the map kept him on course. This allowed him the opportunity to examine the surroundings. For perhaps the first time in his life, he took the time to study the forest and to actually enjoy where he was.

It is so serene here, he thought. There were bushes along the way from which he plucked berries that he popped into his mouth. He was certain he had eaten them before, but he didn't recall how pleasant they tasted. And the air was fresh, too. It smelled and tasted clean and rich. Had it always been like this, he wondered. Why hadn't he noticed this before?

He stopped in his tracks. Something was suddenly different.

"What's wrong?" asked Akmen Milzu. "Why have you stopped?"

B'nair didn't answer immediately. He shook his head, raised his hand to signal for silence, and looked around once more. The woods looked like any other forest. There was nothing special or remarkable about it. He sniffed the air. He could smell the aroma of the pine needles that littered the ground, but nothing more. He looked down at the berries still in his hand.

He raised them to his nose and sniffed. Then he touched them to the end of his tongue. As soon as he did, the colors of the forest became more vibrant, he could hear birds singing in the distance and a cool, refreshing breeze drifted through the trees. Had the berries enhanced his senses, he wondered. Or were they distorting them? He threw them aside.

"Nothing's wrong," he said.

This place is hexed, he told himself. He would have to be more careful. He shook his head once more and took a deep breath.

"I thought I heard something. That's all," he added, and then he resumed walking.

Akmen Milzu and Neraka Ferr exchanged glances, but said nothing. They were well aware of the tricks and traps that the Alchemist was capable of. They both knew they would have to watch the Rebbercand closely. They had noticed nothing out of the ordinary. So far. Akmen Milzu plucked from a nearby bush some of the berries B'nair had eaten. She raised them carefully to her nose and sniffed. She considered tasting them, but thought better of it. She cast them aside.

"What do you think it was?" the Fire Kelpie asked the master when they were out of earshot.

"I'm not sure," Akmen Milzu replied. "I don't believe for a minute that he heard anything."

"What then?" Neraka Ferr persisted. "Why did he stop?"

"He _felt_ something," she answered. "Perhaps something the Alchemist left behind."

"How could he sense that and we could not?" asked her friend.

"That stone he wears," the Mountain Kelpie suggested. "It grows stronger as we grow stronger."

"But the Rebbercand has no powers. Unless…"

"Unless what?" Akmen Milzu asked, turning towards Neraka Ferr.

"That pendant was the source of the witch's power," the Fire Kelpie said. "He holds it now, and, somehow, he's changed. I think that is part of what's changed him. I think even half of the witch's pendant bestows incredible power. That stone cannot be lost to us."

"Perhaps we should simply take it from him," suggested the Mountain Kelpie.

"I'm not sure that would be possible," Neraka Ferr replied. "As long as he holds that axe, the stone will not leave his possession."

"How do you know this?" she asked. "What makes you think this is so?"

"The blade of that axe was forged centuries ago from iron that was drawn from deep below the volcano that was my home," Neraka Ferr said. "It belonged to one of the Rebbercand's ancestors."

"The one who slew the witch!" Akmen Milzu exclaimed.

"Yes," agreed Neraka Ferr. "I believe so. And the legend is that when she cast her dying spells, she broke the stone from the pendant, and a piece of it…"

"Struck the blade of that axe," the Mountain Kelpie finished. "And now half of the stone from her pendant is in the possession of the same person who holds the axe."

"So it seems."

"He's unaware of the growing power within him, isn't he?"

"I think that's safe to assume," agreed Neraka Ferr. "He hasn't demonstrated otherwise – until now."

"We must all be rejoined before the other half of that pendant is discovered."

"We are almost complete. Rovek is nearby and once he is freed, we have only Ollos Foscos to locate."

"We can dispose of the Rebbercand once Foscos is free," said Akmen Milzu.

"In those depths, it will be easier to leave him to the mercy of the Dark Eye," Neraka Ferr whispered. "That axe will not protect him there."

Akmen Milzu turned to her friend, considering this suggestion. She nodded her agreement.

"Should we share this with the others?" the Fire Kelpie asked.

"Not yet," cautioned the Mountain Kelpie. "I don't yet trust Ena Ray, and the imp appears to be growing much too friendly with him. When Rovek is free, I'll find a moment to discuss this with him and Scirios. By then, we may also be rejoined by Saldeti.

Once more than half of us are reunited, it will be easier to ensure the imp's cooperation and exert appropriate control over Ena Ray."

B'nair had been several yards ahead of the two Kelpies while they engaged in their secret discussion. Scirios had been accompanying him, talking to him about irrelevant things. He knew this was an attempt to divert his attention from the clandestine conversation of the other two. It was not successful.

The Rebbercand had noticed a different feeling about himself not long after they left the mines of Djall. He dismissed it at first, but the feeling was persistent. He seemed more...aware. His senses were all on high alert. That was the only way he knew to describe it. It had become more pronounced after they entered this forest. He felt a warmth from the stone around his neck and for the first time since the hobgoblins found him, a tingling in his dead right arm.

Even though they were well out of his range of hearing, he knew what the two Kelpies were talking about. It was almost as if he was engaged in their conversation himself. Scirios' inane conversation did nothing to interfere with that. In fact, he was able to converse with the Lightning Kelpie and still understand the discussion that he couldn't hear, but knew was taking place. He even knew what they were saying.

At one point he reflexively reached for the pendant, but stopped himself. He wasn't sure if Scirios knew what his two friends were talking about; if the Lightning Kelpie had the same ability to hear their conversation. In fact, what B'nair couldn't know was that the Kelpie only knew that the discussion between

Akmen Milzu and Neraka Ferr was intended to be private. He was unable to discern the topic.

B'nair kept his body language, facial expressions and the tone of his voice as neutral as he could. It would not serve his purposes to betray what he knew. He let it all simmer as he considered his own strategies. His thoughts and his conversation with Scirios were suddenly interrupted by the sound of distant howling.

"What's that?" B'nair barked.

Scirios looked in the direction of the sound. The howls weren't very far off. He could hear growling and barking intermixed. He turned towards the other Kelpies and then back to B'nair, with a slight smile on his face.

"Jackals, I believe," he answered.

B'nair knew there were many wild and dangerous animals in this forest, but he had never encountered jackals before.

"It would appear that one of our old friends is nearby," said Angin Topan.

"The Kelpie?" asked Ena Ray.

"No," said Neraka Ferr. "The jackals are the Alchemist's doing. They are meant to protect his sentinels."

"Who are the sentinels?" asked B'nair.

"They are traitors and cowards for the most part," answered Akmen Milzu. "Friends of the Alchemist."

"Then why did Angin Topan say one of your old friends is nearby?" questioned Ena Ray.

"At one time," explained Scirios, "they counted themselves as supporters of our cause, but then the Alchemist and his witch turned them against us. Now they provide support to those others – the ones who have been following us."

"So then why are there jackals nearby?" B'nair asked.

"The jackals are meant to protect the sentinels," said Akmen Milzu.

"From you?" Ena Ray wondered out loud.

"From others who would harm the sentinels," answered Neraka Ferr. "They only serve to warn the sentinels about us."

"So you're saying that there's a sentinel somewhere close," suggested Ena Ray.

"Not likely," answered Scirios. "They are howling more than barking. If I had to guess, the sentinel is long gone."

"Gone where?" asked B'nair.

"Nowhere that should concern you," said Scirios with a smile. "Where they've gone, they will do you no harm."

About a half mile away stood a large tree with an opening in its roots. Through the opening and beneath the roots was a small hut, filled with herbs and potions. The jackals nearby were still mourning the departure of the old woman who lived beneath the tree. They had not seen her since they had cornered the young woman that had visited for a short time, and who was blue when she left.

The Kelpies and B'nair didn't wait around to find out what the jackals were howling for. They continued their trek through the forest. They continued the rest of the day until night fell and they reached a clearing where it was evident a campfire had been set at one time. B'nair stopped and knelt down. He reached into the ashes and picked up a handful.

"One of them has been here," he announced.

"One of who?" asked Akmen Milzu.

"A sentinel?" asked Ena Ray.

"No," B'nair answered. "Not a sentinel. One of those who we are fighting."

He no longer referred to them as the ones who were following him and his group. He knew who they were. He had battled them before, in the mines of the Trepans. Their involvement in the attack on his mining operation was clear to him now. He also knew that one of them had the other half of the pendant and that both groups were after the same thing – the last remaining Kelpies, the stone and the band. He realized this was now a fight.

He looked around at the trees. They were different here. They were very large and very old and unlike the others they had passed in the forest. Their trunks were very wide, and were twisted and gnarled. Branches turned in odd directions, intertwining with one another. In some places they blocked any openings that existed between them.

He also noticed that the shape of the bark, especially where branches had been cut or broken off, looked almost like faces. They were severely distorted, but in a few of them, he could clearly see what looked very much like closed eyes and mouths open in expressions of agony.

"What happened here?" he murmured, not expecting an answer.

He looked closely at one of the trees. It had a large knot in the side of a twisted trunk. The bark was thick and rough. There were two smaller knots – one slightly higher than the other – that could pass for eyes. There was a protrusion of bark that ran between them and that looked like a large and broken nose. Underneath it was a large gouge cut into the trunk, shaped like a wide inverted "U" with one side drooping lower in the same manner as the off-set eyes.

He looked to the next tree and saw another face. This one almost looked like it was gazing skyward, pleading for something. As he turned around, he saw several more. They were arranged in a rough circle around the dead campfire. They all looked different, but each one of them looked like they were in great pain.

And then, almost hidden from view, slightly behind the trees that had grown closest together, he saw another one. This one was much shorter than the others. Its branches drooped to the ground, set their own roots and rose again, intertwining around the trunk. It almost looked as if the tree was choking itself. B'nair moved closer and with his free hand, pulled aside some of the branches.

The bark on the trunk was thicker than the others, more deeply gouged and scarred. The leaves that hung on the tree were all black and dead. He pulled on some of them, but they didn't come off. He looked closer. He could make out another face. It was not pleading or in agony like the others. This one seemed to be filled with hatred and rage. The ugliness made B'nair take a step back. He had found Rovek.

"Is this him?" asked Akmen Milzu. "Is this our friend Rovek?"

"Yes," answered B'nair.

"Then release him," demanded Neraka Ferr. "What are you waiting for?"

"Nothing," B'nair said over his shoulder.

He circled the tree once, and then again. He moved the thick twisted branches aside until he found a small notch in the back. Then he raised his axe and brought it down swiftly and heavily. The blade sliced through the bark, deep into the trunk. A foul odor and a rasping gasp were released. The branches quivered and then went limp. The halves of the trunk cracked and drooped to either side.

"What have you done?" shouted Angin Topan. "Have you killed him?"

"No," said B'nair dismissively. "I've released him."

The limp branches turned black and withered, eventually dropping to the ground. Then the bark on the trunk shook like a dog shaking water out of its fur. Pieces flew in every direction, revealing a figure not much different than the tree from which it sprang. It stepped forward and raised its head.

Rovek was short and thick. His skin was rough and deeply creased, and as dark as the surrounding trees. His face was filled with features that seemed exaggerated. His chin was large, wide and protruding. His thick lips were stretched in a perpetual sneer. His ears hung on the sides of his head, knotted and twisted. His eyes were deep set under a heavy and pronounced brow. His hair looked like twisted vines of poison ivy.

His arms hung low down his sides, thick as heavy tree limbs. His short thick legs were little more than stumps. He shuffled a few feet forward and looked around. He turned towards Ena Ray and peered at him - up and down. Then he turned back and looked at B'nair, giving him little more than a quick glance. When he had closely observed each of them, he stopped and turned towards Akmen Milzu.

"I see I am not the last," he growled.

His voice sounded like limbs that were being twisted from trees in a windstorm.

"I also see I was not the first," he added.

"We had to be as quick and efficient as possible," answered Akmen Milzu. "There are others who are trying to stop us."

"The Alchemist and the Enchantress?" he asked.

"No, but others like them," answered the Mountain Kelpie.

"Pantano Izaki and Ollos Foscos remain?" he asked.

"Pantano is lost to us," Akmen Milzu said. "Only Ollos remains."

"We need all eight," he said. "Seven will not do."

"Yes," she agreed. "But we have another: a protégé of the witch."

She gestured to Ena Ray as she spoke. The protégé didn't know if he was supposed to step forward and bow or simply stay put. He elected to stay put. Rovek barely even glanced at him, clearly not impressed.

"And the one with the axe?" Rovek asked. "Who might he be? Another replacement? Or another minion?"

"Another friend," was the answer. "We can explain later. Right now you need to replenish yourself."

B'nair felt a sudden wave of anxiety rush through his body. He sensed danger. He moved around the Tree Kelpie and close to Akmen Milzu. He was so close that the Kelpie took a step back. B'nair closed the gap and began to whisper.

"We need to leave," he said in a hushed tone so that only the Mountain Kelpie could hear him.

"We will," she said. "Once Rovek has regained his strength."

"Leave him," B'nair said. "We need to go now."

Akmen Milzu was not accustomed to being ordered by anyone, least of all a Rebbercand. Her stony face hardened even more. She leaned forward over B'nair's head and looked down at him. She stepped even closer, trying to physically exert her power over him. He remained where he stood, staring up at her.

"We will leave when he is ready and not before," she hissed at him.

"Leave someone with him, then," B'nair persisted. "We need to go and we need to go now, if you expect to save your last Kelpie."

"The others can't possibly have gotten through that forest," she said. "Angin Topan left enough traps to occupy them for months."

"That was a useless waste of time," argued B'nair. "I'm telling you we need to go."

"You forget yourself," Akmen Milzu snapped indignantly. "I decide when we go; not you."

She ended the conversation and stepped around B'nair moving towards Rovek. She regained her composure before she spoke.

"What do you need?" she asked.

"Listen to me," B'nair demanded.

He was shouting now at the back of her head. He knew he had crossed the line, but he needed for her to understand the risk they were facing by staying here any longer than absolutely necessary. The Kelpie's body froze. She turned slowly and faced the Rebbercand. She raised her hand. He tightened his grip on the axe, waiting for the showdown.

Akmen Milzu saw that B'nair had set himself to deflect any spell she cast and was prepared to defend himself. She slowly lowered her hand and regained her composure. She forced her body to relax and she stepped toward the Rebbercand. He did not step back or change his stance.

"I appreciate your caution," she said in a low voice. "We will leave when I give the command to do so."

Without waiting for any further response, she turned back to Rovek and asked him again what he needed. Rovek looked past her at the Rebbercand. Seeing that he was not making any further foolish demands, he looked around and saw the circle of trees – the ones that had spoken one night not long ago to a young woman who was wrapped in a purple cloak and whose skin was blue.

"Them," he answered, pointing at the trees. "I need the one with the axe."

B'nair stepped forward, glanced at Akmen Milzu out of the corner of his eye and imperceptibly shook his head. This was madness, he thought.

"What do you need?" the Rebbercand asked, repeating Akmen Milzu's question.

"Cut these trees down," the Kelpie ordered. "One by one. And when they've been cut down, chop off all the limbs."

B'nair turned back to the Mountain Kelpie. He saw clearly that she expected him to do as asked. No, he thought; not asked. Ordered. So be it, he thought. I tried to warn her. What follows is on her now. He moved to the nearest tree and swung his axe near the base of the trunk. As it struck, he heard a muffled scream. He turned to see where it was coming from.

"Don't stop," Rovek ordered. "Keep cutting."

He swung again, driving the axe blade deep into the trunk. Once again he heard the muffled scream. He moved around towards the front of the tree to make another cut. He looked at the trunk — at the knots and gouges. He was certain they had changed. For a second, he was certain that the knots had opened and that a pair of eyes was staring back at him.

"What is this?" he demanded.

"They are — or were — the leaders of the village of Kalayaan," answered Rovek. "They dared to stand against me with the Alchemist."

"I never heard of that village," said B'nair.

"I destroyed it," said Rovek. "Enough of this. Keep cutting."

B'nair looked to Akmen Milzu for support. This was ridiculous. Any one of them could destroy these trees – this entire forest. Why make him cut them down? It was a waste of precious time. Why couldn't they understand this?

"When did you destroy it?" challenged the Rebbercand. "You've been in this prison for what? Two thousand years?"

"Exactly," shouted Rovek. "I destroyed this village and turned its leaders into these trees. The Alchemist trapped me and imprisoned me with them. They, however, could speak. They could come to life once a month."

"Once a month?" shouted B'nair. "They could come to life once a month?"

"I was sentenced to two thousand years of silence!" Rovek shouted back. "Two thousand years! Now do as you were told, and cut them down!"

B'nair reacted to the demand. He lowered his axe to his side and stepped menacingly towards the Kelpie. Akmen Milzu stepped between them and placed a hand on B'nair's shoulder.

"Please," she whispered. "Do as he asks."

B'nair's eyes shot up to hers. Asks? He was about to point out that he had been ordered, not asked. He wanted to point out that this delay was putting them in jeopardy. Instead, he just glared. She leaned in closer.

"Please excuse his behavior," she went on. "Until you have been in our places, you can't understand what it's been like to have been suspended for two thousand years. We will leave as soon as you have done what he's requested. The more quickly you work, the better it will be for all of us."

She resented having to plead with him, but she could see no alternative. They couldn't leave without Rovek – they wouldn't leave without him. And he couldn't leave until he had been revitalized. She would make the Rebbercand pay for this insolence. Neraka Ferr had suggested leaving him to the Dark Eye. She thought this was too quick and merciful of an end. She had much better ways to make him suffer.

The hand she had on his shoulder was inches away from the stone the dangled from his neck. She fought the impulse to yank it from his neck. She knew the power of the axe he carried. She doubted she could relieve him of the stone and cast a spell on him before he could cut her in half with that blade. She wasn't about to find out.

She stepped back and motioned towards the tree he had begun to cut. Reluctantly, B'nair turned back to the tree and continued to chop. Once the trunk had been cut through and the tree fell to the ground, there was no need for him to remove the limbs. The trunk, the branches and the leaves quickly turned black, and then white, shriveling up and turning to dust. When he had finished the last one, morning had arrived.

Rovek seemed fully revived. He hadn't needed to eat the trees or feast on anything like some of the others had. They each seemed to get replenished in different ways by different things. In this case, the total destruction of the trees that had been the village leaders was enough. Rovek didn't look any different. He merely seemed more alert and clear headed. B'nair didn't really care. He was certain they had wasted too much time here. He could feel the others were far ahead of them; perhaps too far. He wasn't sure what would happen then.

Scirios summoned the Lightning Riders, but before he was enveloped in the electrical current, Rovek turned back to the forest and cast a departing spell. As they were lifted into the air, B'nair could see the spell take effect. Hundreds, and then thousands, and then millions of borer beetles appeared. They sprang from the dead campfire and attacked the trees nearest to them, boring deep into their cores.

The trees begin to wither and die, dropping to the ground having been eaten from the inside out. In minutes the infestation spread in a widening circle throughout the forest, killing everything. B'nair wondered how far the beetles would go before they stopped – if they stopped. He wondered if these Kelpies would leave anything behind.

Chapter nine

The bubble had proven to work almost as Lochen had hoped it would. Almost, but not quite. It shielded them from the rain that was coming down in sheets. However, the cascading water made visibility difficult. Stella was continually waving her hands to clear away the rain and after a few minutes, her arms were getting tired. Lochen was trying to guide Liam, who was on his right, and Quinn, who was on his left, to step forward or back as a means of steering the giant ball. He was having minimal success.

"Quinn," he said as patiently as he could. "When I say to back off, I don't mean you should stop walking. I only mean for you to slow down."

"Sorry," groused Quinn. "I can't read your mind."

"You don't have to read my mind," grumbled Lochen. "You just have to do what I ask."

"But you keep changing what you ask," he grumbled back. "Speed up, slow down. Make up your mind."

"I'm trying to keep the pace balanced," he said through clenched teeth. "You do fine for a while, but then you get going and take those long steps and throw everything out of whack."

"I can't help it," he whined. "I'm taller than the rest of you. Why don't you just shrink me? Like Solveig?"

As soon as he said the words, he regretted them.

"Sorry, Solveig," he said. "I didn't mean it."

"That's all right," she said. "It's not your fault."

Lochen was at the front of the globe, in the center. They were able to simply walk in order to propel the ball, but he needed to have the two on either side of him adjust their pace to help steer it. The problem was that Quinn was so much bigger and his stride so much longer that his adjustments tended to overcompensate one way or the other. The result was that the bubble zigzagged to the right and left sporadically. When Lochen told him to slow down, he would once again overcompensate and slow down too much, sometimes almost coming to a stop.

To make matters worse, whenever they came to a rise in the field, they slowed down and had to push the walls with their hands to move the ball upwards. Sean and Natalie, who were at the back often slipped, creating a counter-weight and dragging them all backwards. In the middle was Stella, sweeping one arm and then the other back and forth frantically.

Once they crested the rise, they found that Sean and Natalie were insufficient counterbalance to keep them from rolling down the other side of the hill with any degree of control. It took several chaotic moments for them to develop a rhythm and use the downward roll as momentum for the next climb.

At one point a gust of wind caught them at the top of a rise, spun them sideways and rolled them downward. Inside the bubble, they had all lost their balance and collided with one another, coming to a complete stop in a shallow valley.

"That wasn't as bad as I thought it might be," Lochen announced when they all recovered.

"Not as bad?" squawked Summer. "Try sitting inside this hood the next time. Solveig! Where are you?"

"Here," came a muffled response. "I'm here. I'm OK — just tangled up a bit."

She had dropped down deep into the folds of the hood and was buried. She was now down to about an inch and a half in height. Stella had been able to cast a spell to amplify her voice; otherwise it would have faded as she continued to shrink. She was slightly less than half Summer's size now, and Summer was worried that she might fall on top of her friend and crush her, if they had another tumble like this one. Solveig thrashed around trying to unwrap herself. Lochen's flapping of his hood to straighten it out only made things worse.

"Stop that, please," she shouted. "It's like an earthquake. I can get out by myself, thank you very much."

"I'm sorry," he responded. "If there was another way to transport you..."

"She can ride on my back," Summer interrupted. "My wings have grown back and she's small enough to fit."

She instantly felt embarrassed about having drawn attention to how much Solveig had shrunk. Solveig could see Summer's face redden slightly, and cut in.

"Don't say you're sorry," she ordered.

"I'm sorry," Summer said.

"I told you not to say you were sorry," Solveig said in an exasperated tone.

"I just meant that I was sorry for almost having said I'm sorry, that's all," Summer tried to forget it. "Anyway, what about it? I'd be glad to carry you."

"Anything would be better than smothering in this hood," she growled. "Thanks, Summer," she added apologetically.

Summer climbed to Lochen's shoulder and Solveig got on her back. Summer spread her wings and gave them a strong flap. It felt great to be able to fly again, even if limited to the inside of the bubble. Solveig held on to her shoulders and tried to enjoy the ride. Summer spun in a tight circle around the top of the bubble.

"Enough," said Solveig. "I know you're happy to be able to fly again, but let's not get crazy."

"I'm..." Summer started.

"Don't," Solveig cut her off. "Just don't."

"All right, then," said Lochen. "Let's get this thing moving again."

They had to struggle to get started since they were going uphill from a dead stop. He, Liam and Quinn pushed forward while Stella, Natalie and Sean followed as closely behind them as they could. In a few minutes, they were back to rolling on their former, erratic way. Fortunately there weren't very many hills, and the wet grass made it even smoother for the bubble to slide across.

By late afternoon they could see that they had made considerable progress across the plains and along the valley that separated the forest they left from the forest they were trying to skirt – the same forest to which the Kelpies were, at that time, headed. What they hadn't anticipated was the river.

Ice and snow from the mountain range to the south – the mountain range where Solveig's and Lochen's home was soon to be demolished – melted and ran down the sides into the valley that ran between and separated the two forests. At the beginning, the water ran in several small streams cut into the rock. As these streams dropped to the lower levels, they intersected and combined. By the time they reached the valley, they united into a single, swiftly flowing river.

The left-right motion of the bubble's progress lessened as Quinn, Lochen and Liam adapted to each other's pace and to the terrain over which they were crossing. They reached another open and relatively flat stretch of field and were moving straighter than they had all day. It looked fairly flat as far as they could see – at least as far as they could see through the rain.

"This is great," said Quinn.

"We're really making great time," agreed Liam.

"I only wish we could see a little bit better," muttered Lochen.

"We're doing fine," countered Quinn. "Quit complaining."

"I'm not complaining," Lochen disagreed. "I'm merely making an observation."

"That's a good one," laughed Quinn. "You're making an observation about not being able to observe. Sometimes you really kill me. I think we can go a little faster."

He picked up his pace slightly.

"Not so fast," said Liam, who immediately increased his speed to keep up with Quinn and to keep the bubble on a straight trajectory.

"Hey," shouted Sean from behind. "What's going on?"

"Yeah," said Natalie. "Where's the race?"

"Lochen said we needed to hurry," answered Quinn. "So I'm hurrying."

He picked up the pace a little more, stretching his legs.

"I said no such thing," Lochen objected. "You need to slow down."

He now had to run to keep up. Liam was doing the same.

"Yes, you did," said Quinn. "You got us up before dawn and said we had no time to lose."

"Yes," answered Lochen. "But I never said we should be reckless."

"Quinn," gasped Liam, who was now running alongside Lochen, struggling to keep pace with Quinn. "Slow it down, will you?"

"What's the matter?" he teased. "Can't you keep up?"

He walked a little faster.

"I can keep up," answered Liam, running nearly full out and beginning to tire. "But I can't see where we're going."

"You're moving too fast for me to keep the front of the bubble clear of the rain," shouted Stella.

"Don't worry about it. Besides, we need to take advantage of this long, flat plain," argued Quinn. "It's..."

He didn't finish his thought. The ground dropped out from beneath them. They had reached the edge of the field where the river had cut a deep gouge. They dropped down the steep incline more than twenty feet, careening wildly. None of them could keep up with the speed the bubble was reaching.

They all started to trip over one another and then were flying head over heels, bouncing from one side of the bubble to the other and from top to bottom and back again. Then the bubble hit the river with a splash and was pulled by the current. It was spinning in one direction from the roll down the hill and twirling in another direction from the drag of the rushing water. Everyone was dizzy from the fall down the hill and disoriented from the churning from the river.

"I'm going to be sick," shouted Sean.

"Be sick in another direction," Liam shouted as he pushed Sean's face away from him.

"Not this way!" shouted Stella. "Get sick over there."

She pushed his head towards Quinn, who quickly deflected it towards Lochen, who pushed him in another direction.

"That's not helping, everyone," Sean shouted.

"Oh, wow," said Summer. "He's starting to make ME sick. They all are."

"Don't look at them," Solveig said into Summer's ear. "Keep watching the surface of the river on the outside of the bubble. Forget about them, and forget about the bubble. Focus on the horizon – on the river."

She rode Summer like a horse and pulled her shoulders back, lifting her head. Summer had been fixated on the flying bodies all around her. Consequently, she was spinning out of control. Solveig settled her by getting her to watch the horizon instead. In a few seconds they settled down and hovered – stabile amidst the tossing and tumbling going on all around them.

"We need to get out of this bubble," shouted Liam.

"I agree," shouted Lochen. "We're going to injure each other if we don't."

They both reached out to avoid colliding into one another, only to find themselves bouncing into and off of someone else.

"I can make it disappear," shouted Natalie. "But we'll end up in the water."

"NOOOO!" wailed Sean. "Not the water. Please."

"We may not have a choice," Lochen shouted back. "We can't continue like this."

The bubble bounced from one side of the narrow raging river to the other, as well as up and down with the rises and falls around sand bars and boulders. Along the way it collided with rocks over a long stretch of rapids and then dropped over a low series of waterfalls. The occupants were getting dizzier and had reached their breaking point.

"Go ahead, Natalie," shouted Lochen. "Do it now. Quickly!"

"No!" shouted Solveig. "Not yet."

Natalie raised her hand and then, at Solveig's insistence, lowered it. Since Solveig and Summer had stabilized, she had a better view of what was coming at them. The bubble crashed into a large rock in the center of the water, bounced up into the air and dropped to the right, striking the bank and ricocheting back to the other side, tossing everyone helter-skelter.

"OK," Solveig shouted again. "It's safe now. Go ahead. Do it!"

Natalie raised her arm.

"Stop," shouted Sean. "Not yet."

She lowered her arm. He was pressed face down on the bottom of the bubble. From his vantage point he could see several pieces of debris that had been washed down by the river and were below the surface. They were passing over several tree limbs and sharp branches. If the bubble were to burst now, they might be impaled.

"OK," he shouted once they passed over the branches. "It's all clear. Do it now."

Natalie raised her arm again.

"No," shouted Quinn. "Hold on."

He was pressed against the side and the shore was uncomfortably close. He could see that they were approaching a bend in the river. The bubble was headed for a large rock. If it burst now they'd be splattered against it. As it was, the bubble struck the rock head on, slowed for a second and then was washed around it and further downstream.

"It's clear," he shouted. "Pop it now. Pop it now!"

"Wait," shouted Liam. "Not now. Don't pop it."

He could see they were approaching another series of rapids. The water was crashing into a field of rocks and small boulders that littered the bed of the river.

"Will you all please make up your minds," shouted Natalie.

They had passed the rapids and were in a narrow channel where the water was racing.

"Do it now," shouted Liam. "Quick, before something else pops up.

Before anyone could tell her to stop, Natalie waved her arm and in a blink, the bubble disappeared. Summer shot up into the air with Solveig on her back, fighting against the downpour of rain. The others slid into the river and were shooting through the channel – some head first; some feet first and some tumbling wildly.

"Oh, no," gasped Solveig.

"What?" asked Summer.

She could barely see, the rain was coming down so hard. Solveig leaned close against Summer's back and moved the hand that had been shielding her eyes to point.

"There," she said. "Just ahead."

The channel opened up to a small pool, but the pool emptied out over the edge of a cliff. The waterfall that poured over the lip dropped over a hundred feet into a larger body of water that was flowing slowly towards the sea.

"Oh, poop," muttered Summer. "What can we do?"

"Keep an eye on them," said Solveig. "That's about all. We have to see where they all end up and try not to lose any of them."

Liam and Lochen went over the edge first. Liam waved his arms in what looked like a futile attempt to fly. Lochen spread his arms and legs out as widely as he could, hoping his robes would catch the wind and carry him like a flying squirrel. It didn't work. He wasn't able to get far enough out in front of the falls.

Liam cut into the water feet first, hit the sandy bottom and pushed himself up. Lochen hit the surface face first with an enormous belly flop, the water from the falls crashing on top of him and pushing him under. Liam tried to swim over to him, but only managed to position himself directly under Quinn, who came rocketing down like a ton of bricks.

He landed on Liam's head, pushing it back down to the bottom. Quinn was able to push off, reaching down and grabbing Liam as he did so. He never saw Lochen and didn't think to look for him. He kicked to the surface pulling Liam with him. When his head broke the surface, he looked to the shore and swam in that direction. Unfortunately, he swam to the wrong side.

Natalie and Stella were able to adjust their positions in mid-drop and entered the water like experienced high divers. Being Sprites, they sliced the water neatly and swam beneath the surface, heading for the south shore. As soon as the water was shallow enough, they stood up and walked ashore. Natalie was hunched over and holding her injured shoulder, but otherwise, she and Stella were fine.

Sean kicked his legs and waved his arms wildly as if that would keep him from dropping into the lake. Instead, he landed butt first and sank to the bottom. When he struggled to the surface, he found himself directly beneath the falls. The pounding water kept pushing him back down. He thrashed about, trying to move one way or another, but the sand beneath his feet kept giving way and the falls kept holding him down.

Summer saw him go under, but not come back up. She darted to the south shore where Natalie and Stella were standing, shouting along the way.

"Help him," she screamed. "Natalie. Stella. Help Sean. He's drowning. He's under the falls. Save him."

Stella shouted to Natalie to stay put and dove into the water without waiting for an answer. She pulled and kicked with all her might, heading straight for the bottom where Sean had last been seen. She was there in seconds, but found no sign of him. She stayed under water and searched in a continually widening circle, but couldn't find him. It was no use. He wasn't there. Maybe he was washed downstream.

213

"Where is he?" she shouted after she popped her head above the surface. "Where did he go? Can anyone see him?"

"He was just there," Summer yelled back.

She was hovering immediately in front of the falls, pointing to the spot where the water was crashing down. She wiped the rain out of her face to get a better look, but the gesture was useless. The rain kept pouring down. Solveig leaned forward almost to the point of falling off Summer's back, but she could see no sign of Sean, either. Summer darted back and forth like a dragonfly, trying to see some sign of him.

From behind the falls, up against the face of the cliff, hidden from view, came Lochen's voice.

"What are you looking for?"

"Sean," answered Stella frantically, trying to see through the cascading water.

"Me?" Sean shouted. "Why? What did I do? This wasn't my fault. I'm not the one who told Natalie to pop the bubble. Don't blame me. I get blamed for everything. Most of the time, I admit it, that maybe I deserve it, but not this time. This wasn't my fault! But if it was, I'm sorry. But I'm pretty sure it wasn't."

The adrenalin racing through his body was causing him to ramble. He was struggling to tread water and keep his head up, although it wasn't necessary. Lochen had a tight grip on him.

"You can relax now," Lochen told him.

"I AM RELAXED," he shouted back.

"And you don't have to shout," Lochen added. "I'm right next to you."

"I'M NOT SHOUTING!" he shouted. "I'M JUST TRYING TO KEEP FROM DROWNING."

"Then stand up," Lochen said calmly.

"WHAT?"

"Stand up," Lochen repeated. "There is a ledge behind the falls. The water is only about two feet deep here. All you have to do is stand up."

"Oh," said Sean.

He stopped thrashing, found his footing, but slipped and fell on his butt. He waved his arms and jumped up. When he saw that Lochen had been right and the water wasn't even up to his waist, he took a deep breath and turned to Lochen.

"Hey," he said, chuckling nervously. "That wasn't so bad? Was it?"

"No," said Lochen. "Not bad at all, but we need to get to shore."

"Right," said Sean. "Shore. No water there. Must get to the shore."

Lochen moved to his left and Sean moved to his right.

"No," said Lochen, grabbing Sean's arm. "It's this way."

He pointed to the south shore.

"OK, but then why are Quinn and Liam over there?" Sean asked, pointing to the two on the north shore.

"Wonderful," muttered Stella, who turned to see where Sean was pointing.

She swam over to where they were huddled on the grassy verge. She treaded water a few feet in front of them.

"Jump in and hold on to me," she told them. "I'll swim you over to the other side."

"Get back in the water?" Quinn objected. "Do we have to? We just got out of the water. Now you want us to get back in?"

"It's not like you have to worry about getting wet," said Liam.

"But…" stammered Quinn.

"It's raining," said Liam. "And you're already soaked anyway. Get a grip."

He didn't wait for any further discussion. He jumped in and put his hand on Stella's shoulder. He heard Quinn splash in behind him, and turned to see him flailing his arms and kicking his feet. He reached back and yanked Quinn's collar, pulling him close and then nodded to Stella to start swimming.

By the time she got to where Natalie was waiting, the others had arrived, and were on shore. They helped her, Quinn and Liam out of the water and then all sat in the grass to catch their breath. As they sat there, the rain finally stopped falling, but the sky remained dark and gray.

"Let's not do that again any time soon," said Stella.

"As harrowing as that was," said Lochen, "it allowed us to gain quite a bit of time. If I'm not mistaken, we're not far from Satamakau."

"No, we're not," said Liam. "We should make it soon after nightfall, unless we decide to camp someplace first."

"I don't think that's wise," said Stella. "By now the Kelpies will be on the move again and headed to this forest to the south. They may even be there already. I haven't sensed anything, but it could happen any time. We have to get to the last one, or we've lost everything."

"I agree," said Lochen. "And...oh...oh, my. Oh, no."

His face went dark. He looked like he had lost his best friend. He turned towards Solveig, but couldn't speak.

"What's wrong?" she asked. "What is it? What's happened? Lochen? Lochen, say something."

"Our home," he whispered, swallowing hard.

"What about our home?" Solveig asked.

"It's gone," he answered.

He sat down hard on the ground and held his head in his hands. Everyone looked at him, not comprehending what had happened.

"What do you mean your home is gone?" asked Sean, putting his hand on Lochen's shoulder, trying to comfort his friend and trying to understand what he meant.

"It's been destroyed," he said, raising his head.

"The main castle?" asked Solveig. "Where we live? How can that be?"

"All of it," Lochen clarified. "The entire palace and all the surrounding buildings. The entire village. Everything."

"What are you talking about?" demanded Solveig. "How do you know?"

"The Kelpies," he said. "The Mountain Kelpie. She did this."

"Why?" asked Solveig. "I don't understand."

"She is Jainkaso," Lochen said.

Solveig paled noticeably. She nudged Summer toward Lochen, slid off her back and onto his knee. She could see tears welling up in his eyes.

"Who is Jainkaso?" asked Quinn.

"That's impossible," said Solveig. "That's just a myth. It's not real. She's not real. She was made up to scare little children."

"She's real," said Lochen. "As real as the Malkia that Summer saw."

"NO!" shouted Summer. "I tried to convince myself that what I saw wasn't real; that it was my imagination. Now you're telling me that was actually the Malkia?"

"What's a Malkia?" asked Quinn. "And who is Jainkaso? Will somebody please explain?"

"They are the equivalent of the one your people call the Nelabas," Lochen answered. "The Kelpies we have been trying to contain are the monsters of our respective folk lores."

"I knew it!" Quinn nearly shouted. "I knew it all the time. I knew they were real. Others in the Ice Kingdom told me they were only myths, but I never believed them. I was right. I was right all the time!"

"I'm not sure that's something to get all excited about," said Sean. "It actually sounds kind of creepy."

"Oh, yeah. Sure," said Quinn, containing himself.

"Are you saying that this Jainkaso destroyed our home?" asked Solveig, trying to get back to Lochen's earlier pronouncement.

"Yes," he said. "She's destroyed everything."

"You mean the main building where we live?" Solveig persisted, hoping the destruction was less than Lochen was implying.

"I mean everything," he said. "Every building, every tower, every wall. All my books and scrolls – all if it has been destroyed."

"What about the people?" asked Natalie. "Are your people...are they...?"

"They may have evacuated," Lochen replied. "I can't be sure they are unharmed, though."

She didn't want to put into words what she imagined. Lochen looked up at her, shaking his head at the thought of what might have happened. He turned to Quinn, whose people had also suffered at the hands of a recent attack.

"Many of them may have sought refuge underground," he said. "But most of them wouldn't have escaped."

"This can't be happening," moaned Solveig.

Lochen cleared his throat and took a deep breath. He stood up, scooping Solveig in his hand. He held it out, indicated that she should return to Summer's back. He then smoothed out his still soaked robes, trying to gather his thoughts.

"From the little bit of the Alchemist's book that I've been able to translate thus far," he began, "I've learned that the myths we have all grown up with are based more on truth and actual events than we may have ever believed. Each of our civilizations spawned a villain who grew to become incredibly ruthless, as we have recently witnessed in the Ice Kingdom and now in our mountain home.

"So far we have seen only hints at the extent of their power and their brutality. As more of them escape the prisons in which they have been confined for two thousand years, their power will grow. We should not in the least underestimate the danger they pose, not just to us, but also to our homes. Whether we like it or not; whether we want it or not, we are in a fight to the death."

"Do you think we can reverse what they've done?" Solveig asked.

"I have to believe the Alchemist and the Enchantress have left us with the tools to do that," he answered. "The trick will be to find those tools."

"Is there anything else you can tell us about what the Alchemist wrote down?" Liam asked.

"Soon," said Lochen. "I have more to review."

He reached into his pocket to pull out the scroll with the letters and symbols. The soaking from the river had reduced it to pulp. It hung in a sodden mass in his hand.

"No!" gasped Stella.

"Please tell me you memorized it," said Sean.

"Unfortunately," said Lochen. "Not all of it. I found two references in the book that I found no translations for. I was hoping to unravel those mysteries with the scroll."

"Maybe we'll run into another sentinel," said Liam. "One that can help you."

"Perhaps," said Lochen. "But for now, we need to make haste. We know now exactly where the Kelpies are. Soon they will be in the forest searching for the Kelpie hidden there. That will leave the one remaining. We must get there first. At all costs."

"If what you said is true," said Natalie. "And I have no reason to doubt you, but that means the Kelpie we're going after is the Sea Sprite, Banrian."

"Yes," said Lochen. "I believe that was her name. Will you be able to face her?"

Natalie thought for a second and then nodded. Whatever it takes, she said to herself.

Chapter ten

*T*he impact of Lochen's words was still settling in several hours later. No one had to make the suggestion; they all knew there was no time to rest or to camp. They needed to keep moving. They followed the river for miles until Liam motioned for them to veer slightly to the south. Night fell and they continued without stopping.

For a while Lochen had generated another orb of soft light to guide their way. Eventually they found themselves on an old dirt road and knew they were getting close to the town. Lochen doused the light and everyone crowded closer together. In spite of the need to hurry, the need for stealth was more important. They crept like thieves, looking in every direction for signs of potential threats.

In the early hours just past midnight, they entered the town of Satamakau. The streets were deserted, as they had expected; but there was a stillness that went beyond that of a village asleep. It seemed dead. There were no sounds of stray cats, or of dogs barking, or of late night revelers, as one would expect in any ordinary port town. Instead, it was eerily quiet.

They were crowded tightly together, moving as one, each on tiptoe, hunched over and peering left to right, back and forth. They entered the town along the main road. As soon as they came upon buildings, they hugged the walls and peered around corners before crossing intersections.

Satamakau was not a very big town. There was a main street running perpendicular to the road that ran along the shore. From the main street there were fewer than half a dozen intersecting streets, and a few alleys crossing them. The streets were dirt, rutted in places from wagons that had hauled goods back and forth from the port. There was an old wooden sidewalk that ran along the front of the buildings.

All the shops were locked tightly, although it looked like they hadn't been opened for some time. Windows were coated with dust and dirt. Cobwebs hung in doorjambs. Many of the stores had empty display windows.

They passed a bakery and Sean's stomach grumbled at the thought of freshly baked bread. He wiped the dirt away from the large pane of glass in the storefront and peered inside. All he could see was a stale and moldy roll that looked anything but appetizing.

Liam had spent almost all of his life in the Swamp. His only other venture into a town was another port city: Nohkmar Cambin. That one had been bustling with people. He looked around at the different buildings, but didn't see anything that looked like a house.

"Where do all the people live?" he whispered to Lochen.

"Many of them live above their stores," he answered. "Others have homes outside of the town. I have to assume they are south or north of here, since we didn't see any on our approach."

They came upon the second intersection. This one was a little wider than the first. Lochen stopped and everyone stopped behind him. He leaned forward and peered around the corner looking down the side street. Everyone else leaned into him to get a look. He was being nudged forward into the open.

"It serves no purpose for each of us to look at the same time," he whispered. "Especially if you all push me out into the street. That would seem to work at cross purposes with our efforts at stealth."

They all backed away. He then turned to Summer.

"Has your ability to blend into your surroundings returned with your wings?" he asked.

"I think so," she said. "Do you want me to scout ahead?"

"Yes," he answered. "That might be preferable to all of us trying not to draw attention to ourselves."

Solveig slid off Summer's back onto Lochen's shoulder and Summer rose into the air and then moved up against the nearest building. It was an old clapboard construction. The boards had once been painted a bright blue, but had long since faded to a dull, weathered gray. The building housed a business that provided farming and fishing tools.

Summer quickly blended into the background and looked like little more than a water spot against the wood. She inched her way forward and was soon out of sight. In the meantime, Lochen suggested that Sean and Liam go down the side street in one direction and that he and Stella go down the side street in the other direction.

"Natalie, I'd like to leave you and Solveig here with Quinn in case Summer returns before we do," he said.

"Liam and Sean," he added, "see how far this side street goes and if there are any other roads running parallel to the main street that may lead to the shore. Don't go down them; just see where they lead and then come back here. Stella and I will do the same in the opposite direction."

Liam and Sean nodded their understanding. They looked left and then right, and then as quietly as possible they quickly crossed the street, coming to a stop at the grocery store on the opposite side. Sean's stomach rumbled again. He wiped away the grime from the store window and looked in. Again, there was nothing in the display except for two cans of artichoke hearts.

"What's the deal?" he whispered. "Don't these people eat? There was no food in the bakery, and there's no food in the grocery."

"Maybe there aren't any people here," answered Liam.

He pressed his body against the building and rounded the corner. There was so little light, that he couldn't see more than a few feet in front of where he was standing. He looked back to see that Sean had followed him and was close behind.

"I can't see squat," he whispered. "What about you?"

"I can't see it either," he answered. "What's squat?"

"It's nothing...it's...never mind."

He sidestepped along the grocery, feeling the wall with one hand outstretched. Sean put one of his hands on Liam's back to make sure he didn't get separated from him. He had his slingshot in his other hand. Almost without warning, the building ended. Liam took another step and fell off the boardwalk. Sean stopped, but felt Liam fall away from him.

"Where are you?" he hissed.

"Down here," whispered Liam. "The boardwalk ended.

He got to his feet and grabbed Sean's hand.

"Be careful," he said. "There's a step down right in front of you."

They looked to their left and could see nothing but blackness. To their right they could see a narrow street that led to the shore, but that, too, was shrouded in darkness. They continued forward about twenty feet and came to a stable.

"Do you smell anything?" Liam asked.

"No," answered Sean. "Do you?"

"No," said Liam. "But we should. Stables always smell. This one doesn't."

"Do you think we should go inside?" asked Sean.

"I think we should go back," he said.

"Good," answered Sean. "Because if you said you wanted to go in there, I'd have said, 'Have a nice visit. I'm staying out here.'"

"There's something wrong with this place," said Liam. "I don't think there have been any animals in this stable for a long time. Judging by the condition of the buildings and the display windows, I don't think there have been any people here for a long time, either."

They crossed the street to the side opposite the grocery and headed back. This building was lined with windows, all of which were coated with dust. Liam wiped a circle on one and peered inside. It appeared to be some kind of restaurant. It was filled with tables and chairs. The chairs weren't around the tables, though. They were scattered randomly around the room. Some of them were knocked over.

"It looks like people left in a hurry," said Liam.

"Why?" asked Sean.

"Beats me. But it's all the more reason to get out of here."

On the opposite side, Lochen and Stella were making their way away from the intersection. They had stayed close to the bakery and quickly lost sight of Natalie and Quinn.

"Should we generate a small light so we can see?" asked Stella.

"I think it would be more prudent to keep our presence here as much a secret as we can," Lochen answered. "At least for the time being."

"What are we looking for?" she asked.

"I don't know, exactly," he said. "It seems as if this town is deserted. I had hoped to find some indication as to why."

"Does it matter?"

"Perhaps not," he answered. "However, if this had been a stronghold of the Kelpies, they may come back here before venturing out over the ocean. On the other hand, if it was abandoned because of something the Alchemist or the Enchantress did, then the Kelpies may tend to avoid it."

"Or take revenge on it," Stella offered.

"Hmmm. A good point," Lochen said. "I hadn't considered that."

They reached the end of the building and came upon a large building. Lochen sniffed the air. He took a cautious step forward and sniffed again. There was a pair of large doors at the front and a smaller one off to one side. It was made of the same weather beaten wood boards as the other buildings. At one time this one had been red.

"It's a blacksmith shop," said Lochen.

He tried the handle on the door, expecting it to be locked. It wasn't. The handle turned with a low grinding sound. He pushed open the door, which gave out a muffled squeak. He waved his hand and the door was silenced. He opened it all the way and stepped in.

"What are you doing?" whispered Stella. "Where are you going?"

She stepped up to the door, but didn't go in. She tried to see inside, but it was so dark that she couldn't make out anything. She was startled when Lochen's face suddenly appeared out of the darkness.

"Don't do that!" she hissed.

"I'm sorry," he answered. "Come inside."

She reluctantly stepped through the doorway. It was totally black inside. Then she heard the door shut behind her and raised her hands, ready to cast a spell or a hex. Before she could, she heard something snap, and then saw a very dim light appear It slowly grew brighter and rose towards the ceiling. It was enough to illuminate the interior.

There were several large circular bands of metal hanging from a beam near the right. In the back was what looked like a large fireplace with a bellows at the side. In the center was an anvil. There were hammers and other tools scattered on the ground. Lochen was standing near the forge, sniffing.

"What are you doing?" she asked.

"This forge has been cold for a very long time," he said. "And these tools – they're scattered haphazardly. No self-respecting blacksmith would show such disregard for his equipment. The occupants here left in a hurry."

"This whole place is freaky," Stella replied. "We should get back."

"I agree," he replied.

As soon as they were both at the doorway, Lochen doused the light, and then opened the door. They stepped back out into the night and made their way back to the others. They returned shortly after Liam and Sean got back. They exchanged information just as Summer reappeared.

"There is nothing of use to our right or left," declared Lochen, "other than information. It's clear that this town is deserted and that the residents left rather suddenly."

"It's not completely deserted," said Summer.

"You mean some nut job is still here?" asked Sean.

"I couldn't see who or what it was," said Summer. "But near the marina there's an old wagon and next to the wagon is a campfire. I didn't stick around to see who lit it, though."

"You did exactly the right thing," said Lochen. "We need to be cautious."

They continued down the main street heading for the harbor. Summer had told them that the road ended at the north end of the shore. That was where the wagon and the campfire had been. The fire had provided sufficient illumination for her to see the shapes of several boats anchored in the water, but couldn't tell what condition they were in.

They reached the end of the line of buildings as well as the boardwalk and could see the wagon several yards ahead. The campfire was burning near the side of the wagon and provided enough light for them to see. It was quite long and box-like. The bottom section was rectangular – about twenty feet long, six feet high and eight feet wide. There was a second level that was another rectangle. This one was about sixteen feet long, ten feet high and as wide as the base.

The entire structure was carried on large wooden wheels; except that one of the wheels had several broken spokes, and the frame at that end was supported on layers of blocks. There was a wide seat at one end that stretched from side to side, and a long tongue that extended from the frame – long and large enough for a team of at least four horses.

The wagon had at one time been brightly painted in red, yellow and blue; but those colors had faded over the years. On the side of the upper level could be seen a large sign that said, "The

Amazing Artabarat," in an arc across the top. Beneath that, in straight lines were the words, "And His Astounding Acrobats."

"It appears to be some kind of circus wagon," whispered Lochen. "I've heard of these traveling entertainers, but I've never seen one before. How interesting."

As they were gazing at the wagon, it moved slightly. Out of one end, over the seat, a man emerged. He climbed down awkwardly from the wagon and turned towards the campfire. He was dressed in an outlandish costume.

He wore red pants with a yellow stripe down the side. He had on a jacket that was cut to the waist in the front, but extended with tails down the back that went to his knees. The jacket was blue with large, frilly epaulets on the shoulders, like a tin soldier's. Beneath the jacket he wore a white shirt with a ruffled front. On his head he wore a black top hat.

At one time the colors of his clothing had shown brilliantly. Now, though, they were as faded as the buildings in the village, and were tattered and worn. The seat of the pants was shiny with wear and patches had been sewn on the knees and on the elbows of the jacket. There were stains on the clothing and the hat was torn near the top.

The man himself was equally odd. He had long skinny legs that ended in long, narrow feet that were covered in what appeared to be faded red slippers. His arms matched his legs in that they were also long and skinny, hanging down nearly to his knees, and ending in hands that were large and thin.

His body, though, was short and round. He wasn't fat, but his shape was circular. His head replicated the shape of his body. It was round as a ball. His ears were short and round, like tiny flower buds, and were pressed close to his head. His hair was black and looked like it was dyed. It was greased and combed straight back, and the ends were cut unevenly along the back of his collar.

His eyes were close together and deep set underneath a single black eyebrow that ran across his forehead. His nose was small and round, and separated two round and rosy cheeks. His mouth was also small and bud-like, with thin lips that seemed to be painted a deep pink. His chin was small and round with a dimple in the center.

He walked like a stork in a clumsy and stiff manner, with his arms out to his sides, bent at the elbows. He was mumbling something that appeared to be some kind of song, but the words were indistinguishable. Although the eight who were watching him hadn't made a sound, he reacted as if he heard something.

He turned slowly in their direction and held his hand to shield his eyes, even though the night was completely black. He bent forward at his waist and squinted. He turned his head directly to where they all were standing.

"Welcome," he called to them. "Come stand by the fire. It will take the chill off the night air."

The air in fact was warm, but no one commented on this. At first they didn't move, thinking that he might have been addressing someone else. His voice was high pitched and reedy.

"Don't be shy," he called again. "I've been expecting you."

"It appears we've been discovered," said Lochen. "Be on your guard, just the same."

As they came closer and could see the figure more clearly, they could see that he was wearing what appeared to be makeup. His face was covered in an off-white powder, and the rosy coloring in his cheeks had been painted on. The line of eyebrow that stretched over both eyes was, for the most part, colored in. The skin around his eyes was deeply lined and creased; his neck was pencil thin, but the skin hung loosely under his chin.

When they were near, he doffed his hat and bowed to them, bent deeply at the waist with his head nearly touching the ground. As he did, they could see that his hair was extremely thin in a large circle around the top of his head, but his scalp had been painted or dyed to hide the bald spot.

"Allow me to introduce myself," he said.

His voice had changed from the high-pitched, hoarse strain to a deep and resonant bass.

"I am the one, the only, Amazing Artabarat, artist and acrobat renown! Entertainer to the world! Performer before kings and queens, princes and princesses! Permit me to demonstrate."

He straightened up from his bow, wincing slightly and pressing his hand to his lower back. He then turned in a circle several times, like a dog looking for a comfortable place to sleep. When he seemed to either be satisfied that he had found the best spot, or come to the realization that there were no better spots, he stopped turning.

He lowered himself slowly and awkwardly to his knees, placed his palms on the ground, and then lowered his head. His long, thin fingers were splayed, and revealed long, yellowed nails. They appeared to be covered with some kind of glossy finish. As an afterthought, he removed his hat and then placed his head on the ground in front of and in the middle of his hands, forming a triangle with his head and hands.

Then he lifted one leg into the air and struggled to lift the other one. He wobbled back and forth, his legs both bent at the knees; one in the air and leaning forward and the other jerking to and fro in an effort to maintain his balance. It didn't work. He overcompensated and started to topple onto his back, almost as if in slow motion.

Quinn moved to stop him from falling, but wasn't sure what to grab. Instead, he and the others, looked on in shock as the long, lean figure crashed to the ground, flat on his back.

"Oh, my," he said, his high-pitched, reedy voice returning. "That didn't go as planned. I seem to be a bit rusty. Shall I try again?"

"NO!" they all shouted.

"That won't be necessary," said Natalie. "We're sure you were...are quite talented."

He turned over onto his stomach and slowly got back on his feet. As he stood, his body seemed to unroll into an upright position. He dusted off the front of his jacket and his pants, even though he had fallen on his back. Then he bent down to pick up his hat and replaced it on his head. All his movements were slow and exaggerated – completed with great flourish.

"I was much more agile in my youth," he said. "I'm afraid those days are gone."

"You said you had been expecting us," said Lochen. "Are you…"

"A sentinel?" he asked, finishing Lochen's question. "Yes, as a matter of fact, I am."

A collective sigh of relief ran through the others.

"What can I do to help?" he asked.

"We need to get to a distant location in the Viridian Ocean," Lochen began.

"Excuse me," interrupted Solveig. "Hello? I think there's something a little more pressing at this time."

She had been sitting on Quinn's shoulder and had been completely forgotten. Artabarat heard her voice, turned in her direction and squinted. He extended a long, skinny finger in her direction.

"Oh, my," he said. "You're quite small. You seem to have encountered Angin Topan – the imp! And it appears you in some way incurred her wrath. How unfortunate."

"Yes," said Solveig, backing away from the approaching finger. "But can you stop the shrinking? Can you fix this…fix me?"

237

"Hmmm," he muttered. "I believe I can."

Without another word, he climbed up over the seat and disappeared into the wagon's interior. There was a loud crash, followed by a shout of "I'm all right," and several more crashes. The wagon shook left to right and, a minute or two later, the sentinel emerged with a small container in his hand.

"This may do the trick," he announced as he stood on the seat and held his hand high in the air.

He climbed back down from the wagon and moved closer to the campfire. He sat down with a plop and criss-crossed his legs. Then he reached in the pocket of his jacket and fished around, searching for something. Not finding it, he dug into the other pocket and pulled out something that looked like a syringe, but without the needle. Instead there was a short, narrow hose attached to the plunger mechanism.

"Why would somebody have something like that in their pocket?" Sean whispered to Quinn.

"I don't even know what it is," Quinn whispered back.

"I call it an extractor," said Artabarat.

He looked up and noticed them all still standing away from the campfire and the wagon.

"Sit, sit," he said, gesturing to the campfire. "Please. As for you," he said, pointing to Solveig, "You need to come closer."

He cleared a spot in the dirt between him and the fire and motioned for her to stand there. Whether she wanted to or not, Quinn lifted her from his shoulder and deposited her in front of the sentinel and then stepped back with the others, who remained where they were. Artabarat didn't seem to notice they hadn't moved any closer.

"Now you probably won't like this at first," he said to Solveig. "It takes some getting used to, but it should stop the shrinking."

He opened the container, which was filled with a thick amber liquid. He inserted the extractor and drew back on the plunger. When it was filled, he took it out of the container and resealed it, placing it on the ground next to him. He held the extractor over Solveig's head, and without warning or explanation, he squeezed the contents out.

At first it came out as a thick liquid, but as it hit the air and descended over Solveig, it grew thicker, to the consistency of honey. In seconds it dripped down and covered her completely. She raised her arms and thin strands stretched from her body up towards her fingertips. She looked like she was coated in layers and layers of spider webs.

It coated her hair; it seeped down over her face; it penetrated her clothing – even the cloak she had been given by another sentinel. She turned back to the others with a plaintive look on her face. She had to wipe the goo away from her eyes to see them, and from her nose and mouth to breath.

"Mwunbderfwwl?" she mumbled. "I cnn brly mbrthe."

"What did she say?" whispered Stella to Natalie.

"She said, 'Wonderful. I can barely breathe,'" answered Artabarat.

"How can he hear us?" Sean whispered as softly as he could, hiding his mouth with his hand.

"I don't know," the sentinel answered. "It's a curse, I suppose. I've had no one to talk to for centuries, but I can hear every sound made throughout Satamakau, day and night."

He watched as the sticky substance was absorbed into Solveig's body. Gradually, it began to fade away, and she was able to move more easily.

"Oh, my," said Artabarat. "I see you've met Beebee."

"Yes," said Solveig, cheerfully. "I did. She gave me this cloak. She gave me some...How could you know...wait a minute. Am I blue again?"

She spun around to face the others. She could see by the look of shock on each of their faces, that she was, once more, blue. She jerked back to face the sentinel.

"What did you do?" she demanded. "You were supposed to fix me."

"I did," he replied. "You didn't tell me you had been blue before. You only asked me to stop you from shrinking any further."

"Stop me from..." she sputtered. "Hold on. You mean I'm not going to go back to my original size? I said to fix me. This isn't fixing me!"

"Actually, your request was to stop the shrinking," he replied. "You said nothing of returning you to your former stature."

"He's quite right," interjected Lochen.

"Shut it!" she snapped at him. "You're not helping."

"I'm afraid there's nothing more I can do," the sentinel said apologetically.

His voice was getting thinner. His skin, even underneath the makeup, was becoming gray and even more wrinkled. His head was slowly lowering to his chest, and his eyelids began to droop. He was running out of time, and Lochen was quick to notice this.

"We'll find something else, Solveig," he said, interrupting her. "But right now we need to know if you can help us get out into the middle of the ocean."

"But...but..." Solveig whined.

"Later!" Lochen nearly shouted at her. He turned back to the sentinel and stepped closer. "Can you help us?"

"Ah," Artabarat said; his eyes popping open and his head rising up. "You're going to try to find Ollos Foscos, aren't you?"

"Yes," Lochen admitted. "And we don't have much time."

"It won't matter how much time you have," the sentinel replied. "She is well hidden and under several layers of spells. The Alchemist made sure she and her friends would never see the light of day again."

"Most of her friends have escaped," said Stella. "And they're headed in this direction."

The sentinel's face went from gray to white. A look of shock and panic contorted his face.

"All of them?" he gasped.

"All but one," said Natalie. "One of them was destroyed."

"How?" he asked.

"I stabbed it with this," said Solveig, pulling the tiny dragon's tooth from her belt. "But now it's too small to be of any use. Thanks in no small part to you."

He leaned forward and squinted. She raised the tooth higher for him to see.

"A dragon's tooth," he said in amazement. "I would love to hear how you obtained it, but there's no time left for that." He looked up at her and added, "It will be sufficient when the time comes. Trust me."

His eyes rolled back slightly and his lids fluttered. His head drooped to his chest again, and everyone thought he was leaving them. Then he summoned another burst of energy, opened his eyes and raised his head.

"Be sure to test the point on your thumb before you strike," he told Solveig.

He dropped his head again and then leaned to one side. Without opening his eyes, he stretched out one arm and lowered himself to the ground as if to sleep. He stretched out his legs to get comfortable, and then curled them up to his chest, tucked one arm under his head and hugged his knees with the other.

"Now what?" asked Liam.

"I don't know," said Lochen. "We still need to get out to sea. Maybe we can find something suitable in the marina."

"I have a boat," mumbled the sentinel.

His eyes were still closed. He raised the arm that was wrapped around his knees and pointed to the harbor.

"It looks similar to my wagon," he said softly. "Hard to miss. You should have no problem finding it. Be sure to leave...and return...at...high...tide. Don't...be...late."

His voice had dropped to a whisper and his breathing had slowed so much it was imperceptible. He was dying and they all knew it.

"Awwww, no!" moaned Sean. "Why does this always have to happen?"

"Because it's time," the sentinel wheezed. "My debt...is paid. I am...free now. Be...happy...for...me."

243

He exhaled those last words and made no further movement. Slowly at first, his body crumpled in on itself and then dissolved into dust. In a minute or two, he was gone.

"We need to leave," said Stella.

"Can we at least pay him our last respects?" asked Quinn. "He seemed like such a nice person. It's horrible that he just...you know."

"No," said Stella. "The Forest Kelpie has been released. They'll be heading out to sea soon."

"Besides," said Lochen. "He was only recently nice."

"What's that supposed to mean?" asked Sean.

"I'll tell you more once we are on the water," Lochen replied. "Right now, Stella is right. Time is of the essence."

He turned towards the harbor. Recalling what Artabarat had said about talking to himself for centuries, Lochen realized that there was no longer any need for stealth. He snapped his fingers and generated another orb of light to guide their way to the docks. The others began to follow him. Quinn bent down and scooped Solveig up in his hand.

"Ewww, yuck," he said. "You're still sticky all over."

"Tell me about it," she replied.

"This stuff won't turn me blue, will it?" he whimpered.

"And if it does?" she glared.

"Oh, I didn't mean anything," he sputtered. "That would be OK, I suppose. I just hope it doesn't, you know, turn me, you know..."

"You better quit before you make things worse," she told him.

"OK," he said. "I can do that."

They all ran to the marina, which was not far away. The harbor was in the shape of a large U, with an enormous sea wall that lined the edges. The water was near the top of the wall. There were several small boats tied up tightly along the wall, but it was easy to see that they hadn't been used in a very long time. They were in poor condition, and some of them were taking on water. Others had already sunk and were hanging from their mooring ropes.

At the end of the line was the one that apparently belonged to the sentinel. He was right: it was hard to miss. It was painted in the same garish colors as his wagon and had the same sign painted on the side. It was constructed similar to the wagon in that it had a box-like compartment on the deck towards the back of the boat. In the center was a mast with a single sail folded to the spar. It was also in the same dilapidated condition as the wagon.

"Are you sure this thing is going to float all right?" Natalie asked.

"OH," moaned Sean. "Why did you have to say that? Now that's all I'm going to think about."

245

"You can confine yourself to the interior," suggested Lochen. "As to its seaworthiness, I don't see a more viable alternative, do you?"

Quinn jumped on board and examined the deck, the gunwales, and bulkheads, kicking at the old wood.

"Don't do that!" whined Sean. "It's enough of a wreck as it is. Kicking it isn't going to make it float better."

"It'll do just fine," announced Quinn.

The rest of them scrambled aboard. Liam lowered the sail and tied it down. Quinn took charge of the wheel and steered the ship out of the harbor where Lochen then filled the sails with wind. Stella provided the direction while Natalie, Summer, Solveig and Sean went below deck. It was still hours before dawn, not that there was any expectation of clear skies. Fortunately, none of them had been able to see the name on the ship's transom: *The Ill Wind*.

Chapter eleven

Those below deck took the opportunity to get some rest. Lochen, Liam and Quinn took turns at the helm. Liam and Quinn caught some sleep when they weren't steering the odd looking boat. Summer elected to stay above, but soon the exhaustion of the last few days won out and she fell asleep.

For several hours they coasted across the water in almost total darkness. It was a condition they were all becoming much too familiar with and used to. When the sky lightened at first dawn, they were met with another condition they were much too familiar with – a dull gray and overcast sky. Added to that was a thick mist on the sea, which limited their vision to a twenty foot diameter around the ship.

Lochen had received a clear mental image of the location to which they were headed from Stella, and directed the ship that way.   As they sailed through the night, he used the time to continue with his translation. He had completed the third layer of the initial accounts, using a combination of the letters with the symbols. Some of his earlier assumptions had been proven to be true, although there were a few things that remained a mystery.

Below, Sean was the first one to wake up. He sat up and looked at the others. Seeing they were still deep in sleep, and not particularly interested in seeing nothing but water around them – knowing it was on the other side of the ship's walls was bad enough – he decided to explore the interior.

When he and the others had clambered down the steep ladder, they entered a small galley and dining area. In the center and going towards the bow of the ship was a narrow hall. On one side of the hall was a long room that was filled with hammocks. Artabarat had never said how many acrobats were in his traveling road show, but there were places for eight to sleep.

He quietly tried to roll out of the hammock he was sleeping in. This was a new experience for him. As he shifted his weight, the hammock spun. He dug his fingers into the webbing, wrapped the leg he had swung over the side around the ropes and shoved his other foot into the net to keep from falling out. He found himself upside down, facing the floor.

He tried to wiggle and shift his weight in order to turn right side up, but was only able to swing back and forth. He was getting dizzy. When he stopped moving, he unwrapped the one leg and extended it towards the floor. Fully stretched, he was still two feet above the deck. He carefully disengaged his other foot. His weight dropped down, and his toes touched the floor; but his fingers were stuck in the hammock.

He yanked one way and then the other, trying to free his hands. First one, and then the other, quickly and unexpectedly pulled free. He spun around in a circle, lost his balance and crashed to the floor. He held his breath; looked back to see the others were undisturbed, and then quietly got to his feet and walked out of the crew's quarters and into the hall.

On the opposite side of the hall he opened the door and found several storage compartments lined against the wall. They were filled with nets, hoops, bars, boards and other paraphernalia that Sean assumed were used by the acrobats. All of it was painted the same red, blue and yellow as the ship and the wagon. Like these two vehicles, the equipment in the storage compartment was worn and faded. He ran his hand across one of the bars and discovered it was coated with a thick layer of dust.

This stuff hasn't been used in years, he thought. Centuries, probably, he corrected himself. That made him wonder how old the boat was, and if it was in the same general condition of disrepair as the wagon and this equipment.

"Don't go there," he said aloud. "You'll only make yourself crazy."

He knew any thoughts about the lack of seaworthiness of the ship would only raise his anxiety level several more notches higher than the already too high level that it was now. He closed the door to the equipment compartment and went forward to the bow. There he found nothing but a few coils of rope.

He reached down to pick one up and it crumbled in his hand. The hemp was so wet and rotten that the fibers had lost all their strength. He nudged one coil with his foot and it collapsed in a pile of debris.

"Great," he mumbled. "Hope we don't need any rope."

As the rope crumbled, he thought he saw something skitter across the floor. He pulled out his slingshot – not that he had anything to load into it – and moved some of the debris aside with his toe. Whatever it was skittered again.

"Whatever you are," he whispered, "you picked the wrong boat to ride in."

He backed out the way he had come, walking quietly by the door to the sleeping quarters into the galley. He turned around towards the stairway to the deck that was in the center. On the left was a long table and some benches – room enough for eight, he noticed – and not much else. On the right was a counter with a sink and an oven and stove. Above them and on either side was an assortment of cabinets.

He opened the one on the near end at the top and found plates, bowls and cups. In the next one, he found some herbs and spices in different sized canisters. He removed one of them and looked at the markings on the side of it. He didn't recognize the letters. He opened the top and looked inside.

It was filled halfway with a granular mixture. It was mostly gray with flecks of red and yellow. He was about to stick his finger in to take a pinch to taste, but then thought better of it. He didn't want to turn blue, or green or any other color, and he didn't want to shrink or start speaking in some unintelligible language. He quickly put the lid back on and put it back in the cabinet. The other canisters looked the same, and he decided they weren't worth opening.

In the next cabinet he found some sacks of what looked like rice. At last, he thought. Something to eat. He removed one of the sacks and opened it over the sink. As he pulled the top open, the sack disintegrated, much the same way as the rope in the bow. The contents spilled into the sink. Mixed in with the grain, which turned out not to be rice or anything Sean was even remotely familiar with, was a swarm of tiny insects.

He jerked back, shaking his hands and slapping them against one another, trying to fling off any of the little critters that might have gotten on him. When he was certain that any of them that had climbed onto him were off, he inched toward the sink and stretched his neck forward to see better. The few remaining ones were scurrying around the sink and down into the drain. He reached across and turned on the tap to wash them down.

The old pipes below the sink clanked and thick brown goo sputtered out of the faucet, followed by a gasp of air. Sean quickly flicked the handle back, turning it off. Guess I won't be getting a drink from there, he thought. He looked in the cabinets below the counter. He found some cleaning supplies that were older than the ship, and nothing more.

He then went to the ship's stern. There was a door immediately behind the stairs that opened up to a large cargo hold. Inside the hold there were several crates. Most of them were nailed shut. Sean examined one after another. Most were labeled with such things as "costumes," "sawdust," tents," and so on. He found a box near the back bulkhead where the wood of the crate was so old and decayed, that the nails could be pulled out by hand.

He lifted the top and pushed it aside. The box itself was about four feet wide, two feet deep and three feet high. When the lid was removed, an odor of decay wafted upward. It wasn't very strong, but it was enough for Sean to know that the contents had been sitting here for a very long time. He saw that it was filled with clothing – costumes to be more precise. There were stretch pants, frilly shirts, wide skirts and lacy blouses. There were boots and shoes of different shapes and sizes and colors.

Everything was faded, but he could see that at one time it had all been shiny and glittery. Many items were covered with sequins, although many of them had fallen off. All of it now, though, was a dull red, yellow or blue. Some of the shirts had a large "A" sewn or embroidered on them. When he picked one up, it fell apart in his hand. Some of the items further down, which had been protected from the moisture, were intact.

He looked back towards the entryway and the rows of crates. The ones on the bottom had water stains on them. Sean knew that the contents in these boxes would be worthless. Boxes that were stacked on top of the lower ones were in better condition. He wondered if any of them had anything besides costumes or acrobatic equipment.

"What a dump," he said as he exited.

About the time he completed his exploration, the others were awake and making their way on deck. He reluctantly followed them upward, but stopped when he got to the top of the stairway. From this position he could see to the back of the ship where Quinn was now taking his turn at the helm. Natalie and Stella were sitting cross-legged on the deck to his left and Liam and Lochen were sitting to his right.

Summer and Solveig were in the center of the deck between him and Quinn and between the other four. Solveig was so small, that he worried that she might fall into one of the cracks in the wood of the deck. He had gotten used to seeing her blue before Sarnanok had changed her back. He almost didn't notice that she was blue once more. He wondered why everything, her skin, her eyes, and even her clothing turned blue, but not her hair. It was still red. Weird, he thought – just plain weird.

"Sean," called Summer. "You can come up on deck and join us, you know."

"I'm fine right where I am," he answered.

"It's so peaceful out here," said Liam. "It almost makes you forget where we're going and why."

"Almost," agreed Natalie, "but not quite."

"I just hope this old bucket gets us where we're going and back," said Sean. "Mostly 'and back.'"

"Did you find anything useful below?" Liam asked him.

"Not really," he answered. "Mostly just old, rotten, smelly stuff – and a bunch of bugs."

"A bunch of bugs?" asked Lochen. "What kind of bugs? What did they look like?"

"I don't know," Sean answered. "Just bugs little black ones. Or maybe they were brown."

"Black or brown?" Lochen persisted. "Which was it?"

"I told you, I don't know," Sean repeated. "What difference does it make?"

"Where are they now?" Lochen asked, getting to his feet.

"They went down the drain."

"Down the drain? All of them?" demanded Lochen. "You mean they were released into the sea?"

He was moving towards the stairs, nudging himself between Sean and the entryway, as he climbed down the stairs.

"Yes, all of them," Sean called after him. "At least I hope it was all of them. I suppose they went into the sea. So what? Good riddance. They were creepy. What's the big deal? You weren't planning on eating them, were you? Tell me you don't want to eat them."

"Show me where you got them." Lochen called back to him.

"They were in that cabinet on the left over the sink," answered Sean.

He climbed down the steps into the galley and pointed to the cabinet in which he had found the sack of grain with the infestation of insects. Lochen opened the door and pulled down one of the other sacks. He ripped it open.

"Careful," Sean warned. "They might crawl all over you."

There was nothing in the sack but small kernels of some kind of grain. Lochen sifted his fingers through the particles, but saw no signs of the insects. He tasted one of the granules and quickly spit it out.

"What?" asked Sean. "Doesn't it taste very good?"

"It's poison," Lochen answered. "Very lethal."

He opened another sack and found the same thing. There was one more. He pulled it down and tore into it. Again, it was filled with the same grain as the other two – some kind of poison, but no insects. He yanked open the cupboard door beneath the sink. The pipes ran from the basin through the flooring of the ship and into the sea.

"What is it?" asked Sean. "What's the matter?"

By now the others, except for Quinn, had crowded into the stairway to see what Lochen was looking for. Solveig was hanging on to Summer as she fluttered above the others.

"What's wrong, Lochen?" asked Stella.

"I'm not sure," he said.

"What would someone need with all that poison?" asked Natalie.

"A very good question," answered Lochen.

"What about the bugs?" asked Sean. "What was so important about them?"

"Maybe nothing," said Lochen. "As I suspected, though, the drain empties out into the sea. Whatever they were, they're gone now. Without seeing what they looked like, I would only be speculating as to what they were and if it matters. "

"So speculate," said Solveig. "Out loud. To all of us."

He motioned for them to return to the deck. They climbed back up the stairs and Sean resumed his spot in the stairwell. All eyes were on Lochen.

"This ship was used during the Kelpie rebellion," he began. "But not on the side of the Alchemist and the Enchantress. It was used on the side of the Kelpies."

"What?" asked Quinn. "You mean they took it from Artabarat – against his will?"

"No," said Lochen. "He provided it of his own free will, although, I will admit, he may have been coerced. Still, he did it willingly."

"How do you know?" asked Summer.

256

"Are you sure?" asked Natalie. "He seemed like such a charming person."

"Is that what you meant back there when you said he was only recently nice?" asked Sean.

"I've drawn some conclusions from the material I've translated from the Alchemist's book," he answered Summer.

"Yes, I'm sure," he said to Natalie. "And I agree that he's charming – now. Back then? Not so much, I'm willing to wager."

"And yes, again," he answered Sean. "That's exactly what I meant back on shore. If you recall, he said he had paid his debt – just before he..."

"I got it; I got it!" interrupted Sean. "Just before he...um...just before he wasn't."

"Yes, I suppose that would be correct," Lochen pondered Sean's description. "Just before he wasn't. I believe the debt that he needed to pay was in some way connected to his relationship with the Kelpies at the time of their rebellion."

"Let's back up a little," said Liam. "You have the advantage of knowing more of what happened than we do. It might help if we all understood the same thing."

"You're quite right," Lochen agreed.

He shared his translation of the Alchemist's book – at least as far as he had done. He told them much the same thing that Scirios had related to B'nair in the moments before Akmen Milzu destroyed the mountain castle. He described the identification and development of sorcerers and enchantresses, which had not changed even to the present day. Stella filled in some gaps and told about her training and her connection or bonding to Natalie.

He then told them all about the history of Ena Ray and Tebaga – two people they knew all too well. His account explained a lot about where these two had come from and how they had ended up where they were.

"I know a little bit about Meri Hocto," said Stella. "I learned about her when I was being mentored as an Enchantress. Not very much was known about her, though, so there were a lot of missing parts in the history. Now I see why. Things kind of got out of hand back then, didn't they?"

"Yes," said Lochen. "Very much out of hand."

He continued with the description of how the Kelpies grew to power and became the bases of the folklore of each of the cultures.

"Why do they have two different names?" asked Quinn. "Why is the Nebalas of the Ice Kingdom also called...what did you say his name was?"

"Saldeti," answered Lochen. "From what I can tell, Saldeti was or is his actual name. The term Nebalas was the word that described what he was – pure evil. It comes from myths that go back much further than two thousand years – back to the very beginnings of each of our civilizations. Those words – Nebalas,

Banrian, Bathala, Paligu, Malkia, Mengassi, Jainkaso, and Kurat – all those names we each grew up hearing horrible things about; they all represent what's worst about ourselves. They aren't actually names, but a description of malevolence. Over time, they became names: the names of those who became that evil – the Kelpies."

"Then what I saw wasn't my imagination," said Liam.

"What did you see?" asked Natalie.

"The Mengassi," he answered. "The creature that probably destroyed my people."

"When did you see him...it?" asked Quinn.

"After we split up," answered Liam. "When we left the Swamp and crashed in the desert. I only caught a glimpse of it, so I wasn't positive, but it sure looked like what was described in the myths of my people. And now you're telling us those things were real?"

"Yes," Lochen answered. "And returning to life."

They were all silent for several minutes as they absorbed what he had told them. Each of them was recalling the stories of their childhood. Each of them had grown up learning about a villain that had created havoc among their people. It was hard for them to come to grips with the fact that these villains were real and that this was who they were facing now.

"But why us?" asked Quinn. "Why are we the ones who have to destroy them? We didn't even know each other until not too long ago. And why now?"

"Two things. First, because," Lochen started, "we are the direct descendants of the leaders of our respective people. Except for Stella and myself."

"What?" shouted Sean.

"That's crazy," gasped Summer.

"You're not serious, are you?" asked Quinn.

Lochen let the furor of his comment die down before he responded.

"I am merely the messenger of this information," he finally said. "Not the originator. Trust me. I found it as hard to comprehend as you do."

"Are you telling us that this book of the Alchemist...this 'Quest of Eight' thing...actually names us?" asked Liam.

"No," admitted Lochen. "It doesn't go that far, but all the indicators are there."

"That knock on your head must have really scrambled your brains," said Sean.

"Whatever disturbance to my thought and communication faculties that occurred to my brain does not alter the contents of the...." Lochen started to reply.

"Arghhhh!" Sean shouted. "Get to the point!"

"Too many words," Quinn mumbled.

Lochen looked around at the faces that were all looking at him expectantly. He closed his eyes for a second and took a deep breath while he tried to find the easiest way to explain things.

"The Alchemist's book describes our ancient leaders," he began. "The ones who faced the Kelpies when the wars first began. Some of them were destroyed and others disappeared – never to be found. It was thought that they were either captured or destroyed as well. Regardless, though, the Alchemist's account is not merely a history. It's a diary that was added to over decades – possibly even centuries. But it's also a prophecy.

"He has also included an accounting of the lineage of the leaders, although it's admittedly incomplete. However..." he continued, raising his hand and cutting off the anticipated objections, "however...he has described the conditions that occurred when we were first brought together – the alignment of the planets; the appearance of the Fury; the rise in power of Ena Ray, even though he was still imprisoned; and the possession of a piece of the Enchantress's pendant."

He turned to Summer and waited until his silence caused her to look directly at him. Then he continued, "A piece that had, of its own power, changed its size. A piece that was the center of the pendant. A piece that was in the shape of a triskelion."

Summer reflexively reached for the amulet that she had worn around her neck. It was now attached to another piece of the stone and hung from Stella's neck. She jerked her head around and saw it in Stella's hand.

"That stone?" she asked breathlessly.

"Are you aware of any other?" he asked.

"That may explain Summer," said Quinn. "But what about the rest of us?"

"The prophecy spoke about eight strangers coming together to fend off the resurrection of evil," Lochen said. "That seems pretty clear, doesn't it? It said that these strangers were direct descendants of the eight ancient leaders. That seems pretty clear, too, doesn't it?"

Quinn sat down hard. He managed to keep his hands on the wheel, but he was no longer paying any attention to the direction in which they were headed. By this time, though, it no longer mattered. The ship was steering itself. When Lochen cast the spell that filled the sail with wind, he had directed the wind towards their destination. Manning the tiller had only been something to help some of them keep their mind off what they were headed towards.

"All right," said Liam. "Even if all that is correct – and I'm not necessarily agreeing that it is, but for argument's sake, let's assume we are all descended from the leaders of our cultures. Why us and why now? There have been generation after generation before us. Why not one of them?"

"Ah!" said Lochen, raising his finger in the air. "An excellent question."

"Do you have an answer?" Solveig asked.

"I do," he answered. "As I mentioned, the book is also a diary. It includes an accounting, although a bit incomplete at times, of our various family trees. That is one factor that explains why us and why now. Each of our people age differently – some live much longer than others; some have met with untimely ends. Over the last two thousand years, believe it or not, there has never been a time when each of the descendants of our leaders has been at the same or equivalent levels of maturity."

"Levels of maturity?" asked Sean. "What's that supposed to mean?"

"It means," explained Lochen, "that in spite of our actual years, we are of nearly equal ages."

"Summer is a hundred and thirty," exclaimed Sean. "None of us is that old!"

"I AM NOT!" she said indignantly.

"Well, you're close," Sean clarified.

"Exactly," said Lochen.

"Exactly what?" asked Natalie. "How does that explain anything?"

"Faeries live much longer than the rest of us," said Lochen. "As a result, their aging and maturing process is different – slower. She should live to be nearly four hundred. On the other hand,

Quinn's people only live to be about a hundred. Although he's quite a bit younger than Summer..."

"Hey!" she interrupted. "Not THAT much younger!"

"Somewhat younger," corrected Lochen. "Somewhat younger; at this point in time, they...you and Quinn...are of an equivalent age of maturity."

"I think I've just been insulted," muttered Summer.

"I don't mean mental or emotional maturity," Lochen tried to clarify.

"Hey!" complained Quinn.

"I meant physical maturity," Lochen finished. "We're all about the same physical level of maturity. That is to say..."

"I get it," Summer cut him off. "You said that all of us except you and Stella were descended from the leaders. What about you two?"

"I said we were not descended from the leaders of our respective civilizations," he clarified. "We are, however, the direct descendants of the leaders of the sorcerers and enchantresses – of Ceannaire and Vezeto Landoo."

Stella was unusually quiet. The others had expected her to have the same reaction to this news as they had. On the contrary, she remained silent.

"Did you already know this?" asked Natalie.

"Not for certain," she said. "But I suspected."

"When?" Natalie wanted to know. "For how long?"

"I had...I don't know how to describe it – maybe a sensation?" she tried to explain. "Or, maybe a suspicion. Lately, though, that feeling has been stronger. As hard as all this is to imagine, I think what Lochen has told us is right. Whether we like it or not; whether we're ready or not, we're the ones all this has fallen to."

"You said there were two things," Natalie reminded Lochen.

"Yes," he said. "I did. Quinn had asked why us and why now. I think I've answered his question about why us. As for why now, I think there are a number of contributing factors. One is the alignment of the planets. That happened two thousand years ago and had the effect of altering or enhancing certain powers.

"The Alchemist suggested in his diary that the unusual gravitational pull of so many large bodies added to the other conditions at the time; not the least of which was the number of sorcerers who revolted against the leadership. Also, at this time, the center of the Enchantress's power – the pendant – was destroyed."

He went on to describe the creation of the Fury that coincided with the planetary alignment and the rise of the Kelpies. Those same conditions were replicated when the planets once again aligned. He reminded them of the reappearance of the Fury. He then described some of the translations of the Alchemist's daily accounts.

He told them of the search for the shattered pieces of the Enchantress's pendant; how he had found the one he had hidden in his fortress. The Alchemist had known about the center piece – the triskelion – but hadn't been able to locate it for several years, until he saw it in the armband of a Forest Creature.

"Wait a minute," said Sean. "You said he was blinded by one of the Kelpies. How could he see the stone in an armband?"

"I can only tell you what he described," said Lochen. "Since I wasn't there, I can't say to what extent he was blind or to what extent he could actually see."

"That doesn't make any sense," said Quinn.

"Try to remember the old man we encountered in the mines of the Trepans," suggested Lochen. "He was clearly blind, and yet, he maneuvered through those caves and tunnels better than those of us who had the use of both our eyes."

"Come on," said Solveig. "We've seen stranger things than that. So he was blind, but he could still see. Keep going, Lochen. What about the other pieces of the pendant?"

"Well," continued Lochen. "He had located a second piece much later and hid that one in a shop in that walled and dead fortress where we ran into the troll. The last piece had fallen into the hands of a Rebbercand. That, combined with the weakening of the spells that Meri Hocto had cast imprisoning Ena Ray, and the alignment of the planets and the return of the Fury – all of it is what brought us together at this particular time."

"I don't suppose there could be an alternate theory," mumbled Quinn.

"I'm afraid not," said Lochen.

As he was speaking, Stella's attention was directed back the way they had come – back towards the shore that was well out of sight. She felt a stirring. The color drained from her face. At that instant she felt something else, and turned towards Solveig.

Solveig's legs had suddenly weakened and she sat on the deck to keep from falling. She felt drained. She felt a wave of despair sweep over her, and she felt an extreme urge to cry. A terrible sense of loss filled her. She jerked her head up and looked towards Stella. Liam, who had been sitting opposite them, noticed the change in both their expressions.

"What's wrong?" he said. "What happened?"

Everyone turned towards him as he asked. Everyone except Stella and Solveig. They both exchanged knowing looks. Stella reached out and Solveig touched her tiny hand to an extended finger.

"They released another Kelpie," said Stella. "The one in the forest."

"Then they'll be on their way towards us soon," said Lochen.

"They are already moving," said Stella.

"But there's more," said Liam. "Isn't there? You both know something else has happened. What is it?"

"When I was lost in the forest," said Solveig. "I came across the last remaining survivors of the town of Kalayaan. They had been changed into trees. They could only speak once a month."

"What about them?" asked Sean.

"The Kelpie – the one they last released," said Solveig. "He's had them all destroyed. He's had them all cut down. I could hear their screams. I could feel them."

"They are getting much stronger," said Stella. "I can feel their power growing."

"How much further do we have to go?" asked Liam.

"Not much," answered Stella.

"Would a bit more speed be in order?" asked Lochen.

"It wouldn't hurt," she replied.

"Unless it starts to break this old tub apart," said Liam. "Be careful how much more stress you put on it."

"I'll be cautious," answered Lochen.

He waved a hand and the bow of the ship rose higher into the air as the wind in the sails became stronger. Within seconds, the buffeting of the hull against the sea started to reverberate through the entire ship. Summer and Solveig, being the smallest and lightest began to bounce with the vibrations and slid towards the stern.

Sean crouched lower into the stairwell; Liam and Natalie held on tightly to the bulkhead and Quinn tightened his grip on the wheel. Everyone's eyes shifted from the sail to the deck to the sides to each other and back to the sail.

"If this thing breaks apart," shouted Sean, "it won't matter if we get where we're going first. I think we need to slow down."

Lochen eased off a bit, and the rumbling of the old wooden hull quieted a bit.

"Turn right," Stella shouted. "Actually, turn back. We've gone too far."

"Are you sure?" asked Lochen.

He stopped the wind without waiting for Stella to confirm that she was certain. Quinn spun the wheel and turned the boat in as small a circle as he could.

"Yes," Stella answered. "The map in my head didn't seem to take into consideration the shifting of the sand and the water near the bottom. Wherever the Kelpie is hidden looks like it's been moved a little."

Lochen raised his hand to fill the sails with wind and send the ship back the way they had come, but Stella raised her hand to stop him.

"No," she said. "This is it. We're here."

In the excitement of learning more about the Kelpie wars, their connection to the ancient leaders of their respective cultures, the mysteries of the pendant of the Enchantress, and now, the arrival at their destination, they had all forgotten about the insects that had crawled down the drain and out to sea.

Chapter twelve

Saldeti had been a reluctant participant in the Kelpie rebellion. When Rovek had first asked him to find a place where he and some others could meet – a place far from prying eyes – he hadn't bothered to ask why. He also hadn't been expected to be included in the meeting. When he was, he was surprised to see so many sorcerers from such far-reaching locations. He was overwhelmed by their presence and didn't focus clearly on their intentions.

He initially thought that their plans were more along the lines of effecting a series of pranks. They had been somewhat circumspect in their discussion at first. By the time he started to really pay attention to what was going on, he was too involved to back out, or so he felt. He was not a leader, and he felt intimidated by the more dominant personalities. He could have distanced himself from them in the beginning, but the longer he waited, his indecision and his inability to stand up for what was right in the face of strong opposition became his undoing.

When Rovek asked if he could find a secure location, he suggested a large lake in the southern area of the Ice Kingdom. In the warmer weather it was not frozen. Rovek had told him that one of the meeting attendees was from the sea creatures and could cast a spell to create a pocket beneath the lake's surface so they could all breathe. Under the water was an ideal location. In the winter, about two feet of the surface froze over – enough to keep others out, but not enough to prevent a passage from being cut so that the meetings could continue.

It didn't take long, though before Saldeti found himself as one of the eight sorcerers who were plotting an overthrow of all the civilizations. The thought of this made him nervous.

"What have you gotten me into?" he demanded of Rovek after one of the meetings.

"I've opened a door to you that leads to unlimited power," he answered.

"I don't want such power," replied Saldeti.

"You will," the Forest Kelpie said. "Once you get a real taste for it, you will crave even more."

"But what you are all talking about is...is...it's treason!" he pleaded.

Richard Reda

"What WE are talking about," Rovek reminded him. "You are just as much a part of this as the rest of us."

"I never signed up for this," Saldeti objected.

"You never walked away," Rovek pointed out.

"Well, I'm walking away now."

"I think now is too late," said Rovek. "You know too much about the plans – OUR plans. We can't afford for you to decide now that you don't want to be a part of this."

"What's that supposed to mean?" asked Saldeti. "Are you threatening me?"

"It was meant to be a point of clarification," Rovek answered. "This is not a game we're playing. We all knew the stakes when we started."

"Perhaps you should have been a bit clearer. I certainly didn't know the stakes."

"Don't play stupid now," hissed the Kelpie. "What did you think this was all about? A childish game? You knew very well what we were discussing – and from the very start."

"I most certainly did not!" objected Saldeti.

"Come now," chided Rovek. "Do you think your claim of ignorance will be believed? Because I don't – not for a minute. You're in this up to your neck, just like all the rest of us. You might as well make the most of it."

Even then, even with the implied threats, Saldeti could have walked away from them. He could have sought out the guidance and help from the leader of his people – Galvenais. But he did not. He could have appealed to others, like the Alchemist. But he did not. He could have summoned an ounce of courage and faced the intimidation of the Kelpies regardless of the risk. But he did not. Instead, coward that he was, he submitted.

As much as he could, he played a minor role in the rebellion; but he never stood against it. He knew that his compatriots had instigated a war between the small people and the Forest Creatures. He did nothing to intervene or to oppose it. He sat safe in his land far to the north and assumed the conflict would never reach him.

When it spread, forcing the Mountain People high into the peaks and the Sea Sprites deep under the sea, he refused to acknowledge his role in any of it. He turned his back on any pleas for help and held fast to the belief that it would all go away and that his home would not be affected.

When the Kelpies' plans went awry and they began to terrorize towns and villages, he went along, standing on the sidelines, assuming that this was enough to demonstrate that he was not a part of what was going on. He was wrong.

When Pantano Izaki was captured and imprisoned, he fled back to his home, hoping his part in the revolt would go unnoticed. He returned to the lake and attempted to eliminate any sign of the meetings and preparation that had been conducted there. He attempted to erase any sign of his involvement. When he was certain he had been successful, he returned to his own home and began to destroy whatever evidence was there.

As he was doing this, Galvenais approached him. The leader was merely seeking his guidance on how to protect the people of the Ice Kingdom, but in his shame and suspicion, Saldeti was certain he had been discovered.

"What is it?" he demanded. "What do you want?"

"I need to speak with you about the sorcerers who are rebelling," said the patriarch of the Ice Kingdom.

"Why? What makes you think I know anything?"

"You are one of them," was the answer.

Galvenais had only meant that Saldeti was a sorcerer as were the ones in revolt. He never thought that Saldeti was a party to their treason. But that was not how Saldeti understood the statement.

"Come with me," said Galvenais. "I have arranged for you to see the Alchemist."

The words were not an order, but an invitation. The meeting with the Alchemist was not to capture and imprison the sorcerer, but to discuss a solution to the problem. But Saldeti knew his own culpability. He knew deep in his heart he was as guilty as the Kelpies; that he, himself, was a Kelpie. All his efforts at minimizing his involvement did nothing to absolve him of his role in their duplicity, and he knew it.

Still, he was a coward at heart and believed he could escape retribution. In a momentary lapse of reason, he spun on Galvenais and struck him full on with a spell. As soon as he cast it, he regretted his action.

The leader was unprepared, not that he could have stopped the spell, but he could have sought to clarify his comments or to reason with the sorcerer. The spell was instantaneous and lethal. He was immediately frozen solid and dropped to the floor.

"What have I done?" Saldeti said in shock.

He darted out of his room and looked around to see if anyone was nearby. He was alone. He turned back and looked at the body of ice on the floor. He wrung his hands in desperation, wondering what he should do now. No spell could undo what he had done. He knew that. He should report this, he thought. He should turn himself in, he thought. He should find the Alchemist, he thought. But he did none of these things.

Instead he ran. He had no destination in mind and ran blindly, until he met up with the brothers, Anea and Afea.

"You have to help me," he pleaded. "Something horrible has happened."

At first they were reluctant to help, but because he was the sorcerer to the people of the Ice Kingdom, they agreed. He didn't tell them exactly what had happened until they arrived in his room and saw the frozen body of Galvenais. The brothers looked at each other and then turned to Saldeti.

"How did this happen?" asked Anea.

"It was an accident," he claimed.

"Then just report it," said Afea.

"I can't," argued Saldeti. "You don't understand. I have been critical of the leader recently. If this gets out, it will appear that I did this on purpose. We have to hide the body. If you do this for me, I will make sure you are amply rewarded. I have some very powerful friends."

The brothers looked at each other and an acknowledgement passed silently between them. They nodded and then covered the body, disguising it. They moved it secretly out of the village in the dark of night.

"You must come with us," said Anea.

"Where we are going, we will need you to help," said Afea.

"Of course," said Saldeti. "Whatever you need."

They loaded the body onto a sled. They could take no dogs with them for fear that the dogs would remember the destination and take someone else there. The sorcerer provided the spell that propelled the sled across the ice and snow far to the north.

They came to a large body of water and the brothers motioned for Saldeti to continue. He drove the sled over the surface of the water, trying to keep it above the waves. Eventually, they reached the shore of a new, much larger ice shelf. Ahead of them was what appeared to be a wall. They removed the body from the sled and carried it on their shoulders.

"What place is this?" Saldeti asked.

"One that is known to few people," said Anea.

"One that will keep your secret," said Afea.

They moved closer to the wall. Saldeti was waiting for them to stop; to indicate some kind of opening in the wall. They both looked to the sky, as if seeking a bearing. Then they continued on, walking towards an image of a gateway that seemed to appear from nowhere. All the time it looked like nothing more than an apparition, but instead of stopping, the brothers simply walked through it.

"You can come, too," said Anea.

"There is nothing to fear," added Afea.

The wall of ice was extremely thick, but the passage from the outside to the inside was like walking through a thin veil of water. Saldeti suddenly found himself inside a large open area. There was very little light inside.

"We need some light," said Anea.

"Use your powers," said Afea.

Saldeti waved his hand and a burst of light appeared. It shimmered off huge crystals of ice that hung from the ceiling and jutted from the walls. He could see that the floor of the cavern was smooth. He looked around, turning back towards the way they had come. It was gone – as if it had never been there.

Without waiting for him, the brothers began walking. The path wound narrowly through the crystals and beneath stalactites, twisting and turning. There were often side paths on either side of the main route. Most of them were very narrow or the openings were very low. It's a labyrinth, thought Saldeti. Do they mean to get me lost and leave me here, he wondered.

"How are we going to keep from getting lost?" he asked.

"In the land of ice there is a way," said Anea, without any explanation.

"With many paths that go astray," said Afea.

Saldeti recognized the rhyme immediately. Every child in the Ice Kingdom had grown up chanting it. He had never given it much thought, other than that it seemed to make no sense. Now he understood the meaning.

"Learn the course from start to end," said Anea.

"Or with dangers great you will contend," added Afea.

"Four counts left then one to the right," Saldeti chimed in. "Keep your goal well in sight."

The paths twisted back and forth so often that Saldeti was not able to keep track of where they were going or from where they had just come. Some of the turns they took seemed like they were clearly the wrong choices. In some sections he had to stoop down so far, that he was duck walking through some of them. The brothers often had to put the body down on the ice and drag it. The entire cavern was absolutely and eerily silent.

The wind and noises from outside were completely absent. They had diminished shortly after Saldeti and the brothers had crossed into the cave, but the silence now was unnerving. The light that Saldeti generated created strange shadows on the walls. Beyond their small circle the light faded. Actually, it was more like the light was smothered by the darkness.

The further they traveled along the path the thicker the darkness became. The turns became harder to see, but somehow the brothers knew exactly where they were and walked with confidence as they mumbled the ancient rhyme. The deeper they crept into the labyrinth, the more oppressive the darkness became. It enveloped them like a dank musty old blanket. The darkness wasn't the only change they noticed. The air was becoming thicker – staler. It left an acrid, metallic taste in their mouths as they breathed.

They all also detected a pervasive odor that got stronger the further they went. It smelled like rotting garbage. Saldeti wondered how many other bodies these two had brought here. He wondered if they would try to leave him here as well. Finally, they stopped walking.

Deep inside, at the end of the path, they came upon a deep gorge cut across the floor of the cave. There they stopped.

"Be careful," warned Anea.

"There is no returning if you should fall in," said Afea.

They rolled the body to the edge of the chasm and the wind seemed to draw it in and down. In an instant the body of Galvenais, leader of the people of the Ice Kingdom, was gone – never to be seen or heard from again. And with it, Saldeti's fate had been sealed. The return trip was uneventful. Saldeti wondered if he could trust the brothers, and decided he didn't have much choice. Killing Galvenais had been an accident. He didn't have it in him to purposely murder anyone.

He never mentioned his deeds to any of the other sorcerers, but he was certain that somehow Akmen Milzu knew. At least she knew that something significant had happened; something that now committed Saldeti to the rest of them. She never said anything, but he was convinced she knew, just the same.

He resigned himself to this new destiny and became more active and involved in the plotting. This involvement cemented his connection to the Kelpies. When Pantano Izaki disappeared, the rebels hadn't understood that they were being singled out and hunted down. When Angin Topan was taken from them and buried in the desert, they realized something was happening.

Being the coward that he was, Saldeti fled back to the Ice Kingdom. He didn't wait to see if the other Kelpies were mounting a counter-attack. He didn't explain where he was going or why. He simply fled. He didn't seriously believe he would be safe, but he hoped he would go unnoticed.

When he returned home and entered the village, he found someone waiting for him. An old man with long white hair was

281

sitting on a chair in the middle of his room. The man had milky white eyes and appeared to be blind.

"Hello, Saldeti," the old man said when the Kelpie arrived.

"Do I know you?" Saldeti asked.

"We haven't met," the stranger said, "but I believe we know each other. I certainly know who you are. I am the Alchemist. Perhaps you've heard of me."

Saldeti froze in his tracks. He looked around to see if anyone else was present.

"We are quite alone," said the Alchemist.

That caught the Kelpie by surprise and unnerved him even further. The old man looked blind, he thought. How can he see what I'm doing?

"What do you want?" Saldeti asked.

"I'm looking for Galvenais," the Alchemist answered.

"What makes you think I know where he is?" demanded the Kelpie.

"You are his sorcerer," was the reply. "How can you not know where he is?"

"I've been gone," Saldeti answered. "I've only just returned."

"Still," persisted the Alchemist. "I believe you know exactly where he is, don't you?"

The sorcerer could taste the fear growing inside him. Beads of sweat broke out on his forehead, and he could feel a churning in the pit of his stomach. He looked around the room and took a small step backwards. The Alchemist rose to his feet. The unexpected move caused Saldeti to panic.

He raised his arm casting a spell – the same one that had frozen Galvenais. The Alchemist, however, was better prepared and deflected the spell easily. Saldeti then thrust his other hand forward, sending a blast of energy at the old man. As easily as swatting a fly, the Alchemist diffused the burst, leaving a sound of static and the odor of something burning in its place.

Saldeti turned and bolted from the room. The Alchemist walked out following him. The sorcerer ran out of the village – out into the open air. He ran blindly. He saw someone approaching on a sled. He pushed the riders off, and with a flick of his wrist, he cut the reins that led to the dogs. He spun the sled around, waved his hand and the sled shot forward. He looked back to see the Alchemist steadfastly marching towards him.

He waved his hand again, and the sled increased in speed to a near perilous rate. He looked back to see how much distance he had put between him and the Alchemist, but there he was, a few dozen yards behind, still walking casually.

How is that possible, he wondered. Some more of the Alchemist's sorcery, he concluded. He increased his speed again. Every time he looked back over his shoulder, the

Alchemist was standing not far behind. In actuality, the Alchemist had never left the village.

When he brushed aside the burst of energy that Saldeti threw at him, he cast a spell of his own that projected his image behind Saldeti. That image would appear whenever the sorcerer turned to look. The Alchemist knew that the leader of the Ice Kingdom had been slain and was certain would never be found.

Saldeti was clearly not going to admit to anything. He knew he could not catch the Kelpie, and really had no need to do so. His time would be better spent locating the accomplices and dealing with them.

The Kelpie drove faster and faster, eventually heading for the lake and the hidden retreat of his comrades. He crested the ridge that surrounded the water. It was still summer and the lake had not yet frozen. As the sled rose into the air, he lost control and spun off, sliding across the ground to the water's edge.

He got to his feet and stretched out his arms. The water did not open as it had in the past. It did not separate and allow him to descend to the hidden chamber on the floor of the lake. He tried again. Still nothing happened.

"What is happening?" he shouted in frustration.

"Your powers are no longer of any use," a voice answered.

He spun around, expecting to see the Alchemist. Instead, he saw the Enchantress. Before he could react or even defend himself, she had thrust both arms forward and encased him in an energy field. She lifted him into the air and out over the center of the lake.

Only then did the water part. But there was no hidden chamber beneath. There was nothing. She thrust him downward. As he hit the sandy bottom, he could feel the air around him suddenly get extremely cold. In the blink of an eye, she sealed him in a solid block of ice – colder, harder, and more impenetrable than any before.

Once the block had set, she allowed the water to close over him. Then she cast a spell on the lake itself, freezing it completely. It would remain frozen – winter or summer – until broken open two thousand years later by Saldeti's partners in crime.

When Akmen Milzu sent him into the caves of the gargoyles with the instructions to amass an army, he was somewhat relieved to be separated from them all. The Rebbercand made him nervous – wearing a piece of the witch's pendant. And when he learned where Ena Ray had been held prisoner, he could feel his skin crawl.

He knew the Kelpies would not think less of him for having killed Galvenais, but the thought of what he had done shamed him – even this long after the incident. He wondered what had ever happened to the brothers Anea and Afea. They were probably long gone.

It didn't take him long to find the first group of gargoyles. He could smell them long before he saw them. It also didn't take much to instill fear into them and to get them to do his bidding. He had come across a small group devouring some kind of animal. He couldn't tell how long the animal had been there.

Some of the stench he detected was from rotting meat. It didn't seem to bother the gargoyles.

He let them finish their meal and then gathered them together and got them to lead him to another group. One group was added after another as they wound their way through the extensive tunnels. Sometimes they doubled back, but overall, they were heading in an easterly direction towards Satamakau.

As he accumulated his soldiers, he studied them. He picked only the largest, fastest, and most brutal. The rest he told to stay behind. From the time he began until he was near the end of his journey, he had assembled over five hundred beasts.

They reached a point in the tunnels where the gargoyles told him there was a portal. It would shorten the time it would take to get to their destination. If it was open. The gargoyles had told him that this exit had been blocked for centuries, but now they believed it may be unlocked. Whoever had kept it impassible either no longer cared if it was secure, or had left it unattended.

Saldeti, in an uncharacteristic show of bravery, opened the portal and went first. He pushed aside the door from the inside of the tunnel. On the other side, the door had been a shelf containing several containers of herbs and potions.

The room into which the portal opened was small and relatively neat. There was an odd pile of white dust on the floor in the center, next to a table on which sat a skull and a cup. Saldeti looked into the cup and saw the remnants of tea leaves. The leaves had long since gone cold and had an unusual bluish cast to them. He picked up the cup and carefully sniffed.

"Hexed," he said to no one in particular.

This was the home of someone adept at making potions, he considered. On the other side of the small room was a stairway that led up between some large roots. He climbed up and out, finding that the portal had opened to a room inside the base and root system of a large tree. When he emerged, he found himself in a forest.

He recognized the forest, or at least he thought he did. It had been two thousand years since he had been here, but he felt he was near the place Rovek called home. The trees had all grown, died and been replaced hundreds of times over, but there was something about the area that Saldeti felt was familiar.

"There was a town," he said.

He looked around, trying to get his bearings. Then he pointed to his right.

"Kalayaan," he said. "It was the village of Kalayaan."

Then he remembered what Rovek had done to the leaders of that village, and to the village itself. He elected to avoid that location. He would find out later that the Kelpies would be there before the next day was done.

He arrived in Satamakau hours after the boat that had belonged to Artabarat had sailed off into the Viridian Ocean. He directed the majority of his following to make camp outside the town while he and a select group entered and searched.

He found the same desolation that he predecessors did. Moving along the outer perimeter of the town, he eventually discovered the old wagon. There was a campfire that had gone dead, but he could tell had been recently hot. There was another pile of white dust next to the wagon.

"Artabarat," he called. "Artabarat, my old friend, where are you? It's Saldeti. Come out and greet me."

But no one answered. He had to remind himself that the acrobat had lived two thousand years ago and was probably long forgotten. Still, his wagon was here, Saldeti noted. After all this time? He bent down and picked up a handful of the white dust. As soon as he did, he knew what it was.

He jerked his hand back, dropped the dust and tried to wipe all trace of it from his hand.

"The Alchemist!" he hissed.

He looked around for any sign of life. Sweat broke out on his forehead, and he could feel the old familiar grip of fear. What traps had the Alchemist left behind, he wondered. He, too, must be long gone, the Kelpie thought.

He turned towards the harbor, and ordered his small team to follow him. When he reached the sea wall, he could see that the tide had gone out. There were a number of old and decrepit boats scattered randomly along the sea wall. He thought it was odd that they were all tied tightly to the top of the wall. They hung in the air far above the sand below.

He looked towards the horizon and well off in the distance he could see the Ocean. The shore extended hundreds of yards from the sea wall to the water. He then noticed mooring lines that dropped down the side of the sea wall. A boat had been here, he realized. Those others were ahead of them.

He went back into the village. He found no signs of life, but he could detect the presence of the others who had been there hours earlier. He moved his army into more strategic positions in the town and along the harbor. If they returned this way, he thought, they would receive a warm and very inhospitable welcome.

As he was thinking of what other measures he could take, he could feel the air above him heat up. It was charged with electricity. When he looked up, he saw a massive current appear above him and begin to descend. He watched with a mixture of fear and curiosity until he recognized the shapes of the other Kelpies.

The Lightning Riders lowered to the ground and slowly deposited their cargo, and then fizzled into nothing. Saldeti stood back and waited until Akmen Milzu had taken in their surroundings, noting in particular the army he had gathered and the strategic deployment.

"Well done, my friend," she said. "What have you learned?"

"They've already been here," he said.

"How long?" she asked.

"It's hard to say," he answered. "I believe they have the use of a boat."

He took her to the harbor and showed her the mooring lines. He admitted that he couldn't know for certain, but all the other lines were attached to boats that were still in the marina. He mentioned the wagon, and recalled that the acrobat also had a boat at his disposal. There was no sign of the boat.

"But that was centuries ago," the Mountain Kelpie said dismissively.

"Yes," agreed Saldeti. "But I think the Alchemist had a hand in this."

"What do you mean?"

He went on to explain the portal through which he and the gargoyles had come and the pile of white dust he found in the room under the base of the giant old tree. He told her that he hadn't thought anything of it until he found another pile next to the acrobat's old wagon.

"Are you sure it's the same wagon?" she questioned him.

"Yes," he said. "I was very familiar with it. It has aged, certainly, but not as much as it should have in two thousand years. When I felt the dust, I knew...I sensed that it was the remains of the acrobat."

"The Alchemist slowed his aging?" Akmen Milzu asked. "Is that possible?"

"I believe it is," Saldeti answered. "He managed to keep us alive that long in a suspended state. Why not others?"

"To what end?" asked the Kelpie.

"I'm not sure," said Saldeti. "Possibly to thwart our efforts?"

"No," said the Mountain Kelpie as the pieces of at least part of the puzzle fell into place. "To help those who are trying to stop us. That's what he's done. He's scattered them all over – wherever help might be needed."

"Help? What kind of help?"

"Like a boat, when a boat is needed," answered Akmen Milzu. "I think you're right. They have a boat."

She began to smile.

"You seem amused at this," Saldeti said. "Why, if I may ask?"

"Because," she answered. "That boat may help them get to Ollos Foscos faster, but it will also make them easier to find, and more vulnerable to what we can do to them."

She headed back into town to rejoin the others; Saldeti following close behind. When she reached them, she explained what Saldeti had shared with her and the news of the boat.

"I remember that boat," said Rovek. "It was the same distasteful colors as that ridiculous wagon. We should have no difficulty whatsoever in finding it."

"And in destroying it," added Neraka Ferr.

"And all on board," Angin Topan finished the thought.

"Scirios," called Akmen Milzu. "Summon your Lightning Riders once again. We have our destination."

"What of me?" asked Saldeti.

"You remain here," she ordered. "If they somehow escape us, I need you to make sure they get no further than this town."

He knew she was trying to make his assignment sound important, but deep inside, he knew she didn't trust him. He had acted cowardly before; she believed he would do so again. She could read this in his face.

"My friend," she said. "You have amassed a more formidable army than I could have imagined. You have deployed them as a field general would. I need you to guard our flank. We will release Ollos Foscos and return here. I trust you to make certain that no one but us – only us – comes back to this harbor."

"I understand," he answered.

With that, Scirios summoned the Lightning Riders. The electrical charges enveloped all but Saldeti and his army of gargoyles. He watched as they were lifted into the air and disappeared into the clouds.

He looked back at the harbor. He decided they needed to have an early warning, in case the worst should happen. And a contingency plan in the event that a landing was attempted further down the shoreline. He divided the army into thirds. He sent one third under one commander to the southernmost end of the sea wall. He sent the second third to the opposite side and he kept the remaining third with him.

He instructed the commanders to arrange their armies so as to force anyone returning into the channel and towards his forces. If they tried to escape in either direction, they were to be annihilated. If they saw the forces on opposite sides of the sea wall, and tried to escape down the center, the commanders were to light signal fires to alert him and his army. There would be no escape this time.

Chapter thirteen

Lochen stopped the boat's movement. Liam looked around for an anchor, but could find none. What kind of boat is this that it doesn't have an anchor, he wondered. Lochen told him not to worry about it and waved his hand over the boat. He assured them all that it wasn't going anywhere. They all looked at him, at the waves across the breadth of the sea, and back to him.

"Trust me," he said. "The boat is securely anchored."

"Any idea how far down this thing is?" asked Sean, who was still crouched in the stairwell.

"It's at the bottom," said Stella. "I can lead the way."

"I'm going down," said Natalie.

"I'm not sure that's a good idea," said Liam. "The wound to your shoulder hasn't fully recovered."

"It's recovered enough," replied Natalie. "I'm going. That's all there is to it."

"So am I," piped up Solveig.

They all looked down to where she was standing. Next to her, Summer looked like a giant – three times Solveig's height. No one responded immediately; not even Lochen. Finally Sean spoke up.

"If nobody else is going to say something, I will," he announced. "Are you completely mental?"

"What's that supposed to mean?" she asked defensively.

"It means, have you lost your mind altogether," Sean answered.

"I think she knows what the phrase means," said Quinn. "I think she wants to know why you're asking her that."

"I don't need a translator," she shouted at Quinn.

"Sorry! I was just trying to help," he muttered.

"I know what the phrase means," she said to Sean. "I want to know why you're asking that."

She realized that she had repeated Quinn's words almost verbatim. She stole a guilty look in his direction, regretting that she snapped at him. Then she turned back to Sean and glared at him.

"Well, duh!" he said. "Look how small you are. What do you think you're going to do? Flick this Kelpie thing on the nose? Or are you planning to talk harshly to it? That'll probably work."

"I'm going to stick it with this," she replied, pulling the dragon's tooth from her belt.

"Oh, yeah," he said mockingly. "That will really worry her. I know it's scaring me. I'm quivering."

Solveig took a menacing step towards Sean.

"All right," he said holding up his hands. "All right. Please. Don't stab me with that splinter. You can't seriously think you can do some damage with that, can you?"

"It worked on that other Kelpie," Solveig answered defiantly.

"But it was much longer," said Stella.

"Solveig," said Natalie. "I appreciate your bravery, but I think Sean is right. You and your dragon's tooth have become so small, I doubt that weapon would penetrate the Kelpie's skin, and you might be putting yourself in jeopardy needlessly."

"We have to hurry," urged Stella. "The others are on their way."

"But what can either one of you do?" Solveig objected. "You can't cast spells with the same power as either Lochen or Stella, and Stella's spells won't work. If they did, we could have destroyed the other Kelpies by now."

"We'll think of something," answered Natalie. "But I really don't think the tooth will be effective."

"I'm not so sure," interjected Lochen. "We have no indication that the Kelpie must actually be stabbed with the tooth. It's possible that a simple scratch may suffice. I don't think we have a choice but to allow Solveig to go with you."

"What if I take the tooth?" asked Natalie.

She reached out her hand. Solveig looked at it, and then back to the tooth. It was impossible for her to hide her disappointment. Her shoulders slumped and she held the tooth up towards Natalie. Natalie reached down, with her palm open and Solveig handed the tiny object over.

"Ow!" Natalie shouted. "Take it back! Take it back. It's burning me. Hurry!"

She forced herself to keep her hand still so the tooth wouldn't drop to the deck and fall through the cracks. She could hear the skin on her hand sizzling with the heat generated from the tooth. When Solveig snatched it back, there was a small mark where the tooth had left an imprint. It had gotten so cold that it felt like fire.

"Are you all right?" Summer asked.

"Yes," Natalie replied. "I think so."

She shook her hand ineffectually. Stella reached over and took it. There was nothing she could do to relieve the burning. Solveig smiled at the fact that the tooth was back in her possession and then immediately felt guilty that her friend had suffered.

"I guess that means I'm going with you," she announced.

"Well I hope you don't get eaten by a fish or something," said Sean. "You're going to look like bait down there."

"Thanks for the kind words," Solveig shot back.

"I'm just saying," he said. "You may have that tooth, but you're still tiny."

"We'll protect her," said Stella.

"How do you expect to breathe?" asked Quinn.

"I can wrap her in a bubble," said Natalie.

"And I can make it so we can speak and hear," said Stella. "But we have to hurry."

"Yes," said Lochen. "Go. Go now."

Natalie climbed over the side and dropped into the water, cutting it like a knife with almost no splash at all. Stella followed her with the same ease and grace. Lochen bent down and picked Solveig up to carry her to the side of the ship.

"Please be careful," he said to her. "If I thought I would be of any use, I would join you."

"No," said Solveig. "You're needed more up here. I'll be careful."

He hesitated a moment as if he had more to say, but then leaned as far over the side as he could, extended his arm and let her slide off his hand into the water. She disappeared instantly from sight.

As soon as she was under water, Natalie and Stella joined her. Natalie waved her hand in a large circle around Solveig. Solveig didn't notice anything different, nor did she feel any different, except that she could breathe.

"Wow," she said, surprised that she could also talk. "This is great."

"Don't get too far away from us," cautioned Natalie. "It's hard to see you. Your blue color blends in with the water."

"Yeah," agreed Stella. "Your red hair floating behind you looks like algae or kelp."

"Don't worry," answered Solveig. "I'm not letting either one of you out of my sight."

They exchanged glances and then let Stella take the lead. She closed her eyes for a few seconds to bring up the map, fixed the location of the Kelpie, and then turned towards the ocean floor. She looked over her shoulder to make sure the others were ready and then gave a strong kick with her legs. Solveig followed immediately behind, and Natalie trailed after Solveig.

The deeper they went, the darker the water became and the less visible Solveig became. At Natalie's insistence, Stella slowed down as they sank lower and lower. Before long, all that Natalie could see of Solveig was her hair. Other than that, she was completely invisible. The white of the dragon's tooth in her belt was merely a speck.

Without explanation Stella suddenly stopped. Motion to her right caught her attention. They were close to the bottom by now and she spotted an outcropping of coral. She darted into it to take shelter and Natalie and Solveig followed right behind.

"What is it?" asked Solveig. "What did you see?"

"Look," she said, pointing to what seemed to Solveig to be nothing more than a shadow.

"What?" Solveig asked again. "I don't see anything."

"Eels," answered Natalie. "Hundreds of them."

"And jellyfish," added Stella. "Hundreds of them, too."

Solveig strained to look. Still she could only see what she had assumed was either a shadow, perhaps of the boat above them, or a reflection of the clouds. Then, as the black mass got closer, she could see distinct shapes.

"Oh, poop," she muttered. "Those things are huge."

"They're dangerous, too," said Natalie.

"I thought eels were smaller and sort of...you know...harmless?" Solveig said.

"These are moray eels," said Stella. "They can get to be as big as fifteen feet long. And they are far from harmless."

"They have big teeth and a strong bite," added Natalie. "Their rear teeth are hooked, so when they bite into something, they can't let go."

"Wonderful," said Solveig. "I guess I don't have to worry about that. I'd just be an appetizer. I suppose it could be worse. They could be poisonous."

"They are," said Stella. "At least this variety is."

"It looks like they're shaking their heads," Solveig said. "What are they doing?"

"They're communicating with each other," explained Natalie. "They're preparing to hunt. This coral isn't going to be safe pretty soon. They can get into some really narrow places."

They dropped down to the sandy bottom and inched away from the coral. To their left was a shelf, which lead to a drop further down into the ocean. Stella headed there, keeping an eye on the school of eels. She carefully stepped over the edge of the shelf and floated downward with Natalie and Solveig following. The eels circled in and out of the coral above them, but the jellyfish appeared to be following them.

"I was afraid of that," said Stella.

"That's not something that I want to hear," said Solveig. "What now?"

"The jellyfish," she answered.

"Those are Medusa jellyfish," said Natalie. "They get pretty big, too – as much as six feet across."

"I can barely see them," said Solveig. "They don't look so mean. Don't tell me they have teeth."

"No," said Stella. "No teeth, but those tentacles can be as long as twenty feet. And, before you ask, yes; they're poisonous."

"Where did they come from?" Solveig asked. "Are they normally in these waters?"

"No," said Natalie. "I've never heard of them being this far out in the ocean, or this deep. And I've never seen so many in one place."

"The bugs," said Stella.

"What bugs?" asked Solveig. "What are you talking about?"

"The bugs that Sean found," she answered. "The ones he said disappeared down the drain in the boat's galley."

"That's what was in those sacks?" exclaimed Solveig. "Oh, man, it's a good thing we didn't try to eat that stuff."

"The granules in those sacks must change into eels or jellyfish – or both – when they enter the water," said Natalie.

"Why would Artabarat have something like that?" wondered Solveig.

"To prey on the Sea Sprites," said Natalie. "We're their favorite food."

"I wish they'd go away," said Solveig.

"I think they know where this Kelpie is," said Stella. "And I think that, although they can't release it, maybe they intend to keep us from destroying it until its friends get here."

"Do we have much further to go?" Natalie asked.

"No," said Stella. "I think what we're looking for is in that cave."

She pointed to a cleft in the rocks and the sea floor that was about twenty feet in front of them. They burrowed into the sand and crawled across the expanse, keeping watch on the predators above them and avoiding the trailing tentacles of the jellyfish. Once they reached the mouth of the cave, they were out of reach of the jellyfish, but in danger of being trapped by the eels.

"What now?" asked Natalie.

"There's no other access to this cave," said Stella. "I can't tell you how I know that. I just do. The Kelpie is in there somewhere."

She knew that she should stand guard at the entryway in case the eels made an appearance. She hoped that her powers would enable her to fend them off. But there was no way she could suggest that her Princess put herself at risk by going into a cave without knowing what was ahead.

She also knew that she should be going into the cave to ward off any spells or tricks of the Kelpies. Unfortunately, she saw no way to be in both places at once. Natalie was quick to come to this same conclusion, and made the decision for both of them.

"Stella," she said. "I need you to stay here at the opening. Protect us from anything that may try to get in and stop us – or at least buy us some time."

"But…" Stella started to object.

"No," interrupted Natalie. "But nothing. If those eels or jellyfish or anything else comes in here, it's for one purpose only: to keep us from destroying that Kelpie. Nothing is going to wander in here by accident. We need you and your powers to let us do what we need to do."

"Yes, your Highness," Stella answered begrudgingly.

"This ought to be great," Solveig muttered. "A wounded Sea Sprite with no special powers and an hors d'oeuvre taking on the Demon of the Deep. Sounds like a bedtime story."

"Let's just hope it has a happy ending," said Natalie.

At that, the two slowly swam deeper into the cave. The depths outside of the cave had been dark, but now the darkness enveloped everything. As soon as it became completely black, it started to lighten. Natalie stopped and motioned for Solveig to do the same.

"What now?" whispered Solveig.

"Dragon fish," Natalie answered.

"That doesn't sound good," Solveig whispered even more quietly.

"It's not," said Natalie.

"Worse than eels?"

"Different," Natalie explained. "They're not as big, and they're not poisonous, but their teeth are bigger – and sharper."

"Where is the light coming from?"

"Them."

"What?" asked Solveig. "How? Can they cast spells?"

"They have these sensors all over their bodies or dangling from these antenna-like things that hang in front of their mouths."

"In front of their mouths?" Solveig asked.

"Yes. The light attracts smaller fish."

"So what is the light...oh," said Solveig, finally understanding that the light was bait. "This just keeps getting better."

"One good thing, though," said Natalie. "They don't see very well."

"That's good."

"But their sense of smell is incredible."

"I didn't need to know that part."

They slowly maneuvered their way through the school of dragon fish, careful to stay away from any dangling lights. Then they came to a narrow fissure in the rock. The dragon fish swam back and forth in front of the opening as if on sentry duty.

"I think we've found the Kelpie," said Solveig.

"We need to figure out a way to get by the dragon fish," said Natalie.

"No," said Solveig. "We don't need to do that. I do. Is there any way you can create a diversion?"

"I can generate a burst of light."

"I'm not sure that will do much," Solveig said. "With a light hanging right in front of their faces, I don't think a burst of light will have much effect."

"I think it will," Natalie disagreed. "Their light is generated by something in their bodies. It's a soft light. Look at it. You can stare at it and not be affected by it. I think a burst of a brighter light and from something else will create enough confusion for you to get inside that chamber."

"I hope you're right."

"Me, too," said Natalie. "Just in case, don't look at the light and be ready to hide."

Solveig moved as close to the opening as she dared. She didn't trust the fact that Stella and Natalie had a hard time seeing her. These fish lived in the dark. She was certain that, if nothing else, her red hair made a tempting morsel. She lowered herself into the sand and prepared to spring up and into the crease in the rock.

Natalie slowly floated to the top of the cave. About a half dozen dragon fish noticed something moving and lazily swam in that direction. Natalie stopped and waited until it seemed like they lost interest and went back to where they were. She continued upward until she was at the top. She hoped Solveig was well hidden. She could see no sign of her friend.

She closed her eyes and hoped that Solveig was doing the same thing. Then she brought her hands together the way Stella had once shown her and concentrated on creating a small ball of energy. A tiny static burst appeared and she flung it forward. It was disappointingly small, and not very bright. She was afraid she had not only failed, but that she had alerted the dragon fish to her location.

In spite of her doubts, the flash had the desired effect. The dragon fish were startled and their limited vision was further diminished. They reacted with a frenzy, darting forward and backwards, bumping into and snapping at one another. The water was filled with churning fins, bouncing lights, flashing teeth and each other's blood. In the chaos, Solveig propelled herself by them and into the even darker chamber.

All the other Kelpies had been encased in some kind of material – ice, rock, wood, etc. Ollos Foscos, however, was not. She had been sequestered inside a small dark cavity inside a deep dark cave and held in place by generations of dragon fish. Solveig had no idea what to expect.

She pressed herself against what felt like the side of the hole and waited until her heartbeat slowed back to normal. Before that happened, she felt the wall she was leaning against move. She froze.

Outside, things were returning to normal. The dragon fish resumed their languid floating from one side of the cave to the other and back. As they passed the opening to the nook in which Solveig now found herself, thin beams of light penetrated the dark.

Solveig waited for the next passing and focused on what was causing the wall to move. What she saw was not a wall. It was an enormous tentacle. It was smooth and black on the outside, but the inside was a dull gray and covered in large suction cups. In the center of each of the suckers were two curved and very sharp talons that faced one at the end of the sucker that was larger.

This is not good, Solveig thought. She moved her arms to swim away from the tentacle, but the motion she created alerted the creature to her presence.

"Who is here?"

The voice she heard was so deep that she could actually feel its vibrations. She froze. The sound attracted one of the dragon fish which turned its face towards the opening of the crypt. When it did, it illuminated the interior.

Go away, Solveig shouted to herself. She felt incredibly exposed. However, all that was visible was her hair drifting like gossamer in the water. The creature next to her shifted. The giant tentacle against which she had been leaning seemed to uncurl. It went on forever until the end eventually appeared. It was shaped like an elongated diamond and was covered by more and smaller suckers and teeth.

The tip flipped and then turned away from her as the body repositioned itself. A massive head floated within inches of Solveig and she willed herself to the ocean floor to avoid making contact. The dragon fish lunged forward, snapping its jaws and then as quickly resumed its position. It was as if it was firing a warning shot, keeping the Kelpie in its place.

The creature corkscrewed itself around once more. Tentacles whirled through the murky water over and around Solveig's head. She moved as stealthily as she could to avoid making contact, but the Kelpie knew something or someone was in the cramped quarters with it.

"Who is it?" Ollos Foscos demanded. "Is this another curse from the Alchemist? Show yourself."

Solveig had no intention whatsoever of showing herself. As the giant head rotated once more, she found for an instant that she was face to face with the monster. A single orange eye came into view. Beneath the eye was what Solveig could only assume was the center of the Kelpie's face. She caught a fleeting glimpse of a large beak. It moved in and out of a mass of puckered skin. It was disgusting, she thought.

She wondered where the voice was coming from; if the Kelpie spoke through that beak thing. Then she wondered why she was thinking such thoughts or why she even cared. She needed to stop wasting time thinking about stupid things and destroy this creature. She pulled the dragon's tooth from her belt.

She looked down at the tooth. It had shrunk at the same rate she had. Sean was right. It was a miserable excuse for a weapon. She looked up at the giant creature above her. Its skin must be inches thick, she thought. There's no way this tiny speck of a thing will have any effect at all. What was I thinking, she wondered.

She was about to give up, but then realized she had nothing – well, almost nothing – to lose. She could stick the creature or scratch it and scurry out of the cave. Maybe she could do some damage, although she seriously doubted it. She was about to take a jab at the Kelpie when she remembered something.

Artabarat had said to test the tip first. What did he mean by that? What was that supposed to prove? Could the tooth have gotten dull? Was he warning her that the tooth may not even cause a scratch? Why hadn't she done that before she came down here? Has my brain shrunk, too, she asked herself.

She held the tooth in her right hand. With her left hand she felt along the side from where she was holding it, moving upward to the tip. When she reached the top, she repositioned her thumb and pressed it against the point of the tooth. It was so sharp that she could barely feel it penetrate her skin. It sunk in almost half an inch before the nerves she was cutting into sent the message to her brain.

Ouch, she said to herself. It was more than sharp enough. Why had the sentinel thought otherwise? She pulled her hand away as the blood seeped from the small cut. In the darkness she couldn't see the trail of red mix with the sea and spread outward. But the dragon fish could smell it. And Ollos Foscos could smell it.

Dozens of the dragon fish turned towards the smell of blood. They crowded into the opening of the cavity, the lights dangling at the front of their bodies pouring light into the interior. Ollos Foscos flicked a tentacle in their direction and they scattered, but only for a second. Many of them snapped their massive jaws at the slithering arm, but none of them entered the smaller cave.

Solveig tried to curl up into as small a ball as she could and hide from sight. Then she felt a tingling in her left hand. Even with the additional light from the dragon fish, it was hard for her to see her own hand. However, she could feel it start to change. Her hand began to swell and then popped.

In an instant, her left hand was more than ten times the size of the rest of her. Before she could grasp what had happened, her left arm began to tingle, swell and pop. It was as if she was a balloon being inflated in sections. Her forearm expanded and was followed by her upper arm, then the left side of her body, down to her left thigh, her left leg and her left foot.

Then the swelling and expanding moved to her right foot, up her right leg to her right side, her head and then down her right arm to her right hand. The last thing that tingled, swelled and popped back to its original shape was the dragon's tooth.

All this time, Ollos Foscos watched in shock. For two thousand years she had been held captive. For two thousand years she had seen nothing but the images of the dragon fish as they floated past her cave. For two thousand years she had not seen, touched, smelled or heard another living soul. And now this figure that was barely discernible in the blue waters, except for the flowing red hair, was materializing right before her.

Solveig was as shocked as the Kelpie. Their astonishment subsided at almost the same instant. Ollos Foscos had no idea who this person was, but instinctively knew that she was a threat. She reared her head back as far as her cramped quarters would allow. She moved her tentacles to wrap Solveig in a death grip.

As fast as the Kelpie was, Solveig was slightly faster. She jammed the dragon's tooth upward, thrusting it inches below the beak that was quickly extending outward, right at her head. The tooth sunk easily into the flesh. At first it seemed as if nothing happened. Then the single orange eye appeared to register first the pain and then the realization of what had happened.

In a final effort, Ollos Foscos opened her massive beak and made a lunge at Solveig's head. She saw it coming at her, but she was unable to move. The tentacles had closed around her and held her in place. Added to that was her own fear and amazement at what she had done and her apprehension that it had no effect.

As the beak came within inches of her head, it dissolved into millions of bubbles of air. Behind the beak, the head, and then the body and tentacles also evaporated into a gush of air. Outside the cavity, the dragon fish seemed to sense that their duty no longer required their presence. They moved in their normal lethargic manner out of the cave and disappeared into the depths of the sea.

When Natalie saw the dragon fish leave, she worried that something bad had happened. Something changed to cause them to no longer stand guard at the Kelpie's prison. She knew she should have gone with Solveig. If something happened to her, she thought, I'll never forgive myself. She dived down from the ceiling of the cave and made a beeline to the hole that had held the Kelpie.

"Solveig," she called. "Are you...whoa!"

She stopped short. She had expected to have to search the darkness for her tiny friend, as well as defend herself against the monster. Instead she found Solveig returned to her full height, although still blue – it was beginning to look natural on her – and no sign whatsoever of the Kelpie.

"What happened?" she asked.

"I'm not exactly sure," Solveig answered. "I did what the sentinel told me. I tested the point of the tooth before I stabbed the Kelpie. It cut me and when I started to bleed, it attracted the dragon fish, which lit up the inside of this hole. Then that...thing...grabbed me and I...I just stabbed it.

"I thought I was gone for sure. That horrible beak was coming right at me, but at the last minute...I don't know what happened. It sort of evaporated or fizzled...something. It disappeared."

"But you're back to your normal size," exclaimed Natalie.

"Oh, yeah," said Solveig. "That happened, too. I guess I forgot."

"You forgot you were no longer small?' asked Natalie, not understanding. "OK. I guess. You're sure you're all right?"

"I'm fine," Solveig answered. "Let's just get out of here. Quickly. This place...and that thing give me the creeps."

They left the interior cave and carefully exited the outer chamber, making sure none of the dragon fish were lingering behind. When they got to the opening, they slowly poked their heads out to see if the eels and jellyfish were still a threat. They saw no evidence that they had been there. Stella sensed someone behind her and turned to see Natalie and Solveig.

"What happened?" she asked in amazement. "You almost look normal."

"I suppose that's a compliment," said Solveig.

She gave Stella a brief account of what she and Natalie had found inside and of how she had destroyed the Kelpie. Then she commented on the fact that there was no sign of the eels or the jellyfish.

"They're gone," said Stella. "It was the weirdest thing. They seemed to know where we were or where the Kelpie was and were headed this way. I couldn't decide if I should try to cast a spell on them or if one would even work. Then I felt this pendant begin to hum or vibrate, or something. I grabbed it and it actually felt hot. The next thing I knew was that there were all these air bubbles all over the place. And when they cleared…"

"The eels and the jellyfish were gone," Solveig finished her sentence.

"Yes," she said. "How did you know?"

"The same thing happened to that Kelpie."

"We should get back," Natalie interjected.

"You're right," agreed Stella. "The rest of the Kelpies were headed this way. They can't be too far behind. We need to leave this place – to get away from this ocean."

They started swimming upward, still keeping a watch out for any predators. They swam back to back in a tight triangle. Every once in a while Stella would look up towards the surface to keep them on course to the boat. Even though it was midday, there was little light coming from above.

They were all stunned when a sudden burst of light appeared. They stopped moving and looked upward. Over their heads appeared a large circle of red and yellow. A few seconds after it materialized they were pushed downward by a tremendous shock wave.

"What was that?" exclaimed Solveig.

"An explosion of some kind," said Natalie.

"The boat!" they all said at the same time.

Solveig lunged for the surface. She almost slipped past Stella and Natalie, but Natalie managed to grab her ankle and pulled her back.

"What are you doing?" she asked. "We need to see if the others need help."

"Look closely," said Natalie, pointing to the large red circle. "That's fire."

"Fire?" shouted Solveig. "All the more reason we need to help."

"No," said Stella. "The surface of the water is on fire. If we go up, wel'l rise into the middle of that inferno. We'll all be burned."

"We can't just do nothing," Solveig objected.

"We have to," insisted Natalie. "We won't do anyone any good if we get ourselves burned alive."

The ring of fire illuminated the surface – except for the dark rectangle in the center: the rectangle that was the boat. All Solveig could think of were Lochen's last words to her, exhorting her to be careful.

Chapter fourteen

B'nair looked over the collection of gargoyles the Ice Kelpie had assembled. He had to give the sorcerer credit. He had probably picked the best of what there was. The problem was that gargoyles were stupid and undisciplined. He would have a hard time getting them to do anything right. But that was not his problem.

The Lightning Riders reappeared, duplicated and interlinked themselves, once more wrapping their passengers in a fine electrical web. B'nair closed his eyes and summoned the map. One spot remained. It was far out into the ocean. He had never been fond of the sea. Flying over it only made things worse.

Quest of Eight Part Seven: Ad Paria

Richard Reda

He had done his best to encourage Akmen Milzu to leave Rovek behind and to get to this last Kelpie as soon as possible, but the Mountain Kelpie would not consider that option. He was dumbfounded when she elected to stop in this toilet bowl of a town and check on Saldeti. He was speechless at her seeming lack of urgency.

It was nearing midday, not that anyone could tell the difference between midday, mid-morning or mid-afternoon. The dull gray sky seemed to be a permanent fixture for as long as the Rebbercand could remember. In fact, he thought, he really couldn't recall the last sunny day.

When he opened his eyes, they were rising above the marina and headed out to sea. His stomach churned at the sight. Maybe it would be better if he kept his eyes closed, he thought. He no sooner shut them than the fatigue of the last several days overwhelmed him and he fell asleep.

Within minutes, the dream returned. As all the times before, the dream started with him falling. That's because you're so high in the air, he told himself. No it's not, he answered himself. You weren't in the air the other times you had this dream. He wondered which of his dream voices would win this argument.

As the old familiar sense of panic rose once more, he tried to tell himself to wake up, even though he knew he couldn't. As he was continuing his mental debate, the scene changed. He was on a bridge deep inside a cave. I've been here before, he thought. No, he corrected himself. It looks familiar because you've seen it before in this same dream.

I'm not going to argue, he told himself. He instinctively turned to see if the Kelpies were behind him, even though he knew they weren't. Where were they when you needed them, he asked. He didn't bother to answer. He had no answer.

When he turned back, he saw on the other side of the bridge what looked like a door. He had asked himself before where the light was coming from that allowed him to see the door. He hadn't received an answer before, so he didn't bother asking the question again.

He felt the presence of someone behind him but knew that no one was there. Still, he jerked his head around, hoping to get a glimpse of whatever was causing that sensation. As before, he was alone. He turned back to the door and could see it more clearly. He knew he would see it more clearly and wondered why he hadn't been able to see it as well from the beginning. What a strange dream, he thought.

He had forgotten about the tingling against his chest until he felt it again. When he looked down and saw the flash of light coming from the stone he was wearing around his neck, he knew that this, too, had happened before. What comes next he wondered. As hard as he tried, he could not recall, until it happened.

He pulled the stone from under his tunic and the chamber in which he was standing was illuminated. He looked at the stone and then back to the door. More light was coming from

319

something in the center of the door. I knew that, he thought. He tried to move towards the door, but couldn't. His inability to move his feet caused a sense of panic to sweep over him.

Relax, he told himself. You've dreamt this before. You know it all works out in the end. He just couldn't recall how the end actually worked out. As he was thinking this, he realized that the light was coming from the band that the Kelpies had mentioned. He could see the strange markings on the outer part of the rim.

Yes, he said to himself. The band. He said it as if he knew what it was and what it meant. But what does all this mean, he quickly asked himself. He could feel the answer. He could feel it just beyond the reach of his memory. In the instant he was certain it was all becoming clear, he felt a burning sensation in the center of his chest.

It distracted him. He forgot about the band, the light and the markings. He looked down at his right hand. The axe was still in his hand, but one of the blades was driven into the ground. The pain increased. It was becoming unbearable.

He moved his free hand to the spot where the pain was most intense. He could feel, but not see, something protruding from the center of his body. He couldn't recall anything burning so intensely. He felt the object from where it seemed planted in his chest and reached outward. He opened his eyes. Scirios had his finger pressed against his chest.

"You were asleep," the Kelpie said with a strange smile on his face.

"I closed my eyes for just a second," B'nair said.

"You need to tell us how close we are," Scirios said.

"Of course," answered the Rebbercand.

He closed his eyes for a second or two, summoned the map and then opened them. He pointed straight ahead and said they were only a few miles away. At that instant he felt something change. He closed his eyes again and the marker for Ollos Foscos began to fade. He knew the Kelpie was gone. They were too late.

He decided not to say anything. They would find out soon enough. In fact, they found out sooner than he thought they would. He could feel a shift in the mood of the Kelpies. He realized they had immediately sensed what he had seen.

"NO!" shouted Neraka Ferr.

Neraka Ferr was so agitated that the others began to worry that he would disrupt the web of the Lightning Riders. He was furious. He began to scream incoherently and to thrash.

"We share your anguish," said Akmen Milzu. "We will have our revenge on those who have done this."

321

Quest of Eight Part Seven: Ad Paria
Richard Reda

In a few minutes they could see the ancient boat of the acrobat. It was sitting idly on the waves. They could see several figures on the deck. The figures spotted them and scurried below, as if that would save them. B'nair believed that there was nothing that would protect them from the wrath of the Fire Kelpie.

- - - - - - - - - - - - - - - - - ******* - - - - - - - - - - - - - - - - -

When Lochen had lowered Solveig into the water, he had grave misgivings, but he was unable to determine the source. Ultimately, he dismissed those feelings, assuming they were due to his being separated from her while she placed herself in harm's way. It was a situation he was not comfortable with and had difficulty accepting.

"What happens if Natalie, Stella and Solveig are able to eliminate this Kelpie down below?" asked Liam. "Does that stop them from whatever they're planning on doing?"

"I don't know," said Lochen. "I haven't gotten that far in the translations."

"When we were separated," said Liam, "Sean, Stella, Solveig and I met one of the sentinels in the Ice Kingdom. He told us that we had to maintain the balance; that there were eight in the beginning to face the others."

"That's right," said Sean. "What?" he asked when Liam looked at him in astonishment. "I was paying attention."

322

"Only because you couldn't go anywhere," said Liam.

"Whatever!" replied Sean. "Anyway, he told us that evil had risen again and that it couldn't rain without a checkup or something like that."

"Oh, yeah," muttered Liam. "You were really paying attention. What he said was that evil had to be balanced, that it couldn't rein free – not rain without a checkup. Really?"

"I was close," whined Sean.

"Not even," said Liam. "He also told us that all things had to be in balance; that there were eight to fight the evil that was growing unchecked."

"I told you," objected Sean. "There's that checkup part."

"Evil will destroy all if those who are good do nothing," said Lochen.

"That's right," said Liam. "That's exactly what he said. How did you know?"

"That statement was in the Alchemist's book," said Lochen.

"All right, then," said Liam. "So what does it mean if there are only seven Kelpies, or six?"

"Or none," added Quinn. "I like that better: none."

"I think it was an analogy," said Lochen. "I don't think the exact numbers are important as far as we're concerned; although I think all eight of the Kelpies have to be together for them to gain full control."

"But we already got rid of one," said Sean.

"Yes," agreed Lochen, "but that doesn't seem to have stopped them, which is why I don't believe the exact number is critical."

"Does that mean we have to fight all of them?" asked Quinn.

"Possibly," Lochen answered. "But let's deal with one thing at a time," he added after he saw the look of despair on Quinn's face.

Their conversation was interrupted by a rush of air bubbles that burst through the surface of the water all around the boat. There were thousands of them. The disturbance shook the ship so much that Summer had to take flight to keep from being jiggled off the deck and into the ocean.

When she gained a little bit of altitude, she could see an enormous circle of air bubbles around the little vessel. As soon as they had appeared, they were gone. She was lowering herself back to the deck when she noticed a flash of electrical discharge in the distance. She stayed aloft and turned in the direction of the flickering.

It was high in the sky and blocked by the low, dark clouds. However, it had been strong enough to break through the thick, gray cover. She fluttered a little higher to see if she could get a better view. As soon as she did, she was filled with dread. She didn't know why, but some deep instinct was telling her that danger was approaching. She wasn't alone in that feeling.

"Summer," Lochen called. "Please come back."

She didn't need to be asked twice; she turned and darted back to the deck of the ship. As she was returning, she could see the others were looking up at the sky in the same direction she had. Lochen had moved to the front of the ship; Sean was stretching forward, out of the stairwell; Liam was holding on to the side rail, and Quinn had the wheel gripped tightly in his hands. But all faces were pointed upward.

"What is it?" she shouted.

"Get below deck," Lochen urged. "Now! Go now!"

Sean jumped down and out of the way. Liam scrambled after him, followed by Summer. Quinn was still holding the wheel. Lochen backed away from the bow towards the stairwell. He turned in time to see Quinn riveted in place.

"Quinn!" he shouted. "Get below."

"But what about the boat?" he asked. "I can't let us go off course. Natalie and Stella and Solveig might not be able to find us."

"The ship is anchored," Lochen answered. "You holding the wheel is doing nothing. Now, will you please get below?"

He looked from Lochen to the sky to the wheel and back again, confused. Then realization sunk in. He released his grip and ran to the stairwell. Lochen moved to let him by and stole another glance at the sky. He could feel the power and the anger high above him. The Kelpie below must be destroyed, he thought.

He started down the stairs, but at the last moment, he turned back to the source of the lightning and waved his arms in a sweeping circle. He barely returned them to his sides when he felt a tremendous burst of energy knock him from his feet and throw him down the stairs to the floor below.

As he landed at the bottom of the stairs, he could see an explosion of flame engulf the upper part of the ship. He quickly rolled to one side as a large tongue of fire flicked down the stairwell and then disappeared.

"Quickly," he said, scrambling to his feet. "Move to the cargo hold."

Quest of Eight Part Seven: Ad Paria

Richard Reda

As soon as they were all inside the hold, Lochen pulled the door shut. He motioned for them all to move as far to the front as possible and then looked for some escape route. There was none. He wondered if he had doomed them all.

------------------- *** -------------------

As the figures below them scurried down the hatch to the interior of the ship, Neraka Ferr clenched his fist and hurled a giant ball of flame down on top of them. B'nair watched as the last one of the figures waved his arms uselessly before being blasted into the hold. What was he thinking, the Rebbercand wondered. Did he really believe he could stave off the anger of the Kelpie?

The fire engulfed the ship, attaching itself to the sail and the mast first and then spreading out across the deck. In seconds the entire craft was burning. B'nair looked from the ship to Neraka Ferr. The Fire Kelpie was still enraged. He was looking for something else to destroy, but there was nothing.

"Burn the sea," said Scirios.

Neraka Ferr snapped his head in the direction of the Lightning Kelpie, wondering if he was being mocked. He fought to control his anger. Seeing that Scirios was being earnest, he looked back at the ocean. They might somehow escape the burning boat, he realized. They could swim to safety. His friend had been right. He needed to burn the sea.

Quest of Eight Part Seven: Ad Paria

Richard Reda

He roared in anger as he once more balled his fist and hurled another explosion of flame downward. This one burst before it hit the ship and spread out across the surface of the water in a circle at least a hundred feet across. It wasn't extinguished by the water, but seemed to feed on it instead. B'nair had never seen water burn before.

"What's happening?" asked Ena Ray. "What's wrong?"

He did not yet have the ability to share the sensations that the Kelpies did. While he was a replacement for the one that had been lost, he was still not one of them. He didn't understand what was going on.

"The Kelpie we have come for has been destroyed," B'nair told him.

Ena Ray studied the Rebbercand. How could he know this and I cannot, he wondered. B'nair could read the puzzlement on Ena Ray's face. He debated about sharing how he knew and then considered that there was no reason to keep it secret.

"The map that has been imbedded in my memory," he explained, "allowed me to see that this Kelpie had been destroyed shortly before we arrived."

"And if we had left when you urged us," interjected Akmen Milzu, "we might have prevented this."

B'nair wasn't sure if the acknowledgement of her error was a good thing for him or not. His experience was that people in power did not like it when their underlings pointed out their shortcomings or mistakes. He knew that in spite of all he had done for these sorcerers, he was not viewed by them as an equal. He was an underling and always would be.

"You were right," she added. "I will not fail to follow your urging in the future."

What future, wondered B'nair. As he thought these thoughts, Ena Ray brazenly verbalized them.

"What happens now?" he demanded. "Do we all go on our merry way as if the last two thousand years never happened? Is there no one to take our vengeance on? Do we go meekly into oblivion?"

Is he crazy, thought B'nair. He wished there was a way to free himself from the grip of the Lightning Riders and put some distance between him and Ena Ray. He could see the rage in Akmen Milzu coming to a boiling point and he didn't want to be anywhere near when it erupted.

"We need the eight of us," the Mountain Kelpie replied through clenched teeth. "With Ollos Foscos gone, there will only be seven. Do you propose that we split you in half?"

Instead of answering the taunt, Ena Ray turned to B'nair.

Quest of Eight Part Seven: Ad Paria

Richard Reda

"How did you know to find me?" he asked.

B'nair was taken aback by the question. Of what importance was that now? He was uncomfortable with the way this upstart was digging himself deeper and deeper into trouble. He was going to cause the Mountain Kelpie to do something rash and they would all suffer for it. He looked from Ena Ray to Akmen Milzu and back. He swallowed hard before answering.

"An indicator appeared on my map. It told me that someone or something was present where we found you. It was a marker similar to the ones that identified where the Kelpies were located. It hadn't been there before, but once the first one was destroyed, and we got closer to where you were, it became more distinct."

"And how do you read this map?" Ena Ray asked.

"It is in my mind's eye," the Rebbercand answered. "I see it when I close my eye."
"Then close it now and look at your map," directed Ena Ray.

"And what am I looking for?" asked B'nair.

"When I was being trained by the witch, there was another with me," he said. "We were both banished by her at the same time. If I can replace one of the Kelpies, he may be able to replace the other."

"Where am I to look?" B'nair questioned.

"I have no idea," said Ena Ray. "You found me without help. Do the same now."

"She had two protégés?" asked Akmen Milzu.

"How was this kept from us?" asked Angin Topan.

"Where were you trained?" the Mountain Kelpie asked Ena Ray, ignoring the question from the imp.

"It was a citadel of some kind," Ena Ray answered. "It was enormous, but it was all hidden inside a tree in the middle of some village. There was a portal that we passed through to go from her citadel to the town and back. I don't know where the village was, though."

"Boravak," Akmen Milzu gasped. "I thought that was only a myth."
"Boravak?" asked Ena Ray. "That was the name of the village? Do you know where it is?"

"I see it," announced B'nair, cutting off all other conversation. "It's well south of here. It looks like it, too, is in the middle of the ocean, but there appears to be some kind of island."

"We need to leave at once," declared Akmen Milzu. "Scirios, please direct the Lightning Riders."

331

"No," objected Neraka Ferr. "Not until I'm sure they have all been devoured by the fire."

"Burn more of the sea," said Angin Topan. "Make it so there is no place for them to surface."

The Fire Kelpie did not find this a satisfactory answer, but knew they had to make haste. They could not allow these intruders to thwart their efforts again. He half-heartedly delivered another ball of fire to the conflagration below. As soon as it had been sent downward, the Lightning Riders lifted their passengers higher into the air and turned to the south.

- - - - - - - - - - - - - - - - *** - - - - - - - - - - - - - - - - -

Inside the hold of the small boat, the air was becoming extremely hot. Lochen had moved away from the hatch he had shut, but it, too, was starting to burn. Above them, fingers of flame had worked their way through the decking and were searching for more fuel to burn. Quinn had scooped Liam, Summer and Sean and was huddled over them in an effort to protect them.

"We need to see if we can puncture the hull," said Lochen. "Does anyone see any tools or other implements that we can use to create a hole?"

"You want to poke a hole in the bottom of the boat?" asked Sean. "Are you completely mental?"

332

Quest of Eight Part Seven: Ad Paria
Richard Reda

The room was filling with smoke and it was becoming difficult to breathe. Quinn started coughing. Pieces of the deck were breaking up and flaming chunks were dropping into the hold. Lochen ran from one to another stomping on them to extinguish the fire.

"Do you have an alternative idea?" he asked.

"You'll drown us," complained Sean.

"We either take our chances in the water, or face the certainty of this fire," he shouted over the roaring flames.

"The only tools I saw were at the other end of the boat," said Sean.

"I'll get them," offered Quinn.

"No," said Lochen. "You're too big. You wouldn't be able to run fast enough and keep your head low enough at the same time. The smoke will be too thick."

"I'll go," said Sean. "I'm the smallest, except for Summer, and she couldn't carry anything back. Besides, I'm the only one who knows where that stuff is."

"All right," said Lochen. "Be quick and be careful. Wait."

He cast a quick spell on Sean and he found himself drenched in water.

"What did you do that for?" he asked. "You know how much I hate water."

"It will keep the flames off you," said Lochen. "At least for a short while. Don't waste any time. If you don't find anything right away, get back here."

Lochen grabbed the door latch and pulled it open. As soon as he did, he cast another quick spell, shooting a torrent of water at the flames. This wasn't an ordinary fire, and his spell didn't have the same power against it. There was a loud hissing sound and a lot of steam. The flames were temporarily smothered – long enough for Sean to make a mad dash across the galley to the equipment room.

Lochen left the door open and kept generating water to hold the fire at bay. He could tell he was losing ground. The Kelpie's spell had been too powerful. He only hoped he could hold things off long enough for Sean to get back with something.

In a few seconds, he saw the Forest Creature running towards him with a long pipe in his hand. As he darted past Lochen and back into the hold, Lochen could see that much of Sean's hair had been burned and the skin on his neck and back was raw from burning. What a mess I've gotten them into, he thought.

"What did you find?" Quinn asked excitedly.

"This was all I could find," Sean answered, holding up the pipe.

"It's a bar," said Quinn dejectedly. "It's a pole. It's round at both ends. We can't pry anything loose with that!"

"I thought maybe we could ram it into the wood," Sean offered.

"Ram it into the wood?" repeated Quinn. "You're not serious, are you? Do you have any idea how thick this wood is?"

"Can you cast a spell on it and break it apart?" Liam asked Lochen.

"No," he answered. "Consider how old this ship is – more than two thousand years. How do you think it has lasted so long? It's been protected by spells more powerful than mine. I think we have to give Sean's pole a try. Perhaps with enough force we could dislodge some of the planks."

"Wait a minute," said Summer. "What happens if we only make a small hole and all it does is let the ocean in – before we can make it big enough to get out?"

"You have a point there," admitted Lochen. "I hadn't foreseen that."

"We have to do something," Quinn sputtered between coughs. "The smoke is really getting bad, and so is the fire. Give me that thing."

He grabbed the pole out of Sean's hand and moved Liam out of the way. He looked for a spot near the front of the hull, where he hoped the wood would be the weakest. He raised the pole as high as he could and rammed it downward with all his strength. He aimed for a seam between planks and struck his target. Nothing happened.

The pole struck the wood and left a mark in the grain, sinking into the waterlogged hull about a half-inch. When Quinn pulled the pole up to strike again, the indentation disappeared. Sean was standing behind him with his arm wrapped around one of Quinn's legs, looking on. Summer was hovering over Sean's shoulder, and Liam and Lochen were trying to look around the both of them. All eyes were on the spot where the pole had been driven into the wood.

"Try again," urged Summer.

Quinn drove the pole once more into the wood. Once more the pole dug into the hull, sinking about a half inch. Once more, when Quinn raised it to strike again, the indentation faded away.

"Maybe the wood is soft because of the water," suggested Summer. "Hold on a second."

She dropped down to feel where the pole had contacted the hull. She could find nothing different. The wood all around was completely solid. The pole was having no effect.

"Nothing," she said. "I think that's a waste of time. I don't think we're getting out of here."

As she spoke those last words, a long, white, pointed object drove through the planks mere inches from her feet. She jumped up with a shriek.

"Hey!" she shouted. "What was that?"

When the object receded, no water came pouring through as they had expected; however the hole remained. Again, the object shot up through the hull. This time it was a few inches away from the first hole. And again, when it receded, no water poured through.

"It must be some kind of giant sea creature," said Liam.

"Oh great," whined Sean. "If we don't get burned to death, or choked to death by smoke, or drowned in water, we're going to get eaten by some sea monster. I don't think I can make a decision about which way to go. There are too many choices."

The piercing of the hull came faster and faster and took the shape of a large circle. One hole after another appeared, but still no water came through. Once the circle was completed, more holes in between the first line were drilled by the object until they all touched upon one another like a series of connected dots. Then a pair of fingers appeared and pulled the inner circle away from the deck.

Everyone backed away, expecting a gush of water to flood the compartment, but instead, a head appeared.

"Don't just stand there," shouted Solveig. "This ship is burning up, and Natalie's bubble won't keep the water out much longer."

Summer didn't wait for any more of an invitation. She darted by the others and out through the hole. She found herself inside a large bubble of air that Natalie had attached to the exterior of the hull. That explained why no water seeped in. She looked at Solveig, who was her normal size, but still blue – although the shade of blue seemed to be a bit lighter. In her hand was the dragon's tooth, also returned to its normal size. Solveig had used it to create the hole.

Quinn grabbed Liam and pushed him through the hole and then shoved Sean out. Sean resisted, fearful of getting soaked, but Quinn easily overpowered him, picking him up by the scruff of his neck and tossing him unceremoniously through the opening. He reached for Lochen next.

"I can manage on my own, thank you," Lochen replied.

He quickly lowered himself out of the cargo hold. Quinn went last. As he did, the flames finished devouring everything above, and the ceiling above him caved in at the instant he disappeared into the sea.

The entire boat came apart, splitting along the keel and breaking open. As it did, Natalie's bubble had nothing to hold to and it too broke open. The contents of the cargo hold dropped into the water. Some of the crates dropped towards the ocean floor, while others bobbed to the surface.

Lochen began to swim upward, but Solveig grabbed his leg and motioned towards the fire that could be seen for hundreds of yards circling above them on the surface. Lochen made a gesture indicating that it was all right, gently removed her hand from his leg and continued upward.

Sean was flailing more than necessary, fighting against Natalie, who was trying to keep him from the surface. She gave up when she saw Solveig release Lochen and watched as Lochen casually swam upward. The rest of them followed him. When they broke the surface, they found a wide layer of air between the water and the fire.

"Where did this come from?" asked Stella.

"When I saw the Kelpies coming," answered Lochen, "I assumed they would try to harm us. Fire made the most sense. It would destroy the boat, and strand us in the ocean. I created this layer of air in the event the three of you tried to return to the surface without knowing what was awaiting you. I had no idea that the rest of us would need it as well."

"What now?" asked Natalie.

"We need to get to shore," Lochen answered. "I have more information to share with you and our next destination lies in that direction."

Chapter fifteen

he Kelpies made their way south, bypassing the port town of Nohkmar Cambin. It was just as well. The town was now deserted. There were no ships in the harbor, and no signs of life in the town. The Kelpies soared across the sky and over the sea – far out into the ocean until the tiny island came into view.

They arrived at the time the tide was receding and the volcano was emerging from the sea. The water was being sucked down into the shaft, creating a large whirlpool. Unlike the last visitors here, they had no problems landing on the shore of the tiny island or entering the mouth of the volcano. The Lightning Riders lowered them to the beach by the interior lake.

During the descent, Scirios generated a ball of light and illuminated the shaft. Once they landed and were all released from the electrical web, they surveyed the interior of the volcano. What they saw was a graveyard of ships of various types and sizes. They were the same wrecks that had been here for centuries, drawn down into the giant whirlpool that was created each time the tides shifted and the water that normally covered the volcanic cone rose and lowered.

"Where do we go from here?" asked Angin Topan.

She was flitting around the large cavern, searching for a sign as to where to go. All she saw were the broken hulls, shattered masts, and rotted sails that littered the basin. In the meantime, B'nair had crossed the sandy beach and had been walking along the walls that encircled the far side of the cavern. He knew there had to be a passageway somewhere. He could feel the proximity of the sorcerer that would replace the last Kelpie, but could see no sign of a crypt.

He looked up at the shaft through which the water was tumbling down and the pool into which it was emptying. The water was still falling at a steady rate, but something was not right. He studied the water. The level of the pool was not rising, he realized. The water must be going someplace, he thought.

He continued walking along the edge of the pool, oblivious to the grumbling questions of the Kelpies. At the far side, he saw a small, low opening that ran under the cavern wall. There was a break in the side, and the water was flowing under the wall and through some kind of trough in an underground stream.

"This is the way," he announced.

341

He stepped into the shallow stream, not waiting to see if he was being followed, ducked under the wall and disappeared into a tunnel. It was a tight fit for him. He knew that Akmen Milzu and Neraka Ferr, who were much bigger, would not make it through. Then he heard a rumbling sound as the Mountain Kelpie pushed the walls and ceiling of the tunnel out.

B'nair hoped her actions wouldn't threaten the stability of the rest of the volcano. He knew how fragile something like that could be. When he oversaw the mining operations of the Trepans, he had witnessed the effects of careless displacement of walls and what happened to those who acted carelessly. He had no wish to be buried alive.

After about a hundred more yards, the tunnel ended at a larger vault. The water from the stream continued a short way past the opening to the vault and then dropped over the edge of an immense waterfall. The path continued in a circle around the falls to the other side where it widened out. At various points on the path there were five large fissures in the walls. They were doorways, he realized.

B'nair could sense immediately which of the openings was the right one, but waited to see if any of the others had the same sensation. They all looked to him with blank expressions waiting for him to decide.. Either they had no clue or were very good at masking their knowledge. He was certain they had no clue.

As he walked past the first fissure, there was a rumble, followed by a grinding sound. He looked in the direction of the sound.

"Trap doors," he explained, as if he knew what they were.

He was as surprised as the Kelpies, but felt he needed to keep control of the situation by letting them believe he knew what to expect. He surmised that the Alchemist, or the witch, had created this place. If so, there were certain to be traps. He was right. Once they had all walked by the doorway, it shifted and revealed a different path on the other side.

He continued walking. When he came to the third opening, he felt a prickling against his chest. He casually reached into his tunic and removed the pendant. It was warm to his touch – warmer than merely from the contact with his skin. The stone had also faded from gold to a brownish red. He decided to take a chance.

"In here," he said, and he stepped through.

The others followed. Before them was a long, narrow passage, as far as they could see, until it faded into the darkness. On each side of the passage were dozens of openings. Some were large, and others were quite small. Scirios snapped his fingers and a line of light rose to the ceiling and stretched out ahead of them, illuminating the tunnel.

"That should help you see that stone more clearly," he said.

"Thanks," B'nair replied when he couldn't think of anything else to say.

He looked down some of the openings, but didn't go in. He could see this was a giant labyrinth. As they all proceeded along the maze, the openings behind them sealed up, cutting off the exit and creating another, possibly false, passage.

"More of the Alchemist's petty trickery," said Akmen Milzu. "I could easily push this all aside."

"I wouldn't do that," replied B'nair. "He may have expected you, or someone else, to do exactly that. You could bury us all."

She begrudgingly admitted he was probably right. They continued on, twisting and turning to the right and to the left in no apparent pattern. The passageway grew narrower and narrower until they were required to walk in a single file. The Mountain Kelpie again raised her arms and pushed the walls apart, ignoring B'nair's earlier warning.

"I hope you are being careful," B'nair finally said.

"If we can't fit through," she replied, "it won't really matter, will it?"

In spite of her bravado, Akmen Milzu dropped her arms and looked up at the ceiling and then to the walls. She breathed a silent sigh of relief when she saw no signs of damage. They continued in silence through several more turns until they finally came through the last opening into an antechamber. In the center of the chamber was a large stone box.

"I believe the one you need is in there," said B'nair, pointing to the crypt.

The Kelpies moved cautiously to the large cube. They looked down at the surface and could see that the dust that had accumulated over the last two thousand years had been swept aside not too long ago. They could see the image of a creature in the center of an inscription.

"Beware the treachery of Tebaga the Betrayer, placed in this sarcophagus by the Enchantress, Meri Hocto," read Akmen Milzu. "I think I like this person already."

B'nair assumed this tomb was like all the rest. He stepped forward and was about to swing his axe and cut into the stone, when Scirios stopped him.

"If this prison was created by an Enchantress," he said, "perhaps we should let one of her kind attempt to break the spell."

Everyone turned to Neraka Ferr. He wasn't sure what he was supposed to do. He hesitated for a few seconds, and then moved past the others and up to the cube. He raised his hands and brought them down with all his strength on the top. The block shuddered, shifted color slightly, but remained intact. He raised his hands again and began to cast a spell, but stopped before he even began.

"I don't know what spells were cast to create this prison," he said by way of explanation. "I don't know how to undo them."

Frustrated that they still had to rely on the Rebbercand, Akmen Milzu turned to him and gestured towards the block.

"Please," she said. "Let's see if your success can continue."

B'nair could feel the stone against his tunic vibrate. He didn't have to look at it to see that the color was changing to a blood red. He could feel the power of the pendant surge through his body and concentrate in the arm that held the axe. It was the same sensation he had felt in opening all the other tombs. This would be no different.

He brought the blade down swiftly into the center of the image. The blade cut through the stone as easily as if it were cutting through sand. It slowed to a stop as it reached the base of the stone. The engraved top separated and the sides slowly dropped to the floor, falling away like a shell. In the center was a mound of what looked like finely crushed gravel.

All eyes turned to the pile of cinders. It was moving. Gradually the pieces began to separate. One pile swirled around, creating a second, smaller pile. The larger one began to take shape from the ground upward. A pair of hoofed feet appeared, followed by legs that looked like those on a mountain goat.

"What trickery is this?" shouted Neraka Ferr, but he was unable to look away.

None of them had seen Tebaga before, except for Ena Ray, and none of them knew what to expect. As they watched, Ena Ray saw a familiar form take shape. As the rubble continued to take shape a distended abdomen appeared, bulging forward, while a tail started growing in the form of a snake.

The trunk of the body followed, hunched forward like a question mark, the back covered with barbed spikes. Muscular arms appeared, cocked towards the back like chicken wings, but far more powerful. The huge shoulders led to powerfully built upper arms and then to large forearms, and ended in three talons with razor sharp claws.

Finally the head took shape. The chin was long and pointed, extending outward like a bird's beak. Thick lips gave the face a snarling look. Deep set eyes under a heavy brow made it look sinister. A large hooked nose sprouted from the center of the face and curved down almost touching the chin. The top of the head widened and was marked by extremely large ears the size and shape of conch shells on either side. Aside from the goat-like legs, there was no hair on the body whatsoever.

When the reassembly had finished the gravel consolidated, filling the seams and gaps, and the entire body turned blood red in color, except for the eyes, which glowed a deep yellow. And then the creature sucked in a deep breath and let out a bellow. It took a staggering step forward and then turned its gaze on everyone who was looking at him.

It scanned the small group and then fixed on a figure it recognized. Its body went rigid and its eyes widened.

"How nice to see you again," said Ena Ray. "Although I must say, you've aged poorly."

The curse Meri had placed on Tebaga had twisted his features, exaggerating most. He was the same person Ena Ray had known, but at the same time, different. Meri's curse had changed his appearance to reflect his soul. In doing so, she had personified all the deceit, hatred, and evil that had corrupted him. Still, there were enough of his original features that Ena Ray recognized him.

"YOU!" Tebaga bellowed.

He staggered forward menacingly, but staggered to a stop. Ena Ray stood his ground. As quickly as Tebaga had moved towards his former classmate, he noticed more clearly the others standing around staring at him. Although he had seen them initially, it was as if he was now seeing them for the first time.

347

His mind registered the fact that he and Ena Ray were not alone. He took his time surveying the others. His eyes were caught by the sight of B'nair. He raised his head and cocked it to one side, his focus pinpointing on the Rebbercand. He took an unsteady step forward and looked more closely at B'nair.

"Another one?" Tebaga asked.

"Another?" B'nair asked back.

Tebaga looked down at his feet at the second pile of cinders. As he did, these, too, began to move. They swirled in the same manner as before, and quickly rose into the air, reassembling into another shape; much different than the first. In a few seconds a second creature appeared, fully formed.

"Hello, brother," B'nair said.

"B'nair!" exclaimed Bacham. "Where did you come from? What happened to me? Who are all of you?"

"So many questions," said Scirios. "So little time."

Bacham either didn't hear or chose to ignore Scirios' comment. He looked in shock at his brother. It had been a long time since they had last seen each other. Bacham had changed little, but B'nair was very different. The burns and scars he had accumulated from his mishap in the mines of the Trepans had altered his features greatly.

B'nair was well aware of how much different he must look because of those injuries. What he couldn't know was how much more he had changed as a result of the evil that had corrupted his soul in the short time since those injuries. He eyes were more deeply set than before; there was a perpetual sneer on his face, which was oddly contorted by the toll his sins had taken.

Bacham rubbed his eyes and tried to clear his head. He felt unsteady on his feet. He took a deep breath and shook himself.

"What happened to you?" he finally asked.

"Too much to recall," B'nair answered vaguely.

"And has what happened to you, Ena Ray," interrupted Tebaga, "also been too much to recall? Because of you, I was cast into this...this...hole for an eternity. Where, exactly, were you all this time?"

"Unfortunately," said Akmen Milzu, "we must dispense with the normal formalities. We are in a hurry."

"Indulge me," insisted Tebaga, dismissing the interruption by the Mountain Kelpie. "It's been a very long time since I've had someone to speak to. I feel the need to be brought up to date on current events. But I want to hear it from him."

Akmen Milzu gestured to Ena Ray to go ahead, but to make it brief. The sorcerer looked to the Kelpies, who also reluctantly motioned for him to respond. He provided a quick synopsis of who the Kelpies were, where he had been for the last two thousand years, and the roles he and Tebaga were being called upon to play.

"And I should trust you?" Tebaga asked. "You are the reason I ended up here."

"I never forced you into anything," Ena Ray shot back. "You were a willing partner."

"I didn't ask for this!" shouted Tebaga, gesturing to the cave that had been his home.

"Trust me," replied Ena Ray. "My accommodations were no better."

"Trust you?" Tebaga exclaimed in disbelief. "NO! I do NOT trust you."

"Enough!" shouted Akmen Milzu. "We have an opportunity to return to the power that is rightfully ours. You two can sort things out later. For now we must hurry."

Tebaga took an aggressive step towards the Mountain Kelpie, but then thought better of it. He resented being ordered around, but could see that he was outnumbered. If Ena Ray was right about the level of their power, it would be better for him to swallow his pride – at least for the moment.

Akmen Milzu turned to B'nair and added, "Can you locate the band? The piece that held the stone?"

At the mention of the stone, Bacham jerked his head towards his brother. B'nair was distracted by his sudden reaction and looked questioningly at Bacham before turning back and answering the Kelpie.

"Yes," he said. "I'm sure I can locate it."

His suspicions about the importance of the band were now confirmed. He was puzzled, though by the look his brother was giving him. He noted that Bacham's eyes were fixed not on him so much as on his chest. He looked down and saw the stone hanging from his neck. When he looked up, he saw Bacham glaring at him.

"That stone!" Bacham shouted. "It's mine. How did you get it?"

"What are you talking about?" B'nair asked.

"You know exactly what I'm talking about," growled Bacham. "That stone around your neck. It's mine. It belongs to me. Where did you get it?"

"Sorry to disappoint you, brother," B'nair replied. "The stone is mine, and how I got it is of no concern to you."

He recalled how oddly Bacham had acted the last time they were together. He had been secretive about something and ranted incessantly about searching for a source of power of some kind. That was about the time B'nair had been mining the materials for the statue to Reng'n. He had found his brother's actions distracting and childish, and had dismissed him. Now, though, he wondered if he had been wrong. Could he have known about this stone? But how is that possible?

"Liar!" Bacham shouted, interrupting B'nair's thoughts. "You know that stone is mine. You know I found it."

B'nair was shocked at the sudden burst from Bacham. As brothers they had never been particularly close, but B'nair was a higher-ranking leader among the Rebbercands. His position alone warranted a greater degree of respect. Bacham, in spite of all his failings, had at least shown him the respect of his rank. Something had changed.

"Be careful the names you throw around so easily," warned B'nair. "And how you address me. I am still your superior."

"You are not in charge of me now," Bacham spit back at him. "You banished me. Remember? I owe you no allegiance. Now give me my stone."

"This is NOT your stone," B'nair shot back. "It never was and it never will be."

Bacham stepped forward, his fists clenched. B'nair stood his ground, but turned slightly, moving the axe behind him, readying it to strike. Scirios intervened.

"What have we here? Sibling rivalry?" he asked. "Have we unleashed quarreling children, or powerful sorcerers and warriors?"

He gestured to the Rebbercands and then to Ena Ray and Tebaga. He had turned to the other Kelpies and said the last with a slight laugh. It was his attempt to diffuse the situation, but instead, it only made things worse.

"We are not siblings," Ena Ray and Tebaga shouted irately at the same time.

"Does that mean, though, that you are quarreling children?" Scirios mocked.

He held his hand up in dismissal to the two of them and turned to Bacham and B'nair before either of the sorcerers could respond.

"Can you two hold your spat in check until we are finished?" he added.

Bacham glared at the Kelpie, and then turned to look at the others. Realizing he was at a severe disadvantage, he backed down, but his rage was far from being in check. He recalled finding the stone several years ago. He recalled the feeling of power the stone gave him, and the knowledge and insight that came with it.

He recalled trying to convince B'nair to focus his efforts on something other than that mining operation and the building of that foolish statue to Reng'n. Such a typical, bootlicking effort on B'nair's part, he thought. Bacham had refused to participate. Then he recalled how B'nair had summarily dismissed him – banished him, in fact. He had never taken Bacham seriously throughout his life.

All this was too much for him to accept meekly. The feeling of power that stone had given him – the implied promise of even more – was unyielding in its pull. If he didn't retrieve it now, he was afraid the opportunity to do so later would never come. He would have it, no matter what he had to do to get it.

He turned away from B'nair for a second, but then spun back and ran up at him. B'nair had seen his little brother behave this

353

way before, and was ready for him. Growing up they practiced their combat training with one another. Bacham never deviated from his tactics. B'nair could tell he would repeat that mistake now. He let Bacham think he had dropped his guard, and waited until the last minute. As soon as Bacham was within reach, B'nair stepped to the side.

Bacham's momentum carried him past his brother. He was too slow in stopping and changing his direction. B'nair brought his fist around and struck Bacham across the side of his head, driving him to the ground. He pulled his fist back, ready to strike again. He carefully stepped closer to Bacham, but avoided coming within reach.

"Really, little brother," he taunted. "I expected you to have learned some new tricks."

Bacham had unsuccessfully tried to stop his fall. He slid across the ground; his arms sprawled out in front of him. He scrambled to his feet, but his head was ringing from the blow and he was slightly dizzy. He stood up too fast and lost his balance. B'nair took advantage of his brother's defenselessness. He struck him again.

"You never learn, do you?" he muttered to the fallen body.

This infuriated Bacham even further and when he finally got to his feet, he was in a rage. He waited until his head was clear, and then started to storm towards B'nair, who immediately took a defensive stance and readied his axe. Akmen Milzu intervened. She didn't care what happened to Bacham, but she couldn't afford to have B'nair hurt enough that he wouldn't be able to lead them to the band.

"There will be sufficient time later for you two to resolve your dispute," she said. "This is not the time, nor the <u>place</u>."

She spoke with such authority, that Bacham caught himself. He stopped his advance, but he was still breathing hard, his anger still boiling, his head throbbing from the blows he had received from his brother. He glared at B'nair as he rubbed his head. He felt Akmen Milzu's hand on his chest and stopped himself from shoving it out of the way. He looked up at her and realized that this would have been a foolish action.

She fixed her gaze on him and did not lower her hand until she was convinced that the Rebbercand's anger was under control. He looked from her to B'nair and then back to her. Eventually, he took a step back, and the Mountain Kelpie lowered her hand. She did not, however, turn away from him. He took a few steps away, turning his back on B'nair and the others.

"This isn't over," Bacham shouted at B'nair over his shoulder. "That stone belongs to me, and you know it."

Any response B'nair was about to make was cut short. Akmen Milzu turned towards him and gave him a withering look – one that clearly told him to let the matter drop; at least for the time being. B'nair allowed a slight smirk to creep into his face, but said nothing.

"Once we are out of this cursed place," said Neraka Ferr, "you two can annihilate each other for all I care."

"Let's hope it will not come to that," interjected Akmen Milzu.

I'm sure that would please you to no end, B'nair thought. More and more his suspicions about his future with these Kelpies were being confirmed. Now that there were eight of them again, he believed his usefulness was coming to an end. It didn't help that he also had to protect his back from his brother.

He knew from his history with Bacham that he wouldn't have to wait long for his brother to make another try for the stone. He would have to try to resolve that problem before it presented itself. If he could separate Bacham from the Kelpies long enough to explain what was going on, perhaps he could convince him to be an ally, even if only temporarily. This would take some finesse, he thought. Bacham would not be easily convinced.

The Mountain Kelpie moved close to Neraka Ferr and in a quiet voice admonished him for his outburst.

"We need the Rebbercand to find the band," she reminded him. "Don't encourage the two of them to kill each other. Once we have what we are looking for, you can dispose of the both of them, if you like."

Neraka Ferr bridled at being reprimanded, but held his tongue. He knew that she was right, but he had had his fill of the Rebbercand's display of self-importance. He wasn't a sorcerer and never would be, no matter whether he possessed the pendant or not. The sooner they were rid of him, the better, the Fire Kelpie thought. In fact, he would be glad to be rid of both of them.

B'nair didn't have the powers that Stella had, so he was not able to short cut the return of his party to the lake under the volcano shaft. He and they had to go back step by step the way they had come. He held the stone closely in his hand and hoped that Bacham would control his impulses until a time when he could confide in him. Fortunately, Bacham was towards the end of the line, so B'nair didn't have to worry about him for now.

Many of the passageways were too narrow for Tebaga and some of the others. Akmen Milzu repeated what she had done on the way in. Each time she moved the walls of the corridors, B'nair cringed, expecting the entire structure to cave in on them. Finally, they came through the last entry and found themselves at the underground lake, and he breathed a little easier.

Tebaga stared at the wrecked ships and up at the ancient volcano shaft. He could see the gray sky far above them and wondered where this strange place was. Bacham looked around at the wreckage as well, but saw nothing that indicated he and several others had been here before.

How long ago was that, he wondered. He remembered holding the Sea Sprite princess captive and the battle of spells Tebaga and the princess's enchantress engaged in. He thought for sure the enchantress would be disposed of. The last thing he remembered was a giant wolf, a flash of light and then nothing.

He found himself in darkness, but he knew he was not alone. He could not speak, see, nor hear. He could not feel or taste, but he was awake. He never slept and had no need for sleep. His mind never rested. He was left to his own thoughts with no concept of time. He could sense, but not communicate with, the entity that was trapped inside with him. He assumed it was Tebaga, but didn't know for sure until they were released.

He couldn't tell if minutes had passed, or years. The only indication of time he had, he gleaned from the appearance of his brother. It was evident that he had been badly injured, and that alone had aged him. Other than that, it was hard to tell how much time had gone by since he had seen him last, or since he had been placed in that box with Tebaga.

His resentment at being cast into that box only fueled his anger at his brother. He looked around at the wreckage. There had been no sign he had ever been there. There was nothing left with his people that indicated he had ever walked among them. His own brother had not even noticed he had disappeared.

He looked back at his brother. For the first time he noticed the axe held in a withered hand. Where had that come from, he wondered. Something else he had probably stolen, in addition to my stone, he thought.

He and the others were crossing around the rim of the lake. Off to his left, he saw debris from one of the many broken ships that had been drawn into the whirlpool created when the tides rose and covered this small volcano island. He saw an old piece of a galleon that had broken apart when it landed on the rocks.

In the scattered pieces, he saw a long, round piece of iron. He had no idea what it could have been used for. It was about three feet long, narrower at one end than the other. It looked to him like a club. He bent down and picked it up. It was heavy – about the same weight as a battle-axe. It felt good in his hand.

He looked back at his brother. He had his hand on the stone that hung from his neck. My stone, thought Bacham, his thoughts of the axe immediately erased by his thoughts of the pendant. B'nair was standing off to one side, but on the edge of the group of Kelpies.

So pompous, thought Bacham. As if he was one of them, he said to himself. You're only fooling yourself. You'll never be one of them. You just don't understand. You never did. That's always been your problem. The words swirled in Bacham's mind, stirring his anger more and more.

"Bacham," called B'nair. "Get over here."

B'nair looked skyward and through the opening at the top of the volcano, he could see the Lightning Riders beginning to form up. He heard the first crackles of electricity and saw the first small lines begin to descend. They would be here shortly to carry them all off. He looked back at Bacham. His brother was just standing there, glaring at him.

What's wrong with him, B'nair wondered. He must have been locked in that box far too long. What was he doing here in the first place? How did he ever get here, of all places? B'nair decided he would have to ask him about that. He wondered if it had anything to do with the stone. He was certain the stone he wore around his neck was not the one Bacham believed was his.

He continued to stare back at his brother wondering what tricks of fate had brought the both of them to this place. Perhaps he had formed some kind of alliance with that Tebaga creature, although that didn't appear to have been a possibility. They were an unlikely combination and the creature seemed to pay him little attention.

"Bacham," he called more forcefully, waving at him with his empty hand. "Get over here now!"

Bacham continued to glare at his brother. The same thoughts repeated over and over in his mind. He thinks he's better than I am. He's always thought that. He's always ordering people around. And me. He's always ordered me around. Even now he does that. In front of these others. To show off how important he is.

B'nair felt the stone tingle slightly against his chest. He reached up to hold it once more. Bacham's eyes followed the gesture. My stone, he thought. His rage grew. He's holding my stone. His grip on the piece of iron tightened. He'll never give it back to me, he thought. I'll just have to take it, he decided. That's what I'll do. I'll take it from him now – when he's least expecting it.

He stepped forward while B'nair was still several feet from the Kelpies. He raised the iron club above his head. His eyes were fixed on the back of B'nair's head. He moved as quickly and as quietly as he could. At the last second B'nair turned to face him.

B'nair had called a second time for Bacham to move up with the rest of the group. He was standing off by himself like a pouting child. The more he thought about his brother, the more he grew impatient. He had always been like that – trying to be something special instead of simply doing what he was supposed to do.

Perhaps I should have been more of a mentor to him, B'nair thought. Perhaps I have been too hard on him. He would have to try to change that. Once they were in a position to separate themselves from these Kelpies, he would...his thoughts were interrupted by a burning sensation in his chest.

It was the same feeling he had in his dream. He squeezed the stone more tightly in his hand and an image appeared in his mind. Someone was advancing on him with a weapon. One of the Kelpies, he immediately thought. He spun around, swinging his axe in a wide arc to threaten whoever was coming up on him.

When he turned he saw the face of Bacham. It was frozen in an expression of surprise. He held an iron club in his hands above his head. His arms were motionless, suspended in the air. His brother looked like a statue.

The club fell from his hands and dropped to the ground behind him. The noise alerted the Kelpies who turned to see what had happened. They saw B'nair with his axe extended out to his side. He was facing Bacham who was about four feet away from him. The iron club he had been holding was now on the ground and rolling away.

"My stone," gasped Bacham. "You stole my stone."

The words caused B'nair's anger to rage. He took a step closer to Bacham and readied his axe. He needn't have bothered. When he spun around the blade had cut quickly and deeply across Bacham's midsection. It had happened so fast that even Bacham wasn't aware of what had happened.

As he gasped his last words, his knees gave out and he fell to the ground. The upper portion of his body rolled away from the lower portion. However, instead of blood, thousands of tiny flies escaped and his body dissolved as the flies dispersed. In seconds, he was gone completely.

In his anger, B'nair kicked at the sand where his brother had been and swatted his free hand at the swarm of flies as they buzzed around him and vanished up the shaft of the volcano, past the Lightning Riders and to the sky beyond.

He looked up at the several pairs of eyes that were watching him. He said nothing, and neither did the Kelpies.

Chapter sixteen

The fire that surrounded the damaged boat extended in a large circle and, as Lochen had managed, hovered about five feet above the water. Still, the air between the fire and the sea was hot. They needed to get out from under the heat very quickly. Stella and Natalie, having lived in the water, were able to move smoothly. Summer fluttered a few inches above the sea. The others were struggling.

Quinn grabbed one of the nearby crates that had bobbed to the surface. It seemed to be in good shape. He reached out and pulled Sean over so he could hang on to it as well. The two of them then steered the box towards the others, each of whom held on to one of the edges. Once everyone was accounted for, they began kicking to propel the container towards shore. Unfortunately, they were all kicking in different directions.

Natalie looked over her shoulder and saw them all splashing in the water, but going no place other than in circles. They all stopped at nearly the same time, pointed towards the shore and began kicking again. She shook her head in disbelief. They were still just making circles.

She swam towards them, dodging around pieces of the still burning boat as well as larger and smaller crates and other debris. When she was close enough, she whistled to get their attention.

"You all need to get your act together," she said. "Quinn, move to the middle of the box."

He inched his way over towards the center. His weight caused the front of the box to rise up into the air, carrying Sean with it.

"Put me down!" he sputtered. "I can't believe I'm asking someone to drop me back into the water."

"Slide around to the far side," Natalie instructed him.

He looked down at her and then stretched his toes out to the corner of the box. He used his foot to pull himself towards the side, sliding his hands across the top. He stepped over and around Liam to move towards the back corner, next to Quinn.

"Good," said Natalie. "Liam, you can stay where you are."

"Thanks," he said. "I wasn't planning on moving."

"Lochen, can you move to the other corner on the other side opposite of Sean?"

Lochen simply let go of the box and swam around to the back next to Liam. That resulted in Quinn being in the middle, Solveig hanging on to the back of the crate on his right, and Liam on his left. Sean and Lochen were on opposite corners and partially on the sides, but everyone was facing generally the same way. Even though the front of the crate was higher in the air, it was more aerodynamic.

"That's better," said Natalie. "Liam, which is the most direct route to the shore?"

Liam scanned the horizon and then pointed slightly to his left. With that, Natalie took the lead and Stella swam behind the crate while the rest resumed kicking – this time all in the same direction.

"I don't understand," Natalie shouted over her shoulder. "You all can get out of the most difficult situations and overcome enormous obstacles, but you can't manage to push a box in the same direction."

"It seems the difficult we can manage," answered Lochen. "It's the mundane that is our undoing."

"You said you had more to share with us," commented Sean. "What is it?"

"Yes," said Lochen. "I did. I have translated more of the Alchemist's book."

"When did you do that?" interrupted Quinn.

"As we were sailing out here," Lochen answered.

"Weren't you paying attention to where we were going?" asked Sean.

"Of course I was," he replied. "I was multitasking. I can do that."

"What did you find out?" asked Solveig. "Was it more about our ancestors?"

"No," he said. "I believe we know all there is on that subject. The new information pertains to the origins of the gargoyles and the hobgoblins we encountered at the Alchemist's fortress. It seems they have a common ancestry with a people we are unfortunately well acquainted with: the Rebbercands."

He then described the spell that Meri Hocto had cast when she banished Ena Ray and Tebaga, cursing the Rebbercands who formed their armies and invaded her citadel. Both the gargoyles and the hobgoblins were relegated to the underground. For the most part they kept themselves separate from one another and their civilizations evolved in slightly different directions.

While they were cursed to live in permanent exile beneath the earth, the Rebbercands who occupied the village that surrounded her citadel became nomads with no fixed home. This had nothing to do with any curse she had cast. At the time she created her citadel, the Rebbercands were relatively inoffensive.

Lochen pointed out that they were still narrow-minded and stubborn, but somewhat harmless. It was likely that Meri's presence in their midst, even though it was largely unknown to them, was the driving factor in keeping them from becoming confrontational and aggressive. Once she was gone, that influence was gone as well.

"Wow," said Solveig. "She must have been really powerful to have had such an effect on an entire community without even trying."

"Yes," said Lochen. "She was an immensely powerful Enchantress."

"Are you sure she was from this planet?" asked Sean.

"Oh," said Lochen. "I hadn't really given that serious consideration. I'm not sure where else..."

"I was joking," Sean interrupted. "Sometimes you can be really dim for someone so smart."

"I see," Lochen answered icily. "Perhaps I should look into the lineage of the Forest Creatures to see how long it's been since you left off living in trees."

"Funny," muttered Sean. "Real funny."

"Did you learn anything else?" asked Liam, anxious to get back on subject.

"Yes," answered Lochen. "As powerful as the Enchantress was, her power seems to have been magnified by the pendant she wore."

"You mean that stone that Stella has?" asked Solveig.

"What Stella has seems to be only part of the stone," he said. "It was much larger – and it was encompassed in a band. The band served to amplify or pinpoint the power."

"What do you mean?" asked Quinn.

"I mean it harnessed the power of the stone, increased it even further and allowed that power to be directed with incredible accuracy."

"Are you talking about that band we found in the Crystal Citadel with Ena Ray?" asked Summer.

"Yes," said Lochen. "I believe they are one and the same."

"How did he get it?" asked Solveig.

"As far as I can tell, he must have reached for it at the instant he was converted from his natural form into the form as we saw it, and when he was transported from wherever he was at the time to the Crystal Citadel. I think it simply went with him."

"This is the same band that sealed the portal and kept the gargoyles locked up?" asked Liam. "The band with those markings on it?"

"Yes," said Lochen. "That band."

"And that's what the Kelpies want to find, isn't it?" asked Liam.

"Yes," Lochen replied. "That and the stone that Stella has."

"It kind of makes you wonder," said Summer. "Who's chasing who? We've been following them to keep them in their prisons, but it looks like they're going to be following us to get the stone."

"I think that's an accurate assessment," said Lochen. "They will want the stone and the band."

"But we don't even know where the band is," said Sean. "And we're the ones who put it where it is."

"That's right," added Quinn. "I remember us all putting our hands on it...wait! How could we do that if it was small enough to fit around the stone that Stella has?"

"It can change sizes," said Lochen. "Just as the stone can. If you recall, the triskelion that is at its center was a pendant worn by Summer when we all first met. It fit into the indentation in the armband that Sean wore. Both of them changed size when Stella placed the band on her head. The triskelion changed size when it was joined with the other piece of the stone we found."

"So when...or if...we find the band," concluded Solveig, "it will alter itself to fit around the stone again."

"Exactly," said Lochen.

"How are we going to find the band," asked Quinn, "if none of us can remember where we put it?"

"I believe Stella will be able to tell us," answered Lochen.

They all turned to look back at Stella who was swimming right behind them. At the sound of her name, she looked up. She had heard them talking, but hadn't really been paying attention. She was focused on guarding their backs instead.

"What?" she asked.

"Close your eyes," said Lochen. "And bring forth the image of your map."

"Why?" she asked. "All the Kelpies have been freed or destroyed. There aren't any left to see."

"I think that map has more to tell," answered Lochen.

She did as he asked. She could see faint smudges where the Kelpies had once been located. The most recent indicator was in the same location as the volcano far out in the southern part of the Viridian Ocean – a place she was glad they would not be returning to. She assumed they had found the crypt of Tebaga and released him.

She let her mind float over the map. In a few seconds, something new appeared. It was different than the markers for the Kelpies. She instantly knew what it was: the location of the band.

"Yes," she shouted. "I see it. I know where it is."

"I hate to change the subject," Natalie shouted over her shoulder. "But has anyone else noticed how fast we're moving?"

They all looked around them. They seemed to be in the midst of a series of strong, low rushing waves. The waves were heading for shore, which was now visible through the mist, but still a long way off.

"And what's that noise?" asked Summer.

In addition to the increasingly rapid movement of the sea towards the shore, there was a low rumbling sound that had been growing steadily. They could feel the sound vibrations beneath them

"Maybe it's just high tide," said Liam.

"This is moving pretty fast for only being the tide," said Natalie. "Lochen, what do you think?"

"I think I am out of my depth," he said. "No pun intended. You forget. I live in the mountains. We don't have tide there. I would defer to you, or Stella, or perhaps Liam."

"Oh, poop," said Quinn. "I know what this is. I saw this once on the western side of the Ice Kingdom."

"And are you going to share with the rest of us?" asked Sean.

"It's a tidal bore," he said, his voice little more than a whisper.

"You mean like a pig?" asked Sean.

"No," said Quinn. "Not a boar, b-o-a-r; a bore, b-o-r-e."

"Oh, yeah," said Sean. "Clear as mud. Thanks."

371

"What happened with the one you saw?" Summer asked Quinn.

"It was in this bay," he said, "where it was wide at the part that faced the sea and then narrowed down and led to a river. There was a large wave front followed by a bunch of smaller waves right after it. It made a noise like a stampede."

"Hey," said Sean. "Isn't there a wide bay at Satamakau that leads to a river?"

"Yes," said Natalie. "And that's exactly where we're headed."

"Then this boring wave should get us there quicker, right?" asked Sean.

"It'll get us there a lot quicker," said Quinn. "But it's like riding a tornado. That's the rumbling we're beginning to hear. It's churning up the water and the rocks and whatever else is under us."

"That's not a good thing, is it?" Sean concluded.

They were beginning to notice bubbles rising from the bottom directly beneath them. Mixed in with the bubbles were sand, stones, seaweed, and small bits of the destroyed boat that had trailed them from the burn site.

"Can somebody do something about this?" Sean said, his voice rising. "Like a spell or something?"

Those riding the crate held on tighter. Natalie eased back until she was pressed against the front of the box. Stella kicked a little harder and closed the gap between herself and the others. By now, the shore was coming at them at an alarming rate.

Meanwhile, in the harbor, Saldeti had positioned and repositioned his army of gargoyles half a dozen times. He had placed a third at the south side of the bay and a third on the north side, keeping the remaining third in the harbor. Then he pulled them all back to the harbor. Worried that he'd miss something, he moved half of them to the south, then pulled them back only to move them to the north.

He finally settled on small outlooks at the north and south sides of the bay, but his uncertainty was eating at him. He paced back and forth, debating about another move when he began to feel a low and steady vibration beneath his feet, followed by the deep rumbling. He began to pace back and forth in a panic. He had no idea where the sound and tremor were coming from.

The gargoyles, not comfortable being on the surface, began to grumble. They looked around for a passage that would lead them back underground, but there was none to be found. They looked for lower ground. The ones closest to the sea wall saw the long, sandy beach at the bottom of the wall. Some of them started climbing over the side and dropping to the shore below.

Saldeti paced even more. He would cast a spell of some kind, if only he knew where to cast it. The roaring sound and the trembling beneath his feet grew steadily stronger. He couldn't determine the direction from which they were coming. In his anxiety, he was oblivious to the gargoyles slipping one by one over the sea wall and down to the beach. It didn't dawn on him to look in that direction.

Quest of Eight Part Seven: Ad Paria

Richard Reda

He ran back into the town, searching for some place to gain a higher vantage point. Many of the buildings were locked or boarded up. Seeing there was nothing to help, he ran back to the marina. Still he was blind to the number of gargoyles who were deserting to the shore. He ran along the north side of the sea wall towards the sentry at that end.

He was almost all the way up to the sentry's post when he noticed the wall of water rushing towards the town. What he saw was the tidal bore front wave. He had never seen anything like this. He could see the water rushing towards the opening of the bay. It took him several seconds before he realized what was happening.

He stepped back and forth several times, trying to decide what to do. He looked back at the town and the marina towards which the waves were heading. That was when he saw his army of gargoyles pouring over the wall and onto the sand below.

"What are they doing?" he screamed. "Are they mad?"

He realized they had no idea what was coming. He looked back at the leading wave, which was already at the mouth of the bay. He reached out his arms, throwing everything he had into a spell. The face of the rushing water froze as the impact of the spell reached it, but the immense power of the sea behind was too much.

The wall of ice Saldeti had cast collapsed under the pressure like a house of cards. The cracking and crashing of the ice was lost in the roaring of the tide. Over the top of the front wave he could see a series of smaller waves immediately behind. In their midst he could see several pieces of the shattered boat, pieces of equipment from the broken crates, and one box that appeared to have people on it.

They were moving too fast for him to cast a spell on them, and he wasn't sure who they were or whether they posed a threat. Instead he turned his attention to the gargoyles, who still hadn't understood the danger they were in.

He began to run back to the marina, waving his arms and shouting as he went. His voice was no match for the rumbling onrush of the sea. The few gargoyles who spotted him had no idea what he was saying or what his frantic gesturing meant. A handful turned towards what they finally determined to be the source of the noise and the tremors.

They saw the rushing water moving at them with incredible speed and began to panic. They turned back towards the wall and tried to fight their way back to the top of the marina. There were too many of them pushing against them, still climbing over and down to the shore. They began to scream.

Saldeti tried another spell to stop or slow down the rush of water. At first he thought he had been successful. The water seemed to slow down. Then he realized that this was a natural part of the advance of the bore. The rocks, sand and debris that were churning in the front wave were scraping along the floor of the bay, generating more turbulence while reducing the speed of the tide.

He had forgotten about the crate with the people on it. They were high in the air atop one of the several secondary waves. He was focused on the fact that nearly his entire army was trapped on the beach between the incoming water and the sea wall. He searched his brain for some way to save them.

At the last second he thrust his arms forward once more. This time, though, instead of targeting the front wall of the tide, which by now was racing past him, he targeted the gargoyles. He coated them in a giant block of ice, freezing them in place. It ultimately did nothing to protect them.

The tidal bore crashed down on the encased gargoyles, crushing the ice, breaking parts of it into small pieces, driving most of the pieces and the frozen gargoyles into the sand, and pressing the rest against the boulders and mortar that made up the sea wall.

The sea wall had been built long ago to contain the regular tidal bores that rushed through the bay and up to the village. It had been built high enough to keep the roaring sea from crashing over and flooding the town. However, it had not been built on the assumption that there would be a massive block of ice at its base.

The massive slab created by Saldeti in his failed effort to try to stop the wave merely provided a wedge against which the front of the tidal bore was lifted up and over the face of the wall. The water washed through the marina, over the streets between the buildings and beyond the site where Artabarat had his wagon and campsite.

On the crest of this wave were several items of the wreckage of the boat that had been set ablaze by Saldeti's fellow Kelpies, as well as two Sea Sprites, and a crate carrying several passengers. Above all of it fluttered a tiny faerie. Saldeti watched as all of this passed by him and disappeared on the far side of Satamakau.

As the tidal bore had gotten closer to the sea wall, Natalie had called back to the others, telling them to hold on tight. They were headed for a crash. She then moved to the side of the wooden box so as not to get crushed by it when they all landed.

"A spell would be real nice," Sean repeated his plea.

"And what, exactly, do you have in mind?" asked Lochen, tightening his grip on the edge of the crate. "I can't make us all fly."

Summer made a couple of circuits flying over the crate, sprinkling faerie dust, but the box was too heavy. It rose up a few inches, but was still being propelled by the wave. Stella moved from behind the crate to the side near Natalie. She tried to free her hands to cast a spell, but the waves were too close together and she kept getting beaten down whenever she stopped swimming.

"I think you're going to have to ride this out," she shouted.

"I was hoping for a different Plan B," Sean shouted back. "Between the two of you, can't you combine your spells?"

"It doesn't work that way," answered Lochen. "You see, the training sorcerers receive and the nature of the spells they can cast are quite different..."

"I don't really care," interrupted Sean. "I mean, I'm sure that's all very interesting, but right now? It's not something I need to know."

"Can you at least slow us down?" asked Quinn.

"Oh," replied Lochen. "Slowing down is another matter. That I may be able to do."

"I thought you couldn't cast a spell!" sputtered Sean.

"Slowing us down is something quite different," Lochen replied.

He pulled himself towards the front of the crate and reached over the edge to steady himself. He looked down at the water and then up towards the rapidly approaching sea wall, trying to determine the best place to cast his spell. He shook his head and then waved his arm in a low arc across the front of the crate. Then he wiggled back to his earlier position.

"There," he said. "I think that's the best I can do."

"Nothing happened!" shouted Sean. "That's it? That's all you can do? Nothing?"

"I beg to differ," answered Lochen, somewhat indignantly. "By my calculations, our speed has been reduced by nearly ten percent."

"I have to agree with Sean," said Liam. "It doesn't seem to have changed much at all."

It was at this moment that Saldeti had cast his own spell, trying to freeze the front edge of the approaching tide. Instead of stopping the water, it caused the frontal wave and the smaller ones behind it to rise up a few feet higher until the sheet of ice shattered under the pressure.

"Look out," shouted Natalie. "There's something up ahead."

She and Stella slowed down and moved behind the protection of the wooden box. Pieces of ice flew at them across the air and through the water. Several pieces struck the front of the crate, shattering into hundreds of smaller shards. Lochen was able to snap his fingers and melt the pellets. Large droplets of water sprayed the passengers, smacking them in the face.

"What was that?" spit Quinn.

"Someone on shore is trying to freeze the water," shouted Natalie.

"What's that ahead of us?" yelled Summer.

"The sea wall," answered Liam. "You know? That thing we're going to crash into?"

"Not that," she shot back at him. "Those things on the sand at the bottom of the wall."

"People," said Quinn. "There are people down there. Hundreds of them."

"Those aren't people," said Liam. "They're gargoyles."

"Oh, wonderful," whined Sean. "A welcoming party. If we don't drown or aren't squashed, we have gargoyles waiting for us."

When there were less than a hundred yards out, as they prepared to meet the wall head on, Liam saw the results of Saldeti's second spell. A thick coating of ice covered the army of gargoyles that had finally understood what was coming at them, and were trying frantically to get back to the top of the wall.

The ice kept growing, climbing over the scrambling army and up the face of the sea wall. It created a giant wedge over which the rushing sea slid. The mass of ice managed to cut the base of the wave out from under the top, slowed the approach, and reduced the impact on the wall. It also raised the ocean floor by several feet, causing the wave to shoot over the top of the wall and through the village.

The crate and the Sea Sprites were carried by the wave over the wall, through the town and past the wagon and campsite of the sentinel. Stella and Natalie skidded on their stomachs across the water and grass, trying to get their feet under them. They fell, tumbled and got up again, slipping and sliding, twisting and turning, trying to avoid trees, rocks and pieces of wreckage that were washed ashore with them.

The crate rode across the wave, slowing down as the water was absorbed into the ground or spread out across the fields. It spun in circles when one of the front corners struck some unseen object. The passengers held on as long as they could, but Sean and Lochen were spun off. Liam and Solveig grabbed Quinn's arms to keep from being thrown, but they all fell off when the crate collided with a large rock and came to a sudden stop.

"I can't believe we made it in one piece," said Quinn.

"Is everybody all right?" asked Liam.

"Lochen? Sean?" shouted Solveig. "Where are you?"

"They're all right," Summer answered. "It looks like everyone's all right."

She darted from one to the other, back and forth, checking everyone out. Natalie and Stella had finally stopped foundering and were walking towards the others. Stella saw Sean off to one side, covered in mud, sitting on his bottom. He was trying to wipe off his face, but his hands were so thick with muck that he was only smearing it around.

"Here," she said. "Let me help."

She flicked her wrist and a burst of water appeared from nowhere and soaked him. He gasped in surprise, kicked his feet and rolled over onto his stomach. As he scrambled to get to his feet, he slipped and fell face first into the mud.

"Sit still," Stella ordered. "You're only making things worse."

"Can't you just get rid of it?" he argued. "Do you really need more water?"

"Quit complaining, or I'll leave you caked in mud."

Natalie ran over to where Lochen was sprawled. He was on his back spread-eagled. At first she thought he was unconscious, but when she came up to him she could see he was staring at the sky.

"Are you all right?" she asked.

"Yes," he said. "I'm fine. Have you noticed that it's been weeks, perhaps even months, since we've seen a clear sky?"

"Seriously?" she asked. "We are nearly burned to death, nearly drowned, nearly smashed against a sea wall and all you can think of is when was the last time we had a sunny day? Did you hit your head again?"

"No," he said, sitting up. "I'm fine. Truly. I only realized I hadn't noticed the continual gray clouds overhead until I was looking up at them. That caused me to wonder how long there has been no change."

"I'm sure the others will be glad to have a weather report," she said, shaking her head. "Let's go find them."

She helped him to his feet and they started walking to where the crate had come to a final stop. Along the way they were joined by Sean and Stella. The four were met by Summer who had flown back to check on them.

"Come on," she said. "Everyone else is up ahead. Everyone's all right."

The crate had stopped next to a tributary that led to the sea – the sea from which they had all recently been deposited. Normally, the water ran from the inland sources, westward to the ocean. However, in light of the tidal bore, the water was now traveling in the other direction towards a large lake not far away. In a few hours that would be reversed, and the current would once again flow to the ocean.

Quinn, Solveig and Liam were sitting on the ground with their backs against the crate. They seemed to be laughing – a release of the tension, and their realization that they had survived the landing. They all looked up as the others approached.

"I can't believe it," said Quinn. "What a rush. I could almost do it again."

"No thanks," said Sean. "Once was twice too many times."

"That doesn't make the least bit of sense," said Solveig.

"It does to me," said Liam.

"Does anybody know exactly what happened?" asked Solveig. "It looked like we were going to crash into that wall, but then there were those gargoyles and then they all of a sudden got covered with...what was that?"

"Ice," said Lochen. "I believe one of the Kelpies was left behind, probably to trap us if the burning of our ship was not sufficient."

"Where do you think they went?" asked Sean.

"Back to where that Rebbercand took Natalie," answered Stella. "I could see another marker appear on the map right after Solveig did her thing on the last one. I'm not sure what for, though."

"To find a replacement," said Lochen. "I believe that is why they freed Ena Ray. He was a sorcerer being trained by the Enchantress, as was the creature the Rebbercand led us to at the base of the volcano."

"Is this more from that book you've been translating?" asked Natalie.

"I've mentioned most of it before, but I've only recently put some of the pieces together," he replied. "It is clear that it is essential for there to be eight of them. Their power is magnified when they are all resurrected. Solveig has thwarted those efforts to a certain extent, but they've managed to find replacements. It's not clear to me why the Enchantress, of all people, would have been training them."

"It would have been part of her responsibility," interjected Stella. "It's part of being an Enchantress. Anyone we encounter who has the capabilities – we must help them develop their skills and steer them towards the proper use of those talents. She really had no choice."

"But it appears they turned against her," said Lochen.

"There is always that chance," said Stella. "We can train them, but we can't force them to use their powers for good. That is their decision. It's the decision we all must make."

"Yes," Lochen agreed. "That makes sense. We must all be responsible for our own decisions; our own choices. It seems that the two who the Enchantress was training chose poorly."

"So you're saying that they're at what...full strength?" asked Sean. "And we're sitting here discussing it? Shouldn't we be doing something else?"

"Yeah," agreed Quinn. "Like getting away from here as fast as we can?"

"That sounds like a great idea, but where do we go?" asked Solveig.

"To find the band," said Lochen. "The stone – part of which Stella is wearing – and the band in which it was held are the keys to their power. We must ensure that they don't possess them."

"How do we find the band?" asked Liam.

"Wait a minute," said Summer. "You mean the band that we all held on to in the Crystal Citadel? The band that somehow transported us someplace underground? The band that sealed the doors and locked up the gargoyles? That band?"

"Precisely," said Lochen. "As to how we find it..."

He turned to Stella. Without being asked, she closed her eyes and brought forth the image of the map. After a few seconds she opened her eyes and looked towards Liam.

"It's in the Swamp," she said. "The access is where the first Kelpie was released."

"It'll take us days to get there," said Liam. "We can follow this river most of the way."

"The sooner we start," said Lochen, "the better. I don't know how far away the one Kelpie left behind is, but I'm sure he's close. The others will be along soon."

"We don't have any supplies of any kind," groaned Quinn. "We should open this crate and see if there's anything inside we can use."

"An excellent idea," agreed Lochen.

Quinn moved towards the front where the box had collided with the rock. The crate had held strong. There was no break in the boards. He tried to pry off the top, but it was sealed tightly.

"Allow me," suggested Lochen.

Quinn took a step or two back while Lochen twirled the index finger of his right hand. The nails holding the top popped out one by one. Then the lid lifted up and fell away. Quinn moved back to the box and looked in.

"What the...?" he muttered.

He reached in and pulled out several items. He turned to face the others and displayed the contents.

"Hats," he said. "Nothing but hats."

Chapter seventeen

Quinn held up his hands to show what he had pulled from the opened crate. They were, as he had stated, simply hats. In his hands were three or four of different kinds, each a different shape and a different color. He looked back inside the box, hoping there was something more. He fished around, moving the remaining contents from side to side before turning back to the others.

"Nope," he said. "Nothing but hats."

"Fat lot of good a bunch of crummy hats will do us," groused Sean.

"Hats?" repeated Stella. "Hats?"

"You heard right," confirmed Quinn. "That's what I said. Hats. You know? Those things you wear on your head?"

"Hats," repeated Stella.

She had a puzzled look on her face. Her brow was furrowed like she was trying to work something out. She motioned for the others to keep silent while she wracked her brain for the answer.

"Hats," she repeated.

"YES!" said Quinn, growing frustrated at having to repeat it. "That's what I said the first three times. HATS."

"That's what he said," replied Stella.

"Yes," said Sean. "We were all here when he said it – and said it and said it. Does he have to say it again? Hats! Would it be better if I said it? Hats. Hats. Hats."

"Thank you. I think I heard him quite clearly," said Stella. "But I wasn't referring to Quinn. I was referring to the sentinel. What was his name? Anea! He said, 'Wear the hats.' We thought he said, 'Where it's at,' or 'where are the bats' which didn't make any sense at all; not that 'wear the hats' would have made any more sense at the time."

"Who are you talking about?" asked Natalie.

"The sentinel that Liam, Sean, Solveig and I met when we were in the Ice Kingdom."

"Are you sure?" asked Lochen. "About what he said, that is. Is it possible that he said something else and now, because you see these hats, that's what you think he said?"

"Anything is possible, I suppose," she replied, shaking her head. "But I'm pretty sure he said to wear the hats."

"But you weren't sure that's what he said the first time you heard him, were you?" asked Sean. "Remember? I thought he said 'where are the bats,' and none of us could remember seeing any bats anywhere."

"We saw bats," said Summer. "It wasn't a pleasant experience."

"Maybe he did say 'where are the bats,'" repeated Sean. "And the bats Summer saw were the ones he was talking about."

"I didn't think he said 'where are the bats,'" interjected Liam. "I thought he said 'where they at.' Maybe he was talking about Lochen, Quinn, Summer and Natalie, since only the four of us were there with him."

"This is getting us nowhere," said Lochen. "And time is of the essence. Stella, are you certain you recall what the sentinel said?"

"Well...no," she answered. "But of all the things to find in this box, why would it be filled with hats?"

"It's not filled," said Quinn.

"What?" asked Summer. "What do you mean?"

"I mean it's not filled," he said, holding his hands and the hats in the air. "There are only eight."

Everyone stopped talking. They exchanged glances, each waiting for another to say something. If the crate had been filled with dozens of hats, Stella's insistence on what the sentinel might or might not have said could be easily dismissed. The fact that there were only eight hats – and nothing else in the crate – gave her assertions credence.

"OK," Summer finally said. "So there are eight hats. That doesn't mean they were meant for us."

"Um…, well, no," said Quinn. "I think you're wrong."

He held up one of the hats with one of his fingers. It was a bright yellow sun hat with a wide, floppy brim. It had two or three small yellow flowers on the side. It looked like it had never been worn. It also looked small enough to fit only Summer. She stopped flying, dropped to the ground and sat down. Her head was spinning.

"That's just too freaky," she gasped.

"Fine," snapped Lochen impatiently. "Then let's take them with us and leave. I really must insist. We cannot afford to waste any more time than we already have. Quinn, pick them up and take them with you. We can sort all this out later!"

"NO!" shouted Stella.

Everyone kept completely still. All eyes turned to her. Even Lochen stopped in his tracks. Stella's reaction was so uncharacteristic of her that it took them all by surprise.

"No," she repeated less forcefully. "The sentinel said to wear the hats, not take them with us. He must have had a reason for saying it the way he did."

"That's if he was talking about hats," muttered Sean, "and not about bats. I still think…"

He was cut short by the glare that Stella turned on him.

"Enough with the freaking bats, already," she nearly growled at him.

She slowly turned towards the others, keeping her icy glare fixed on Sean. When she was sure he wasn't going to bring up the bats anymore, she faced the rest of the group.

"Just put them on," she ordered. "We've already spent more time debating this than it would have taken to put them on our heads."

"But," Quinn sputtered.

Stella turned a withering eye towards him. He slumped his shoulders and lowered his head like a puppy that had been scolded.

"I just wanted to know – aside from the hat for Summer – who gets what. They're all different."

"Take a guess," Stella snapped. "Just get it done."

"When did she get so bossy?" Sean whispered to Liam.

"Don't press your luck," he whispered back.

Quinn held up his hands and looked at the assortment of colors, shapes and sizes. He quickly spotted a snow white knitted cap with a large white pompom on top. It was much larger than the rest. He wondered why he hadn't noticed it before.

"This one's easy to figure out," he said.

He put the hat on his head and it fit perfectly. He handed the yellow sun hat to Summer. At first she thought the wide brim would interfere with her wings, but once she put it on and flapped, she discovered that it was as if the hat wasn't even there. Her wings swept right through the material.

"Weirder and weirder," she said.

Quinn shifted the rest of the hats from one hand to the other. He found one that was pointed in the front, with the brim folded up against the sides like wings. In the band was a dark green feather.

"Here," he said motioning to Sean. "This looks like something someone would wear in a forest."

Sean took the hat and turned it around several times in his hands. It looked like a large triangle from front to back and from top to bottom. He put it on and moved it to adjust it. Quinn had been right. It matched perfectly with his personality – and it fit perfectly on his head.

"Neat," he said.

Next Quinn pulled out a bright blue pill-box hat. It was round and about three inches high. The material was soft and smooth. The sides had tiny blue flowers along the edge. He looked up and the first person he saw was Natalie, with her bright blue eyes.

"I think this would look good on you," he said.

She smiled dubiously as she took the hat and studied it. There wasn't much use for hats in the ocean, she thought, but she had to agree, this one looked nice. She looked inside for some indication of which part was the front. It didn't seem to matter. She plopped it on her head – another perfect fit.

"What about me?" asked Solveig. "I'm the one who is blue. What do you have that goes with blue skin and red hair?"

"Blue and red?" asked Quinn.

He looked at the rest of the hats. For the first time he noted that they had been changing colors. He found he was holding one in his right hand and the rest in his left hand. His eyes were immediately drawn to the purple beret in his right hand. He held it up and smiled at Solveig, still wondering how that one had been separated from the others and when it had turned purple.

"Purple!" she exclaimed. "I love it."

She put it on quickly, lowered one side down on the left and puffed up the front. As she did so, and as the hat conformed exactly to her head, the blue color of her skin began to fade away as if being absorbed into the hat. Within seconds, it was all gone and she had returned to her natural coloring.

"You're not blue," said Sean.

"No," said Solveig. "Natalie is blue; I'm purple. Were you not paying attention?"

"No," answered Sean, pointing at her. "I mean, yes, I was paying attention, but no, that's not what I meant. Your skin – it's not blue anymore."

She held out her hands to get a good look.

"Finally," she sighed. "Now if I can only stay this way."

"Do you have one for me?" asked Liam.

"Ladies first," answered Quinn.

He held out a bright red tam for Stella. It was made from the softest yarn any of them had ever felt or seen. The color was so vibrant it almost looked like fire. Once it was in place, Quinn held out his hand towards Liam. In it was a tan canvas hat with the brim folded up on one side.

"This looks like it was made for you," Quinn said.

Liam took that hat in his hands and turned it over. He had to admit, it looked really cool. He couldn't keep himself from smiling as he put it on. Like all the others, it fit him exactly and complimented the clothing he was wearing.

Only Lochen was left. Quinn looked down and saw there was only one hat left. He was sure this same hat hadn't been there before, but he couldn't recall what was. He looked from the hat to Lochen and back.

"Absolutely not," said Lochen. "I refuse to wear that."

In Quinn's hands was a dark brown hat that rose up about a foot to a point. It had a brim around the bottom that was slightly bent in a couple of places. The cone shape of the hat itself was also slightly bent.

"It looks like a dunce cap," objected Lochen. "I will not agree to this."

"It looks like a sorcerer's hat," said Stella.

"Really?" asked Lochen as he slowly became more interested. "Do you think so?"

"It looks cute," said Solveig.

"That does not encourage me," Lochen snapped at her. "It looks all beaten up."

"It looks like it belongs to someone wise," said Quinn.

"Wise?" repeated Lochen.

He studied the hat. He tried to straighten out the brim, but it was hopeless. He tried to straighten out the crook in the cone, but the hat only returned to its original shape. He looked at it with mild distaste. He had been right, though. All the others looked as if they had never been worn, but the one Quinn had handed to him appeared to be old and well used.

"It looks too big," he grumbled.

"It looks majestic," said Natalie.

"Hmmm. Wise and majestic?" he said, pondering the item. "Well, I suppose…"

He put it on and the hat immediately looked like it had belonged to him forever. It not only fit him perfectly, it matched the color, texture and look of his robes. Like Liam, it was impossible for him to hide his smile.

"Now," he said. "We really have to make haste. If the Kelpie that was left behind doesn't find us, the rest of them are sure to. We must leave here and get to the Swamp."

- - - - - - - - - - - - - - - - *** - - - - - - - - - - - - - - - - -

Saldeti was distraught. He had been unable to stop the massive wave of rushing water, and worse, he had lost almost all of his army of gargoyles. When the few remaining ones saw what had happened to their comrades, they all deserted, leaving him alone. They slipped away before he could do anything to prevent their departure.

As the wave had covered and crushed the gargoyles he had covered in ice, he caught something in the corner of his eye. He thought he had seen some people attached to a large piece of wood riding the waves into the marina.

It had all happened so fast and he had been so fixed on his doomed army that he hadn't paid particular attention to the fleeting image. There was something else he had seen that confused him. He thought he had seen a faerie fluttering above those on the wooden object. He was certain then that he had been imagining things.

He ran along the sea wall towards the town, searching for any remaining gargoyles, but knowing that they were all gone. He debated for a few seconds about going back to the caves and tunnels underground to find replacements. He knew that was futile. He would never find any of them. Besides that, he didn't relish the idea of returning to that stench.

"What am I going to tell Akmen Milzu?" he fretted.

He knew lying to her was pointless. She would see through him in an instant, and then he would have to suffer her wrath for trying to deceive her. He would have to be forthcoming. There was no other way.

By the time he made it back to the town, the flooding from the water that had poured over the top of the sea wall had subsided. There was mud and debris everywhere. He walked carefully, trying to avoid the larger puddles of water and muck. That was when he heard voices. Or at least he thought he heard voices.

At first he considered that he might be imagining things. Then he thought the deserting gargoyles were taunting him. He was becoming suspicious of every sound and of every movement. He spun in circles trying to determine if the voices were real and where they were coming from. Then they stopped.

"Get a grip on yourself," he said out loud. "Think."

He looked at the mud he was standing in and then back to the sea. The tidal wave, he realized, had come in this direction. If he had been right about what he first had seen, and there were people on some piece of wood being swept ashore, they would have come this way. He turned to face the opposite direction.

He could see the campsite with the wagon and beyond that there was something more. He mustered his courage and headed that way. As he passed the campsite, he moved more cautiously. There was something ahead. Moving even more slowly, he crept up to the crate.

He could see that there was no top on the box. He looked around and saw no sign of a lid. How had this managed not to fill with water, he wondered. He carefully stepped up to the box and looked in. It was empty. He looked around and saw no signs of anyone else until he stepped in another soft area of mud. He looked down at his feet and noticed tracks of several others.

He stepped back and examined them more closely. They were of different sizes and, as far as he could discern, there were seven sets of footprints. Furthermore, they were clearly not made by gargoyles. He had been right. Someone had come ashore on the wave, crashed here and now was gone. Not someone, he corrected himself; some others.

"They must be the ones following us," he said to no one.

He turned sharply back towards the sea. If they had come from out there, he considered, then they had escaped. Either they had escaped detection by his counterparts, or they had escaped confrontation. In either case, the fact that they had eluded the other Kelpies was not good news.

"Where are they now?" he asked. "Where could they be going?"

He moved beyond the crate and saw a winding river nearby. They were going east, he reasoned. But why? Should he follow them? He had no idea where the other Kelpies were. He found it inconceivable that they could all be lost or destroyed. He would have sensed something; he was sure. But he felt nothing.

He had no way of knowing it would be almost a full day before they would return. He had no clue that they had traveled far to the south in search of Tebaga. He was filled with indecision. If even one of the gargoyles had remained with him, he could leave a message for the Kelpies. But then he considered that he could never trust a gargoyle to follow orders.

He went back to the town, searching for something on which he could write a message. There was nothing. He returned to the marina. This was the most likely place they would come, he thought. He decided he would leave word for them here and go after those who had slipped past him on the crest of the wave.

He returned briefly to where the empty crate was. He stretched out his hands and raised the box into the air. He moved it to the marina and placed it at the end of the sea wall. It looked so out of place, he was certain it would attract their attention. However, to make certain he moved his index finger through the air and burned a message into the face of the box.

Army destroyed; chasing enemy; follow river - Saldeti

Satisfied he had done all he could to alert the other Kelpies, he went in search of the voices he had heard. The slight breeze carried the sound in his direction. Before, all he had heard was a buzzing, but enough to know someone was speaking. As he strode past the rapidly deteriorating wagon of the acrobat and to the location where the crate had been found, he could make out something more clearly. He was certain he heard someone say, "I agree."

- - - - - - - - - - - - - - - - *** - - - - - - - - - - - - - - - - -

"Don't you think the colors of some of these hats will attract attention?" Liam asked Lochen.

"If we don't start moving soon," he replied, "I don't think it will matter in the least. I really must insist."

"Lochen's right," added Stella. "I can feel someone nearby."

"I can go back and scout things out," offered Summer.

"No," said Lochen. "We have too far to go and too little time to get to the Swamp."

"We could sail," said Quinn. "At least part of the way."

"On what?" asked Sean. "I don't see any boats around here, and I don't think you seriously expect us to go back to the marina and untie one of the ones there."

"No," said Quinn. "I was thinking more of a raft."

He gestured to the lid of the crate that had been pushed aside when it was pried from the top.

"But the river won't be flowing to the east for much longer," said Liam. "It's only going that way because of the tidal flooding."

"Maybe so," said Natalie. "But it's better than nothing."

"Besides," said Solveig, "even if we only use it for a little while, it's better and faster than walking."

"Awww, not in the water again!" moaned Sean. "That thing isn't seaworthy and it's not big enough. It's a lid! It's not even a real raft."

"We can make room," said Summer. "I can fly and you can sit in the middle."

Lochen was growing extremely impatient with all the chatter. Without entertaining any more discussion, he gestured with his hand and the lid rose up into the air, flew across the grass and sand and landed on the shore of the river. He looked at the others with an expression that asked, "What are you waiting for?" They ran over to the raft and climbed on.

Once they were in place, Lochen waved his hand and the raft propelled itself into the current. As they picked up speed and pulled into the main channel of the river, Stella felt a shiver run through her. She looked back to where they had shoved off as it slowly disappeared while they followed the bend in the river. Once it was out of sight she leaned in close to Lochen so only he would hear.

"I feel that we got out of there just in time," she whispered. "I think they are closer than we thought."

He lifted his head and looked back in the direction she had been facing. He studied the shore and the trees as the raft followed the river. He looked back at her and saw the tension in her eyes. He then snapped his fingers and increased the speed of the wooden platform and felt the breeze blow past him, as he replied.

"I agree," he said.

------------------ *** ------------------

Saldeti walked to the edge of the river. He looked upstream, but saw nothing beyond the trees and brush where the river curved out of sight. He then looked down at his feet. He could see an indentation in the sand. There was an indication that something large and square had been here very recently. He studied the shape and size. He recalled the crate on which he had left his message in the marina. That was where the lid went, he realized.

He looked down and saw the same footprints that were around the crate imprinted here in the sand. He had been right. There were others here. And they had escaped by floating along the river. He thought for a minute, and then ran back once more to the marina.

He looked at the old boats tied to their respective moorings along the sea wall. He found an old fishing boat that seemed to be in acceptable condition. He looked it over quickly to make sure there were no rotting boards and that it was not taking on water. He flicked a wrist and the mooring lines untied. Before the boat could drift away, he thrust a hand forward and raised it into the air.

Walking back to the river, he held the boat in the air over his head. At the shore, he lowered it into the water. Holding it in place with one hand, he snapped the fingers of his other hand and extended the gangplank. When it stretched out and touched the sand, he walked aboard. Snapping his fingers again, the gangplank returned to the boat.

He then thrust out his hand and pushed the boat into the middle of the channel. With a flick of his wrist, he put the craft in motion and followed the current. He moved cautiously, keeping a sharp eye as far out ahead of him as he could. He wished Angin Topan had been with him. He would have appreciated having her scout ahead for him.

He was intent on not getting caught or trapped by whomever he was following. He was also determined to make up for the loss of the army of gargoyles. He would find out who these people were and what they wanted. He would deliver them to Akmen Milzu, no matter what it took.

Chapter eighteen

When the Kelpies reached Satamakau, it was early the next morning. Saldeti was well on his way upriver in pursuit of the voices he had heard. His associates had left the volcano island with Tebaga added to their company. They had made the trip in almost total silence. As evil and violent as they were, what B'nair had done to his own brother had shaken them. Akmen Milzu was particularly concerned that the stone in the Rebbercand's possession was giving him powers that he would not normally have – powers which he was not prepared to handle.

Dealing with that would have to wait. Now that there were eight Kelpies, even though two of their numbers were not the originals, they had to retrieve the rest of the stone and find the band. She debated how much she could share with B'nair

404

compared to how much she would be required to share in order to find the band.

She assumed the ones who had been following them, and who had been left to burn in the sea, had the other half of the stone. She wondered if the Rebbercand's map would show exactly where that stone was. She also wondered if they should go in pursuit of the stone now or go back and find Saldeti.

Finding Saldeti, she determined, was more important. Whoever had been following them had the capability of destroying Kelpies. She couldn't afford to lose Saldeti, regardless of how ineffectual he had been in their rebellion. Useless or not, he had committed to their cause and he was one of them. His safety needed to be secured.

As the dawn struggled to break through the gray sky, the Lightning Riders lowered their passengers to the ground. All seemed to be as it had been when they left. The tide was in; the marina was full; and the town was empty. It was all the same as it had been when they left Saldeti behind – except for the odd looking crate at the end of the marina.

"Stay close," ordered Akmen Milzu.

The Lightning Riders had released them all and had dissipated into the air. The Kelpies, the sorcerers and B'nair relished the feeling of solid ground under their feet. But Akmen Milzu wanted only to retrieve Saldeti and leave. That was when she and Neraka Ferr saw the message.

"Curse him," shouted the Fire Kelpie. "He can do nothing right. He had a simple task – amass an army of gargoyles and wait here. I see no army and he's not here."

"The gargoyles are not easily commanded," said Ena Ray. "They are not especially intelligent."

He had seen the crate and came up next to Akmen Milzu to see what she and the Fire Kelpie were looking at. His comment about gargoyles brought Tebaga, B'nair and the others up as well.

"If you know so much about gargoyles," said Angin Topan, "perhaps it should have been you to amass the army rather than Saldeti."

"Saldeti was well chosen to lead gargoyles," said Rovek. "He has the ability to do little else."

"No," said Ena Ray, ignoring the comment by Rovek. "I led them once before, when they were in their original form."

He cast a glance at B'nair, but saw that his comment had no reaction on the Rebbercand. Tebaga understood the reference and looked to B'nair as well.

"I don't think he understands," Tebaga said.

B'nair realized they were both looking at him.

"Understands what?" he demanded.

"You and the gargoyles," Ena Ray began.

"And the hobgoblins," added Tebaga. "Don't forget the hobgoblins."

"And the hobgoblins," Ena Ray continued. "You and the gargoyles and the hobgoblins all come from the same ancestors. You're related. Didn't you know?"

B'nair had learned of his shared lineage with the hobgoblins after he had been rescued by them in the mines of the Trepans. They had healed him as best they could and restored him to health. They had provided him with the axe that was now permanently sealed to his hand. During his time with them they had explained their relationship. He knew nothing, though, of being related to the gargoyles.

"I can see by the look on his face," said Tebaga. "This is all news to him. No wonder the Rebbercands were so easy to manipulate."

Tebaga and Ena Ray had preyed on the Rebbercands who inhabited the village in which Meri Hocto had secreted her citadel. It had been inside a massive tree in the middle of the town, accessible through a portal unknown to the Rebbercands. The two sorcerers had used the local residents as pawns in their games – until things got out of hand.

Those that had followed Ena Ray had been transformed into gargoyles and relegated to the underground. Those that had followed Tebaga had been transformed into hobgoblins and sent to a different life in the caves and tunnels under the surface of the earth. With the collapse of the citadel, the remaining Rebbercands – the ancestors B'nair and his brother had grown up with – became nomads.

"And all because of that pendant of hers," said Ena Ray.

"So that was what you were after," said Tebaga.

He finally understood that he, too, had been a pawn. He had been used by Ena Ray for the sole purpose of stealing the pendant of the Enchantress. He had been deceived into violating her trust. He had been deceived into misusing his powers to manipulate the Rebbercands. The war games they played had all been a ruse.

He could feel the rage inside him boiling up. For two thousand years he had focused his hatred at the Enchantress. He had blamed her for overreacting; for not seeking an explanation; for not giving him a second chance. He hadn't understood the reason for her fury. Until now.

He charged towards Ena Ray. He raised his hand to cast the most damaging spell he could. Before his arm could come down, he felt a tremendous pressure engulf him. Everything slowed down. He could see Ena Ray and the look of panic on his face. But he could also see that the sorcerer had not reacted quickly enough to stop him. The spell he felt was coming from somewhere else.

He slowly turned his head. He could feel the pressure squeezing him. The air gushed out of his lungs. He couldn't breathe in. His arm would not move forward. The sounds around him quickly faded away. All he could hear was a ringing sound. He realized the ringing was coming from inside his own head. His head stopped turning when he was facing Akmen Milzu. All motion stopped when he saw her.

Her hand was extended forward, directly towards him. It was clenched in a fist. He knew instantly that it was her spell he was under. She had stopped him. She was crushing him; squeezing the life out of him. Slowly, he could feel the pressure easing, but not leaving completely – only enough for him to breathe.

"Enough," she said.

She eased up a little more, only to allow him to speak.

"She cursed me," he gasped. "She sent me into oblivion for centuries. I could not see. I could not hear, or smell or taste. I could feel nothing. I was dead, but not dead. I suffered that punishment because of him."

"You made your own decisions," Ena Ray shouted at him. "You were responsible for your actions. Don't blame me. Besides, I suffered the same as you."

"We all did," exclaimed Akmen Milzu. "Neither of you is special."

"But I didn't deserve that," Tebaga argued. "It wasn't my fault."

"Silence," shouted the Mountain Kelpie. "He merely gave you a choice, poor though it was. You decided to accept what he offered. Every choice you made; everything you did had its consequences. You alone are responsible for the decisions you made. You deceive yourself when you blame others for those decisions."

Tebaga bristled at the Kelpie's words. He didn't want to believe her. He struggled, but she held him tightly, and continued to do so until his anger evaporated. It melted into self-pity. She still held him.

"You have an opportunity to change things," she said to him when she was more certain he was listening.

She turned to look at B'nair. Now seemed as good a time as any to reveal everything. She would have to trust that the Rebbercand would be willing to give up the stone for a greater reward later on.

"This opportunity extends to you as well," she added.

She could see that she had his undivided attention. He had been shocked at the revelations Ena Ray and Tebaga had shared. He had been lost in his own thoughts. Now he had put them aside.

"I'm listening," he assured her.

"The stone you wear around your neck is part of the pendant that belonged to the witch — the one known as Meri Hocto. As you can tell, there is a part or parts that are missing. But there was also a band that encompassed the stone."

"I had that band," said Ena Ray. "It was in my grasp when I was banished to the Crystal Citadel."

"A pity you couldn't hold on to it," snarled Rovek.

"I had no physical form," replied Ena Ray. "I had no hands, thanks to the witch. It was suspended above me — in my possession, but out of my reach — for centuries."

"The Alchemist," muttered Scirios.

"He had nothing to do with it," said Ena Ray. "I reached for it at the instant the spell was cast on me."

"I know he had nothing to do with where it was," said the Lightning Kelpie. "He was responsible for leaving it there."

"What do you mean?" asked Tebaga.

"He knew the pendant had been destroyed," continued Scirios. "He would have searched for the pieces for as long as it took, and once he found them, he'd have to hide them."

"Why?" asked B'nair. "And what does that have to do with the pendant?"

"Because he knew there would come a time when the spells on us would be weakened," continued Scirios. "When the planets were aligned – the same as they were when we began our rebellion. When that happens, the powers of all sorcerers and enchantresses are magnified. When they commit themselves, as we did, that only further amplifies our power."

Ena Ray began to understand how he had been able to control elements – the Fury – far beyond the Crystal Citadel.

"And the band does the same thing," he added.

"More than that," said Akmen Milzu. "It channels the power. It becomes unstoppable."

"So when the band was hovering over me, as a reminder of my imprisonment," Ena Ray said. "It was also channeling my power."

"Yes," said Neraka Ferr. "That's right. And it would also have caused the spell on you to weaken."

"If I had been in a solid form," Ena Ray concluded, "I could have escaped? Is that what you're saying?"

"Perhaps not," said Akmen Milzu. "But it would have been much easier for one of us to release you."

"But why would the Alchemist leave it with him in the Citadel?" asked Tebaga.

"He was hiding it in plain sight, so to speak," answered Scirios. "No one would think to seek out the Citadel. None of us knew of the existence of either of you, so we would have no reason to search for you. He could take his time finding the pieces of the pendant and hide them in places only he would know."

"Like the fortress at Virkio," said B'nair. "Or in that glass shop inside the fortress of the Thumpers."

"How could you know where those pieces were?" asked Rovek.

"The hobgoblin who gave me this axe," B'nair explained. "He told me the myth behind it. He said it belonged to the person who killed the witch. Before she died she shattered the stone, but a splinter of it glanced off the axe blade and lodged in his forehead. It served as a beacon for the other pieces – pieces he searched for over decades.

"The hobgoblins, over the centuries, had learned that one of the pieces was in the fortress at Virkio. They also discovered a way to break into it. They led me there. Once I had one of the pieces, I could sense the location of another piece."

"The piece your brother claimed belonged to him?" asked Angin Topan.

"No," said B'nair. "Neither of the pieces I have was ever in his possession. I found the second piece in a refuse barrel in a shop in the deserted village inside the fortress of the Thumpers. I have no idea what he was talking about."

"He had one with him when he released me from my crypt," said Tebaga. "I don't know how he came by it. He had taken a Sea Sprite hostage in an attempt to trap her Enchantress. He somehow knew where I was and how to release me. He lost the stone in the fight with these others you have mentioned – the ones who have been following you."

"You mean the ones that it now appears Saldeti is chasing?" asked Rovek.

"And where does all that leave us?" asked B'nair.

He was certain that it was all leading up to a request or demand that he give up the stone. He wasn't sure he would be able to fend off any spells they would cast on him. He had seen all too clearly the power they were able to exert over one of their own. Tebaga was still being restrained by Akmen Milzu.

"We need to find the rest of the stone," said the Mountain Kelpie. "And then find the band. I believe you may be able to tell us where both are. Until the stone is placed back inside the band, its touch will do us great harm. Therefore, we would be grateful to you if you retained possession for the time being."

"And once the stone and the band are together again?" B'nair asked.

He decided it might be good, once and for all, to get everything out in the open. Depending on the answer he received, he would decide how cooperative to be. He expected the Kelpie would tell some kind of lie. He was curious to see what form that lie would take. At the same time, Akmen Milzu was considering how much she should reveal and what reaction the Rebbercand would have to whatever she said.

"I will ask you to give the pendant to me," she said, surprising him as much as she surprised herself.

"And why would I do that?" B'nair asked.

"Because it will open a portal that can't be opened by you," she said.

"You've gone too far," hissed Rovek. "You've told him too much already."

"He has earned the right to know," Akmen Milzu replied.

She kept her eyes fixed on B'nair's. She needed him to trust her. She concluded that she had to be honest with him. Perhaps not completely honest, but enough to convince him. Part of her resented Rovek's outburst, but when she saw the flicker in B'nair's eyes, she realized the Forest Kelpie's outburst served her purpose. It convinced the Rebbercand that she was telling him the truth.

"It will open a portal," she continued. "On the other side of this portal, our power will become permanent – no longer dependent upon the stone or the band. It will be limitless."

"And how does that benefit me?" asked B'nair.

"We will not forget the person who made this possible," she said.

She gambled that if she told him he would have unlimited power, he would know it was a lie. Telling him something less – that he would be rewarded because of his loyalty even though this, too, was a lie – she hoped would be more convincing.

"I expect you won't," he answered.

It was not the commitment she had hoped for, but it was enough. B'nair had gone through the same thought processes as the Kelpie. If he told her she would have his full commitment, she would know he was lying. He, too, gambled that by telling her something less, she would believe him. In the end, neither truly trusted the other, but both had decided they had no choice but to trust each other if only for the time being.

"Good," she said. "Then I suggest we collect Saldeti and head back out to sea to find the remaining piece of the stone."

"It's not in the sea," said B'nair.

"How is that possible," roared Neraka Ferr. "I burned them all myself."

"It seems they must have escaped," replied B'nair. "At least the one with the stone did. I can't tell exactly where it is, but I know it's not in the sea. Perhaps your missing Kelpie knows where it is."

"Maybe he's not as useless as you thought he was," Angin Topan muttered to Neraka Ferr.

"That remains to be seen," the Fire Kelpie growled back.

"Can I trust you to put the past behind you?" Akmen Milzu asked Tebaga.

The sorcerer turned towards Ena Ray and fought against glaring at him. This was not over, he thought to himself. However, he turned back to the Mountain Kelpie and nodded. She then released her grip on him. He took a deep breath, glanced once at Ena Ray and then walked in the opposite direction a few steps.

"Scirios," called the Mountain Kelpie. "Summon the Lightning Riders. It's time we found Saldeti."

The sorcerer did as requested. The small electrical charges dropped from the dark sky above and slowly spread out, encompassing the Kelpies, the sorcerers, and the Rebbercand. Once they were enmeshed in the webbing, they rose towards the clouds.

"Not too high," Akmen Milzu said to Scirios. "We need to keep the river in sight."

The mass moved in staccato bursts over to the water and then made short surges forward following the current, which was still heading east as the ocean tide continued to push against the flow coming westward from the mountains.

- - - - - - - - - - - - - - - - - *** - - - - - - - - - - - - - - - - -

Several miles ahead, moving away from Satamakau, Lochen was still steering the wooden lid along the water and propelling it with short, quick gestures. He looked like a conductor leading a symphony only he could hear. The river snaked back and forth, limiting visibility both to the front and the back to less than a hundred yards.

Shortly after they had launched the makeshift raft, Stella's attention had been diverted back towards the town. As the turns in the river had gotten sharper, Lochen had slowed their speed down to avoid running ashore or into unseen obstacles.

"Don't slow down," Stella whispered.

Lochen looked at her. He could see that she was intently focused on something behind them. He glanced at the others and then back to Stella.

"I have many talents," he whispered back. "But seeing around boulders, trees and shrubs is not one of them. If I don't slow down, we may collide with something that may halt us altogether, or worse, sink us."

"Yes," she replied, her voice still low. "I understand, but try not to slow down any more than you have to."

"What do you see?" he asked.

She looked over her shoulder to the others. They had arranged themselves to disburse their weight and keep the crate lid balanced – and to accommodate Sean's insistence to be as far from the water as possible. Summer was flying a few yards ahead, keeping an eye on anything in the water that would otherwise be out of Lochen's sight. None of them was looking towards the back.

"Nothing," she whispered. "It's more of a feeling."

"And what do you feel," Lochen persisted.

"I think we're being followed," she said.

"Gargoyles?"

"No. Something worse."

"The Kelpies?" he asked. "Have they come so close to catching up to us? I thought it would take longer."

"It doesn't feel like all of them," she clarified. "And I don't feel the presence of the rest of the pendant. Maybe there's only one."

"Of course," he said. "That would confirm our earlier suspicions."

"That they left one behind?"

"Yes. Natalie had mentioned someone on shore trying to freeze the water," he explained. "I hadn't thought of it at the time, but I recall seeing a figure of some kind on the north shore, and then a flash of light immediately prior to our vault over the sea wall. I have to admit I was preoccupied with surviving the crash of the wave into the harbor. I dismissed what I thought I had seen."

"So you were right about them leaving one of the Kelpies behind."

"So it seems," he said. "Although it also seems somewhat risky for them to have done so, considering we've destroyed two of them."

"Which they've managed to replace," she pointed out.

"Yes, they have. However, I believe they are running out of substitutions. The Alchemist's book only refers to two protégés being schooled by the Enchantress. If our assumptions are correct, then these two have replaced the two Kelpies we, or I should say Solveig has destroyed. If we destroy another, there are not likely to be any more to fill in the void."

"Do you think we should try to ambush him...her...whatever?" Stella asked.

Lochen considered her question and looked towards Solveig. Thus far, she had been the only one capable of eliminating Kelpies. The dragon's tooth she carried appeared to be the only viable weapon against them. He resisted letting her go after the one at the bottom of the ocean. He was not about to suggest putting her in harm's way again.

"No," he answered. "I think it's too precarious a proposition. We would be better off trying to avoid any encounter."

"Then we need to get off the river," she said.

Lochen evaluated their alternatives and options. He immediately recalled how trapped they had been out at sea. While they could move faster on the river, they were more vulnerable to attack and had fewer options to defend themselves or launch a counter attack.

"Yes," he agreed. "We will fare better on land, although we run the risk of the Kelpies – or even only the one following us – catching up to us sooner rather than later."

"What do we tell the others?" Stella asked. "I don't want to worry them."

"I have found," Lochen replied, "that in such dire circumstances as these, the truth is normally best."

Stella looked at him and thought about what he said. She took a deep breath and nodded. He was right. They had all been through so much; this was not likely to frighten them.

"We're getting off now," Lochen exclaimed.

"Off?" asked Liam. "Why?"

"Fine with me," exclaimed Sean. "I've had enough water to last more than a lifetime."

"Summer," Stella called. "Come on back. We're getting off the river."

"Is something wrong?" asked Solveig.

"Stella believes we are being followed," Lochen explained. "And I agree that she's very likely correct. We're far too exposed on the water. We'll fare much better on land."

"Who's following us?" asked Quinn.

"We think one of the Kelpies," answered Stella. "I haven't seen anything so I don't think he...or she...what are they, anyway?"

"Hes and shes," answered Lochen. "Remember, they are both sorcerers and enchantresses. Regardless, the one that seems to be behind us is probably not very close, but all the same, we should exercise caution."

Lochen maneuvered the raft to the northern shore and held it steady as the others climbed off. When they were all back on land, he began to walk away, following the river, but several yards inland. After a few steps, he stopped and went back to the crate lid.

He looked at it for a few seconds, thinking about what to do with it. Then he stretched out his hand, palm down and flicked his fingers upward. The wood slid away from the shore and back into the river's current. Then he turned his hand sideways and flicked his wrist. The raft began moving along in the original direction, heading eastward without its passengers.

"Why did you do that?" asked Summer.

She had fluttered ahead, but when she looked back over her shoulder, she had seen Lochen leave the group and return to the shore. Wondering what he was doing, she had followed him. She also wanted to make sure that he didn't get separated from the others. At the sound of her voice, he turned to answer.

"If we're being followed," he explained, "whoever is following us will most likely want to avoid detection. To do so, his...or her...attempts to spy on us will be limited. If he...or she...catches glimpses of the raft, then it's likely that he...or she... will continue pursuit and allow us more time to evade him...or her."

"Why don't you just call them 'it'?" she asked. "It seems that would be simpler."

"I suppose you're right," he said with a smile. "I suggest we make maximum advantage of our ruse."

He strode past her and caught up with the others.

Further back on the river towards Satamakau, Saldeti was guiding his boat along, weaving back and forth, trying to stay close to the shore and out of the middle of the current. He hadn't seen what he was looking for, yet, but he was certain they couldn't be far ahead of him.

He decided to increase his speed slightly. A few minutes later, he floated by the embankment where the wooden crate lid had beached and been divested of its passengers, and then sent on its way. Saldeti hadn't noticed the gouges in the sand made by the raft, nor the footprints of those who had gotten off and began walking.

He moved around the next bend and then another, narrowly missing a large rock in the riverbed and ducking under a low hanging tree branch. Then he saw it. Just the corner, but he could see that there was something ahead that was sailing along the river.

He hugged the shore as much as he could and increased his speed a little more. As he came around the next bend, he caught another glimpse. Still, it was only the corner, but this time he had been looking for it. It was some kind of raft.

"I knew it," he muttered to himself. "They're right ahead of me."

He started to increase his speed again to overtake them. At the last second, he stopped. What do I do when I catch up to them, he wondered. They destroyed Pantano Izaki, and, it appears they may have done the same to Ollos Foscos. They could be more powerful than previously imagined. He could be heading into a trap.

He maintained his speed until he came around the next bend. He was certain he could see more of the raft, although in reality, it was only in his imagination that more of the crate lid was visible. He slowed slightly to allow a bit more distance to grow between him and them.

He considered his options and then decided he would rush the craft ahead of him and whatever passengers were on it and immediately cast a spell freezing them in place. He knew that one of them could be a faerie, but he knew that faeries had no special powers and would not pose a threat to him. Just the same, though, he would be on guard for that possibility.

With his strategy decided, he increased his speed until he caught sight of the raft once again. As it disappeared around the next turn in the river, he surged ahead, rounded the bend and thrust his arms out, coating the crate lid in ice.

It was empty. The spell had covered the wood in frost and stopped its forward motion. Now it was subject to the current, which was slowing considerably as the water from the mountains was pushing back on the flow of water from the tidal flood. The raft, now without the guidance of Lochen's spell, drifted and spun in the eddies until it lodged itself against the nearest bank.

Saldeti maneuvered his boat over to the beached piece of wood and looked at it in stunned anger. How could he have been such a fool? They had obviously placed this thing in the water and set it adrift in the expectation that he would follow it. They probably never left the village. The other Kelpies could be in danger.

He reversed the boat and headed back towards Satamakau. He increased the speed, heedless of the hidden dangers in the bed of the river. He sped around the bends, winding back and forth. In seconds he blew past the place where the raft had deposited its passengers. A few minutes later, he came upon a series of small rocks in the center of the current.

When he had been following the raft, he had kept close to the shore to maximize the cover provided by the overhanging trees and shrubs. He had not been aware of the obstacles in the center of the waterway. He hadn't been prepared for the rocks and ran the boat over the top of them.

The first ones cut the hull like a knife, ripping gashes in the old wood. As the boat took on water, it dropped lower into the water and provided an even larger target for other rocks and a log or two that had been trapped in the bed.

The boat slid over some of the rocks, but one of the logs caught. It jerked the ship to the right before dislodging, and the craft moved sideways along the river. Saldeti was too surprised to react in time. The hull struck a larger rock mid-ship. The boat stopped suddenly for a few seconds.

Saldeti could feel the current begin to pull him back the way he had come – back away from Satamakau. He mistakenly cast a spell forcing the boat against the current, where it slammed into the same rock again before righting itself and continuing on. By now, though, the damage was done. The hull had cracked and the ship was doomed.

In seconds water flooded into the cargo hold and the ship was lost. The river crashed over the bulkhead as the boat sank to the bottom. The water wasn't deep, but it was enough to cover the deck and soak Saldeti to his waist.

In a panic he jumped over the side and sank even further. He flailed his arms and kicked his feet, certain he was going to drown. As his vision blackened, and he felt lightheaded, he thought he heard voices. They sounded like they were coming from somewhere above him.   The water splashing in his ears distorted the sounds, making them crackle.

Before he knew what was happening, he felt himself being lifted into the air and dumped onto the ground on the southern shore of the river on an open field of grass. He rolled onto his stomach and lifted himself to his hands and knees, gasping for breath.

"You should have taken the time to learn how to swim," he heard one of the voices say.

He looked up to see Scirios standing over him.   Behind the Kelpie, Saldeti could see the Lightning Riders discharging and the rest of their passengers stepping out onto the field.   Among them was another strange looking creature.   Saldeti knew then that something had happened to Ollos Foscos.   His associates had found another replacement.

"Yes," he coughed in response to Scirios.   "I should have.   But then I would have deprived you of your dramatic rescue."

"Tell us this was not a waste of time," grumbled Neraka Ferr.

"What happened to the army you were supposed to have amassed?" asked Rovek.

"Didn't you see my message?" he asked as he got to his feet.

"Yes," replied Rovek. "We saw the message, but that didn't tell us what happened. Couldn't you control them?"

"It was the ocean," Saldeti tried to explain. "It was unstoppable. They wouldn't follow my directions and they...it..."

"Enough," interrupted Akmen Milzu. "What happened to a bunch of gargoyles is irrelevant. Did you see the ones who destroyed Ollos Foscos?"

"She's gone, then?" asked Saldeti.

"Do you see her with us?" Neraka Ferr nearly shouted.

"I thought, perhaps, you lost her," Saldeti snapped back.

The Fire Kelpie turned a deeper red, swallowing his anger and choosing not to respond. He had seen in the corner of his eye the admonishing look from Akmen Milzu. He also realized any further discussion was pointless. Saldeti's uselessness was only confirmed in his mind.

"The ones who destroyed Ollos Foscos?" Akmen repeated the question.

Saldeti thought for a second. He was about to tell them about his pursuit of whoever he had seen riding the crest of the wave, but in light of what he had discovered, he realized he had nothing to say. Voicing his speculation would only make him look more foolish than he already felt.

"No," he answered. Anticipating their questions about why he was then on the river in an old wreck of a boat, he added, "I thought they had escaped by way of the river, but I could find no sign of them. I was returning to Satamakau when you found me."

"You were drowning in a river when we found you," corrected Neraka Ferr, able to get in one more dig.

Ignoring the Fire Kelpie's comment, Akmen Milzu turned to B'nair.

"Do you sense their presence?"

"No," the Rebbercand replied. "Perhaps we should search for them.

"The stone will come to us," Akmen Milzu said. "We and they are going to the same place — to find the band. We don't need to waste time trying to find them — or even only the one with the rest of the stone. We must reach the location of the band before they do. There are eight of us now. We are once again intact. When we find the band we will be that much closer to reaching our ultimate power. Scirios. Summon your Lightning Riders."

Chapter nineteen

By the time Saldeti had been rescued by his comrades and they were ready to transport themselves in their further search for the pendant, Liam had led the way for his friends through the tall grasses and small trees and shrubs that lined the river side. He could feel the air temperature change gradually. The water was beginning to stop its eastward flow as the warm ocean tide was meeting a stronger current from the icy mountain streams. The mixture was also beginning to generate a slowly growing, thick fog.

A few hundred yards later, the vegetation thinned out and they approached a wide stretch of clay and sand. A minute or two later, they started seeing several holes dug into the beach. They were of different sizes and depths. When they turned, following another bend in the river, they saw someone crouched at the water's edge. Liam halted everyone's progress until he could study the person and determine if he was a threat.

The figure was squatting down and leaning over the water with his hands in the river almost up to the elbows. His legs were long and thin, although his thighs seemed quite muscular. His arms were thin and sinewy. His body was short and stocky, but it was his head that attracted the most attention.

It was large and oval shaped — much wider sideways than from top to bottom. His eyes were squinted over a wide, flat nose. His ears were small and pressed so close to his head as to almost be non-existent. His chin blended into his thick neck, and his mouth was very wide. His complexion was pale and had a sickly hue to it – grayish to the point of being nearly green.

"He looks like a giant frog," whispered Sean.

As soon as he said this, the creature lunged his head forward, opened his mouth wide and scooped up a large gulp of river water. He leaned his head back, shook it, and then lowered it towards the water again, spitting out a fish.

"He looks pretty strange to me," said Quinn.

"He looks rather harmless to me," said Lochen.

Abandoning caution, Lochen stepped forward and approached the creature. The figure slowly turned his head in Lochen's direction, but made no other move. He eyed Lochen from top to bottom and then looked past him to the others.

"Nice hats," he said in a croaking voice. "Did you steal them?"

"No," said Lochen. "Well...not exactly."

"Which is it?" asked the creature. "No or not exactly."

"We found them," Lochen replied.

"They belong to Artabarat," the creature said.

"That's right," said Stella as she stepped forward. "He loaned us his ship, but it was...well...it sank. The hats were in a crate that came ashore."

"Then they belong to you, I suppose," the creature replied.

At those words, he let out a high-pitched giggle and rolled his eyes. Other than that, he hadn't moved.

"Who are you?" asked Natalie.

"Gulper," he replied, and giggled again.

"That's an odd name," said Summer.

"That's not my name," he answered. "She asked me who I was, not what was my name."

"So I did," said Natalie. "What's your name?"

"Igel," he said. "But you can call me Gulper." And he let out another giggle.

"But if your name is..." started Quinn.

"Let it go," whispered Sean, pulling Quinn back a step or two. "This guy's a nut-basket."

"So, Gulper," said Solveig, "Are you a sentinel?"

"Are you friends of the Alchemist?" he asked.

"Yes," she answered.

"In that case, I'm a sentinel," he replied and giggled, this time a bit more hysterically.

"Have we come at an inconvenient time?" asked Lochen.

"Inconvenient time?" Gulper giggled again. "I have nothing but time."

"I only ask because you appeared to be eating," said Lochen.

Gulper squinted even more, fixing his gaze on Lochen and then moving slowly to each of the others. He giggled again, even more shrilly. His head lolled to one side and a look of sadness came over him.

"I am hungry, but cannot eat," he mumbled. "I am thirsty, but cannot quench my thirst. I am tired, but cannot sleep. I am old, but cannot age."

Instead of standing up, he waddled in his squatting position and moved away from the water's edge. He turned towards the expanse of clay and sand behind him, which, for the first time the others noticed, was covered with hundreds more holes. He looked up and saw the expressions on everyone's face at the sight. His own face seemed to brighten.

"Do you like my holes?" he asked. "It's what I do."

"They're...lovely," said Solveig.

"I think so, too," he said. "I remember a long time ago, there was a young man who was of a different mind. I tried to engage him in a discussion of them, but he simply didn't understand."

He didn't elaborate. Everyone watched him for several seconds waiting for him to go on, but it appeared he was finished.

"What didn't he understand?" asked Lochen.

"Don't encourage him," whispered Sean. "He's wacko."

"He didn't understand anything," Gulper went on, not hearing Sean's comment. "Sez he, 'they're just holes; they're all the same.' Sez I, 'You're wrong,' sez I. 'Each one is different; each one is unique.' Sez he, 'Nonsense, a hole's a hole.' Sez I, 'Yes, a hole's a hole's a hole, no matter how deep or wide.' Sez he, 'Not if you fill it half way. Then it's only half a hole.'

Gulper was beginning to become agitated. His voice was rising and his diatribe was filled with hysterical outbursts of giggles.

"Sez I, 'No such thing as half a hole; it's a whole hole – the hole is whole.' Sez he, 'If it was a whole hole to begin with and you fill it half way, then it's half a hole.' Sez I, 'If you fill it half way, no matter. It's still a whole hole.' Sez he, 'What if you fill the right half? Is it still a whole hole?' Sez I, 'Right half, left half, front half, back half. Doesn't matter. Always was and always will be a whole hole.' Sez he, 'Not if you fill the top half. Then it's gone.' Sez I, 'Wrong again. Hole's just underground, and it's still a whole hole. The whole hole is whole.'"

"This is all very fascinating," Lochen interrupted.

He had no idea how much longer this could go on. He was afraid it could extend for hours. Gulper didn't seem to be offended by the interruption. He opened his eyes wide and they almost bugged out of his head. He focused for a second on Lochen and then resumed his squinting.

"I thought he was my friend," said Gulper with a note of sadness in his voice. "But he wasn't. Not at all."

As he had been talking, the fog had slowly gotten thicker. It was crawling along the shore and rising upward. At the same time, over their heads, there was a sudden flicker of light – a small electrical charge. Everyone looked up. They were stunned to see the Kelpies not far overhead, wrapped in a web of electrical current.

"Lightning Riders!" shouted Gulper.

He began waving his arms frantically and yelling.

"Hallooo. Down here. Can you see me? I'm down here. I've got new holes. Come and see. They're all whole holes; not a half hole in the bunch."

"What are you doing?" gasped Summer.

"They won't come down here," he said to her.

"Of course they will," said Liam. "You're attracting too much attention."

"No," countered Gulper. "If I didn't wave at them, then they'd be suspicious."

"We have to hide," wailed Quinn.

"Hide?" asked Gulper. "Why?"

"Because they'll see us," Quinn shot back.

"I told you he was loopy," said Sean.

"They can't see you," said Gulper.

"What are you talking about?" asked Solveig. "We're out in the open with these brightly colored hats. How can they NOT see us?"

"Because you're wearing those hats," he answered.

"See?" asked Sean. "A total fruitcake."

"I'm not sure I understand," said Lochen. "We're wearing items that should, by all accounts, stand out in extreme contrast to our surroundings and, thereby, make us easy to spot, and you contend that the contrary is true?"

"Now's not the time for a debate," argued Stella. "Quinn is right; we need to hide, if it's not already too late."

435

"Does he always talk like that?" Gulper asked, turning to Solveig.

"Yes," she answered. "All the time, but that's not the point. We thought you could help us, but instead, you're leading the Kelpies right to us."

"I told you," Gulper giggled hysterically again. "They can't see you. Artabarat's hats make you invisible to them. You're quite safe."

Nearly as suddenly as they had appeared, the Kelpies were gone. The mass of electrical current sparked and then disappeared.

- - - - - - - - - - - - - - - - - *** - - - - - - - - - - - - - - - - - -

Shortly after Saldeti had been reclaimed, the Kelpies headed towards the Swamp and the exact location of the band. Akmen Milzu had instructed Scirios to stay low to the ground in the event they came across their adversaries. She didn't want to pass up an opportunity to settle the score and to relieve them of the other half of the stone.

They surged ahead, stopped and surged again. In one of the stops they could see below them a strange creature squatting near the shore of the river. He appeared to be near hundreds of holes in the ground, many of which were barely visible through the growing fog. He looked as if he was talking to himself.

"Wait," said B'nair. "Maybe we should investigate."

"Don't bother," said Scirios. "It's only Gulper."

"Who's Gulper?" asked Ena Ray.

"He had been one of my minions during the revolt," explained Scirios. "I thought he would be reliable."

"That was an error in judgment on your part," said Angin Topan.

"What went wrong?" asked Ena Ray.

"He proved to be useless," said Scirios. "Completely insane. He engaged me in what felt like an endless discussion about holes. He argued that there was no such thing as half a hole; that all holes were whole."

"He was right, wasn't he?" asked Ena Ray.

"Don't get him started," said Rovek. "He was as bad as Gulper."

"That's not true," Scirios shot back defensively.

"Who kept arguing with him?" asked the Forest Kelpie. "You, as I recall."

"Let's move on," said Akmen Milzu. "There's nothing for us here, but the mad man."

In a blink they were gone. No sooner had they left when B'nair felt a sudden burst of energy strike his chest. It was the same location as the burning sensation he had felt in his dreams. He reached into his tunic and felt for the pendant. It was still there, but as soon as he touched it the surge of energy jolted him.

"Go back," he shouted.

"What for?" asked Scirios. "I've already told you. Gulper will offer us nothing useful and will only waste our time."

"Not him," shouted B'nair. "The stone. The other half of the pendant. It's down there."

"Where?" demanded Akmen Milzu.

"Where that creature was," he answered.

He was struggling against the electrical current, trying to turn back towards the shore where the hundreds of holes were.

"Stop moving," ordered Scirios. "You'll disturb the connection and we'll all be lost."

"Then turn back," B'nair ordered back at him. "I'm telling you. The other half of the pendant is back there."

"Go ahead," Akmen Milzu instructed. "Reverse course."

In an instant they turned back. The first surge didn't take them far enough. They hovered for a few seconds to ensure their bearings and to scour the ground beneath them. Satisfied they needed to go back further, Scirios steered the Lightning Riders once again. The second surge brought them back, directly over Gulper.

"I told you," Gulper had said as he giggled hysterically. "They can't see you. Artabarat's hats make you invisible to them. You're quite safe."

Only seconds after the words were out of his mouth, the static burst of electricity that swept the Kelpies away, returned.

"Perhaps I was wrong," Gulper said.

The cluster of current holding the Kelpies hung over his head as he and the others looked skyward. Slowly it descended. It was clear that they weren't going away. They were getting closer.

"These hats make us invisible to the Kelpies from above," said Quinn. "What about face to face?"

"I'm not sure about that," said Gulper.

"I think discretion is the better part of valor," said Lochen.

"Whatever," said Sean. "We need to get out of here."

"I believe that's what I said," Lochen replied.

"No," shouted Gulper. "Stay close. The fog is rising rapidly and you may get lost."

He was right. It had risen much higher in the last few minutes. Liam looked around and noticed he couldn't even see the river, which had to be within twenty feet of where they were standing. He looked up and could see the Kelpies still descending, but the fog was rising and beginning to engulf them, too.

"Grab each other's hands," he shouted. "Don't get separated."

They did as he said, and at the same time moved away from where they thought the river was. Meanwhile, Gulper stepped into the mist. His voice, though muffled by the fog, was also reflected by it in the same manner as an echo. No one could tell from which direction it was coming.

"My old friends," he shouted. "You've come to visit Gulper after all. How nice. I have new holes."

The descent was taking too long for B'nair. The near proximity of the other half of the stone was too much for his patience to bear. He wrenched his arms trying to free himself from the Lightning Riders. He couldn't see the ground now and had no idea how high they were or what was immediately under them. He guessed they were close enough to where he could jump, and that they had to be near the shore. He guessed wrong.

As he broke the electrical connection with his thrashing, he could hear a crackling and sizzling sound. The web began to disintegrate and its hold on its passengers evaporated. One by one they dropped downward. B'nair was the first to escape, but he pulled threads of the electrical current with him. Instead of touching down on the sand and clay shore, he landed in the river.

The clash between the water and the still active lightning resulted in a tremendous shock that jerked every muscle in his body. He went completely rigid, arching his back as the wave enveloped him completely. He splashed into the water and began spinning in the eddies created by the converging currents.

The icy waters from the east were colliding with the warm ocean waters from the west. The current where he landed swirled and churned. He spun one way and then the next, crashing into rocks and shoreline brush before getting caught up in some debris trapped on the shore opposite from Gulper. He was temporarily paralyzed from the electrical shock, but his head had lodged up over the top of a log, keeping him above water. Otherwise, he would have drowned.

Ena Ray and Tebaga had been closest to him. Tebaga dropped first, and Ena Ray landed on top of him, driving him into the muck near the water's edge. Tebaga pushed downward, lifting his face from the water and trying to push Ena Ray off of him. When it didn't happen immediately, he turned onto his side and rammed his elbow into Ena Ray's back. The two began thrashing and fighting until they felt enormous hands clamp down on them and pull them apart.

Akmen Milzu managed to land on the shore, but heard the splashing behind her. She stepped carefully through the mud until she came to the source of the sound. She had expected to find one of her comrades struggling to keep above the water. Instead, she found the two sorcerers wrestling like children. Her anger boiled and she grabbed the both of them, yanking them up and tossing them to the shore.

Rovek and Saldeti had managed to jump at the last minute. Although their jump had been blind, it had been accurate. They landed on the shore, a few feet down from Akmen Milzu. Behind them they heard the sound of Neraka Ferr falling into the shrubs that lined the shore further up, beyond where Gulper had his holes.

Scirios had made a last minute lunge and threw himself as far as he could away from where he believed the river to be. He had succeeded in that regard, but had landed in the area where Gulper's holes had been dug. He dropped one leg into one of the holes and his momentum had carried him too much further. He had broken his leg and was in extreme pain.

Only Angin Topan had managed to escape unharmed. She flew in small circles, widening with each revolution, in an effort to locate the others and, perhaps, get a fix on their adversaries. She reached Akmen Milzu first, after Ena Ray and Tebaga had been thrown to the shore.

"Stay where you are," she instructed the two sorcerers. "And try not to kill each other. I will bring the rest here."

The fog had gotten so thick that she couldn't see more than a few feet in front of her. The imp was able to keep a steady course, though, in spite of this. The squabbling from Ena Ray and Tebaga echoed and bounced through the mist and was not only distracting, it was covering all other sounds. She darted back.

"And keep your mouths shut!" she admonished them. "If our enemies are here, we will never find them with all your childish chatter. Shut up!"

She didn't wait for any reaction. She turned and swept from left to right and back, widening her arc as she did. She knew Akmen Milzu had to be close by. She had heard the Mountain Kelpie muttering curses when she flung the two to shore. In a few seconds she found her.

"I knew you would find me, my friend," she said to the imp.

"This way," Angin Topan said in a low voice. "I don't think any spells are going to lift this fog or allow us to see through it. I have established a central place for us to gather."

"You shouldn't have difficulty locating Scirios," the Mountain Kelpie said. "He's wailing like a wounded dog."

"I'll save him for last."

She returned to her sweep until she found Rovek and Saldeti not far behind where she had left Ena Ray and Tebaga. They both had the sense to stay where they were, knowing the imp's ability. Even though they could hear her voice and the sound seemed close, they knew the fog played tricks on sound.

When she discovered them, she led them back to where the others were waiting. It took her longer to locate B'nair, and he was still unconscious when she did. She created a small whirlwind and transported him to the shore. While she went to find Neraka Ferr, Akmen Milzu brought B'nair back to his senses.

"You endangered us all," she said quietly to him.

"Then you should have told me of all the rules before wrapping me in those creatures and transporting me," he said. "And you should have listened to me when I first suggested we search this area."

"Your point is well taken," she replied through her clenched teeth. "This, though, is not the time for debate. Can you conjure your map and locate the stone?"

He was doing that when Angin Topan returned with the Fire Kelpie and finally went to retrieve Scirios. B'nair concentrated. The map had never before shown the location of the other stone, and he didn't expect it would now. Still, he felt he had to try. When he confirmed that the map was of no help, he pulled the pendant from his tunic. He felt nothing.

"It's either gone," he said. "Or well disguised. Can't any of you do anything to eliminate this fog?"

"No," Akmen Milzu replied curtly as she mended Scirios' damaged leg.

"We can't remove it," said Neraka Ferr, "But it provides no protection from fire."

He didn't wait for approval. He began to methodically cast spikes of molten heat into the dense mist. He would fire two or three and then stop to listen. They all could hear the sizzling and crackling as the bolts struck unseen objects. If anything had been nearby, it would have been impossible to avoid being struck.

A side effect of the barrage of heat was that the fog slowly burned off. When they could see, although it was still not much more than a few yards in any direction, Neraka Ferr, Scirios and Rovek volunteered to carefully search the surrounding area.

They moved as stealthily as they could, keeping completely quiet. Rovek moved west, following the river and moving to his right and left in a sweeping pattern. Neraka Ferr did the same, traveling to the east, also following the river. Scirios covered the sector between them, moving north, careful to avoid the holes Gulper had dug.

They inched their way along, creeping slowly, and avoiding making any sounds. Rovek soon came upon some footprints in the clay. He could see where several people had recently come this way. He changed his direction and bent close to the ground, following the tracks. By his count there it appeared to be from seven people of different sizes.

He followed them back to the shore where he saw another set of marks. Gulper, he realized. He located the exact spot where the strange creature had been standing. Then he saw the tracks lead away from the river. He came upon several holes and heard movement. He froze, ready to cast a spell.

Through the fog he saw Scirios appear. He gestured, trying to attract his companion's attention. The Lightning Kelpie spotted the motion. Immediately he understood that Rovek had discovered something. He nodded his understanding and motioned that he would follow a parallel course. Together they would be able to trap these intruders once and for all.

They moved quietly and carefully, not making a sound. Those they had left behind remained completely silent. The only sound was the gurgling of the water from the river as it faded while they moved further away from it.

Rovek studied the tracks. He found a place where it seemed that whoever left them had stopped walking. This must have been the spot where Gulper had been standing when he waved to them. Why hadn't they been able to see the others who had been standing near to him, Rovek wondered. More of the

Alchemist's tricks was all he could reason. He looked closer at the ground. He noticed something different.

The tracks seemed to disappear altogether. He wondered if their owners had sought refuge in the holes that were scattered all about. Then he spotted something else. He couldn't tell what it was. He bent down to look closer. It appeared to be a pile of something white. He reached down and grabbed a handful. It was dust. It slipped through his fingers and scattered on the light breeze, disappearing as it blew away.

---------------- *** ----------------

"My old friends," Gulper had shouted, and then giggled wildly. "You've come to visit Gulper after all. How nice. I have new holes."

"You really are trying to get us killed," muttered Sean.

"Are you all holding hands," Gulper asked in a low voice.

"Yes," Quinn answered.

"Do you want us to hold hands to make it easier for the Kelpies to kill us all at once?" asked Liam.

"Do you trust the Alchemist?" Gulper asked.

"Yes," said Solveig. "Of course."

"He left me here to serve you," replied Gulper. "Now you must trust me."

They heard a loud splash as B'nair dropped into the river. They felt Gulper move them through the fog. They had no idea where they were, where Gulper had placed them, or where the Kelpies were. Summer burrowed in Lochen's hood, holding on tightly to her yellow sun hat. What good is this thing, she wondered.

Then they heard a loud thump not far from them followed by a scream. Scirios had landed and broken his leg. His screams unnerved them even more. Fear gripped them all. Lochen, who had grabbed Stella's hand, leaned in close to whisper in her ear.

"We may have been betrayed by this sentinel," he said as quietly as he could. "Our survival may be in our own hands."

"What do you propose?" she whispered back. "Maybe Natalie could cast a bubble around us."

"That may protect us for a while, but it wouldn't last long," he replied. "This may call for something more drastic."

"Like what?" Stella asked.

"Do you think Liam can lead you and the others out of here?"

"Through this fog?" Stella questioned him. "I suppose. He'd have to tell you for sure, though."

"I will leave that to you," he said. "Just go north. Keep going as far and as fast as you can."

"And what do you plan on doing?" she wanted to know.

"I will attempt to distract them," he replied. "I will cast a series of spells. I can divert their attention, move slightly one way or another and strike again. They will think there is more than just one attacking them. Liam should be able to lead you, and you can protect your retreat. You must get to the Swamp before the Kelpies. At all costs."

"OK," she said. "You cast a couple of spells and then try to find us? I don't think that's going to work very well."

"I wasn't planning on trying to find you," he said.

"What?" Stella hissed.

"What are you two whispering about?" asked Quinn. "It's not like I can't hear you. I'm standing right next to you."

"Lochen wants to stay behind and distract the Kelpies while the rest of us escape," Stella said.

"LOCHEN!" whispered Solveig. "NO!"

"I don't exactly WANT to stay behind," he tried to clarify. "I think that's the most viable option."

"And you all think I'm trying to get you killed," Gulper interrupted.

They all jumped at the sound of his voice.

"Where did you go?" muttered Summer.

"To get what I needed to help you," he replied.

He raised his hand to cover his mouth and stifle his giggle. When the sound escaped his lips, he ducked down and looked back over his shoulder. Everyone else looked where he was looking, too – not that any of them could see anything. They heard voices that were uncomfortably close. They could hear Ena Ray and Tebaga scuffling and then being admonished by Angin Topan.

It sounded like they were only a few feet away. Lochen wondered how much of his conversation with Stella had been overheard. Any element of surprise would certainly have been lost if they had.

"What did you get?" asked Sean. "And don't tell me it's another boat."

"Better," replied Gulper.

He held up his hand. In it was a milky white stone about the size of an egg. Lochen recognized it immediately. It was a transporter stone. He reached out to take it and looked up at the person handing it to him. He could see the lines of age quickly creasing Gulper's face. His large eyes were beginning to droop and film over. His time was near. His service had ended.

Lochen reached out with both hands. He wrapped them around the stone and around Gulper's hand. He pulled the sentinel closer so he could whisper in his ear.

"Come with us," he said.

Gulper pulled his head back and tilted it slightly to one side, staring back into Lochen's eyes. Moisture began to form in the corners, but he blinked it away.

"Thank you," he said with a strained voice. "But there would be no point. They can do me no harm, and it's time for me to go home."

Lochen nodded. He reached back with one hand and held on to Stella.

"Safe journey," Gulper whispered.

In a flash, they were gone.

Chapter twenty

When they reappeared, they found themselves near a shallow, marshy stream. There were signs of a large slab that had once held the body of a Kelpie, but had been torn open. The shape of the slab, reflected in the water gave the impression of an arrowhead. Where they were standing was on stones that led to the slab. Now, it appeared instead to be an opening to a deep cavern.

"Is everyone all right?" asked Lochen. "Is everyone here?"

They looked at whoever was holding their hands and then at the others. The only one unaccounted for was Summer, until she popped her head out from Lochen's hood and fluttered into the air.

"The hats are gone," she announced.

"I suppose they served their purpose," said Natalie.

"I sort of liked mine," said Solveig.

"And I was getting used to seeing Lochen's," added Stella.

"I am quite fine without it," he replied.

"What now?" asked Sean.

"Is this place familiar to you?" Quinn asked Liam.

"More or less," he replied. "It's on the edge of the Swamp. I've been by here before, but I never paid it much attention until we came here looking for the Kelpie. He was gone by the time we arrived."

"And was this opening there?" asked Lochen.

"Not that I can recall," he said. "And I think I would have noticed a big hole in the ground."

"I don't remember it being there, either," said Solveig.

Sean and Stella concurred, which led them all to wonder if the opening had been created from above or below, and by whom. Lochen stepped to the edge and peered inside. He snapped his fingers and created a small burst of light.

"There are stairs," he said. "I think we should descend."

He put one foot down the opening to the first step. He could tell by the feel of it against his foot that it was made of stone and covered with a light layer of dust or perhaps dirt.

"Wait," said Liam. "How do you know it's not a trap?"

"I don't," he answered, raising his head and turning back towards Liam. "I can only surmise. However, since the Kelpies are not here, who else would set a trap for us?"

"It doesn't have to be a trap specifically for us," Liam responded. "It could have been set by gargoyles for anyone who happens to come by."

"I thought you said no one ever goes into the Swamp," said Quinn. "If no one ever goes by, who would they trap?"

"I keep telling you they aren't all that bright," Liam said.

"Then the rest of you stay here," said Lochen. "I'll exercise the utmost caution and explore."

He turned back to the opening. The light he had created had faded out. He took another step downward.

"I'm not staying out here," said Solveig. "And I'm not letting you go off by yourself."

"Really," Lochen objected, stopping and turning back towards Solveig. "I am actually quite capable of defending myself."

As he was talking, he had started to turn again and take another step, but went a little too far. His foot landed on the very edge of the step instead of in the center. The dust and dirt that coated it gave way under his weight and his foot slipped, skipping over the step and hitting the next one down. In an effort to keep his balance, he overcompensated and tumbled downward.

"Way to go, Grace," Sean shouted after him. "I guess we're all going in, now."

"Hold on a second," shouted Liam.

He looked through the brush and debris at the mouth of the opening until he found some long, hard sticks. He gave the longest one to Quinn and a shorter one to Solveig and kept one himself. The staffs were as long as each of them was tall.

"It's dark down there," he said. "We can use these to keep from falling."

"Like Lochen did?" asked Quinn.

"Exactly," replied Liam. "We can take the lead. The rest of you stay close behind."

They all quickly, but carefully, entered the pit and followed the steps to a landing at the bottom, a few yards down. Quinn, Liam and Solveig tapped along the steps while the others reached out to the wall on either side of the steps until they realized they had no idea what they were touching. Summer flew slowly right behind Quinn's shoulder.

When they reached the bottom, they nearly tripped on Lochen, who was trying to get back to his feet and to generate another ball of illumination at the same time. When he finally did, he could see that he was not alone.

"I've been expecting you," a voice from the shadows said.

It was thin and reedy, but not at all threatening. Still, each of them jumped at the unexpected sound. They turned in the direction of the voice and could make out a silhouette in the shadows. They could see the figure move a hand in a sweeping motion and were all prepared for some kind of hex or spell, but, instead, a glow of light appeared.

Before them was a small and withered old man – a Trepan. He had white, wrinkled skin with deep lines in his face that seemed to all point to his mouth, or looked like rays emanating from the corners of his eyes – they went every which way.

They had never seen anyone who looked so old. He had very little hair, and what he did have stood out in wisps from the top of his head. His ears were large and hung low on the sides of his head, looking like pieces of worn and deeply lined leather. His skin looked like thin parchment, and was lined with blue veins.

He was sitting in a niche in the side of the wall, on a stone bench. He was wrapped in an old white cloth of some kind that looked strangely like a toga. His feet were bare and as wrinkled as the rest of him.

"You're a sentinel, aren't you?" asked Liam.

"Yes," he answered. "I am Ock."

"Ock?" asked Lochen. "That's an odd name for a Trepan."

"There is more to my name," he said. "But Ock will be sufficient."

"We are looking for..." Stella started to say.

"I know," interrupted Ock. "The band. You are looking for the band to the pendant of the Enchantress, Meri Hocto."

"You seem to know much more than the other sentinels," said Lochen.

"I've been sitting here for two thousand years," Ock replied. "I've had little else to ponder. Besides, I am the last sentinel and much has been entrusted to me."

"The last?" asked Natalie. "How many are there...or were there?"

"I have no idea," he said. "The Alchemist was very careful about that in case any of us were to be discovered by the Kelpies. I only know I am the last."

"The last one...alive?" asked Sean.

"Another question I can't answer," he said. "Since I don't know how many there have been or how many you've encountered. But you are at your journey's end. After me you will need no others. After me, we will all be gone. Our debts will be paid in full."

"One of the other sentinels said that, too," commented Solveig. "What does that mean, exactly?"

"When the Kelpies revolted," Ock told her, "there were some who aided them. In some cases the aid provided was minimal, sometimes not. Sometimes it was voluntary, sometimes not. In any case, it was wrong. We were all responsible for our choices – for the decisions we made. Everything has a consequence. The consequence for our betrayals was our consignment to become sentinels – for as long as it took until we were needed.

"When the Kelpies were captured and imprisoned, the Alchemist knew their captivity would not last forever. He anticipated each of you. You are the chosen ones, the direct descendants of the leaders of each of your people. He expected that you would discover the shattered pieces of the Enchantress' pendant and return here to bring it all to a conclusion."

"All what to a conclusion?" asked Lochen. "I don't understand."

"The Kelpies cannot be killed," answered Ock. "Evil doesn't die. It can only be contained."

"But we destroyed two of them," objected Solveig.

"Only temporarily," replied the sentinel. "They will rise again."

"So what are we supposed to do?" asked Quinn.

"Recover the rest of the stone, secure the band and then seal the portal," said Ock.

He was fading faster than the other sentinels had. He had been much older than they when the Alchemist slowed his aging process. His voice was already weakening.

"But how?" asked Summer. "And what portal are we supposed to seal? And then what happens?"

"He knows," replied the sentinel, pointing at Lochen.

"I beg to differ," Lochen said in a surprised voice. "I know nothing of the kind. I am as mystified as the rest of us."

"But you were given his book," wheezed Ock.

"Yes, but..."

"It's all in there," Ock cut him off. "And I can see that you've read it completely."

"I...well...it was lost...and I...uh...translated it," Lochen sputtered.

"Then you have all the answers."

The sentinel's voice was so thin it was difficult to hear him. He was leaning to one side now, propped up against the wall. His hands had dropped to his side and his eyelids were fluttering.

"I've translated it," objected Lochen. "But that doesn't mean I understand it."

"Understanding will come. You have what you need."

"But...but..." Lochen was perplexed.

He searched his brain. He knew there were portions he could guess at, but there were things he thought were key that he still didn't understand. He knew that the sentinel would expire in minutes – maybe even seconds. He tried to think of what the most important items were.

"Wait," he shouted, as if he could stop death. "Two things. Explain two things to me."

The sentinel's eyes closed and he let out his breath. Everyone stood staring at him, certain he was gone. Then he inhaled with great difficulty and opened his eyes. Lochen didn't wait for him to speak.

"Boravak," he shouted. "And another phrase – ad paria. What do they mean?"

The sentinel smiled and closed his eyes. Lochen's shoulders slumped. He believed he would never have the answers. But then the old eyes opened one last time.

"This is the Boravak," he gasped. "All of it – everything. And ad paria is what the symbols on the band spell. That will become clear to you in due time."

Lochen stared at him waiting for more. Nothing came. The old Trepan did not take another breath. He did not open his eyes one more time. He did not speak another word. A look of complete peace fell over him, and all who were watching him knew his debt had been paid.

"What do we do now?" asked Solveig.

"I...uh...well," Lochen was at a loss.

He took a deep breath, shook his head and looked around. Think, he told himself. You have all the answers. You merely need to sort them out.

"We go deeper," he said. "We must find the band."

"What about the other part of the stone?" asked Summer. "Don't we need that, too?"

"Yes," said Lochen. "We do, but I'm sure that will come to us. The Kelpies are on their way. We must be prepared for when they arrive. Stella, can you see exactly where the band is?"

"I don't think that's really necessary," said Liam. "There's only one way to go."

He was pointing past the small landing to a narrow hall. He was right. The only other way was back the way they had come. Lochen snapped his fingers again and a small burst of light shot out ahead of them.

"Then I believe we should go that way," replied Lochen.

They stayed close together as they walked through the corridor. It slanted downward, going deeper under the ground. After about twenty feet, it opened to a large circular cavern. It looked as if it had been carved rather than naturally formed.

"Wow," said Natalie. "Who could have done all this?"

The cavern opened up below them. From the end of the passage through which they had come, it formed a large and deep circle. Steps were dug into the side to the right, descending to a second level. They ended about twenty feet down to a wide ring that circled around the structure.

Halfway across, on the opposite side, another series of steps appeared. Unlike the first set, these were cantilevered – jutting out from the rock wall. These, too, dropped about another twenty feet down to a third level. This level was smaller and the ledge that circled the center was narrower. At several places along the wall there were small grotto-like niches cut out. It was unclear what purpose they served, other than to make the whole scene more ominous.

At random locations along the walls of the first and second level were large columns. It seemed as if the columns supported the ledge of the layer above it or the ceiling of the uppermost level. There were oddly shaped images cut into some of the columns. It was difficult to make out exactly what the carvings represented; they all appeared to overlap one another.

Streaked throughout the walls of the structure were veins of stone similar to that found in another cave at another time. These veins generated a low level of illumination – enough to allow visitors to see, but not enough for them to observe traps or other dangers. In and around the veins of glowing stone were small cracks in the walls. In some of those cracks, roots from the trees high above could be seen poking through. Shadows were cast everywhere, adding a heightened level of eeriness to the place.

From the third level, there was another stairway that led to a fourth plane. Unlike the others, this fourth one formed a half circle and was connected by a bridge to a landing. The bridge spanned yet another ledge and a deep, black gash in the rock that seemed to drop to the core of the planet.

Sean picked up a stone and tossed it down. It glanced off the bridge, bounced on the landing and then dropped to the ledge where it rolled off and down into the crevice. The sound of the stone echoed as it struck the bridge, the landing and the ledge, but then nothing was heard after that.

"I suppose we have to go down there," Sean gulped.

"Not all the way," said Stella. "But close."

Lochen didn't have to snap his fingers to generate another burst of light. There was enough illumination coming from the streaks in the walls. Besides, he was worried about running into gargoyles and thought the less attention they attracted, the better.

"We need to be cautious," he advised.

"I agree," said Liam. "Just because we haven't seen anything dangerous at the surface or down here – so far – doesn't mean we're in the clear."

"I'll go first," announced Stella. "I can sense where we have to go."

"Quinn and I should go with you," said Liam, raising his staff up in his hand.

"I'll cover the back," said Solveig, raising her own staff.

"And I'll join you," said Lochen. "Summer, I suggest you fly close to Quinn, but don't get too far ahead of him."

"Don't worry," she said, recalling her adventure with the bats.

"Natalie," Lochen added. "You and Sean stay in the middle and keep watch to either side."

Stella headed out with Summer floating a few feet over her head, and Quinn and Liam on either side of her and slightly behind. They were followed by Natalie and Sean and then by Lochen and Solveig.

They moved to the steps on the right side of the structure and carefully climbed down. They were only about two feet wide, and some of them were higher than others, making the passage difficult. Along the walls the streaks of glowing rock pulsated, but never grew really bright. The shifting light made the shadows dance and gave the illusion of movement throughout the cave.

Interspersed among the veins were the tips of thick, white roots. Natalie looked closely at one of them as she passed by and was certain it had moved. She took a step away from the wall and bumped into Sean.

"Hey," he squeaked, startled by her contact. "Not so close."

"Sorry," she whispered, her voice cracking.

He pushed back to move away from the edge of the steps as the group circled down to the next level. Their eyes had gotten somewhat accustomed to the dim light and they could see that not only were the columns engraved, but so were the walls.

"What are these things?" asked Summer.

She fluttered close to the wall and tried to get a better look. It didn't help. It looked like random illustrations, but there was a certain pattern to them all. If she had to guess, it looked like piles of the same thing had been stacked on top of one another and fashioned into walls and columns. Whatever it was, it gave her a bad feeling, and she quickly backed away.

Stella didn't stop when she reached the ledge. She moved ahead to the opposite side and to the next series of steps. Quinn and Liam had to follow in single file. The ledge was too narrow for them to walk side by side. Quinn looked up and could see the top of the cave. It looked like what he imagined a grave would look like from underground.

Dirt was packed tightly across the top in a large dome. He couldn't tell what was holding it up. He wasn't sure anything was. There was some seepage from the nearby river, and water trickled down one side, flowing slowly and silently down the wall, over the ledge to the next level and so on until it disappeared into the narrow black gap at the bottom. Some thin tendrils of roots poked through the dirt and hung limply from the ceiling.

He shivered and reached out his hand to keep his balance on the shrinking path. His hand came in contact with one of the roots, which quickly wound itself around his fingers and withdrew into the dirt, trying to pull Quinn with it.

"Yuck," he gasped.

He yanked his hand free, looked at some kind of goo the root left on his fingers and searched for something to wipe them off on.

"Don't even think about it," Liam said, looking at Quinn's fingers. "Use your pants."

Quinn reluctantly wiped his fingers on his pants and then picked up his pace to catch up with Stella. When she reached the next flight of stairs, she stopped and took a step back, gasping. These steps were not carved into the stone. They were cantilevered from the wall – sticking out from the side with no support. They were far enough apart to see between them from the top.

"Oh, poop," Stella muttered. "I really don't like this."

She reached out her hand for balance, but then thought better of it. She forced herself to focus only on the next step. She placed her right foot down and then brought her left foot next to it. She took each step one at a time, moving slowly and gritting her teeth as she did so.

When she reached the bottom, she breathed a sigh of relief and waited for the others. The air had been cool and damp, but she found herself perspiring. She attributed it to nerves and waited until her breathing returned to normal. A few minutes later, everyone was down on the same level. Lochen turned back to the steps and raised his hand.

"There's no sense in making things easy for them," he said.

One by one, the steps retracted into the wall until they were all flush and there was no sign of any steps to the third level. With the staircase gone, it was clear now that the cavern was getting smaller in diameter the deeper they went. By now the path had gotten narrower and in some places there was room only for one at a time to pass. As a result, the line spread out.

When she had collected herself, Stella continued on. Once more she headed for the opposite side of the cavern towards the next staircase. Along the way, she noticed deep gouges in the wall. She stopped at one, looked around and then pointed her finger into one of them. A small beacon of light darted from the tip into the niche.

There were cobwebs in the top corners and dirt and small stones on the bottom. It was hollowed out about two feet into the wall and then ended. Strange, she thought. What would these have been for, she wondered.

She reached the final set of steps and was glad to see they were just like the first ones. She carefully climbed down and reached the last ledge above the edge of the chasm at the bottom. From here she could see an expanse of stone that reached across the bottom ledge and the pit. There didn't appear to be any way down to that last ledge and she hoped none of them found themselves there.

She was at the foot of the bridge and could see a large landing on the other side. On the opposite side of the landing was what appeared to be a pair of large doors. She studied the frame and thought that it looked like the doors had been welded shut. The edge around the frame as well as the centerline looked as if they had melted. It also looked strangely familiar to her.

"Where have I seen this before," she said to herself. "And what makes me think I <u>have</u> seen this before?"

She crossed the bridge. The landing was larger than she had first thought and except for the front part that was open, it blended into the wall, with the door in the center on the far side. She stepped slowly forward.

In the center of the doors, about three feet from the ground was a small circle – very small. It was the band. She didn't have to get a closer look to know what it was. She could feel it. She was afraid to go any closer. She craned her neck forward to see better, but stayed in place. It slowly came back to her.

The band had hovered above Ena Ray's head in the Crystal Citadel. Summer had flown across another chasm, similar to the one below the bridge Stella had just crossed. Summer had somehow managed to steal the band from the sorcerer and send it flying to them. It had been much larger, though, she thought.

They had all placed their hands on it and were transported – here? Could this be where they had come? But those doors had sealed in gargoyles. If they removed the band, wouldn't that just release them?

She summoned her courage and stepped closer. She listened, but couldn't hear the screams. The screams, she recalled. They could hear the screams of the gargoyles on the other side. The gargoyles were the army of Ena Ray, she realized. Where were they now?

She was about to turn back to the others, when something caught her eye. The band had sealed itself to the door and didn't look like it could ever be moved. She swallowed her fear and stepped closer. She could see the markings. They were faint, but still there. What was it Ock had said? They spelled out the phrase ad paria? Whatever that meant.

She turned back to the rest and stepped towards the bridge. Before she got there, she felt a tremendous tremor. She ducked down and looked up, expecting to see the ceiling collapsing on top of them. Instead, she found she had trouble focusing.

"What was that?" gasped Quinn, who was still on the other side of the bridge.

"I don't know," said Liam.

He looked up and had to rub his eyes. He looked at the bridge and thought he was seeing double. He looked up at Stella and she, too, was rubbing her eyes.

"Something's happened," he called to her. "I'm seeing double."

"I thought it was just me," she answered.

"I'm seeing it, too," said Quinn.

"Get over here," Stella shouted. "All of you, before it's too late."

"What's happening," shouted Sean.

He turned back to find Natalie. She was a few feet behind him and Lochen was right behind her. Lochen was motioning for them to get over to the bridge and cross it. Sean grabbed Natalie's hand and pulled her with him. Lochen assumed Solveig was right behind him. He watched as Natalie and Sean reached the landing. He stretched out his arms for balance and carefully crossed the bridge.

"This is most unusual," he said to Solveig over his shoulder. "I appear to have contracted an unexpected case of double vision. It arose concurrent with the tremor. Are you experiencing anything similar?"

He made it to the other side and was pulled the last few steps by Quinn and Liam.

"Seeing double?" Liam asked.

"You, too?" questioned Lochen.

"Yes," he said. "I'm not sure what caused it."

Lochen turned around to help Solveig across the bridge, but she wasn't there. He was about to go back, when Stella pulled on his sleeve.

"No," she said. "The Kelpies have arrived."

Chapter twenty-one

The Kelpies arrived in full strength, landing at the site where one of their brothers had been imprisoned. The Lightning Riders delivered their passengers at the exact spot the transporter stone had delivered its passengers only minutes before. Once the electrical current had dissipated, Akmen Milzu could see the broken tomb of her former comrade, Pantano Izaki.

In a fit of rage, she had slammed her fist into the remains of the tomb, sending a tremor deep into the ground – the tremor Stella felt when everything began to blur. The tremor had been so severe that the ground shook for several seconds afterwards, creating the double vision of those below.

B'nair wasted no time. He knew the band was close and that the other half of the stone was even closer. He slipped by the Kelpies and headed down the passage to the outermost ring inside the cavern. Along the way he passed a landing where he spotted a pile of white dust. He didn't stop to explore. Let the others ponder that, he thought.

Unknown to him, Ena Ray saw his hasty departure and followed. The Rebbercand's movement was also observed by Tebaga, who watched Ena Ray go after him. The traitor, he thought. He seeks the pendant for himself. He moved stealthily after his former partner.

B'nair moved quickly and quietly to the topmost ledge and then crept down the flight of stairs. On the opposite side of this second level, he could see where the ledge ended. There was nothing below it leading to the next lower level. He could not see the steps Lochen had pushed back into the wall.

The cave looked familiar, but he was certain he had never been there before. How can it look familiar then, he asked himself. Because he had seen it in his dream, he answered himself. He looked behind him, expecting to see the Kelpies, but none of them were there.

Beneath him, he could see another level and a bridge. On the opposite side of the bridge he spotted the ones who had been interfering with his efforts. They were gathered on a plateau of some kind – more like a landing at the end of a narrow bridge.

He looked closer and could see the bridge was several feet above yet another short ledge and a chasm that disappeared into total blackness. That was when he spotted Stella. He could feel the stone under his tunic pulsating. He pulled it out. The color was shifting and brightening. The other half was in his sights.

He needed to get down there fast – before the Kelpies discovered he wasn't with them and decided to follow. He needed to secure both parts of the stone. The band would be his shortly after; he was sure. He looked for another way down, but could see none. He would have to jump.

He positioned himself in line with the bridge, took a deep breath and pushed off. He gasped as he fell through the air. His recurring dream flooded his mind. It had started this way: with him falling. He felt a rising sense of panic and told himself that this was not a dream; it was real. As suddenly as his panic had started, his falling stopped. He landed safely on the bridge right behind one of his nemeses – the one with the long red hair.

When the cavern had shaken and everyone was taken by surprise, Solveig had been lingering behind the others, studying the carvings on the walls. The quake had been so violent, that it had knocked her from her feet. She got to her hands and knees, trying to shake the double vision she was experiencing.

"Lochen," she gasped.

He had been right next to her a few seconds ago. Where was he? She looked up and saw him across some kind of narrow bridge. All the others were there, too. She got to her feet and staggered slightly trying to regain her balance. She moved to the bridge and took a tentative step.

She looked down at the ledge and the chasm below her and the dizziness returned. She closed her eyes, lifted her head and then opened her lids. Her vision was returning to normal. She took a few steps forward and focused her attention ahead of her. Lochen was looking back at her. Something was wrong. She could tell by his expression. She could see he was looking up and behind her. Before she could turn around, she felt a presence behind her.

In the instant he landed, B'nair grabbed Solveig's hair and yanked her head back. He brought up his axe and placed the blade against her throat. Lochen raised his hand, but B'nair merely grinned at him and shook his head in warning. He could move the blade across her throat before Lochen could get out any spell. They both knew this.

Stella lifted the stone from around her neck and held it out in front of her. She moved a few steps forward to the edge of the landing. Her movement caught B'nair's eye and he saw the stone around her neck glowing in the dim light. He smiled his awful smile at her.

"How about you bring that necklace to me," he growled to Stella. "And then I'll give your little friend here back to you."

"No," said Lochen. "You can't give that to him. The moment you do, Solveig is doomed."

"I have no intention of giving him the stone," Stella answered.

She stretched out her arm a little further, dangling the pendant over the edge of the abyss.

Quest of Eight Part Seven: Ad Paria

Richard Reda

"Let her go," she shouted to the Rebbercand. "Or I'll throw this down the chasm."

"That hardly seems like a fair exchange to me," B'nair replied. "How about you give me the stone, or I'll separate her head from her body, and then I'll come after you?"

"Don't do it," shouted Solveig.

"I'd keep my mouth shut if I were you," B'nair whispered in her ear.

He moved the axe slightly. The blade was so sharp, she didn't feel it cut the skin. However, she could feel the warm trickle of blood as it seeped from the cut and rolled down her neck. He focused his attention back on Stella, who hadn't moved. At the same time, Summer made herself as invisible as possible and fluttered over his head, looking for some kind of advantage – some way to free her friend.

B'nair had the strange sensation that something was behind him and he jerked his head around. Nothing was there, but the feeling lingered. He didn't look closely enough to see the wavering motion that was Summer hanging over his shoulder. He turned back to the front and then looked to his left and right. He was alone in this strange place. Where is everyone else, he wondered. Where were the Kelpies?

That was when the increasing light from the band at the center of the door attracted his attention.

He faced forward and on the other side of the bridge he could see in the very dim light something that looked like a door.

Quest of Eight Part Seven: Ad Paria

Richard Reda

Where was the light coming from, he wondered. He looked across the bridge to Stella and then slowly scanned the others, all of whom were watching him. There was another, he thought. A faerie. Hadn't he killed her back at the volcano? He wasn't sure.

He looked back towards the door. It was clearer now. There was more light. Where was it coming from? He felt a tingling against his chest. He looked down and saw a flash of light. It was coming from the stone – the piece of the witch's pendant that he wore around his neck. He saw it dangling and wished he had secured it under his tunic. With his one good hand wrapped in Solveig's hair, holding her off her feet over the edge of the abyss, there was no way for him to move it.

The light from the small stone was growing. He could see the one held by Stella was also glowing. But they weren't the only source of the light. There was something in the center of the door on the far side of the bridge. He tried to cross the bridge but his feet wouldn't move. It felt like they were part of the bridge on which he was standing. A wave of panic swept over him. Elements of his dream returned to him and his fear became palpable.

He looked back towards the door. He could see a circle of some kind. It was beginning to glow. He realized this circle – whatever it was – was the second source of light. He tried to move closer, but was still rooted to the bridge. He bent forward as much as he could. The circle was some kind of band. It was the band the Kelpies had mentioned, he was sure of it.

As if a curtain had been pulled aside revealing something that had long been hidden, B'nair knew instantly that he was seeing the band the Kelpies had mentioned, but failed to explain. In the same instant, the band flashed brilliantly. He could see strange markings all around the outside. This was the band he had seen in his dream, he told himself. This is a message.

Above and behind him, Ena Ray watched in silence. He could see the two pieces of the stone and the increasing illumination from the band. All of it was well within his reach. He held his breath and waited for the drama below him to unfold. Tebaga was immediately behind him. Ena Ray had been so fixed on B'nair and the pieces of the pendant that he hadn't noticed that he had company.

Summer could see no way to get Solveig out of B'nair's grasp. She was furious at her inability to do something. She moved back across the expanse to where Lochen was still standing. All the others, except for Stella, were behind him. Solveig's brave shout to Stella not to give up the stone raised a lump in her throat. She couldn't let the Rebbercand win. Not this time.

She focused her attention on his one good eye and then darted forward. As she did, her invisibility faded and her movement towards him became apparent. B'nair caught the sudden blur that was headed at him. There she is, he thought. She's come back for another lesson. This time I won't be so kind, he chuckled to himself.

He fixed his gaze on her and readied his swing. He'd move the blade from Solveig's throat in one quick swipe. This time, though, he wouldn't aim for separating the faerie from her wings. Instead, this time, he'd cut her right in half. Come on, little one, he thought.

Quest of Eight Part Seven: Ad Paria

Richard Reda

Before anyone knew what she was doing, Summer shot like a bullet at the Rebbercand. When she was a fraction of a second away from the moment he swung that horrifying axe, she dipped down under his swing and then bolted upward, striking him in the eye with her fists. At the same instant, Sean saw the Rebbercand was distracted and that the blade was away from Solveig's throat.

He dropped down, scooped up a handful of stones and fired shot after shot with lightning speed and deadly accuracy at the inside of B'nair's right knee. Pain shot through the Rebbercand's eye, and his missed swing had thrown him off balance. He shook his hand and let go of Solveig's hair, reflexively covering his damaged and watering eye. At the same time, he felt a series of stabbing bursts in his knee. Combined with the staccato pain and his shifting weight, his knee gave out and he began to fall.

He could feel himself falling, but couldn't see anything. He flailed his arms uselessly for balance. As quickly as the falling sensation started, it stopped. And just as quickly, the pain in his eye and knee was replaced by a burning sensation in the center of his chest. It was driving deep into him.

He wiped the water from his eye, but still couldn't see anything. He felt around and realized he was sprawled on the ledge below the bridge, near the rim of the abyss. His right hand hung limply at his side, free of the axe that had been sealed there. The pain in his chest was becoming unbearable. He moved his left hand to the spot where the pain was most intense. He could feel, but not see, something protruding from the center of his body. He couldn't recall anything burning so intensely. He felt the object from where it seemed planted in his chest and reached outward. He opened his eyes.

The axe had struck the ground near the edge of the chasm and stuck in the dirt and rock. The other side of the blade was firmly planted in the center of his chest. It had cut through the strands that held the stone around his neck.

He opened his mouth, but no sound came out. He watched as the stone slowly rose into the air and away from him. He reached out his left hand and swiped at it, but it eluded him, floating higher into the air to join its other half. He gasped and looked back down at the blade that was driven into him.

Like his brother, he began to dissolve into a mass of flies. As his body faded to nothing, his last thoughts were a mixture of rage and confusion. How could this have happened? How could he have been defeated by a Dozor and a faerie?

At the moment B'nair felt the blade of his axe drive into his chest and end his life, several other things happened almost at the same time. Ena Ray saw the Rebbercand fall, and saw the blade cut through the string holding the stone around his neck. He watched as the stone floated upward. He looked in the direction it was rising and saw Stella holding the other half in her hand.

No, he thought. He couldn't allow the pendant to escape his possession. He reached out his right hand and began to cast a spell. The floating half of the stone stopped in mid-flight, and then began to drift toward the sorcerer. He looked back at Stella and could see that she was doing nothing to alter the new path of the stone.   This will be easier than I thought, he muttered to himself.

Except his comment wasn't kept only to himself. Tebaga had been watching the events unfold as well, and stood poised close behind Ena Ray. He saw the stone rise from the Rebbercand's body and head towards the other half. He saw Ena Ray reach forward and change its course.   He knew what his former partner was intending to do.

Tebaga's mind flashed back to the time, long ago, when Ena Ray had duped him into playing a game. It had all been a ruse to create a distraction so that he could steal that pendant from the Enchantress. Tebaga had been foolish to trust Ena Ray back then. He refused to be a victim a second time.

He reached forward, grabbed Ena Ray's left arm, yanked him back enough to turn him slightly and then pushed him towards the chasm. Ena Ray's spell on the stone was broken. He hadn't realized Tebaga was behind him. As he was pushed backwards towards the crevasse, he clutched at Tebaga and grasped an arm, pulling him down.

The pair tumbled over the side, clawing at each other, and landed with a bone-crunching thud on the ledge below, only a few inches from the dissolving body of the Rebbercand. Tebaga kicked and pushed Ena Ray over the side.   The sorcerer tightened his grip, but still slid down the side of Tebaga's body, wrapping his arms around his opponent's legs.

Tebaga began to slide over the side at the same time. Ena Ray thought about casting a spell to stop his fall or to create some kind of landing or bridge, but it would mean he'd have to release his grip. If he did that, he'd fall for sure, and he wasn't certain he would be able to stop his fall. So, instead, he pulled and tried to climb up Tebaga's body to the ledge and safety.

Tebaga could feel the weight of Ena Ray pulling him down. He felt his body slide across the ledge. He scrambled with his hands trying to find something to stop his momentum, but his fingers merely scratched the stone surface. In a final, desperate effort, he lunged for the only thing he could see to grab onto.

He reached out with all his strength for the axe that was wedged into the rim of the ledge. Any sign of B'nair had vanished; replaced by a swarm of buzzing flies that swirled around Tebaga's head and then dropped into the darkness of the abyss.

His hand came down onto the top blade. He tried to hold on to stop his fall, but the razor sharp edge cut through his fingers. The tips dropped off on the far side, leaving the stumps and his hand to drop away uselessly. His fingers were severed from his hand before he even felt the pain. He was already dropping over the side before what happened registered in his mind.

Their fates sealed, Ena Ray and Tebaga continued to push, grab and kick at each other as they dropped from sight. Their shouts echoed along the walls of the chasm until they faded away to nothing.

At the instant Summer drove her fists into B'nair's eye, and he released his grip on Solveig's hair, she dropped from his grip and her body slammed into the edge of the narrow bridge. She thrust out her arms to hold on as the rest of her dangled over the side. She looked back over her shoulder, looking for something to step on, but only saw blackness below her.

She looked back only to discover that the Rebbercand was no longer standing over her. In fact, he was nowhere to be seen. He had dropped out of her line of sight onto the shallow ledge on the opposite side of the bridge. She tried to pull herself up, but the stone of the bridge was too smooth and there was nothing to hold on to.

As narrow as the bridge was, it was more than the length of her arms. Her fingers stretched, reaching for the other edge, but only slid across the surface. She kicked, trying to elevate herself, but only managed to weaken her grip. She couldn't hold on any longer and dropped away.

She could feel herself falling, but was so quickly enveloped in the darkness that she couldn't see anything. Certain she was going to drop to her death, she was startled when her feet struck something solid and she collapsed against the wall.

She froze in place, hoping that her eyes would adjust to the darkness, but they refused to cooperate. When she was able to control her breathing, she felt along the wall, willing herself not to think about what she might be touching. She felt around her feet and discovered that she was on a flat-topped column of some kind, that rose from somewhere below her.

It was less than two feet in diameter and was about ten inches from one side of the chasm. She felt around the wall to see if there were any handholds or footholds. Above her she could see a thin sliver of light and the underside of the bridge from which she had fallen. She also heard a sudden burst of shouting, rumbling, and explosions.

Within seconds, she could feel a rush of wind as something large shot by her. What she couldn't see were the tangled bodies of Tebaga and Ena Ray as they plummeted downward.

Almost immediately after the breeze blew past a small burst of light appeared; and she felt herself rising into the air. At first she panicked. Then she saw Summer appear, fluttering immediately in front of her.

"We thought we lost you for a second," Summer said. "I've covered you with faerie dust and Lochen sent down the light so we can see."

"What's going on up there?" Solveig asked.

"A lot," Summer answered. "We have to be careful. We're going to come up on the other side of the bridge. Once we do, get over the top as quickly as you can and run to the far side of the landing."

Solveig watched as the bridge got closer and Summer maneuvered her to the opposite end and the far side. Once her head was level with the top, Summer darted above her and Solveig felt like she had been ejected from a cannon. She flew up over the top of the rim and landed inches away from Lochen, who seemed to be absorbed with something else.

She scrambled to her feet, raised her head and ran to the back end of the landing, close to the still sealed doors. When she spun around, she was stunned by what she saw.

At the instant B'nair fell and the axe was driven into his chest, Angin Topan realized that he, Tebaga and Ena Ray were all missing. She fluttered around looking in every direction and realized that they had gone deeper into the cave. She alerted the Kelpies and then darted ahead.

She moved quickly and carefully, darting back and forth until she entered the main cavern and could see the Rebbercand standing on a bridge, holding someone by the hair. It was one of those who had been following us, she said to herself. In fact, it was the one she had cursed with the shrinking spell. She had somehow broken that spell.

Then she noticed the others on the far side of the bridge. She was stunned to see that they had gotten so far ahead. Her attention was caught by the sudden reaction by B'nair when he dropped the person he was holding and grabbed his eye. She saw the rapid fire of stones at the Rebbercand's knee and watched as he dropped off the bridge to the ledge below and become impaled on his axe.

She watched as Ena Ray and Tebaga renewed their battle and threw each other to their doom. What was going on, she wondered. How had things gotten so out of hand? She heard the Kelpies arriving at the upper rim behind her. She turned to look back at them and the view was suddenly obscured by some kind of film.

She spun around to see what had happened and then flew forward, preparing to cast a spell to destroy each and every one of these irritating intruders. She fixed her attention on the one closest, the one in robes who was waving his arms, casting spells. Before she knew what happened, she felt something strike her in the center of her body, driving her backwards into the wall of the cavern.

Quest of Eight Part Seven: Ad Paria

Richard Reda

At the instant B'nair fell and the axe was driven into his chest, Akmen Milzu heard Angin Topan call to her and the others. B'nair, Ena Ray and Tebaga had gone ahead of them and were into the bowels of the cavern. She was furious that they had gone off on their own. She motioned to the others and followed the imp into the cave.

She stood at the edge of the uppermost level and stared down at the mass of confusion below. A swarm of flies appeared from nowhere, swirled around and then dropped down into the chasm. She saw Ena Ray and Tebaga dropping from their perch to the lower landing and then into the abyss. She was about to hurl her most powerful spell down on the creatures below when a strange film appeared near her feet.

She thrust her fist down, launching a series of boulders that materialized out of thin air. They struck the substance and bounced off, creating no damage at all. She turned to Saldeti.

"Freeze it," she demanded.

And then to Neraka Ferr she added, "And then burn it."

She then turned to the others and ordered them to do what they could to destroy whoever was on the other side of the film. Rovek raised his arms and muttered an incantation. His spell awoke the long dormant roots in the walls of the cave. They began to emerge and move like snakes, stretching outward and striking at anything close.

Scirios raised a fist and brought it down sharply. The glowing rocks imbedded in the walls sparkled and began spitting out electrical charges. Akmen Milzu screamed in anger and commanded the Kythauls to come forth.

Below the layer of film that separated the Kelpies from the lower levels, the figures carved into the sides of the cavern came alive. They pulled themselves free from the columns and skittered across the walls and the different levels. Their stone eyes blazed red and searched for their targets. Seeing several creatures at the lower landing all huddled together, they began to creep in that direction.

At the instant B'nair fell and the axe was driven into his chest, Lochen saw Solveig fall against the bridge and then drop into the crevasse. He lurched forward, but immediately realized he could not stop her fall. He saw Summer dart into the blackness after her and generated a small ball of light to help out.

At the same moment, he saw Ena Ray and Tebaga drop from higher up, struggle on the lower landing and fall off the edge. He looked up and saw the Kelpies had arrived. He turned to Natalie. Even before he could speak, she had reacted by sealing the top of the cave with a bubble.

"It won't hold forever," she said.

"Any amount of delay will help," replied Lochen.

The words were no sooner out of his mouth when bursts of electricity shot across the cavern. Everyone ducked, except for Lochen, who began casting spells to discharge them. He looked like he was conducting a symphony. As quickly as they shot from the stones, they fizzled and disappeared. However, they were coming faster and faster. That was when he saw something coming towards him. He began to raise his arm to defend himself, but was too busy with the bursts of electricity. He knew he was already too late, though. It was the imp. She would be on him before he could react.

As suddenly as she had appeared, he saw her driven back and smash into the wall. One of the roots that had mysteriously started extending from the wall snatched her in midair like a cobra striking its prey. The root enveloped the tiny Kelpie, bending her in half, crushing her wings and pulling her backwards into the wall.

Lochen turned back to see Sean behind him. It was clear that his friend had spotted the imp and dispatched her quickly and cleanly with a single shot from his sling.

"That was for what she did to Solveig," Sean said.

"And, I hope, for what she was about to do to me," replied Lochen.

"Oh," Sean replied. "Yeah, that, too."

He saw Solveig come rocketing over the top of the ledge and then scramble behind him to where Quinn and Liam were. He continued to battle the spell cast by Scirios when he saw the creatures emerge from the carvings on the walls.

"What the what?" asked Sean.

"They're Kythauls," Liam said. "They're kind of a cross between gargoyles and goblins, only worse."

"Worse?" shouted Quinn. "How can they be worse?"

"They are made of stone," Liam answered, "and you can't kill them. All you can do is try to knock them over the edge into the chasm, or smash them and kick the pieces into the chasm. They are indestructible and exist only to serve their master."

"And which one is their master?" asked Sean.

"Up until recently, I couldn't have told you," Liam answered as he hacked at the intruding roots. "But now I'm sure it's one of those Kelpies. Probably that big, ugly stony-looking one."

He had been busy slicing through the roots, cutting them off and kicking the severed parts off the landing into the chasm; but as fast as he cut, more appeared. When the Kythauls began to move, Sean fired a few shots at them, but to no effect.

"What do you think you're doing?" Liam shouted to Sean.

"You didn't say they couldn't be hurt by stones," groused Sean.

"They're MADE of stone," shouted Liam. "How would hitting them with stones do any damage?"

Quinn held his staff in both hands and began whacking at them. Sean shoved the useless slingshot into his belt, took the staff from Liam and did the same. They swung and poked, breaking and shoving the pieces over the edge before the creatures could re-form.

At the instant B'nair fell and the axe was driven into his chest, the stone from around his neck rose into the air. For a second it stopped and changed direction, but then it stopped again, only to return to its earlier trajectory. Stella watched it rise up and come at her. She backed away, somewhat overwhelmed by the sudden explosion of activity around her and by a touch of fear at the pulsating stone in her hand and the one rising upward on its own motion.

Before she could do anything, the two pieces of stone merged. A wave of power surged through her that she had never experienced before. She quickly put the pendant back around her neck and looked up.

The bubble that Natalie had cast suddenly clouded over. The freezing spell cast by Saldeti had discolored it. Seconds later, it glowed bright red and then shattered into thousands of pieces. Stella raised her hand in an almost dismissive manner, turned the frozen shards off to one side, and then superheated the pieces into as many feathers that floated downward harmlessly.

"Once more, if you please, Princess," she said to Natalie.

"It won't last any longer than the first one," Natalie answered.

"No, it won't," Stella agreed. "But it will last long enough."

Natalie did as she was asked and watched as Saldeti, who she could see far on the other side, once again cast a spell to freeze the layer. As it was frosting over, Stella strode over to Lochen and waved her other hand, distinguishing a series of electrical charges bursting from the walls behind them.

"We can't keep this up much longer," she said.

"No," he replied.

Sean moved next to him on the other side.

"Can't the two of you get us out of here some way?" he asked.

"I don't see any avenue of escape, and I seem to have lost the transporter stone," Lochen said.

"I think that disappeared when we arrived," said Stella. "There is another way, though."

She placed her hand on his arm as she looked back at the door. The band that had blended in and disappeared on the handles was now reappearing and glowing brightly. Instead of turning to see what Stella was staring at, Lochen looked down at the pendant. At the moment she had reached up and touched his arm, his eyes opened widely as if some mystery had been explained.

"Of course," he said. "A Boravak. I understand now. How ingenious. The Alchemist created this...this...other world, so to speak. It was...or is...amazing."

"Now is not the time for a lecture, professor," shouted Sean.

He swung his staff at another Kythaul, shattering it into hundreds of pieces, each of which began to move and reassemble. Sean tried frantically to kick the pieces over the side. Quinn had to reach out and keep him from slipping over the edge.

"We're kind of busy here, in case you hadn't noticed," Sean added.

Lochen turned to look behind him. Summer was doing her best to avoid being hit by the mini-lightning blasts, grabbed by the roots, snatched by Kythauls, or hit by a swinging staff. Solveig had taken a long bladed knife from Liam and was hacking at roots. Quinn was hammering at the stone beasts along with Sean, smashing and scattering them. Natalie was trying to reinforce the bubble that was protecting them from the Kelpies, but it was an exercise in futility.

"Yes," Lochen replied. "I can see that."

As he was thinking, Stella walked towards the end of the landing to the sealed doors. Once she was within a few feet, the band on the handles broke free and shot out at her. Before she could react, the band had attached itself back around the stone. The pendant was now complete once again.

Another wave of power swept through her and at the same time a small hole opened where the band had been. It slowly grew wider and seemed to extend inward, away from the landing, like a funnel. In a few seconds it was about two feet in diameter and had stopped growing. The vortex from the end that was inside the cave to the end that led somewhere else moved in an undulating manner, making it impossible to see what existed on the other side.

Lochen was still swinging his arms, fending off the electrical charges, and the others were struggling against a continually increasing assault by the roots and the Kythauls. Stella, without looking behind her, waved her hand at the instant the second bubble again burst into thousands of shards, and converted the pieces once again to feathers.

"Once more, if you please," she murmured to Natalie, who again plugged the ceiling.

Stella looked back over her shoulder at Lochen.

"A Boravak?" she asked.

"Yes," he replied. And then his eyes lit up again. "And I know what the phrase means. Ad Paria. It's all become clear."

"Can we discuss this later?" wailed Sean. "Because I've got a news flash for you: we can't keep this up much longer."

"They need to get out and we need to cover their retreat," Lochen said to Stella.

She nodded her agreement, and moved closer to him. He called for Summer. She darted in and around all the flying obstacles and hovered over his shoulder.

"I want you to lead the others through that opening," he said to her.

"Are you sure?" she asked. "Is it safe?"

"Yes, and yes," he replied.

"How do you know?"

"Well...I...we...this is a Boravak...It's a world within...oh, just trust me on this, will you?" he stammered.

She took a deep breath and then turned away. She flew over to Natalie and told her to go through the opening. Without looking to see if she did, Summer then went over to Solveig.

"No," Solveig answered. "I'm not leaving anyone behind."

"Please," Lochen pleaded. "We don't have much time. I promise. We'll be right behind you."

Solveig thought for a minute and then reluctantly agreed. She turned and followed Natalie, climbing into the vortex. In an instant she disappeared from sight. Summer then moved to Liam and Sean, and then to Quinn.

"I hope you know what you're doing," Liam said as he hacked at one last root and then leaped through the opening.

Lochen and Stella moved closer to the opening. Both of them now were casting spells one after the other, fending off the attack. They both looked upward and saw the frosted membrane begin to glow red. It would only be seconds before that protection was gone.

Sean followed Liam, tossing his staff to Quinn, who was now wielding both staffs, swinging them like the arms of a windmill. Lochen spun around and thrust one hand at the Kythauls and shouted for Quinn to get through the portal. He threw the staffs at the last of the rock creatures and wiggled through the opening, which appeared to be closing.

"Everyone else is through," Summer shouted to the remaining two. "I'll make sure they're safe and then I'm coming back to make sure you both get out."

"NO!" shouted Lochen. "Don't do that. Once you go through you can NOT come back. Is that clear?"

"Why not?" she demanded.

"Because the Boravak is not only another place, it's another time," he answered. "If you come back, you may not be able to go through again. Promise me you won't try to come back here, and that you won't let any of the others try. Promise me!"

"I can't agree to that," she said.

She was close to tears. She didn't like what she was hearing and what she was certain was not being said. Lochen glared at her and shouted again.

"Promise me!"

"OK," she started to sob. "OK. I promise."

"Now hurry," Lochen added. "The portal's closing."

She hesitated for a second, wiped the tears from her eyes, and then turned to fly through. As she passed from the cave to the other side, she could hear Stella's comment to Lochen.

"We aren't going to make it with them, are we?" she asked.

"I don't think so," he replied.

They were both frantically trying to stave off the attacks and now the bubble above them collapsed. There was nothing to shield them from the rest of the Kelpies. If either one of them stopped casting spells, they would both be lost; and they both understood this.

On the opposite side of the portal, all the others were flopped on the ground next to an enormous tree.

"Where are Lochen and Stella?" asked Solveig.

"They're not coming," wailed Summer, completely distraught. "I heard them say that as I was being pulled through."

"We have to go back after them," demanded Natalie.

"We can't," cried Summer. "Lochen said that this was a time portal; that if any of us went back to get them, we wouldn't be able to get back here."

"Nuts to that," muttered Quinn.

Before anyone could stop him, he lunged back into the portal. Sean and Liam jumped up and were barely able to grab his legs. They held him tightly to keep him from being sucked back into the opening. His body shook and they felt their grip loosening.

When Quinn leaped back through the portal, he came face to face with darkness. Where did everyone go, he wondered. He looked in every direction but could see nothing but black. He tried to wiggle backwards, but nothing happened. He pushed with his arms but couldn't dislodge himself. What have I done, he thought.

Inside the cavern, the Kelpies had eliminated the barrier between them and the pendant. They climbed down to the ledge on the far side of the bridge. Akmen Milzu spotted the stone around Stella's neck and waved her arms, increasing the attacks by the Kythauls. At the same time, she began hurling boulders across the expanse.

She focused her attention on Stella, who became the target of the projectiles. Stella was fighting frantically to fend off the attack, while Lochen was countering the electrical blasts and now disposing of the slithering roots, as well. The Mountain Kelpie saw this as an opportunity to press her advantage and strode across the bridge.

In a flash, Lochen snapped his fingers. The bridge collapsed and a very surprised Akmen Milzu reacted too slowly to stop her fall into the abyss. Scirios and Neraka Ferr became enraged. The Lightning Kelpie raised his arms and commanded bolts of energy from some unseen place above them to rain down on Lochen and Stella.

Lochen lifted his left hand into the air and created a small shield onto which the lightning blasts were deflected. Neraka Ferr raised his hand and the floor and walls began to heat. They turned a glowing red and the rocks began to explode and burst into jets of lava. Only Saldeti backed away. He had seen that these two opponents had the power from the Alchemist and the Enchantress. Even though they were outnumbered, they were too dangerous for him to risk falling victim the way the other Kelpies had. He backed up against the wall and looked for a way to escape.

Quest of Eight Part Seven: Ad Paria

Richard Reda

He had overestimated the power on the other side of the chasm. Lochen and Stella were becoming overwhelmed. There was too much coming at them. In a single, quick motion, Stella yanked the pendant from around her neck, glanced over her shoulder and tossed the stone into the slowly closing portal.

"What did you do that for?" asked a shocked Lochen. "Any chance we have of defeating them is surely diminished without that pendant."

"Don't you remember what Ock said?" she asked. "He said evil couldn't be destroyed. It could only be contained. We can't defeat them. If that's the case, then we couldn't let them get the pendant. I didn't see any other option."

"Then you have to jump through," he told her.

"And what? Leave you here? You won't last more than ten seconds. They'll crush you. You jump through while I hold them off."

"I couldn't do that," Lochen replied, glancing over at her. "No more than you could."

"Then you better come up with some other way for us to get out of here," she said.

"I'm afraid I've run out of ideas," he sighed. "At least the others are safe."

Neraka Ferr thrust his arm forward and an immense ball of flame shot out. Stella and Lochen, still battling every other spell, could only watch as the blast came at them. They moved a little closer to each other, expecting the worst.

Suddenly, Quinn's head appeared, seemingly out of nowhere. He looked as shocked as Lochen and Stella did, but in spite of his surprise, he reached out his arms and swept Lochen up in his right and Stella in his left. He started to kick his legs. On the other side, Liam and Sean pulled with all their might.

They fell backwards, yanking Quinn with them and with Stella and Lochen in his arms. As soon as they were through, the portal clamped shut, allowing only a wisp of smoke and a wave of heat to escape.

"What just happened?" asked Liam.

"Yeah," added Sean. "What were you thinking, Quinn?"

When Quinn turned to face them, they could see his blond hair had turned white. His face had the beginning signs of age; there were deep lines at the corners of his eyes and his face was drawn.

"What do you mean 'just?'" he wailed. "Why didn't you pull me back right away? And you two?" He motioned to Stella and Lochen. "Where did you disappear to? Why did you wait so long to come back?"

"What are you talking about?" asked Summer. "I told you not to go back and you ignored me, just jumping in. If it hadn't been for Liam and Sean, pulling you back out in seconds, you would have gone all the way through?"

497

"Seconds?" shouted Quinn. "Are you nuts? Seconds? I was in there for years! YEARS!"

He was nervous and distraught. He looked at each of the others who were staring at him, not knowing what to say. He could see that none of them had aged. They looked the same as they had the last time he had seen them.

"I couldn't move," he went on, his eyes beginning to tear up. "I tried to get back, but that didn't work. I tried to move forward, but that didn't work. I had to wait there in the dark. There was no one around – nothing – until these two showed up. They just appeared out of nowhere."

He looked directly at Stella and Lochen.

"If you found a way out, why didn't you share that and why did you even come back?" he pleaded.

"Years?" asked Solveig, finally finding her voice. "How is that possible? We've been right here. It's only been minutes – seconds!"

"Yeah," said Sean. "And besides, if you were in there for years, what did you eat? Tell me that!"

"Stop," interjected Lochen.

He took a step towards Quinn and extended his arm, touching his shoulder.

"It was years for him," he continued. "I'm so sorry, my friend. I mentioned to Summer that the Boravak was not only a different place, it was a different time. There was an inherent hazard to attempting to travel back and forth. What seemed like only seconds to those of us on either side of the portal were years to Quinn."

"Then how come he didn't lose any weight?" asked Sean. "He still weighed a ton. It took all our strength to hold on to him and to pull him back."

"More of the Alchemist's sorcery," said Lochen. "It's the only answer I have. Look how long the Kelpies were imprisoned, and yet, none of them starved."

"I can't believe you risked so much to come after us," Stella said to Quinn.

She moved close to him and reached up to touch his face and to wipe away the tears from his eyes. As she did, the last residual effects of the pendant flowed from her fingertips to his face. The lines of age slowly faded and his hair transformed from the white of an old man back to the golden blond of his youth. He reached up to feel the change. As he did so, Stella stepped back, somewhat surprised herself. Before anyone could comment, Natalie brought their attention back to the Kelpies.

"So where are they?" she asked, looking at the knot on the tree that sealed where the portal had been. "And why can't they get out of..."

She motioned to the tree. For the first time it all began to sink in. They had transported from a cave – and an entire other world – through a tree.

"The Boravak?" asked Lochen.

"Yeah," said Sean. "The Bureaucrat...or whatever it is. What exactly is it, anyway?"

"It is a world within a world," said Lochen. "The Alchemist got the idea from Meri Hocto. She had created her citadel inside a tree in the center of the Rebbercand village. He did the same thing on a much grander scale. He encompassed our entire world – the forests, the sea, the mountains, the Ice Kingdom; all of it – inside this tree."

"And what about the Kelpies?" asked Solveig.

"They are contained," said Stella.

"Exactly," said Lochen. "Evil can't be destroyed – only contained. Ad paria."

"Odd what?" asked Sean.

"It was what the inscription spelled out," said Lochen. "Those markings on the band; they translated into the phrase ad paria, which means 'return to balance.'"

"The band!" exclaimed Stella. "Where is it? I threw it through the portal."

She looked at the ground around the tree and where the others were standing. Several of the others stepped back searching as well.

"Nothing came through the portal after Summer," said Natalie. "Not until Quinn pulled the two of you through."

"It's gone," said Lochen. "Perhaps it's back with its owner. One more aspect returned to balance."

"Wait a minute," said Sean. "Go back to that 'return to balance' thing. Explain it – in simple terms, if you don't mind."

"Yes," said Solveig. "You're telling us that with the Kelpies in there," she asked, pointing to the towering tree, "and us out here, everything has returned to balance?"

"That is precisely what I meant," answered Lochen. "At least for the time being."

"And where, exactly, is here?" asked Summer.

For the first time since coming through the portal, they took the time to look closely at their surroundings. The enormous tree was on top of a knoll. It was very wide and its limbs stretched out in a nearly perfect circle and high into the sky.

Below them they could see a lush glen that led to a crystal blue body of water and a pristine shore. As Summer studied the foliage along the shore, she knew that her village was close by. Even though she couldn't see them, she could sense that her friends and family were all there, safe and sound.

Sean followed her gaze and saw the forest that was just beyond the clear water. He couldn't see inside the forest any more than Summer could, but, like her, he knew that his Lodge was there and the forest creatures were anxiously awaiting his return.

Quest of Eight Part Seven: Ad Paria

Richard Reda

Beyond the forest a range of majestic mountains rose against the clear, blue sky. They climbed high above the surrounding land. Lochen and Solveig knew their castle was intact, just as it had always been. Within it, life was carrying on and the people were awaiting the return of their Princess and Sorcerer.

Further down the shore, Natalie and Stella could feel the presence of a large village of Sea Sprites, all of whom were wondering where their Princess and Enchantress were – preparing a celebration for the moment they would come home.

Liam looked up at the sky. He realized that he couldn't recall the last time he had seen such a bright blue – and only one sun. Even though he couldn't see it, he knew there was a large marsh north of the mountains. This marsh, though, was filled with beautiful flowers; abundant vegetation; clear, cool streams; and a large community of animals. He also knew that the people from which he had descended lived in this marsh – his people. He knew he was no longer the last of his kind.

Like Liam, Quinn could not see the vast ice fields, the colonies of seals, dolphins, whales, or birds, but he knew they were there. They were in the same kingdom in which there was a large village and a home where Kelsey and Rover were napping idly.

Without explanation, they all knew where 'here' was. They all knew they were home.

Epilogue

The old man moved slowly through his garden. He had lived a long time and although he was in good health, he wasn't as spry as he used to be. His movements were more deliberate and even more relaxed. His long white hair blended into his white robes. His aged skin was like parchment and nearly as white as his clothing. His eyes, too, where white. A milky film covered the iris and pupils – the result of a spell he hadn't been quick enough to avoid. He had lost his sight in a battle long ago, but he had not lost his inner vision.

He moved through the garden seeing it clearly in his mind's eye. Anyone watching him would never know his sight had been affected.

He approached an unusual looking plant with a very colorful flower. The plant seemed to sense his arrival and the flower turned in his direction. He reached out his hand and the bloom opened even further. It was like an animal reacting to the gentle touch of its master. The plant was a hybrid he had been patiently developing, but not with the success he had hoped. He was working intently on pruning and feeding it when he sensed another presence. Someone had entered his garden. Without turning around, he smiled.

An old woman had joined him, moving as silently as the air across the stone walkway that wound through the garden, and seated herself on an old stone bench near where the old man was puttering. She watched quietly while the old man continued to administer to the flower.

When he was done, he turned in her direction, facing her. He noted that she was wearing the pendant he had given her so very long ago. She could tell that he could see it and reached up reflexively, holding it in her hand and then releasing it. It was a uniquely colored stone with a triskelion in the center that was slightly darker than the rest of it. The stone was bound in a gold band with curious markings on the outer edge.

Just the touch of her hand caused the colors in the stone to shift and swirl. It was as alive as the plant to which the old man had been tending. She folded her hands in her lap and looked up at his misty white eyes.

"Are you almost finished," she asked.

"I suppose," he answered.

He motioned with a small set of clippers towards the plant.

"I've done as much as I can for now," he said, scratching his head. "It's not exactly what I was planning. I can't seem to get it quite right, but I seem to be getting closer."

"Isn't that a..." she began.

"Dragon Spadix," he finished.

They smiled at each other. They had been together so long that they often finished each other's sentences; that is, when they even bothered to start them. They could almost read each other's thoughts.

"Yes," he said. "Quite right."

"I thought those were dangerous," she commented, shaking her head.

"Normally, yes," he answered, again motioning to the plant. "But not this variety. I've been able to resolve that issue. I think it's rather lovely, don't you?"

"Beautiful," she answered. "What seems to be..."

"The problem?" he finished. "I can't seem to get them to..."

"Stop moving." It was her turn to finish his sentence. "That's why there's only one."

"Yes," he said, smiling at both the old woman and then back at the plant. "The others appear to have..."

"Walked off," she finished.

"Yes. Exactly."

"I'm sure you'll figure something out," she said. "You always do."

She watched a little longer and then stood up. She winced slightly when she did. He didn't have to see her grimace to know the pain in her back was bothering her. She had suffered an injury long ago that neither of them discussed. He had found her after an arrow had been driven into her back. Somehow she had managed to make her way to his castle, in spite of all the hexes and spells he had cast to safeguard it.

He found her in the center of the roof of the tallest tower under the protection of one of his "pets." He tried to remove the arrow, but it was too close to her spinal cord to be safely extracted.

He had broken the shaft and done what he could to heal the wound. Over time, the bone grew around the arrowhead, keeping the sharp edges safely away from the delicate thread of nerves. But the consequence was that the steel projectile constantly reminded her of its presence.

"Don't stay out here too much longer," she said to him. "They're all here waiting to see you."

"All of them?" he asked.

"Of course," she said. "And they're getting anxious."

"Really?" he replied. "I can't imagine why."

"Nor can I," she answered.

It was an exchange they shared frequently.

"Then I won't waste another moment with this silly plant," he said, waving at it in dismissal.

They walked together through the garden and into a large, airy room.

"Papa," came the shouts. "Mimi said you'd tell us a story."

"She did, did she?" he replied. "Then I guess I better."

He sat down and looked at each of them before he spoke again. They were all quiet waiting for him to start. He cleared his throat.

"The time was right," he began in an ominous voice. "He could feel it. The planets were perfectly aligned and his powers were at their peak. He had been preparing for this moment for quite some time."

Ad Paria

Quest of Eight Part Seven: Ad Paria

Richard Reda

ABOUT THE AUTHOR

Richard Reda spent most of his life working for various agencies and Departments in the Federal Government. He believes this gave him a solid foundation for writing fantasy and fiction, so much so that he was encouraged to return after retirement to write some more. He lives with his wife in Manassas, Virginia, where he retired – the first time.

The *Quest of Eight* series originated as bedtime stories for his grandchildren. As the grandchildren got older and the bedtime stories got longer, it was suggested to him that he write them down. So he did. One, however, was not enough. The seven stories have been a true labor of love.

Quest of Eight Part Seven: Ad Paria

Richard Reda

www.ingramcontent.com/pod-product-compliance
Lightning Source LLC
Chambersburg PA
CBHW071337020726
47502CB00001B/130